STARSHIP ROGUE

CHRIS TURNER

This is a work of fiction. All the characters and events portrayed in these stories are either fictitious or are used fictitiously.

Cover Art: GooKingSword

Published by Innersky Books
www.innersky.ca

ISBN-13: 978-1-989493-19-9

CONTENTS

CHRIS TURNER

THETIS 3

BOOK I

CHRIS TURNER

Chapter 1

Wandering, wandering…way back in the mists of time I walked the starry mile, across a lightstorm of shattered dreams, a galaxy of endless possibilities, wondering what it would be like to fly a starship. An X-class starship.

Well, I wasn't flying one of those now, but I was certainly captain of two on a dingy VH3 maintenance craft, out in Veglos sector.

Wow, Rusco, you're a real top gun. Gonna pin a medal on that chest myself.

Marty, my partner in crime, a short, heavy-boned bully with fleshy lips and swarthy complexion, was acting navigator. We were off to heist a bunch of beryl on Thetis Station.

Why beryl? The heart of the Varwol space drive, crystal beyond value.

Yet this sector was no safe zone for old men, as near inside enemy territory as could be. A cesspool of warlords, cons, thieves, murderers, creepo gangsters, come to scavenge anything and everything, using Skurgian raiders, those mutant cannibals, as muscle, every low life imaginable.

The free sectors had gone to shit—as had most of the rest of the colonized worlds—except some notable planets fighting for and maintaining their independence, but those were fast falling to scumbag warlords. Marty was a real warthog today—jittery and curmudgeon material, riding my ass about every detail. He'd been cracked high on Myscol, just a few hours ago. Still running paranoid. I told him not to gulp down so much but he patted me on the back and flashed me his fox-like grin, "Relax, Rusco. You worry too much. I need that fix to set my aging nerves straight."

Too many schemes gone bad lately. And Marty had crossed from irritant to pain in the ass.

"When we going to make our approach? How we know they're going to buy it?"

"Everything's in order, Marty, relax."

Gras, our shaven-headed pilot, cast him a sour glance. "Yeah, muzzle it. You're going to jinx this whole mission."

"Yeah, well that blip on our holo-radar isn't just a figment of my imagination." Marty waved a meaty finger. "Check it out."

I scanned the holo grid and swung my gaze about. "Just one of Sharki's patrols. We're all good. The ship is lock tight, drive signatures in order, maintenance logs in place. Our two birds here can't squawk either." I motioned to the two trussed-up bodies, backs huddled against the console.

Marty grumbled and let his fingers crawl over the nav pad.

Timing? Fate? Luck of the draw? To fly a stolen craft with kidnapped crew into the hornets' nest meant a lot of shit-feathers were going to fly. Anything else was just lies.

That cautionary voice went off in my head like a dull schoolbell: Commander Dakker's last commendation before I went completely rogue, *"I'm hiring you, Rusco, because you've done good work in the past. Keep my product out of the hyena's grip, you hear me? Don't mess up."*

Well, I messed up, and here I was on a thieves' run to hijack some high end beryl out from under some serious scumbags' noses. Give me an A for Audacity.

So, life had taken a plunge since I'd lost Dakker's commission and inevitably turned to vice. But in the long run I was just following my path, wasn't I? Whatever destined path that was. Some middling success out in Ganymede had stoked my fires, gained me a bit of confidence and ready cash. I hoped I could make this heist work, that there was some method in the madness. But unexpected upturn plus confidence can set one flat on his ass.

While the captain and what I guessed his gunner struggled at the thick cord wrapped around their torsos, wrists and legs, I thought of all the bad things that could come out of this caper.

Marty seemed to read my thoughts. "These two monkeys are liabilities, Rusco. Let me waste them."

Good old Marty, volatile and violent to the end, ready to plug shells into a problem rather than think it through.

"Remember last time you nearly deep-sixed our pigeons? We needed them and almost got our throats cut."

"Stop bringing that up."

A rough boy with bullet-shaped head, Marty had a patch of mustard-colored hair and eyes cold and unblinking as a viper's. He was as tough as nails, as hardy as they come but maybe too impulsive for what I required at the time. Leaning toward the reckless, he was light on the thinking side. Yeah, Rusco, like the wolverine calling the tiger a predator.

"They're not looking too happy," Marty pointed out.

"Yeah, well that's the price of being in the wrong place at the wrong time."

"You're real compassionate, Rusco."

"Glad you approve."

The larger captive with the tawny hair, rasped. "When Drayer finds out we've gone awol, you're going down—"

"But he ain't, is he?" snorted Marty. "Now shut your gob or I'll stuff it full of lead. We'll be in and out of *Thetis*, and maybe keep this tub here for our own use and ditch you two on a far off planet. Any more lip and it's bye-bye." Marty stuck his piece in the man's ear.

"Dial it back, Marty," I warned. "These minnows aren't worth it."

Our pilot Gras grunted an endorsement.

"Do we need access codes to dock?" Marty jabbed the captain in the ribs. The man thrashed to and fro, giving back an angry snarl.

"He's not going to tell you anything," I said. "Leave it alone."

The captain's buddy beside him, the gunner, gave us an equally black stare. "Drayer's the least of your worries. Boss Sharki's going to murder your asses."

"Sharki can lick it," said Marty.

The captain's eyes bulged. Under the stringy hair plastered to his brow, sour sweat dripped. This boy'd resigned himself to a beating or a grungy death, but I saw pride in those glittering eyes, resentful at being sandbagged down on Tyrone City and his ship commandeered by what he could only assume were a couple of amateur opportunists. Pride among us males is a dangerous thing. He'd be in a shitload of grief when Sharki learned of his incompetence and negligence.

Thetis Station was fast looming up: a long spidery, gunmetal silver weave of steel, somewhat of a dove-tail shape with double docks mid center equipped with landing apparatus. The biggest ore refinery this side of Pegasus. Cargo bays swung to rear and port side. The honeycomb partitions stored vats of beryl. At each end of the station stood massive parabolic reflectors, a solar gun technology channeling the high intensity rays of Thetis's sun for the hyperpolarization and ionization of the beryl that would make superior Varwol crystal for ship drives.

Not going to lose much sleep over Sharki's loss of a shipment or two. Not over one who's selling black market crystal to warlords out to build lethal weapons and light drive engines to enslave worlds.

The plan was to rig some diversion in this beryl-processing station orbiting Thetis, steal one of the ore ships and pocket some serious cash. Whether we needed security codes was another matter. If worse came to worse, we'd have to squeeze the captain with knives and fire.

Gras radioed in and we made our approach. The bright crisp voice came over the com. "Captain Ganx, here. *Algernon*, transmit security code."

Marty spat out a curse, "The code, fucker." He jabbed our Captain in the ribs with the butt of his weapon.

The captain snarled. "Eat shit."

Marty pushed the muzzle of his R4 into the man's mouth. "We ain't playing around here, smart boy. We die, you die, fucker, so I'll ask you again."

The man wheezed out a groan. At last he spat out a monosyllable. "A264. A264. Back the fuck off."

"That's better." Marty retracted his weapon. He nodded to Gras.

Gras punched the code into the console.

"Get ready to abort and hightail it out of here if this gig goes sour," I murmured to him.

The authoritarian voice spoke again over the com. "Maintenance 1 crew, you are cleared for dock at Hangar 6. Proceed to Bay 6. Drop your maintenance supplies there."

"10-4, control." Gras signed out.

I flashed Marty my dog-toothed grin. "See? All good to go." They were falling for it. The docking port opened like a wide oval eye. A few feeder vessels shuttled in and out of starboard port, likely more maintenance craft like ours. We passed under the shadow of the conning tower and on through the main gate.

Algernon swept in and I saw the pressure lock close behind us. We were floating under low impulse through the double bay protection screen past gray-black hypertensized steel walls. The chamber pressurized. Like dutiful soldiers, we headed over to dock at the dim-lit Bay 6 where three other vessels sat parked. Gras dimmed the landing lights. I nodded to Marty. We took our weapons and our makeshift gear: pry tools, portable scanners, compact explosives and a tin of flesh regen in case we got banged up. Gras sat tight to guard our trussed-up prisoners and signal us in case of trouble.

Thus far, the maintenance craft with its artificial grav and solar backup power was serving its purpose. The flight manifest roster had entries detailing the previous pickup of backup spare parts and supplies from Tyrone City proper. A good cover for us— maintenance men garbed in gray uniforms with our black service bags full of 'repair gear'. Just a couple of M-men out for a service check on the power grid at G4.

I regretted we couldn't use my ship *Starrunner* for this op. She was a fast ride that I'd pimped up pretty good and would get us out of here if it came to that. I'd debated camouflaging her to look something like *Algernon* to get inside Thetis Station, but the makeover convoluted what was essentially a simple plan.

We'd studied the schedule. Planned to come in on a shift just before launch of the cargo vessels to the hub world, *Mixr*. A little dodgy if the wrong people got suspicious, but what's to gain without some risk?

I recalled the massive solar guns mounted half way below the parabolas and a shudder touched my spine. The power of reworked tech from the past centuries had fallen into the hands of gangsters like Sharki, accelerating his heating and refining operations and pumping out mega product. Good that some of that loot could go toward the Jet Rusco poverty fund.

Marty grumbled on and was toying with the prisoners again. A belligerent SOB, and mean as a snake, but plenty of iron-hard muscle when it came to nasty business. This was nasty business, kid nobody not. An op run by thugs who wouldn't think twice of pulling out one's entrails and wrapping them about one's neck like a hangman's noose. This heist idea was mostly mine. But feeling the sweat budding under my brow of purple-dyed hair had me wondering what compulsion had thrust me into this hare-brained scheme.

"Play it cool. No embellishments or sudden moves," I said. "All by the book." I swung my long legs down the companionway to the cargo hold. Marty trailed at my heels.

The ship's engines glided us in and I felt a thrill of anticipation touch my spine. Showtime.

Gras parked the craft in as unobtrusive a spot as possible over at the farthest end of the landing depot. I'd studied the layouts on the 3D image. Marty and I hefted our black bags, the weight reassuring on my shoulder while Gras stayed put on armchair alert to monitor the depot on the holo screen. We came out of the cargo hold in our gray uniforms, moving with as much casual ease as possible.

"Remember, 15 minutes max," I hissed at Marty. "Then we're out of here regardless. Anything goes wrong, we come out blasting."

Marty gave me a gruff acknowledgment.

Five ore freighters sat to the side with double cargo doors open showing gleaming bins of treated beryl inside. Two stealth airguard V-Zon ships hung way back, parked at the opposite end of the landing dock. Their purpose, to protect the shipment when the convoy went out into deep space. I didn't like the look of those menacing fuselages or the elongated forward cannon. Could make mincemeat of a few ambitious raiders. One of those ore-freighters was our target. I picked the closest one—for luck. I could read the nameplate on the gray side—'Titan'. Fitting. I wondered if she were a fast ship. I liked the look of her twin cannons. Some extra features were installed there too. Once out in space, Gras would act as rearguard to protect our flanks.

I was glad we weren't using *Algernon* as a getaway vehicle. The maintenance ship was not equipped with much firepower. No fareons or modern blaster tech. If things went awry and we had to hotfoot it, in a shootout we'd be sitting ducks.

I motioned. "I bid for the nearest hauler of those raw supply ships over there. *Titan*. Premium ore. En route to high end worlds like *Mixr*. When the pandemonium is in full swing, we strike."

"What if some security jock decides to board *Algernon* and finds our two pigeons?"

"Gras can stall them. It's a risk we'll have to take. No more than 15 minutes. You chicken-shitting out?"

"Don't insult me, Rusco. I'm always game." Marty gave me a saccharine smile that turned to a feral look that could bring down a charging ox. Good old Marty.

Uniformed, maintenance crew milled about in scrap-happy moods; hauler personnel too, fussing with odds and ends around the loading dock. Last minute protocol. All of these five monster vessels measured 200 feet in length. Impressive, despite their vintage.

"Why even have a refinery here on a station?" Marty asked. "Seems a hell of an inconvenient place."

"I don't know, something about raw beryl not electron charged enough for warp coil production. Needs a vacuum and a serious electromagnetic boost to qualify it for Varwol drive construction. Whatever the case, it's working for them." I motioned to the loaders full of polarized mineral backing up to the last ships.

Over the hum of voices and tumult of forklift engines, a bulky man with raven hair, dressed in a silver spacer's suit barked out surly orders to a gang of dockhands. Likely our space rogue, Sharki. Never met the man, and never wanted to. Heard a lot about the shyster, but one never knows what to believe. A mean brute either way. Killed hundreds, maybe more. Fork-lifts and cranes loaded the last of the vessels with the remaining beryl from the loaders into their cargo holds.

I gripped the stock of my R4. The sleek metal felt warm in my palm. I gave a grunt of satisfaction. Keep them busy over there while we do our business at the control board over here. I snuck up to the control room that fed the station its juice, midway down the depot.

Trouble found us soon enough. Nosy parker security boy, bitchfaced sod waved his R3 at us. "Problem's back there, boys. What's with you running off in such a hurry? Going for a ham sandwich and a pint down in the mess hall?"

I nodded in easy jocularity. "Drayer told us to come down, fix a bad pipe at central control. We've got it writ here on this requisition form. Want to see it? Unless somebody countermanded the order."

He shook his head, a tinge of impatience in the darting eyes. "Whatever. More help is needed on the solar grid at tower B3 than fixing any damn pipe. Four men nearly got bodies scorched the other day."

"You don't say. What gives?"

"Bad gyro."

"Yeah, I heard something along those lines. Drayer shuttled us off to the pipes. Didn't mention—"

"Fuck Drayer. Who's in charge of priorities around here? Fatso Drayer?"

"Seems so, and I hear you, man. Preaching to the choir. Tell you what—we'll get this pipe fixed, then hustle over to B3 to help you guys out. Sound fair?"

He gave a curt nod. "Make it snappy." He moved off before turning back to us. "Whole station's going to shit. Whole place could catch on fire. Yesterday Bonli, working power gyros, near got his head fried."

My lips parted in appreciation. "You know what they say about old stations."

"Yeah, parabola's super old. Solar gun has gigawatts of power, lethal as hell. Not enough maintenance crew here to keep this old rig running safely. Security's a downright pig these days. Any two-bit meister can waltz in and start hacking away with clippers."

I nodded in sympathy. *That's why we picked this joint, you dumb fuck. Now bug the hell off and let us do our work.*

The security man stalked off, mouthing orders into his com.

Marty gave a grim chuckle. "Rusco, you've a knack for ladling out BS."

"Let's just say I've had lots of practice at it. We may not be so lucky if someone else surprises us."

We made it to the steel door of the control room, past some of the hubbub of dockhands and load-lifters but at enough of a distance to keep a sharp lookout on the cargo vessels. The control room, with its small six-inch square thick glass window placed beside the door, lay in plain view. Marty acted as lookout while I set to jimmying the knob with the wrench-like tool I dug out of my bag of tricks. Something like a small Alan key but fancier with better dexterity and some electro-gizmos inside to trip the tumblers that kept the door locked. There was always danger of an alarm going off—sure, nothing to do about that. But I thought I'd covered that base by flashing my kill disc first, which blew the alarm sensor. A common mechanism. Didn't look as if this door had any fancy tripwires or devices. The guy on watch said security was lax here and who would try to steal from Sharki and his cutthroat hirelings? Dangerous thinking, Rusco, but these were dangerous times. Risky—with oodles of wealth at stake for a daredevil. That was the beauty of this operation—no second guessing. Either win big time or get blown to shit. Anyways, we'd know in a second. I heard a snap and a click, some more hard clicks in the tumbler mechanism and the door slid open. I beamed. No strident klaxon or shitbox robot laser thingy beaming down on us. All good. Marty grinned. I slipped in after him.

Ten towers of components stood twelve feet high in a neat row in the center of the room. We'd made it this far. Horseshoes must be up our asses. We were in the control depot that fed the station its juice and controlled auxiliary functions and artificial grav. Luckily I knew where to look. I'd broken into such places before and had a good success rate. That meant diddly squat. Every caper had its pitfalls.

Marty catfooted it past nine towers to the far end of the room and began fiddling with the last tower, particularly the box that contained the control port door stabilizer. I'd coached him how to sabotage it to keep those doors wedged wide open.

The place buzzed with an electrical hum, high voltage, high-powered fluorescent lights. The smell of dust and staleness permeated the air. A disused feel. Nobody had been in this place for months.

While Marty got the faceplate off the upright rig nine towers down and worked at short-circuiting the outer port, I moved to the first stack. In sync we had to undermine the power grid as quickly as possible. If we could get both components to misfire at the same time, we'd have the perfect diversion to steal our cargo hauler and be on our way. One shipload of that rare, treated beryl could weigh in upwards of 30k yols. Not bad for a day's haul by a couple of stone-broke hustlers.

I unscrewed the faceplate off the first stack, crouching at waist level. Just a couple of wires snipped here and there in the right places and joined to the right leads and the overhead energy holo grid would go down. Half the job would be done, just what we needed. Sharki and his goons wouldn't know what hit them.

Marty, however, was slower than dogshit. Too long dicking around with the auxiliary port controller. I hissed into my com, "We're good to go, Mar. On blackout for T-30."

His raspy voice crackled over my ear piece. "This one's a bust, a prick and a half."

"What you mean *a bust?* I gave you the 'easy' job."

"You know how it is, Ruskie. The easiest ones're always the hardest. Some geeks must have parallel-wired the port mechanism, adding triple redundancy or some shit. Have to knock out three of them if we want our door to stay open."

I groaned. "Well, hurry up, or this operation's lizard shit. We could get made. Those doors are under auxiliary power. Could cancel out my blackout magic."

"We can always bail—Damn these snips!" He swore as he made sucking sounds, likely cut his thumb.

"There's no bailing. We invested a lot in this job, Marty. Let's make the best of it. Wait, on second thought, let me handle it."

I heard him swearing filthily as I envisaged him fumbling about with a bloody finger trying to stitch two leads together. Something else crackled over the com, Gras's choked voice.

"Fuck… Gras's made," Marty rasped.

I ducked over to the wall to sneak a peek through the glass, saw two security apes hauling what looked like Gras out of *Algernon's* port doors. Crap! Now what? The two thug security men with brawny tattooed arms were dragging his sorry hide none too gently. I leaned back and groaned. Completely screwed. I told him to fly off or at least lay waste to this pig run if things went sour. Must have tried something heroic and got himself messed up.

"Abort," I hissed.

Marty was at my side, clacking his ugly teeth. "This is bad. What about the doors?"

"Forget the bloody doors. We're screwed! Backup plan." Which wasn't much of a plan if you call a free-for-all shoot out at the OK Corral some kind of fallback. I ran back to the stack knowing we were done for, so hard-wired the main circuit to a full out short. The lights flared, then took a plunge. There was a massive electrical surge. Crackling sizzles from the hardware. Cries and bedlam in the loading deck. Security men were hopping about, R3's hiked and Marty and I were on the move.

The emergency lights flickered on. In the dim periphery sat the hauler, a tempting, easy getaway vehicle. I was itching to get my hide in there. First thing though, we had to try to save Gras's ass. Somebody was going to die. Maybe all of us.

Marty and I moved like lynxes toward the security men, Marty, grim face set, was thinking the same as me.

Before their guns lifted, we took them out, thumping them like sledges on anvils. The first man's face exploded in a tiny ruin as my gunstock slammed down hard. I caught Gras as he slumped, pulled him the hell away from them. Gras choked, getting hold of his senses. His face was white. "I tried to warn you guys…but they snuck in back." His breath wheezed. "Must have had access codes we didn't know about." He was beaten up pretty bad. Two black eyes and an arm hanging limp.

"What about our two stooges?"

"Hid them in the forward bin. Before they stormed the ship."

Bad on me for losing faith in Gras. I nodded. "It's okay. You did okay, Gras. Everything's changed. New plans. Keep your head down and we'll head to *Titan*—" I stared as shells rang out.

Gras's body shuddered to the pump of rapid fire. His head bobbed like an apple as gunfire spat out from the side. His body arched, convulsing around like a dancing manikin.

I jerked back in horror. Gras slid out my grasp. I ducked, returning fire, spraying anything that moved.

Gras died, and he died badly. We couldn't do anything for him yet we pulled him to safety behind the curve of the cargo hauler's rear vanes. He was gone, eyes staring in glassy death. Seconds were ticking.

Marty gave me that wooden, I-told-you-so, empty look. "Got any ideas, Rusco? Better say 'em now."

The moment I realized we were done for, I leaped for *Titan's* cargo door, Marty hard on my heels.

Some dark shape draped in tight leathers came lurching out of the hold, rifle raised.

I surprised her and knocked the R3 out of her hands as she lifted it to my face. Holy shit! But she did some cartwheel thing and landed next to me, smashing me a solid whack across the shoulders. The force knocked me off balance, sending me floating backward like a cloud on ice. In a split of a second I saw the angel-blond hair whip back, tied in a loose pony tail, the length of sleek thigh, hard muscle all round. This was no soft, languid female. Lucky for me I didn't progress to phase 2—Jet Rusco lying in a slimy heap bleeding out on the deck. I whipped up my gun and held it to her vitals. She settled down quick.

I kicked her rifle out of the way. "Don't try anything stupid. Move!" I massaged my neck.

Marty crouched, tagging bodies, covering me from gunfire. Shells raked all around us as we hunched inside the cargo door.

The man in the silver spacesuit came running our way, bellowing orders.

"Into the ship," I rasped. "You too, you stupid creepo." I elbowed her forward.

Silver-face roared, "WTF, Deidra, you gone traitor?" His gun came arching up.

The woman turned around, slack-jawed. "What do you mean, Sharki? I didn't do any—"

"Liar, you're running with scum thieves. You're no different than your rat-bastard father!"

Shots from all angles rang around us, riddling the hull. We ducked, curses in our throats.

"Move, you bitch," cried Marty. He knocked her sprawling forward. "This ain't social hour."

The silver-garbed man cried out to his henchmen: "Kill that traitorous harlot and those good-for-nothing thieves." Sharki's fish cold eyes were black and bottomless like a shark's. I could see where he got his name.

She gave a venomous hiss.

I looked her in the eye. She crouched dazed, her fists bunched, trying to get air back in her lungs from Marty's last love tap. She was no traitor. Just caught in the wrong place at the wrong time.

"Inside, if you want to live!" With a curse, I shuttled her ahead. "Close that bloody hatch." Marty's fingers fumbled for the button. He pulled his fingers back, his left arm grazed by gunfire. Hydraulics whined overhead. Metal sheets came sliding down.

Things were happening too fast. The mind compensates by blurring the edges and giving the brain less information, allowing intuition, intellect and reflexes time to catch up. There was a hollow ringing in my ears. The *rat-a-tat* of gunfire rained down on us like hail, a dull clown's firecracker ricochet off walls at a kid's birthday party. Everything felt in slow-motion from the get-go, some dream within a dream with death lurking around the edges.

The cargo doors slammed shut, sealing us off from Sharki's men. Only the dull echo of gunfire against the armored hull as the blue light set to autolock. Precious moments of a reprieve.

Happy, Rusco? Fabulous handiwork.

We raced down the hall to the bridge, Marty herding Goldilocks and her cursing hide along. Nobody aboard. Marty's door jam hadn't worked back there—our pilot Gras, was lying in a pool of his own blood, so Marty and I'd have to blast our way out, manage the ship alone.

The bridge was a gloomy affair but roomy and designed for comfort. Stacks of tower components to the left. Sensors dead center with console grid and holo displays. To the right weaponry manifold and target equipment. Through the port glass I saw figures scrambling like ants below. I punched at the touch panel. System was locked.

"You captain of this ship?" I growled at her.

She kept a sullen silence. Her lip was curled and out flung in an insolent sneer.

"Answer him, you dumb bitch." Marty came snarling forward, fist upraised, but I herded him off and shook her shoulders. "Unlock these damn controls, or we're all dead."

With a muttered curse she moved to the console like a dazed deer, ran grudging fingers over a touchtab. "All yours, bozos." The fleshy mouth was full of challenge, full cheeks rose-red, brazen tilt to the hips, pretty enough, but a handful for anyone.

"He'll kill us all so why even try?"

"I don't have a death wish. Out of the way." I shoved her aside.

Marty got the ship moving while I shuttered the glass. Armored plates rolled down over the viewing port. I fiddled with the weapons' grid. I could hear shells smacking against our hull. Hundreds of them. The V-Zons'd be on our tail. The things'd be getting ramped up and pretty nasty real soon.

Marty amped our shields up to max. *Titan* surged along the landing pad toward the outer port, our electro-shields catching stray bullets. I trained the ship's cannon at the wall of gray steel approaching in the holo-view. Marty guided us closer on impulse power.

I locked and fired. Shells flared out and the portal erupted in shards and fragments. I kept hammering at the plated metal with guns full on, while our rear shields lit up at the rifle fire from behind. "Hot damn!" Amid the smoke, a gaping hole loomed. Loose material on the landing dock went spinning out in space. I grinned, thinking about Sharki and his gang on deck in a subzero vacuum. The sods'd have a miserable time getting to safety before being asphyxiated.

We were in a ship. We'd gotten this far. Out of the jagged ruin of the port hole *Titan* burst, her rear impulse jets flaring behind us. We'd have to forge the rest of the way on brute strength...and a lot of luck.

Chapter 2

Titan burst out of the station, wreckage falling off her sides in fiery shards. "Yeehaw!" Marty crowed. We headed into deep space on impulse thrust. Marty was pleased.

"Save your yeehaws," I said. "Get *Titan* the hell away from here so we can break out to light speed."

"Too close, Rusco, too close to Thetis. We're at the 10k mark. Grav field still too strong. Seven minutes minimum."

Was it enough time? Activity flared from the station, three hot dark shapes shot out of the burning, ragged hole after us. Didn't take them long to regroup and sic birddogs on our ass.

I turned to Deidra. "Your flyboy boss is a little peeved, I think. Surprised he recovered so fast. Can't believe he's not more worried about his precious station."

She gave a grim laugh. "There've been breaches on Thetis 3 before. The crew always fixes them. Sharki's more worried about the cargo we're carrying." She jerked a finger at the holo display showing three bogies coming straight at us. "Those red blips are stealth V-Zons out to blast you."

"Not if we get to light speed first."

"You'll never make it to light speed before they peg you off. *Titan's* a sloth on impulse thrust. I know it, she's my ship, remember? Too close to Thetis, as your boy just reminded you."

"You're just a fountain of cheer, aren't you?"

"You've made me complicit in whatever scheme you're running by dragging me aboard. Thanks a bunch for signing my death warrant."

"Well, hooking up with scum like Sharki is a surefire death warrant. You can trade a starship's ride out of hell here for a hide full of lead. You should be kissing my ass for saving your butt back there."

Her mouth sagged. She was about to punch back with a retort, instead, she looked over at the holo-view with hopeless eyes.

"Why you so fixated on us getting nuked anyway? Don't you have any ounce of preservation in you?"

"I think I'd rather get blasted to hell than have Sharki on my tail. He'll slap me in a slave shop as he's threatened all along."

I frowned, scratched the cut on my face. "Makes no sense. You deviated before?"

"No, he owned my father."

"You really have no allegiance to him? Aw, screw it. I've no time for mysteries." Ship fire hammered our shields. I set the weapons' grid to lock on the upcoming bogies. They were coming in fast. "Marty, you ready for a tar-and-feather showtime?"

Marty looked casual as ever, as if smoking a peace pipe out on the front deck. Must have been the Myscol he just popped in his mouth. "Ready as ever."

She had hesitated at my last question. Her whole frame tightened with the approach of the lightfighters. "Once you've worked for Sharki, there's no going back. He owns you for life."

Marty guffawed. "That's a pile of shit, woman. Clean up your brain. He's just terrorized you into blind obedience."

Her fingers clenched as if ready to claw Marty's face. She sprang for the spare guns on the rack at the side and I headed her off. "No, not so fast, tigress." She looked ready to claw my eyes out too, or drub me with her bunched fists. "You're all wound up. We're not going to harm you. Nothing you've said changes anything. So get with the program. As I said, from where I'm standing, you should be grateful to be alive."

She let out a rasp. The young woman was not thinking straight. Seeing Sharki's ruthlessness firsthand, I could understand. Her ship had just been hijacked. Her bane, Sharki, had turned on her and promised her a cruel fate.

The first repellor beams came lashing out at our port stern and knocked our shields way down.

"Mother fucker," I breathed.

Flare bombs flashed around us and rocked our hull. Marty's evasion tactics were not working. Jesus, what else could go wrong?

"Can't you fly this thing?" I yelled at her, "or are you just window dressing?"

"I can fly it," she spat.

"Then do it!"

With a sneer, she stamped forward, bumped Marty out of the pilot's chair. Her slender fingers danced over the console, set the ship on a narrow dive, just bypassing one of the V-Zon's repellor beams by a hair.

Our Deidra was coming round, a little late, but I was grateful she was on board.

The V-Zons took another swipe at us, one of their lurid rays catching us hard in the nose, rocking the ship and raising hell on our shields. The other spitfires converged on us like hornets, stingray cannons trained at our fuselage. Whatever could be said of him, Sharki hired good pilots.

I swore. "Shields down to 41%. Fancy moves aren't going to win us the day." I searched the defense systems for any reserve power we could divert into shields. I looked to Marty. "I'm open to ideas here. Only so much I can do with three against one." I punched at the weapons' controls, aiming for the place I expected the closest enemy to dodge to. It was a lucky guess. The torpedo caught the top of the hull full on its nose. Three strikes too many. The hostile's ship flared and went dead, a floating derelict in space. The other V-Zons spiraled in with fury.

Deidra cried, "Monitor frequency K-alpha-2. I put snoopers in place so I could track Sharki's movements. I didn't trust him farther than I could spit."

I adjusted the dial to the requisite frequency. Sharki's decoded voice crackled over the com in poor quality audio. *"Get that ship back. Bring them back alive or dead, I don't care, just preserve that shipment. Out."*

"Roger, Big S. Spiders 2 and 3 are going in."

She flung out a hand. "Quick. Use the cloud mines! Sharki had them installed on all our carrier ships. We were losing too many of them to Skurg raiders."

"Show me."

She leaned in. "Left controls—at two o'clock." Marty took over for her while she tapped fingers to initiate the launch sequence and targeted a particularly irritating mark, V-Zon #2. I remembered the sequence, then grinned as a cloud of green flame engulfed her front section and she dropped back blind.

"What're cloud mines?"

"Flash bombs release an ionizing flare which interferes with com access. Plays havoc with weapons consoles too. Lasts for up to 15 minutes."

"Good. Enough time for us to get away, leave them in a brain fog."

"Look, they're trying to plug a mine on us now." She steered *Titan* wide and sent us lumbering out of its direct path. The tail end caught our stern and disrupted one of our rear vanes.

Marty manned the conventional umbrella bombs. His last missile knocked one of the V-Zons off its trajectory and the dazed craft went corkscrewing off to oblivion.

"Nailed that bastard," he bawled, his face brimming with pride.

"Bravo, what you want, a silver star? Get the next one," I cried.

Deidra scowled. "There's more of them coming in from Thetis Station. Fire everything you have at them! I can't keep flying this hulk forever out of their line of fire."

I released one of the mines and knocked the first ship out of commission. Marty launched multiple torpedoes and tagged the hostile's wing companion. But one slipped through our net as more fire came angling our way, hitting us bowside. *Titan* lurched. I was jarred out of my seat.

T minus 10. We were almost at light drive distance.

Almost is never enough though.

That last enemy hurt us bad, a clean strike whistling off our port, battering our shields down to zero. Ruptured something inside. Smoke swirled from our bridge's component towers. I groaned, pulled myself up, slapped fists on the console. I coughed, waved away the smoke as Marty rubbed his eyes.

How the day was turning sour.

"Varwol sapped out. No chance of warping out," Marty croaked, wiping the sweat and smoke out of his eyes.

I saw the gauges plummet. We'd be lucky to limp to some nearby station or have enough cabin air to make it to the nearest moon.

On reserve power, I sent out the last of the cloud mines. Just as our triumphant V-Zon was about to send in a probe, its hull shone green. The bastard hung disabled in space.

My hopes for success died. I saw a long slog to oblivion, and then lights out.

"What now?" Marty's voice sounded thick in his throat.

"Back to Thetis. No place else nearby. If we can land, we'll have a chance at repairs and think of some way of slipping out from underneath Sharki's net."

"Oh, that easy, is it?" said Deidra.

"You got a better plan?"

Marty scowled at her and she scowled at me and looked away.

We turned about back to the hated, gray-green disc that was coming in fast. *Thetis.* Somehow I'd known that planet would be my bane. My mind was going in too many directions at once. If we came across more V-Zons...

No, don't think like that, Rusco. I thrust my attention back to the woman.

"About this Sharki. What's he got on you?"

I could see it was no small thing this hold of terror the kingpin had over her.

She spoke in a bleak monotone. "Told me if I ever betrayed him, he'd brothel me up, pimp me out on Thetis, Mekeroid, anywhere, till I'm a stinking, used-up piece of flesh."

"Scumbag. Well, if we can get this shipment to Valdair, pawn it off to the highest bidder, we'll have enough funds to keep you out of his clutches. Not a fan of Sharki's modus operandi. He's a slimeball."

She didn't seem too reassured by the plan. "It's a nice dream, but with a broken ship, no means, and right from under the nose of the alligator? He'll kill us outright. I've told you before."

"He'll give up when he can't find us."

"Yeah, right." She shook her head. "Sharki's like a pit bull that sinks teeth into a shin bone. He'll never let go."

"Makes no sense. Why mess with small time peddlers like us? Got enough beryl on Thetis to burn. Doesn't the shitbag have better things to do than chase us? He's wasted three plus ships already."

She exhaled an impatient breath. "You still don't get it, Rusco. He's under the thumb of some megalomaniac warlord. Sharki can't afford to lose one shipment to some rinky-dink raiders, like you, or Skurgs for that matter. This same warlord, some Star Lord he calls himself, will have him by the balls if he reneges on his shipments, even by one crystal. You think Sharki's a cruel bastard. This guy makes Sharki look like a newborn lamb.

"This warlord have a name?"

She shrugged. "Don't know."

Marty just laughed. "Yeah, sure, everyone's got a pressure cooker looming over his head. Warlords, star lords. Some have—"

"Zip it, Marty. Concentrate on landing this crate and dodging lightfighters."

He grunted an oath; he busied himself applying some regen to his left arm still bleeding from gunshot graze. The man seemed immune to pain.

Despite Deidra's fear that Sharki would make a sex slave out of her, all evidence hinted his V-Zons had been out to kill.

* * *

While we still had power, we made our wary descent to the far side of the gray-green planet that waxed in her sun Vala's pale light. Thetis Station we gave a wide berth. We'd taken care of Sharki's lightfighters for now, but I had no doubt he'd send out more on our tails before long.

I ran my eyes over the holo index. AI computer nav said Tyrone City was our best bet for repairs. Blackwater and Narpoon Town were other possibles. Deidra verified each with a sullen nod.

We entered the atmosphere and swung in on a sharp angle, over swamps and mangroves, me gritting my teeth, hoping that *Titan* wouldn't fail us. That trail of smoke behind us didn't look too encouraging.

Thetis was a gloomy world set with perpetual clouds and a windless backdrop of sky, dusky yellow and now morphing into a puce green.

Titan was sputtering, her engines sounding rougher every minute. The thin trail of smoke streaming from her tail piece was ever widening.

The first lights of the capital city winked off in the distance.

"We'll give Tyrone City a wide miss," I confirmed as we swung low over the brooding terrain. "Not an inspiring landscape by any standard."

"Just a few shallow puddles the locals call lakes here," Deidra said, inclining her head to stunted trees and meandering dirt roads.

We followed the line of one of the wider roads. Up ahead, cranes, gantries and other heavy equipment sat lined around the edges of a sizable complex. Would serve as a good cover.

"There—that yard over there. We can hide out and make repairs.

Someone'll have the smarts to fix this ship, judging from all those rigs and cranes."

"You think?"

Deidra thumbed through the index. "Just another crazy *crog* who has multiple businesses going."

"Crog?"

"It means, refinery, man. Lots of 'em here on Thetis. Beryl's as common as sand fleas."

"Good to know. What other businesses he have?"

"Says here, dog yard, or animal yard of some sort, repair station, heavy engines and whatnot, welding shop, yada yada, cutter and refiner of raw beryl."

"Sounds good enough. I'm surprised Sharki hasn't gobbled up places like this. A jealous, spiteful man like that. You'd think he'd string the owners up by the toes, all of them competing against him."

"Nah." Deidra barked out a laugh. "Sharki's got these small-time locals beat with his big ass solar gun. Churns out a hundred times the output of all of them put together down here."

I looked at her with curiosity. An attractive blonde with slender curves and intense sea-green eyes. "Why so glum? You should be happier than a pig wallowing in shit to have escaped him."

"You don't know him. If only you knew the half of it."

Marty spat. "I could give two shits about Sharki. He'll get a fistful of my brass knuckles."

She scowled, turned her back and looked off into space. "Idiot." Her voice was a scornful mumble.

I laughed. We were all going to get along just fine…

Chapter 3

Titan hovered over the refinery and landed amid the sprawl of equipment in the open yard. Deidra moved away from the controls, evidently eager to be first off the ship.

I motioned my firearm. "No, you're staying back aboard."

"Like shit I am, Rusco, I'm in this as much as you."

"Should I bind her?" Marty suggested.

"Do we have to take it that far?"

"Lock her in the forward bin then," Marty advised. I herded her over with my rifle while Marty grinned.

She shoulder-checked by me with a bitter howl. "What the hell are you doing? I thought I was your ally?"

I rubbed the sting out of my arm. "Not just yet. You haven't earned my trust. Remember you were ready to stick an ice pick in my head. Sorry, but if you think for a second, I'm sure you'll agree."

Marty hauled her roughly into the forward bulkhead and slammed the door shut. He set the electromag combo lock to auto and gave it a twirl. "Little birdie'll sit tight till the cows come home."

I grunted a mirthless laugh. "Yeah, you tell 'em. Let's see what we can dig up in this dog yard out there."

Marty took an extra R4 from the wall, his stubbly cheeks creased in a smirk. I gripped my rifle. I was getting sick of that smirk. But then again, I guess he was sick of mine.

We stepped out of the cargo hold, fingers ready on our guns. Low cement walls to either side, wavy wire fence and electro-gates at front and back. Crushed stone along the edges, otherwise gray hardtop up the middle. Smoke came from our rear vanes. I followed the trail of gray curly vapor as it licked around the landing gear then paused, shaking my head in dismay at the gaping hole to left center. Some score marks pocked the middle of the fuselage. Armored plates torn back and colored fluids leaking from exposed pipes. Damn, she'd taken a beating. *Titan* was not looking good. Marty stared, tugging at his bristly chin.

This place was a lonely one. To my ears came an eagle's cry over the distant trees, or something akin. Pale lavender-green sky. High cirrus clouds filtering the faraway sun's light, casting a somber glow on the stark terrain. Must have been a chore to terraform this planet. To either side stood rusted cranes, paint-peeled scaffolding, battered crucibles and metal bins. Air still as death. Hammering drifted our way, and the fires of forges along with men's raucous voices. I caught the hint of movement behind the stacks and tensed.

We were not alone for long.

"Hey, you bozos," a big man called. He came lumbering toward us, waving his arms. "You can't land here. Get that crate out of here."

I held up a hand. "Relax. We just have a few questions to put to the yardmaster. You the head honcho here?"

"Yeah, why?"

A low growl came to my left. I turned, pulse racing, as some creepster animal skulked up. I stepped back, anxious breath on my lips. The creature had a scaly hide like a lizard, smelling of a hog, but smiling through a jowl of yellow teeth. Just what I needed, some slavering, waist-high beast ready to tear chunks out of our legs.

Fear would get us nowhere. I took a giant step forward, but gripping fingers hard on the trigger.

"Easy," the man called. "No need to get mean. Fifer ain't going to hurt you. So long as you don't rile her up. Or smell like cat shit."

I came closer, bridling my unease, knowing it would only antagonize the creature to violence. "Hey, there, Shep." The dog-lizard came bounding over, curling its salivating lip. It whined when I offered it my hand. A rangy orange tongue came out to lick my fingers. I patted the beast. It wagged that scaly tail. Marty threw it an old piece of a synthetic bologna sandwich he'd half finished.

"No feeding the animals, dorkus," the man growled. "What do you want to do, make her sick? What are you, bunch of wise-guys?"

Marty smiled. "Whatever you say, padre."

"It's Kragen to you. What do you fucks want anyways? If you're looking to peddle product on that junker of yours, you've come to the wrong place. Malley over in equipment yard might look it over for trade." He jerked a meaty thumb back behind the tin sheds. "Though that rustbucket of yours won't get you a few k yols." He scrunched up his eyes. "Looks like one of Sharki's rigs. How'd you get ahold of it?"

More bodies came out of the woodwork. Tentative expressions, surly, wary. Men holding tools, drills, ratchet-irons, chains, other implements foreign to my eyes.

I did a quick scan. Most of these worker bees were slaves—they had the blue slave tattoos branded on their necks.

Thetis was one of those old school, backward worlds where slaves were the norm. They still used slave labor here. I recalled the planet's history that'd rolled up on the holo index while Deidra was working it. Some space mogul had capitalized on the destruction of a few innocent worlds and victimized what he could. Brought the 'refugees' or captives, down with other wartorn planets' citizens. Refuge was Thetis's middle name, a planet of 'salvation', if you wanted to call it that, but in my mind, slavery was slavery.

I nodded without enthusiasm. "What do you do here anyway?"

"I'm crog here. We prepare quality beryl for industrial use. Also other gear, like crucibles for the beryl mining operation. See those catwalks?" He pointed toward a trapeze of long-grated steel and railing. "Need four men to monitor the feeders underneath, make sure the sluicers are always pouring in the right mixes. One slip and we lose a batch and Jakren, our distributor, is mighty pissed."

I stared in curiosity. A massive crucible, fifteen feet wide, sat on a low platform joining the first level catwalk. Two more tiers of catwalks ran above that. A chute was attached to the crucible's top where a loader could pour raw beryl into the mouth. Hot flames licked up at the bottom of the vessel. A mix of smaller ones sat on the tarmac. Replacements? When the brew was done? All said and done, this looked like a capable, simple, but ragged ass operation.

Marty gave a curt growl. "Thanks for the breakdown, chief, but we're looking for a bit of slide and dive, if you have it."

I interjected a cough. "What we really want, Kragen, is—"

"I don't care what you want. Getting a funny feeling about you two. Back that rig off and let's call it a day."

"Wait, hear us out."

He scratched at his beard. "I'm listening."

I made appreciative motions at the machinery scattered about the yard. "Nice setup you have. Seems a little out of the way though."

Kragen spat out a wad of brown goo. Local product, likely harvested from the swamps. "Only a few settlements on this wet sponge of a planet. Most of the action is in Tyrone City. Next, Narpoon Town. I like it out here, the isolation, the loneliness, it suits me. You can hear the jackdaw and swamp crake over the roar of an engine, with the howl of firrits like Fifer here thrown in." He patted the mangy hound-lizard on the head.

I signaled to Marty. With an irritated shrug, he turned and sauntered back to move the ship. I heard the whine of engines as he set her down in the adjacent yard. "Happy?" I grunted at the yardmaster.

"Very."

Marty came loping back, looking slightly peeved, but then the hint of a shit-eating grin broke out on his face. "Heard our pigeon thrashing around, Ruskie. What a mouth on that one! Not liking it much in her birdcage."

Kragen's eyebrows shot up and I scowled at Marty, resenting him for his insinuations. Even an old ox like Kragen could put two and two together.

A skinny woman with pale brown cheeks and dust-covered curls edged in. She wore a pair of faded blue overalls. "Boss, that rig is sizable enough for hauling stones from Jakren's new pit over by Narpoon Lake. We could take it off their hands and get these three to work hog down on the feeders."

Kragen smoothed out his mustache. "Not a bad plan, Bessy, if I don't say. Provided these fellows'll oblige."

I gave a sad laugh. "You got it all wrong. See, we're here about repairs, Kragen. We look like a couple of dopes to you? *Take it off your hands...*" I grunted in cynical wonder.

Bessy whined. "Just saying, Krag. We just got off two weeks of loader duty and I was hoping for some kickback. Jakren promised me a fat raise for good work and helpful suggestions after two years."

"You'll get your bonus, Bessy. Be patient. Ain't no raises for slaves, remember? Only perks, like extra fruit cake on Sunday. Now go feed Fifer. She's looking mighty peckish."

Bessy loped away with a jaunty step. The hound bounded after her, its tongue wagging.

"Gotta treat these workers like children," he grumbled to me. "Never get a better worker than Bessy." He cupped his hands and called back to her, "Give her a good scrubbing while you're at it. I see mange patches on that back fur." He turned back to us, blowing air out of his cheeks. "What were we discussing?—"

He stopped short. Several of the yardhands catcalled as Deidra came swaggering up with a viperous look and a rifle in her hands. My jaw dropped. How did she... She sauntered up to me, her face flushed and inches from mine, pissed as hell.

I whirled on Marty. "Hey, I thought I told you to lock down the systems?"

"Relax, Rusco." Deidra chuckled. "Don't blame your boy wonder. Any two bit hack could figure out how to crack that lock and override the password on the ship's systems. It's my ship, remember?"

Kragen laughed. "Well, some mighty fine surprises in that tickle trunk of yours, Rusbo. Any more eye candy hiding back there? I'll get Zeke and Harl to have a look-see."

I raised my rifle. "No you won't."

His smile grew to an icy leer. "I might take whatever load you're stashing there off your hands, if you throw in the girl for free."

I stared in disapproval. "No deal."

Marty huffed. "Why not, Rusco? We don't owe the girl anything. You said so yourself she'd ram an ice pick in your ear."

"Not how we do things around here, Marty."

"Oh, don't be such a chivalrous prude."

Kragen warned, "If you're carrying hot goods, Sharki'll roast you."

"What are you, all a bunch of pussies?" snarled Marty. "The hold's full of quality product. Easy for you to peddle it through your contact, Jakren."

Some of the yardhands stirred. Kragen's eyes narrowed as he contemplated the deal. "No pussies here. How much you want? 20…30?" After some stares and glares, it looked as if a deal might go through at 22. But an inner voice told me that I could get ten times that amount out in Valdair.

One of Kragen's grubby workhands tapped him on the shoulder. He jerked around. "What do you want?"

"Yo, boss, some idgit here to see you. Some greaser the name of Silas." He jerked a thumb over his shoulder.

"What now?" Kragen rolled his eyes. "Thought this was a workplace, not some drop-in joint."

Deidra sprang to attention. "Silas? Shit, that's Sharki's bounty hunter."

Kragen scowled. "Friend of yours?"

"You could call him that," I mumbled.

Kragen growled. "You carrying stuff you shouldn't could get you in trouble. I'll deal with this. You sit tight."

He swaggered across the yard while Marty, me and Deidra

ducked behind some rusted metal bins. No use 'Silas' getting a fix on us. Fortunate that we'd moved the ship to a secluded area.

I caught a brief glimpse of Silas, Sharki's so-called bounty hunter. Recognized his gunmetal garb. Tall rangy sod with a metal-silver shielding up his left arm, the same color as his boss's ugly space suit. He and Kragen spoke at length at the back of the yard, waving arms and raising voices. The yardhands stood around, trading sullen murmurs.

Strident words drifted across the open space. The air was clammy and smelling of swamp stuff like snails and muskeg.

"Their ship trailing smoke was spotted circling around here."

"Sorry, bro, can't help you. Whoever they are must be long gone. Try Smilly's on Barrowfen."

There were grunts and some more curt words traded, then the bounty hunter left. A disc-shaped ship with turbo boosters took off in blue jet blasts and headed toward Tyrone City.

We came out of hiding and brushed ourselves off. "Appreciate your quick cover story," I said gruffly.

Kragen shrugged. "Don't mention it. Considering my good deed of the day, how be you give us something in return?"

"I told you, you can't have the woman."

"Well, if you're not going to throw her in, how about joining in on some recreation? Winner takes all."

"Come again?"

"A little friendly yard play. Nothing to wet yourself over. You win, I get Malley to do your repairs. You lose, we take your shipment, and the girl."

Deidra's mouth sagged. "No fucking way, Rusco."

Marty gave a coarse laugh. I waved them to silence.

"Quite a deal, Kragen. You're a real regular, all round guy."

He beamed. "Glad you approve."

I questioned my wisdom at dropping in on this yard. My fingers flexed around my R4. I liked the warm stock and its feel and toyed with the idea of blasting my way out of here. Not a good plan. Our ship was disabled and we were outnumbered. They all seemed to carry just knives and workman's tools, yet—

"Put that blaster down."

Before I knew it rude hands were groping me from behind. *What the*— Didn't hear them coming. Two rag-bearded fellows, all grins. Someone snatched Marty's weapon and as quickly, Deidra's. Like pros, these weasels.

Now we were even more outnumbered.

"That's better," Kragen rumbled. "A more even playing arena. I don't like strangers with guns in my yard."

"I still don't get—"

"I mean—you against me. Ratchets, Dongels, Hammers, Gongs. You pick."

So, have some sport with the pigeon Rusco. Gain a few laughs and some points with the buds. Okay, I can run with it—old boy throwback tried and true. A bait and impress your yard-dog followers with a trick.

"Ratchets." I could handle this.

Kragen shrugged. "Interesting choice. I see you like pain. No matter." He motioned to one of his men and tossed me a pipe wrench. He gripped one in his own hand and patted one end against his palm. It fit nicely. "Your move, captain."

I raised my weapon.

"Wait," Kragen grunted. "Just to make this more interesting, let's move the arena closer to the workflow."

I flashed him a quizzical glance.

"Sometimes Bessy and Zeke get a little sloppy with their janitorial work. Slop acid drips down from the main crucible. See?" He motioned to a place under the catwalks where acid-scored scaffolding ran up in complex configurations. "Real bitch if somebody steps in those acid pools or heaven forbid, falls in it. Last guy did—well, you don't want to know, Rusbo. I'll leave it to your imagination."

I did and I got it loud and clear. "An amusing game," I murmured. Me, Marty and Deidra followed them over to the crucible pad. "You play this game often?"

"As much as we can. Suffice it to say, a few men are off each week tending to burns and other wounds. This week's unusual though—three guys laid out." He grinned. "Just saying."

I grinned back. "Not surprising." I examined the bilious yellow pools staining the tarmac. A sulfurous reek wafted from the acid-pocked hardtop. One of the massive crucibles had been recently forklifted away and curls of acrid steam still rose from the spillage.

"Shall we? Day's getting on." Kragen gave a terse flourish.

Mumbling in anticipation, Kragen's drones climbed the scaffolding to watch. I cast them a menacing leer and an exaggerated salute.

"After you." I held out my hand to him.

Marty looked on in amusement. "All the luck to you, Rusco." He slapped me on the back a bit harder than necessary. "Break a leg."

Wish he'd given me some Myscol earlier on. Bugger. I could handle this creepo game. We get the repairs done and scram from this joint, before some bitchface, heavy-hitter dirtbag like Silas sidles back looking for us.

Kragen came in strong, beating me back with his pipe and making me sweat. The clinks of cold metal on metal echoed up the yard. Marty moved in closer for a bird's eye view. Deidra stood at a distance, her body rigid. The crowd hollered and cheered for Kragen. I backpedaled, narrowly missing a whistling swing that came a hair's width from my ear. Christ, was the sod trying to kill me? Sure, why not? Gain a free ship and cargo, once he gets rid of Marty and uses Deidra.

I stepped in a puddle and howled as sizzling smoke rose from the sole of my left boot. I hot-potatoed it out of the way, at the same time shucking off my boot while Kragen grinned, shaking his head in admiration. "Tricky business there, Rusbo. You're a real acrobat, doing that jitterbug."

I coursed forward, in a shambling hop, trying to duck under Kragen's next pipe swings which came faster and more furious while I shouldered up heavy and blocked him with my own tool. Now I was lumbering around with one sock foot. Easy prey to more yellow sludge if I wasn't careful. Likely lose half my foot if I mis-stepped.

Kragen's grin grew ever broader. "Good save there, Rusbo. Haven't seen that done in a long time." He guffawed. "Think you just won tipsy award of the week."

He vaulted in and gave me a good wallop with his pipe-wrench that grazed my forearm. Enough of a wicked nick to sting the feeling out of my arm and make me want to howl. But I didn't howl. Never would give that clown the pleasure of thinking he'd scored a point.

Two of his monkeys butted in to shove me closer to his swings.

Deidra came in with both fists to box the first of the two joker's ears. "You buggers ever hear of fair play?" She held her ground, ready to deal out more. Marty was beside her, sleeves rolled up, daring them to go further.

One barked out a lewd remark.

"Yeah, your mother too," Deidra called back.

That last move snapped a wire in my head and now the old Mr. Hyde burned bright and strong. Just an instant hurricane of evil. Not for too long. That mean ugly fucker side wouldn't need it for long. I feinted left then right, ducked his steel and tripped his heavy padded ass. He fell hard and cried out and I beamed him soundly across the back, prompting a howl and a groan. He fell face first to the tarmac, inches from an acid spill. My ratchet head went up to brain him for good but he held up a restraining hand. "Okay, okay, truce, Rusbo. You won that fair and square. No heavy hitting needed. We go get us some brews, dark ones in the back hangar."

"Sure, sure…and it's *Rusco*." I took his hand and helped him up. "What of our guns?"

"Nah, no guns. They scare me."

I rolled my eyes.

"Malley can fix your rig up. He's our best mechanic. I've taken a shine to you, Rusbo, so what's say I swing you a deal? Fair price."

"Rusco."

"If it's structural, be longer. Internal drive conventional stuff."

"How long?"

"A week?"

"Fuck, we don't have a week," Marty cried, fists pumped. "Sharki'll be all over us by then."

I cut Marty off with a chop of my hand. "Not much choice, Marty," I hissed. "We can scout out Tyrone City in the meantime, see what's up."

Deidra's face looked bleak as a cold winter day. "So what now? We just wait around for some sharpshooter like Silas to blow our brains out?"

"You can lay low here," Kragen offered. "No one will bother you. I've got odd jobs for the lot of you—help pay for those repairs."

* * *

So we stayed on and joined part of Kragen's yard gang, working chain rig, hauling buckets of smelt, doing crucible watch, cleanup, any odd piss-pot jobs Kragen had for us. I was soaked with sweat by the end of the day. Deidra too, who lolled at my side, grimed and looking none too happy. Marty raked up piss and shit from the animal yard. He turned to me. "Why they have a rescue station here for every firrit that ever lived is beyond me." He plugged his nose, bawled a curse, plugged his nose again. "Must be a hundred shitters here."

"Because the boss loves firrits, is why," said Edgar the maintenance man. "Keep working. Everybody can have a pet firrit here. Maybe you'll get one too."

Marty shook his head and exhaled a sad breath. "Sure, need one like I need a hole in the head. What I need is one those nightly plunges in the shallow lake nearby."

Turns out Kragen's mini refinery did everything under the sun...and the old-fashioned, conventional way, heating crucibles of mineral with fire then jolts of electricity getting it to proper ionization level. Used loaders and cranes to lift the smelt to a cooling bin before it was cut up into bite-sized crystals then cleaned.

Thetis still had these shops and factories going, though as Deidra pointed out, they pumped out nowhere near the volume of Sharki's operation.

I kept Deidra out of harm's way and under tight watch, a spare tool hid in my back pocket in case anybody got too frisky. That brazen swagger of hers with loose-hipped stride was mighty tempting. Coupled with her full lips, tall bearing and ash blond hair trailing past shoulders was enough to put most men over the edge. Not that she couldn't handle herself. We ate in the mess hall off Malley's yard. Mostly cheap fare, looking like some sort of boiled swamp scallops and white stringy vegetable. But the food was included so I couldn't complain. Marty ate heaping double helpings while Deidra seemed to eat like a bird. All in all, Kragen was a fair host who organized entertainment for us in the evenings, like homegrown comedy hour, dress up night, beer-drinking races, and such, all to the drunken jeers of the slave help. Marty turned out to be a hoot, dressing up like a spinster and giving his ham-handed version of her violent acts with a tire iron when accosted by the rowdy yardhands in an improvised skit.

By day, Kragen worked us hard and Marty was ready to murder someone. "From riches to rags," he griped. "We should be getting that shipment to buyers and be laughing it up."

"But we aren't, are we? So quit your grousing and keep looking to better days. We have the chance to be rich men."

"Yeah, I'll believe it when I see it, Rusco."

Deidra took a more relaxed stance and did her work without complaining. At night time Marty, Deidra and I camped out in *Titan*, spared us having to sleep in the communal barracks. Good thing too. Deidra's good looks and figure would have been a magnet for trouble.

After hours the third day she approached me after the other workers had hit the barracks: nothing more than crude tin lodgings much like an army provides its soldiers, located behind the equipment service yard.

"Still haven't forgiven you, Rusco, for locking me in that closet-crib. Very unnecessary. Who are you anyways? Can't put my finger on you. A wise-ass with some smarts and grit, but unpredictable. Vagabond, thief, rogue, all in one. There's something not quite right about you and that cross-eyed grin of yours under all that murky, cynical exterior, with a few little idiosyncrasies thrown in that don't add up."

I smirked. "Don't think too long, Deidra. You'll never figure me out. Nor will I."

"Clever answer. Why're you chumming around with that hothead bullet-face? Seems a bad match. Surely you can cut loose and do better?"

"Mar's a little rough around the edges, I'll give you that, but a loyal accomplice and one who gets the job done."

"Yeah, that's an overstatement." She shook her head and made a sour face. "Still can't figure you out."

"Forget it. You're in over your head. Concentrate on getting yourself free from Sharki. Until we're off this planet, you're just as much sharkbait as the rest of us."

CHRIS TURNER

Chapter 4

Three days later, Kragen put a rough hand on my shoulder as I was about to haul a bucket of reagent up the scaffolding to drop in the feeder chute. "Repairs done, Rusbo. Warp is still screwed but impulse drive is working fine. A fine ship that is—antediluvian as she may be."

Marty looked up with a growl. "The impulse was working fine before."

Kragen shrugged. "Just relaying Malley's words. The bad news—the ship's clocked up more repair and parts than any of us ever expected. We went ahead, made the repairs anyways. Hope you don't mind and your pals aren't in any hurry somewhere?"

My throat felt dry as I drew in a hoarse breath. "How much repair?"

Kragen winced, wiped his chin, "About 10k yols."

"10k? Get serious!"

"We can amortize the cost over time, relax, Rusbo. Strictly labor. You people seem to be doing a half decent job here." He pointed and smiled. "That'll be three of you working nights. Say about three months work? Maybe two and a half, if you work overtime."

"No fucking way!" Marty bawled. "I'm no roustabout."

Kragen screwed up his eyes in disapproval. "You know, I don't like you, bullet-head. Got a dirty mouth. Seems you need a lesson in humility. To show proper respect for the working class."

Marty reached for the hammer at his feet in the toolbox. "Screw your respect. There's none of that in this twisted universe, so piss off."

"Hold on." I broke up the inevitable fight.

Our heads turned at a sound of a sneering voice. "Hoy!"

Six men came our way, all swagger and heavily armed.

Kragen stepped back with a grimace. My blood ran cold. The old feet didn't want to move but I forced them edging back into the late afternoon shadows. I drew Marty and Deidra with me. My worst nightmare, if ever there was one. We huddled behind some oil drums. Four of Sharki's henchmen stood with R3s cocked alongside that robotic bounty hunter we'd seen with the dart gun embedded in his left forearm.

The firrit at Kragen's side sniffed and growled.

Sharki approached with a palm extended. "What's a matter, pooch? Don't like the smell of a real man?" He laughed.

The firrit scuttled away and sank teeth into Silas's leg.

"Ah, you mother fucker." The bounty hunter smashed down with his metal dart gun arm to brain it but it deked away, snarling. He had only grazed it. The beast made a beeline for Sharki who blasted it between the eyes. The creature fell in a limp heap, convulsing, rotated a few rounds before lying still.

Kragen's face turned beet red. "Hey, you bastard, that was an innocent animal."

Sharki shrugged. "Didn't like the look or smell of it."

"Tough shit. Fifer didn't like you. That's why she attacked. Animal's doing only what it should, protecting its own." He pulled out his knife.

"You might as well slit your own throat with that penknife," Sharki said conversationally. "What you got there is worse than two pairs against a five card stud. Unless you're a knife-hurling ace?"

"What you want? This is a respectable business. Take your bully-boys and get off my property."

"Where you hiding them, crog? Seems I saw brisk activity a

moment ago by those bins."

"Employees is all, under my protection."

"Oh, yeah?" With a vile sneer, he cocked his weapon and pegged a bearded slave trying to creep away. "There's one dead employee. How many more will it take?"

Kragen made to throw the knife but Sharki lifted his weapon and capped the yardmaster in the fleshy part of the leg.

"OW, you son of a bitch!"

Sharki frowned and capped him in his other leg. Kragen rolled, moaning on the ground, hugging his bleeding lower limbs.

Vagas, Kragen's chain gang man, leaped in to club Sharki on the side of the head but the bounty hunter got to him first. A gleaming dart went whistling right through his larynx. He clutched his throat and fell to his knees, gurgling.

"Any more of you pipsqueaks have any objections?"

Dead silence except for Vagas's and Kragen's gurgles and moans.

"No? I thought so." Sharki laid his boot on Kragen's rasping throat.

Kragen had been good to us and I hated to see him die like that. "He's an innocent man, leave him alone," I rasped out from behind the barrels.

"Nobody's innocent, fucknut. Come out and show yourself. Little Tweety-Bird has to pay for lying to the big wolf. See, truth is, Silas here was not that bright and listened to lies the first time round. I ain't the credulous fool he is." He lifted his foot and ignoring Kragen's bellowing protest, stamped down on his neck, snapping it like a rotten branch.

I winced. We slumped behind the oil drums, all three of us gritting our teeth. What an utter cockup. We were dead meat.

Three wasted, more to come. How to get to the ship with six armed men cutting off our escape?

"This voice have a name?" Sharki bellowed. "Let me guess... Jet Rusco. Two bit bandit, demolitions man, hustler, wise-ass. I think you and me have some bones to pick, Rusco."

Damn Kragen. Lost his life, now reduced to a bleeding, shameless heap. Stupid fool and his no-gun policy. We had no weapons to protect ourselves but for a few monkey wrenches, tire irons and cans of paint.

"I made it my personal mission to hunt you bastards down," Sharki went on. "Messed up my station back there. Nobody crosses Sharki and gets away with it. All of them are six feet under, every one of them."

I saw Deidra shudder. She turned pale.

The gangster came marching up the yard, guns in both hands. He leveled barrels to either side, firing indiscriminately while Kragen's yardhands scattered or dropped, and his henchmen grinned and fanned out to cover the exits.

The slaves fled on, up into the catwalk, behind bins, quaking in their boots. Not easy for these two score of workers to flee Kragen's yard with the high wall surrounding the compound and the barbed wire gates at either end. I herded Deidra and Marty deeper behind the drums, my mind brainstorming a plan of action.

Sharki's mop-up man was uglier than sin; a waddler, short, built like a tank, wide-spaced cow-like eyes. Sharki was no better. Warted brute with a sawed off nose, chunky cheeks, shark eyes and buck teeth. Wouldn't doubt he was augmented like his bounty boy. Both garbed in silver kevlar plate with bands of leather wrapped across shoulders and thighs. Both armed to the teeth: R3s, bowie knives, morningstars. I nudged Deidra beside me who was quivering in the dirt and grease. "What's the deal with this kingpin? Is that a nose or a mask he's wearing?"

"Got it in a cat fight in Veglos," she hissed. "Someone tried to teach him a lesson—whipped out a knife. Slice and dice. Let's just say that thug's a hole in the ground."

Sharki marched on, whistling and chuckling. "Come out, come out, wherever you are. Rusco, Jet Rusco, you playing possum on me? That's no way to deal. Lots of little hidey-holes to hunker down in here. We'll find you all. And little Deidra—I can smell your pretty little hide."

A movement to my left. Sharki fired full on into the bins, spraying oil every which way not ten feet away from us. If one of those bullets hit a pressure tank...

A man in coveralls fell, blood-drenched and croaking.

"Oops, excuse me. My condolences, grandpa. Thought you were that rat fink Rusco, the thief who shot up my station. Forgive a fellow an honest mistake."

He blew the head off the maintenance man, Edgar, who tried to make a break for it back in the plum shadows behind a machine-tool rack.

Sharki laughed and recited a kids' rhyme. "*Me, oh, my, folk I do spy, dying in the heat of the day. Hum dee hum.* No need for all this bloodshed, Rusco, if only you'd bring your cowardly ass out and fight like a man."

I ducked back. To my right stood oil canisters stacked three high. A reeking, rancid grease pit. To my left stacks of tools, cellophane and fencing. One of those tire irons might be a good weapon. The whites of Marty's eyes gleamed. The hothead was about to do something rash, with his pipe wrench tightfisted in a hand, so I gripped his shoulder and shook my head. I crept around back, careful not to disturb a pebble, searching for some way to even our odds. No chance. The smart thing was to get that weapon off our bounty hunter or one of his tag-alongs. The stupid thing was to try some heroic kamikaze act, like these other bozos.

I felt sorry for them. They'd no love for Sharki, after what he did to their boss. The ones who ran off got darts in their faces or bullets through their chests. *Rat-a-tat.* It was like a sick symphony.

"That's it, Silas," laughed Sharki as he poked hither and yon with the butt end of his rifle. "Round 'em up like steers."

Silas moved on, huffing, in a wincing limp. They moved up on the crucible platform, and the beginnings of the catwalks.

"Hoof it up, you laggard, you're dragging. One little dog bite isn't anything to get worried about. Just a chicken scratch."

Silas wanted to tell Sharki to bug off. I could tell, judging from the red spreading up his neck, but as they walked under a higher catwalk, a wild shape leaped out of the air.

Bessy, for all her bravery, took a wild plunge from her catwalk level, right onto Silas's back, knocking him backward against the main crucible. Yowling and cat-scratching, she hooked her claws in his face. Silas howled. His left arm pinwheeled and grabbed a hank of hair, flailed into the acid water, singeing half his side and arm. He let out a blood-curdling shriek.

Sharki shook his head in dumb amazement. He bullet-holed Bessy on the spot. "Idgit." Her eyes stared up in glassy death.

"Silas, you witless knob, what the hell have you gone and done? Got yourself dunked like a dumb dog in a poison pool."

"Help me," he begged, writhing on the metal-gridded platform, clutching at his sizzling burns.

Sharki clicked his tongue. "You're beyond help, Silas. Best I can do is put you out of your misery." He lowered his R3 to the back of Silas's skull. Brains flew in three directions.

Sharki barked out orders into his com. "Man down! I repeat, man down. Get your asses over here—Kragen's crib! Full speed."

I looked to the sky, knowing in minutes Sharki's lightfighters would be touching down to fire us full of holes. I wanted the hell out of here. Yet I also wanted to hunt him down and waste him badly. But that would mean the deaths of us all.

I tapped Deidra on the arm. "Try to distract him. Make some noise or something, throw a wrench his way."

She peered at me with owl's eyes. "You insane? He'll shoot us to pieces."

"Do it or we're dead," I rasped. "Only a matter of time before Sharki flushes us out. I'll try to figure something out."

She shook her head in exasperation.

"Marty—go with her," I hissed. "Cover her. Throw pipes, tire irons, whatever. If I can snag that weapon from our dead bounty hunter, our problem could be solved."

Marty grimly accepted the task.

I saw Deidra's sick green look. "He's not that stupid. Not going to kill you…maybe enslave you and your pretty ass, so stall him as long as you can."

I moved out of my hiding place, keeping low to the line of shadows, gauging my time. One, starship, two starships. You're moving too slow, Rusco. Get up on that scaffolding. You're going to—"

Crucible #2 tilted as some yardbird worked the hydraulic controls. A foul slop of chemical slurry poured out on the hardtop. One of Sharki's hirelings screamed, splattered with hot acid.

"Holy fuck!" Sharki bawled. "Kill that bastard who's working the controls."

Fire sprayed up at him on a first level catwalk where the great iron crucible yawed. A bullet-holed body sagged and fell headfirst to the tarmac. The slick spray on the hardtop gave off noxious sulfurous fumes. It was the diversion that allowed Marty and Deidra and me to crawl our way to better cover.

But something crackled behind me. Sharki caught a whiff of movement. Maybe my shadow moving a fraction too fast.

"Hold it." He came waltzing back down the catwalk, gun leveled at my back. "Where you going, spider man? Back it up, don't try to run off."

I exhaled a curse, holding my hands up, rising from my crouch.

He walked up and sized me up. I closed my eyes just as his fist came angling up. An explosion of pain burst across my mouth with the coppery taste of blood. Disoriented, I opened my eyes, wiped off the streaming liquid. I gave him back a twisted grimace.

"You know, Rusco, it's scabs like you make my job harder." He backhanded me another stinging blow in the face. "An honest rogue trying to make a living in this depraved universe gets messed up by a prick like you. It's like having a hot tong jabbing you in a sensitive place. You sticking your nose in business you have no right to. Turning my own against me like that liver-licking Deidra piece of ass who's careening fast to a reckoning in the sluthouse."

He kicked me down to my knees.

"Stay down like the dog you are."

I licked my lips, contemplating my options which were few.

"You're in a heap of trouble here, Rus-boy. Think I'll kill you slow, draw out the pain—for every atom of damage you did to my operation."

"Knock yourself out."

He hoofed me in the gut this time. I was feeling some serious pain right about now. He reached down to pistol whip me but something alerted him at the last minute. He jerked back as a rat-a-tat came at him. He gave back a high-pitched yelp.

At the same time some engine started up behind us, to the side. A forklift, headlights glaring, came to life barreling toward us. What the fuck? Someone managed to get it up and running. Marty?

Shots rang out, shattering the glass. Sharki's #3 boy, crouched and ready, laid into the approaching metal, ripping the cowling to bits. I saw a dark form dive out of the cabin as the thing came whizzing by. Good old Mar!

Where was Deidra? Her bullet caught Sharki on the left toe. He was hobbling around, cursing and hollering, but nowhere near incapacitated. Nothing worse than a wounded shark.

I scrambled away to cover before he decided to pop me.

Marty came out of his roll, smashing into the crouching guard, taking him by surprise. The man fell backward. Marty ripped the weapon out of his grasp.

He tossed a sawed off rifle into my hands as I rushed forward. Must have lifted the other off one of the dead guards. I grabbed it, nestled it against my beating chest. The stock felt warm from the sun. A grin of triumph broke out on my blood-dripping face.

Sharki half limped behind the shell-shot forklift which had crashed into the cement wall and stalled out there, smoke rising from its hood.

Steel whipped out. Marty's carbine flared. He and Deidra took out the last of Sharki's stooges in a burst of crimson and guts.

I followed up with fire of my own, aiming for Sharki's hideaway. He laid into us with all his firepower, shells ripping what little cover we had. Me and Marty scuttled like land crabs on our hands and knees out of gun shot range.

Deidra sprinted in a wild dash beside me. Her hot breath was on my neck.

Sharki called out of his hiding place. "So, the traitor bitch shows her true colors!" He spat phlegm and coughed. "You'll be on the end of a leash before sundown, slut. Mark my words." He shot blind at us.

Deidra howled, a gobbling, gulping sound. I had to pull her back. "No sudden moves, you fool. You'll get gunned down. He's just trying to goad you into showing yourself. We have to think this out."

Sharki was tucked in behind the broken, smoking fork lift, firing blind shells out at us. Anyone tried to get too close to that mad dog would get his legs shot off.

"Come on, let's move!" I rasped. "The ship's waiting. It isn't going to come to us!"

We raced back to the main gate and out into the adjacent yard where *Titan* stood parked. My eyes roved to the sky waiting for Sharki's lightfighters to blow us to bits.

Chapter 5

The service yard was a beehive of activity. Slaves running, firrits barking, shouts, bedlam, general waves of confusion. The gunfire had spooked them. Kragen's no-gun policy had them ill-prepared and running scared. But a few intrepid slaves grabbed up tire irons and gathered to storm the refinery. Good luck to them. Didn't doubt the local law was on its way too. Good time to get the hell out of here. We scooted into *Titan's* open cargo bay and hoofed it to the bridge. Deidra started *Titan's* impulse engines and we blasted off.

"Why don't we buzz Sharki and finish him off?" Marty bawled when we were in the air.

"No, he radioed in for backup, remember? By the time we flush him out, he'll have a battalion of V-Zons on our ass. What we can do is slam his ride. Circle back," I instructed Deidra. She swung the vessel around in a wide arc. Sure enough a high-powered V-Zon sat parked in Malley's smaller yard with a bunch of other vehicles. "Zone in. Let me shred that shitter."

Deidra came in close and I worked the weapons' grid, riddling the enemy fuselage with bullets. Sharki's ship smoked and sizzled. It looked a sorry sight.

Marty grunted in satisfaction. "Why don't we buzz the forklift too he's hiding under?"

"What, and kill innocent yardhands? Sharki's moved on by now.

We spray the yard, innocent people die."

Marty grumbled, "So where to now?"

"We aren't going far until we get this light drive fixed. After all, 10k yols worth of repairs've already been done. Tyrone City, Narpoon Town?" I expelled a breath of frustration. "I just want the hell out of this place. Not going to let this shipment slip out of our hands. Worked too hard for it."

Deidra sighed. "Last place Sharki'll think we'll go is Tyrone City."

"Then Tyrone City it is. He'll be banking we head to some out of the way place again."

"As good a plan as any," said Marty.

A quick mental check. An innocent stop at one machine yard ends in tragedy. I could just see the headline: *Machine yard Bloodbath. Crog and Gangster Slain!* Excellent work, Rusco. How many more people going to die as a result of your recklessness?

The yardmaster didn't have to die. That was our doing. At least indirectly. I hated random, useless deaths. But then this was a dark universe, the colonized worlds were a seething cauldron of violence. Stealing from the bad guys had not been working out too well for us.

"Question is where can we hide the ship?" interrupted Deidra, disturbing my thoughts.

"We can't be gallivanting roughshod with this clunker. It's like waving a red cape in front of the bull."

Marty heaved a sigh. "I don't know, you're the brain came up with the scheme."

"Deidra?"

She winced, catching sight of what must be my swollen face and black eyes. "You look bad, Rusco."

"Yeah, well, not all of us have good days." I pointed to the holo index. "Time's wasting."

She consulted the grid, a 3D enclosed sphere of color and sound. It showed a rotating image of a map and gridded layout with various installations. She pressed tabs on the color-coded menu. A computer voice narrated on. She gave a cluck of irritation and turned it off.

A list of registers came up, layover places, merchant retreats, repair shops, seedy guest houses, smoke shops, other dives.

"A couple of these look promising." Her voice lacked enthusiasm. "*The Midges' Retreat*, or wait, here's a good one, *The Traveler's Depot*—meals to go, underground hanger, extra charge. Every miner's dream."

"Nah, don't like any of them." I scowled. "Too conspicuous. Sharki's scouts'll make us in a second and report us."

She sucked on her lower lip. "I wish that bastard had died down there. I'd feel a lot better." Marty sat, nursing his wounds. I winced at the bruises and bloody scrapes all along his forearm.

Deidra brightened. "Wait, I know a place. Outside town. It might work—an old quarry, adjoining Abashal's mine. We can park this ship in the gully and leave for town on foot."

I rubbed my chin. "Maybe, Deidra...I like it more than the 'Midges' Retreat."

She gave a sigh of defeat. "One of us has to stay back to guard the ship. Guess that'll have to be me."

I snorted. "No doubt you'd volunteer. The answer is no. I still don't trust you. You're coming with us. We all go in as a group."

"What the hell? You're a real hardass." She threw up her hands and glared. "I have a bad feeling about Tyrone. Already told you about Sharki's plans for me."

"Yeah, well me I have a bad feeling too," said Marty. "Boo hoo. Let's suck it up."

"We need flesh regen. Marty's hurting. Also need to find a mechanic who can repair the light drive. If Kragen had come through and fixed that too, we wouldn't be in this mess. I don't trust winging in with this giant. Guess we'll be hitting Tyrone City after all."

Marty set the coordinates for the quarry. Deidra flew us in. The quarry loomed up on our sights, a big open sore amid the wide stretches of bogtree and endless pools of brackish water. We dipped down into the mammoth pit and found a spot along the bottom among the crags and pegmatite rock formations deep in the ravine.

The place was long quarried to death. We set *Titan* back under a natural overhang that hid her from sight from the air. It was damp and humid, populated by creepy crawly things no doubt deeper within, but we didn't investigate. This place'd do for now.

Deidra wrinkled her nose in the muggy air. "Happy now? What's next?"

I motioned her up the carved-out pit along an animal path. Climbing up out of the quarry was an onerous hike. Topside, we took the long slog through lowlands and bogs. We humped it up to Tyrone along the backroads, twelve miles or so into town.

We were running low on food...I had grabbed the last vacuum sealed packs from the ship and we gobbled them down as we walked. Unpalatable fare—freeze-dried mutton with synthetic potato. Food was food and beggars couldn't be choosers. Better than going hungry, I thought. Only some wild firrits, roaming out of the mangroves in packs in curiosity. But their half-lizard hisses and dog-like barks drew out low-lying gators that came snapping at our heels. We did a frantic U-turn to outrun them. Some air cars and supply trucks passed, ignoring us. Ships raced across the lavender-green sky but these were too high to spot us as anything suspicious. Sharki'd be looking for a big ship which he wouldn't find, if all went to plan. Not some hitchhikers and straggler hobos humping it up the backroads out in the boondocks on their way to Tyrone.

Everything on this planet was weird. The spooky light, the queer animals, the creepy, stunted trees, the uncanny windless silence. The odd combo offered an enchanted beauty, one which I could not appreciate at the moment.

We made it to center town at dusk, a weary, disheveled bunch of misfits by the time we caught the last air tram. Narrow streets, puddles of rainwater, hustle and bustle, staring eyes, grifters, hustlers looking for marks. Glitter and chrome, wall to wall billboards and towers, although more rusted and less high than those seen on Gainor and Alphanor.

Night was upon us. Tyrone City lay like a reaper's cloak, the big bad ugly side of temptation and sin exposed in all its malevolent glory. Neon signs glared sickly across the skyline. Echoes of discordant, computerized music. Noise thump-thumping amid the rankness of the city air.

I'd seen worlds like this before. Destitute, reeking of vice. Arenas of debauchery. Violent, lawless towns. A product of the boom of raw beryl like any gold rush town throughout history. Didn't like being forced to dip my nose into the reeking stench but here we were.

Air cars whizzed by. Rowdy youths too, weaving through the crowds on helium-powered scooters.

The city had an alter ego of its own on the other side of the lake, a place called Lagoon City. An underwater network linked up to destinations on the far shore, offering mining incentives as beryl-rich as Tyrone to newcomers. Deidra pulled up data on her pocket coder.

The automated voice droned on:

Tyrone-Lagoon city: Transpo service, manufacturing hub for lucrative beryl industry. Thriving tourist trade. Visitors can witness the rare fish lurking in the lagoons and the canals, from shark hybrids to jelly crabs. Underwater sightseeing booked by Lagoon Travels Limited.

Two-hundred years of terraforming makes Lagoon City the springboard for small business, investment and opportunity.

Yeah, more like a haven for scum like Sharki and warlords to capitalize upon.

Formed in 2531, the golden age of expansion, Tyrone became a settler and slave world. It showed potential but then crashed as warring factions took over..."

The automated voice droned away over the noise of the passing traffic.

Marty turned up his nose. "Interesting, but I'm not here for a geography lesson."

"Nor is anybody, Marty. Well, let's go get you some regen. How many yols you got?"

"Sixty six."

"Between you and me, that makes 100. We should be able to get a small tin. Here—" I pointed to a general purpose utility shop with neon in the windows and a bright sign, "Self serve, Food, Drinks, Utilities for all." On display in the window sat spray cans and firrit food, detergent, canned food and beverages.

I motioned the others to stand by while I slipped into the shop past the painted hookers. I found the regen on a top shelf, also got me some cheap, coin-sized flares in case we needed them. Not enough to do much damage, these mini-explosives, but enough to surprise the hell out of some unwary party. Not much of a line-up in here. I made it out in good time. I smeared some orange paste on Marty's ribs, then doctored up my own wounds and gave the rest to Deidra.

He gave a relaxed sigh as the formula did its work. The goop had a remarkable ability to heal and knit inflamed tissue, cuts and bruised flesh back together. I too could feel it like a balm on my own cuts, scrapes and black-rimmed eyes. "We need to find some mechanic. Deidra?"

"Index says, there's a reputable one down *Wailard's Way*. Seedy part of town, but all there is, unless you want to risk random hopping about? We could run into trouble."

"Any more trouble than we already have?"

Deidra had to laugh at that. Good to see her laughing. For a young one, she was too grim.

Wailard's Way ended up looking much seedier than I imagined though. Blackened brick, broken lampposts, gangbangers and miners roving about with tattoos and buzz cuts. Deidra would have done better to stay back on the ship. *So she could fly off and wave bye-bye to us and never be seen again?* Think again, Rusco, you dummy. Leave the thinking for Bozo the Clown. Didn't like the look of those powder boys and pimps over there staring us down. Too obvious we were, as new fish to town. Fresh marks to prey on. Hoped to hell Sharki hadn't put word out on the street for us—a couple of space grifters wandering about looking for kicks. Likely he had. Bastard. Wondered how he was doing? Enjoying his shot-up foot.

Lots of seedy bars and clubs on this strip. Hoods too. Ex-miners and their sons and daughters gone bad, small time gang people, thieves, cutthroats, pimps in the making, trying to make a name for themselves, but without the experience to back it up.

Live and learn. School of hard knocks. We all live by it.

I hastened us along—not so that we'd look like a bunch of frightened chickens, but that we weren't pausing to examine any wares or looking like goons to get robbed and beaten. I caught a pair of eyes looking our way. I let my gaze move easily past without offering up any challenge.

We hunkered under a low awning, a fruit market, selling all sorts of natural and synthetic goodies. Huckleberries, mincemeat, local jackfruit. Marty popped a handful of grapes in his mouth while the squat, butch-looking vendor had her back turned. Market was selling pretty much everything here: fruit tarts, scarves, bandannas, fermented bog beer. Vendors chortled the worth of their wares in dialects and languages I couldn't understand. They'd mangled the language into something barely comprehensible in this quarter. Needed the pocket computer to translate it. We jostled our way through the milling crowd.

Deidra looked up, shuddering. "Check it, there's one of those sordid places Sharki's threatened to shuttle me off to."

I squinted up, taking in the dilapidated neon tinsel cathouse. "Relax, Deidra. Won't happen to you while I'm on duty."

"I keep thinking it's still my fate." Her shoulders trembled. "Can't seem to shake it off."

I put my arm around her.

Marty snorted. "Well, ain't you the pleasant pair."

"Knock it off, Marty."

My eyes wandered past his brush-cut to a strange-looking woman staring at us across the way. Didn't like the look of her. She'd been staring intently at us for a while now. Rose-red dyed hair done up in a curlicue of weirdness, slight build, jet black eyes like a cat's. She stood up on her heels and whispered something to the toughie beside her— a silent brute with harelip, bare chest, tattooed to the gills with a heaping handful of oiled muscles. The man stood arms crossed by the signpost, as if he were street monitor or something.

A whole story played out in my head—cat woman on the prowl, alert for persons matching our description, especially Deidra's; a savvy watcher able to call on muscle boy to make a move. Call it paranoia or horse sense, I couldn't ignore it.

"Time to make ourselves scarce," I muttered to Marty.

A quick retreat would look suspicious so I grabbed Deidra and pulled her face close to mine. I latched my lips to hers, stuck my tongue down her throat. She grunted, struggled, huffed out an indignant protest, then she relaxed, as if thinking it some strange rough-and-tumble game or fantasy I'd had all along. She eased into a provocative pose, hands groping around my back with a sensual snarl in her throat.

The moments passed and Marty kept walking.

What was I doing? I dipped an eye back. The woman across the way had curled her lip, looking on in disinterest. Just a fly boy out for some cheap piece of ass at the five and dime titty club next door. The ruse seemed to have worked.

Deidra disengaged. She looked up at me with new eyes, a flushed cast to her face and a murmur in her throat. "Rusco. How long you go under for? Didn't know you had it in you to kiss like that. Not bad for an old timer. Like it rough, eh? Never guessed you had the hots for me." Her eyes were all a-flutter. She grabbed at my waist and curled an arm around my butt.

"Sure, baby doll. You're everything I ever wanted." Which wasn't exactly untrue.

While my head was turned, she knuckle-drove me in the ribs. I stifled a groan, massaging my throbbing side.

"Now we're even."

Yes, I could have cued her into catwoman across the way but I didn't want to alarm her and have her running. All good, Jet Rusco. Man of casualty damages.

Call it fate, or bad timing, maybe it was both. Luck wasn't on our side. Some punks, loitering nearby, turned on by our lingering embrace and roughhousing, stepped up to gawp. One made a point to slide too close to Marty and stamped a big boot in a puddle nearby, splashing him up to the knees in brown water as he went past. Marty looked at him with a dead stare. "Want to lick that off, punk?"

"Shouldn't stand so close to puddles, old man. You're on *Black Manxes'* turf. We just want to say hello, to the little lady. Move your lard ass." The hood pulled a switch blade on Marty. Glinted under the neon.

"Woo hoo." Marty pulled out his R4. "You want to sharpen your blade on this?"

The kid backed off, hands upraised.

One of his drunken friends though, thought to get cute and made as if to piss on Marty's leg. Marty who was already in a poor mood, hoofed the douche-bag in the crotch. Things went downhill from there.

Do anything but don't provoke Marty. He smacked the other weasel coming in for retaliation. One got his arm in a quasi head lock around Marty's neck but he slipped out of that hold and rapped the goon in the kidney, doubling him over like a broken rake. Up came the knee. I could see that coming. Ouch.

All fun and games until someone loses an eye. We were supposed to be traveling incognito and here was Marty not making it easy.

I glanced with anxiety over at catwoman. She started to get interested again, especially at the R4 Marty clutched in his palm. I could see her beady eyes narrowing and her elbow nudging bronze boy in the ribs.

"Marty," I hissed. "Two o'clock, across market road."

"Yeah, but the principle, Rusco, the principle. Think, these rat-asses—"

"Fuck the principle. Remember our mission. Incognito. No undue attention."

"Tell it to these bozos, these half assed pricks."

A sudden grabass flurry of motion kicked in as they stormed us all at once, heedless of our weapons. Probably jacked up on street Myscol. I backhanded one of the punks with my R4, reluctant to open fire on him in the street. In the scuffle that followed, the punks snatched Deidra and got the piece out of her hands before she could react. I heard her husky shriek as they pulled her into the alley.

"Fuck! After her!"

They were running, half carrying her down that spidery, black alley before Marty and I could catch up. Others too. Could have sworn they were joined up by bully boys like the bronze one with catwoman. One punk stayed back and shot at us with the gun he'd swiped off Deidra while the others slipped away. We crouched behind some trash bins and fired back at him. He threw the piece away soon enough and scrambled after his buddies. There were plenty of hidey-holes in this scum alley. They'd escaped through one such place like rats in the sewers.

We searched under trash cans, old canvas, burlap, through broken windows. No sign of them. They'd disappeared.

I stood barefaced, chewing my lip. I felt a fool, as the drip-drip of fresh rainwater came splashing on the dirty concrete at my feet from the balconies above. Catwoman was up at the head of the alley, muttering words into her tablet. She dipped back when I lanced her a look. "Rotten bitch." She was gone before we could catch up with her.

Marty blinked and stared and gave a wheezing sigh. "Well, guess that's that."

"What do you mean?"

"Easy come, easy go, Rusco. What don't you get?"

I took a swing at him.

"Hey, slow down." He caught my fist. "You're wound up. Just some chick. She'll find a profitable life in one of these disco clubs along the strip."

I gritted my teeth, shook my head. "Not good, Marty. This is all wrong." We walked slowly away from the market, me fretting and fuming.

Deidra's dark fear had come to pass after all even despite my protestations to the contrary. It seemed incredible. Some protector you are, Rusco.

Easy to walk away, the cowardly way. Taking no action, I'd be complicit in signing her death warrant. What'd I owe her?

Your life maybe, Rusco? Remember the episode back at the yard?

Marty's sense of indifference was warped. He didn't see the big picture. But he was clear-headed enough to know we had to stick together to get through this shitstorm, so he humored me in my quest for the woman.

So we spent the next two days trying to find a mechanic and track her down. Not easy tasks, given we were a couple of wise-guys in an unfriendly town with no leads. I beat myself up, worrying about Deidra's well-being.

We learned a lot of things, snooping around this town. I struck up a conversation with the man behind the counter at Mak's Smoke Shop. Opening the pack of nicoperm I'd purchased, I puffed on what could pass as a homegrown beedi. "Go on, Mak, you were saying something about this guy Sharki."

"Yeah, the bastard's something else. Has ties in Tyrone like you wouldn't believe. Nothing compared to his overlord, some Star Lord, Gong or Bong. I heard on good faith he's like some strutting mogul thinks he's Genghis Khan. Took over a few worlds out in Perseus as if flicking fleas off a firrit's back. My cousin was enslaved by him and taken to his headquarters as a slave for life with a bunch of top people, scientists, executives, that type."

"You don't say?"

"All because of that bastard Sharki, beryl distributor, shyster, the liaison who supplies Lord Bong his light drive engine crystal to fire his warships."

"That's a crying shame," remarked Marty.

"Quiet, Marty. Can't you see there're people's lives at stake here?"

"Bite it, Rusco. Why should I care? What does anyone care of me?"

"They'd care more about you if you kept your mouth shut and respected the dead and the vulnerable."

"Only respect they'll get is at of the end of my R4," Marty growled, lifting his compact, lethal black weapon.

"Let's take it out of the shop, why don't we? Don't be stupid."

Out on the street Marty went full ape. "You're respectful of the innocent? What of Kragen's dead defenders? Who you kidding, Mr. Righteous? Hustling and dealing. Thinking your next angle is the most important thing in the world. Capitalizing on whatever sucker comes along. Hypocrite, that's what you are."

"I admit defeat on that one, Marty. I give you a point. Maybe we're all hypocrites."

He softened. "Yeah, that's about the truth of it."

We were just venting, bullshitting. Barfing up crud on each other for all the wrath we felt in a world that could care less about us, or our individual scrabbling efforts and freedoms. The little guy, the faceless man, the downtrodden worker bee, all were bugs to be crushed under the heel of the powerful. Who was I trying to kid? When had it ever been different? We were just a couple of two-bit vagabonds wishing the universe was something other than what it was.

Maybe I was sore because I'd lost her. She'd been starting to grow on me. On Marty too—but he was just too gruff to admit it.

"What are we doing here, Marty? Scrapping and squabbling like a couple of dogs? We should be off saving that poor woman's ass."

"Yeah, maybe."

"Let's shake a leg and kiss and make up."

"Sure, I'll go get the ring." Marty shoved some more Myscol down his throat.

"Say, you got an infinite supply of those pellets?"

"Yeah, why? And no, I ain't gonna share."

"Good, cause I want to have a whole brain when I start beating on some heads."

"Good."

Only through a chance happening did we start to make any progress at all. That opportunity came soon enough.

Chapter 6

On scouting down *Hell's Acre* looking at various dives, I stopped short. "There," I nudged Marty in the ribs. "Look, that fucking skinhead from the other night. On the corner."

"Yeah, I remember him." Marty's eyes gleamed. "The one who tried to piss on my leg. Didn't you ream him good? Let's pay the knob a visit."

As we approached, I chanced to overhear some street talk. He was bragging to his punk friend, "Orders came from above, Cadd. Slap the bitch in one of the slave houses. We get 50 mekhs for a trade. Not enough though. Should've made that Sharki pay more out of his 30% commission."

I edged in with a crooked leer. "What's this about Sharki?"

"Nothing, pops. Hey, I remember you—the purple-haired dude from the other night. Wow, you looking for something fancy? Some grab and ass tease—"

"Where is she?" I growled.

"Who?"

"My woman you stole, munchkin, remember?"

"Woman? What woman?"

Marty grabbed him by the scruff of the neck and shook him like a rag doll. Marty did something nasty to his nose as it met his knee at a high velocity. Blood spilled everywhere.

Hey, that's not kosher," squealed his friend like a stuck pig.

"Where is she?" I rumbled.

"Dunno, man," Bleeder wailed, snuffling through a flattened nose, dripping blood. "Try *Barflies* on Sunset, or *Cuckoo's Nest*. Last I heard the bitch was there."

"Get out of here," I snarled at him, my fists rapping him hard on the skull. My blood boiled. I was ready to smash his head in but I tempered the impulse.

They huffed off, stumbling and tossing back threats.

Deidra could become some exclusive playtoy rather than a general sex slave. 30% was far too high a payout for that sack of shit Sharki. My mind flashed on the number of hours she would spend on her back for the pleasure of others, passed around from hand to hand, working the slave dives, used and abused. Slaves became factory workers here, as well as courtesans to the public and laborers in every industry this planet supplied. What kept them from fleeing? Only the blue brand on their necks. If they escaped, as soon as they were found out, the authorities would ship them back to slave central in Tyrone. Some might make it offworld, but with that ugly blue brand they would still be looked on with disrespect.

We couldn't afford lodging, so we slumped down under a bridge over one of the canals, smelling of backwater. Our hands were on our chins and we wondered what our next plan of action was.

"Come dusk, we're going in after her."

"Are you nuts, Ruskie? Just because you traded spit with miss hot pants doesn't mean you're beholden to her."

"Get moving. We're going to do something."

"And what may that be?"

"This jughead Sharki rubbed me the wrong way. Killed Kragen and the others. We've got blood on our hands, Marty."

"Like hell we do. They just got in the way. Wrong place, wrong time."

"No way. We created this mess. We have to fix it."

"You're crazy and stupid, Rusco." He walked away.

"Maybe," I called after him, "but I have to do what I have to do. You can bug off and do what suits you, Marty. Blame it on my conscience."

He turned back. "Don't forget, she tried to kill us."

"Yeah, she also saved our asses—if you remember. If she hadn't pegged Sharki after you did your fancy roll out of that tractor, think you'd be walking around whole right now?"

Marty made a sullen noise in his throat. He knew it was true.

* * *

We scouted out the scum dives on Sunset Boulevard. Night time was creepy in Tyrone City and Sunset Boulevard; 'sunset' being a joke—if you could call any of their greenish, haze-covered twilights 'sunset'.

The first, *Cuckoo's*, was the closest to a high end tits-and-ass bar you'd ever get on this scumbucket slag-heap of an industrial world. Front and center were three women climbing poles on a stage up through colored gas tubes, naked and oiled. I wondered what kept those girls at their climbing best. Certainly Deidra would not be doing it of her own free will. Sure enough, she was in Tube #2—doing the nasty, naked ascent while men hooted and jeered in the audience. Patrons inserted their gambling chips into a 'holo jug' at the foot of the stage to put in bids for their pick, the one they thought would make it to the top first. If any of the climbers lagged, electro shocks were administered from the side to jolt unwilling climbers into action. Hard to force a happy face out of any of those nimble gals. Come to think of it, none of their painted faces looked too happy.

With bonus prizes awarded to those who picked winners and the runners-up, this was a win-win scenario. Nobody in the audience could lose. Kind of like electric bingo.

Incredible and sad, but true. This is what entertainment had devolved to.

Marty shook his head in resignation. "You've got to be kidding me."

"Nope, this is real life, Mar. In all its gory clarity. Deidra does look good though."

"She doesn't look too happy."

I saw the blue gleam of the slave mark on the left side of her neck. She wouldn't like that. Too free-spirited. Heard the marks were permanent…forced to wear a scarf for life.

The computerized MC voice spoke over the sound system: "And the winner of the first race raffle is Alfie Borg of Tyrone City! The main prize: a special romp with Miss Angel Heart of TUBE #2. And to go, a stuffed pink elephant, something that Alfie can take back to the missus at home." Bright banners and silver stars and gold spangles lit on the wide screen holo displays spread above the stage.

At a middle table Alfie grinned, a broad gleaming grin on a face with a lot of horse teeth.

"You can claim your prize in the back, Mr. Borg, Foyer 2," the MC voice confirmed. Angel and the other two women were shuttled off backstage while new ones strutted onstage to take their places.

Alfie hauled his heavy bulk up from his table and waddled to the back of the sleazy place. He waved the blue smoke away from his nose, lit a dusky hue by the colored light. We trailed him with grim resolve.

On pretense of using the men's room halfway down, we headed down the hall after him past the bouncer guarding the entrance to Foyer 2. He ducked into the washroom and Marty and I strolled in at a leisurely pace. Out of sight and earshot, I put a hand on Big Alf's shoulder. "You're a lucky man, Alfie."

He turned to face me, his piglet eyes searching my face. "Do I know you? Well, you know how it is. Thought I'd claim my meat early on. Been doing some heavy drinking, didn't want it to interfere with my pleasure. Get my business done early and I have more oomph for extra play later."

I nodded in sympathy. "That's a wise plan, Alfie. You're one of the smarter ones here."

He beamed.

"Actually me and Marty were just wondering if there'd be leftovers for us, after a lucky man like you was done. Angel Heart's a mighty classy piece of woman."

He garbled out an indignant sound. "Not likely, I'm in top form. Now shove off. Don't want to think of my beauty being used by other men, at least not too soon."

"That's a mighty lofty ambition." I grabbed his hand as if to read his palm, feigning a bit of the old drunken love.

"Hey, you poofster, what's the meaning of this?" He took a drunken swing at me and I sandbagged him in the gut. The breath sailed out of his midsection and Marty caught his limp form and dragged him over to the nearest urinal.

"Wait here. I'll be back soon."

Marty nodded and kicked open the stall door and pulled his new deadweight buddy in after him.

I sauntered back down the hall, whistling a jaunty tune, following the path Alfie would have followed had he been conscious. I grinned my cheeky grin, thumbing the coin-sized explosive in my left pocket, wondering how I could use it to advantage.

At a door labeled, 'Angel Heart', a muscled attendant looked me up and down with disinterested eyes. "Name?

"Alfie Borg."

"Well, Alfie, tonight's your lucky night. Go right in. Rap twice when you're done. Angel's ready and waiting."

I saluted, gave him an ear-to-ear grin. He locked the door behind me.

Deidra was slumped on a small cot, her face flushed. She jerked up to her feet on seeing me, a hoarse rasp in her throat. "Rusco! What the hell are you doing here?"

"What's it look like? Getting my money's worth. On your back, bitch. Might as well strip out of those skimpy clothes right away too, dollface."

"Very funny. What's the exit plan?"

I looked around, examining the dingy surroundings. Small, rectangular cage, no windows. Only a single dim yellow bulb glaring from above. Stale air, smell of sex, cigars and sour flesh, name your pick, private parts working hard, no need for luxury.

"We'll get you out of here, Deidra. Didn't much like the thought of Sharki using you like that for the rest of your days."

"That's a kind sentiment, Rusco. You promised you'd protect me. Now look at me, a painted whore." She fluttered her kohl-painted eye-lashes, hands on hips. "Remember that kiss you gave me out in the market?"

"How could I forget? I've a soft spot for—"

"Okay, let's cut the crap."

"Sure, doll. No need to get sore. Follow my lead. Ruff up that hair of yours. Put this on so we can get by these yobos." I tossed her my jacket. She draped it over her slender shoulders. "Cover up your neck."

I rapped twice on the door, held up a finger of silence to her.

The doorman poked his head in. "That was fast, Alfie. More than what you could handle?"

"Naw, just a quick hand job all I needed—" Fast as a snake I chopped him hard in the throat. He was down in seconds. I hoofed him in the side for extra measure then grabbed his neck and pulled him into the pleasure room. Deidra came skipping out, grimacing at the fallen man. I rolled him deeper into the cubicle and drew the dead bolt across the door.

"That was fast," she said.

"I move fast. Let's go."

The thump and beat of the electro-dance music came louder to our ears as we crossed the dim-lit hall. I signaled Marty leaning aside the door to the loo. He fell in step behind us as we made our way to the exit. I made as if to escort Deidra out into the night air. The entrance-door bouncer regarded us with suspicion—two men and a dancer always were—and he held out his arm blocking me. "Slow down, chief. You can't take the merchandise out with you. You pulling a fast one on me?" He pulled back Deidra's jacket and exposed the blue slave tattoo on her neck. "How'd she get out anyway?"

I flashed him my mooniest look and raised a hand. "Look at the little brown fox." My eyes drifted to somewhere behind him.

His head turned. Marty chopped the back of his neck when his eyes were averted. I clocked him in the side of the head for safety. Some wise-ass buddy of his came running toward us. I armed my mini-salvo, lobbed it. Buddy flew high up in the air, the concussion taking out half the wall beside him. Buddy ended up buried under a heaping pile of plaster and metal.

I stared down at him. "Tough break, chief." We left in a hurry out into the rain-soaked street. Deidra clung to my arm and trembled with gratitude to be out of her servitude.

That little blast'd give the lap girls and pole dancers a night off and keep those degenerates busy…though we'd have a few more enemies on our tail tonight.

CHRIS TURNER

Chapter 7

We legged it to the market, shouldering our way through the crowd and on past the dark alleys, the smut shops and the dives. Shouts and bootfall echoed behind us. We weaved in and out, through the crowds, the squares. There we lost our straggling pursuers. Finally to reach the seedy docks off Lagoon Lake.

It was well past the witching hour when the thugs come out to play and I felt no guilt at our desperate acts. I was sure there were more debauched deeds in progress than our violent rescue tonight.

We slumped down at the base of a bronze monument—an exultant miner overlooking the water. We traded blank looks, laced with that 'what now' look. A distant lamppost cast a dim yellow glow our way.

A seaweedy smell drifted across the black water; a foghorn blew amid the gathering mist, a mournful dirge-like sound, some barge likely making its way between the sister cities.

Deidra was handling herself very well, but I could see her control starting to crack at the seams. Her lower lip quivered; her eyes teared up in the glowering light.

"That shitbag Sharki owned my father for many years—before he finally killed him out on Farsi. Sharki took me to pay back my father's debt. Dad didn't deserve to die like that."

I looked away. "I'm sorry, Deidra."

She shrugged. "It's okay, Rusco. I'm tough. It's over and done."

"How'd it happen?"

"Dad got mixed up in Sharki's schemes. His lies." She spat venom. "By the time he figured it out, it was too late, the damage was done. Father used to do runs from world to world, gathering data, speculator prospects, intelligence from the great beyond. A high end envoy, part-time spy and diplomat. I was young at the time. He taught me how to fly a starship, other tricks of the trade. Organized a posse of vigilantes to hunt down Sharki.

"It soured. He underestimated Sharki's slyness, his trickery. Bullet-holed dad right in front of my face. When he died—" her lip quivered "—let's just say I resolved to keep a fire of vengeance burning inside. For him, for me. When I was on that pole tonight climbing to oblivion in front of those fucking lowlifes, I was thinking of my promise to my dad. And now here I am." She brushed away a tear and snorted her defiance.

"I feel your pain, Deidra."

She sniffed. "Haven't been able to escape that mad bastard Sharki ever since. Because of my flying skill, he made me captain of a ship, *Titan*, and automatic accomplice to his larcenous schemes. My purpose, and only purpose, was to make him a profit. Small wonder he said to me, if I ever double-crossed him, he'd string me up like a skinned cat to dry, make me regret it for the rest of my days. Only the past month he left me on my own. And now our shared past's come to a head. At least I got a shot in and nailed that bastard's foot." She sneered. "Hope he gets gangrene and dies."

I hooked an arm around her shoulder. "Glad you see it like that. You happy now you stumbled across us?"

She stared off in a distant daze. "Not really."

I nodded in understanding.

We counted the spaces in between foghorn blasts, sitting in silence like statues.

Marty peered at me at last in suspicion. "Rusco, what are you thinking? Don't like that look."

I rubbed my chin, staring right through Deidra who still seemed detached from reality. "You know, Marty, Deidra getting snatched and this whole caper going bad, gives me an idea. Maybe it's not all about the money this time."

Marty gave a sour grunt.

"Larger stakes are at hand. Like that drive crystal. We gave Sharki a slap on the wrist—but maybe we could hurt him worse. Spare a lot of planets some pain."

"You're talking gibberish, Rusco."

Maybe, but somehow I couldn't leave it alone, even though every bit of logic told me to take our shipment and never look back. The first instinct was not always the best one. Right now it felt pretty sour.

Deidra spoke at last, "You mean blow up the station or something kooky like that?"

I looked away, said no words.

She licked her lips. "But it's—"

"Insane, like a stupid idea, Rusco, suicide?" Marty grumbled. "Forget it. We got the beryl. We get *Titan* repaired, then we truck out."

"In a simple world, yes, Marty, all fine and nice."

"What's not simple about it? Do the math. How complex can it be? If worse comes to worse, we could dodge enemy eyes, waiting it out as we go back and forth to *Titan*, fencing the beryl."

This sinking feeling in my gut would not let me act as Marty wanted me to. "No. We can't be caught out here in the open with Sharki's goons on our tail."

A sense of duty, some attempt at justice, prevented me from taking the easy route. Some noble feeling I'd cherished at an earlier age. Though over the years I'd wandered and gone astray many times. If we took that money, without doing the right thing, we'd choke on it right down to the bitter end. Marty couldn't see it. He was floundering badly, getting all worked up and worried. In the end he threw his arms up in exasperation. He knew he couldn't buck me. Without me, he'd be nowhere, especially now. He gulped down some Myscol and I even took a pop myself. We hoofed it out of that place to central station before some rat bastard honed in on us.

A quick raid on the impound yard and we 'borrowed' a beat up air car while darkness was still on us. Morning was coming on fast. The first glimmering rays of dawn poked over the greenish horizon, lighting the city skyline a lurid hue. The stacks and towers of the city resembled stick-like surreal things.

We found a reputable mechanic in *Hell's Acre* that day. Dawn was a much safer time to be roaming about. The mechanic was a man who declined our business but recommended us to *Balen's Yard* just outside the city precinct. "They'll fix you up for a decent price," he said. "I don't work on such heavy machinery myself." I mulled over his words and thought to kill two birds with one stone: getting supplies in town and prepping *Titan* with camo before we took her aloft to *Balen's* or any other place.

"Thing is, it isn't going to be easy to get past Sharki's scout ships out in space," I said to my partners-in-crime. "Remember we have no light drive until we clear grav and I don't want to lose our beryl shipment by being boarded or blown out of the sky."

"You and me both," echoed Marty. "So, we trade *Titan* in for another ship."

I winced. "It's too complex and time consuming. We'd have to transfer the beryl to the other craft. Many things could go wrong."

"Or maybe just wipe the drive signature?" suggested Deidra.

"Could work. But still risky. Some Johnny Joe keener could recognize the ship by size and configuration."

"It's a risk either way," Marty grumbled.

"No, this is how it'll work. We camo the ship, wipe the drive signature and fly into Thetis station on pretext of picking up a load. Then we blast the solar guns to smithereens."

"Just like that, eh? As clean as the last time?"

"Sure."

It was a wild but simple plan. Me, Marty and Deidra loaded some beryl in the air car and pawned it off in town for cash yols: quick money for food and supplies. We carted back with us a mountain of blue paint and collapsible ladders to the quarry. Deidra was fast recovering from her degrading experience. We painted *Titan* an ultramarine dark hue, making sure we hid the telltale *Titan* plate and put a new name on her—"*Marmot*".

She was a fat marmot with a fortune in beryl in her hold.

"We go in disguised as a supply ship", I murmured, "blow the solar amplifiers and beetle out of there."

Marty still gave his head a grave shake. "I mean, what could go wrong, Rusco?"

Deidra approached, her eyes narrowed in pained doubt. "I admire you for being courageous here. As Sharki's my witness, I didn't have the guts to do anything meaningful while I had the chance. But this—well, it's kind of crazy and I value my life—I don't think I have the nine lives you seem to have."

"Relax, Deedee. Trust me. I've lived this way this long. Not about to die yet."

Marty exhaled a sour breath. "Yeah, and that's a wonderful fucking mystery, Rusco. All the gods up there questioning how you managed to survive so long."

"Come on Marty, how hard can it be to take out a few parabolas? If it looks bad, we bail. Deal? Nothing ventured, nothing gained."

Marty shrugged. He was on board, but just.

* * *

We visited *Balen's*, got the ship fixed up, selling on the ready black market some of the beryl for cash to pay for the repair work. At last we were in orbit around Thetis and made our approach to the station. A lot of nail-biting this time as we stayed glued to the bridge: Marty on nav, Deidra piloting, me working weapons. Much activity played out around Thetis's dovetail futuristic fuselage. Repairs in motion. Scout ships flying in and out, repair craft with extensible crane arms locked onto port doors, maintenance vessels and new ore carriers drifting hither and yon. We were just another supply craft of the dozens coming in from Tyrone City to drop off some materials to repair the damaged parts.

Like ants these drones worked away—hodging together a new anthill the next day. So much for the breach we had created a week back.

Our weapons were still out of range. We'd have to get a lot closer in order to target those monster parabolas and solar guns.

I cast Marty a clown's grin as I spoke into the com. "Delta control, this is *Marmot*. Request access to Deck 3. Over."

"*Marmot…*" the station voice paused. "You're unregistered."

"Affirmative, we know. Got a call from a Mr. Sykes at Engram Enterprises on Tyrone for delivery of piping and platform slabs to Thetis Station. Looks like a rush job. Last ship couldn't make it, so we were called in. Over."

There was a long pause, a pregnant one that had us worried. I stared over at Marty, my fingers ready on the impulse engines, ready to blast out of here if things looked sour.

"You're cleared, *Marmot*. Proceed. Landing designation, Bay 6. Talk to Jraden, the commissions officer. Unload your product as quickly as possible and move out. We have a dozen other vessels scheduled to land in the next few hours."

I could barely suppress a laugh. Easy as that. What a joke. Security must be laxer than ever. Old Sharki hadn't learned a thing, the arrogant fuck. But then again, what idiot in their right mind would try to sabotage the station so soon after the last stunt? The ultimate double-bluff. Rusco at work.

The oval portal slid ajar and Deidra took *Titan* in closer to the massive station. Parabola #1 veered over us on station northwest like some thing from an alien planet. I cued up Deidra for our attack ascent to rip into the tower containing the parabola.

Just when I thought we were going to pull off this impossible feat, a repellor beam caught us broadside. I'd had to keep shields low to maintain the whole charade. It cost us. We were on a quick dive to hell—down.

"Of all the idiotic things!" yelled Marty. "You just lost us 100 grand in yols and our lives, Rusco."

"Get us moving! Out of here, Deidra," I cried, ignoring him.

The ship was toast, finished. No question. But I seized the controls at the last minute. Thrust *Titan* in toward the closing portal before our nav was completely dead.

"You crazy, Rusco? That's an enemy station staring at us."

"Better than burning up out here—or would you rather get pegged by those bastards?"

Titan surged in through the portal on sheer momentum, caught the tail end of sliding metal before lurching through, knocking us roughshod into the landing bay.

The bottom of her fuselage sheared off, crushing her landing gear, smashing her beyond repair. She ploughed through the closing portal, careening down on the platform landing, knocking us on our asses.

Systems went haywire; every buzzer and red light went off.

"Into the suits! Quick!" I grated. I knew we'd be in vacuum while the outer port stayed jammed. I scrambled for the wall, tore down the lightweight gray-silver suits. Marty was at my side, seeing the writing on the wall. I avoided his 'I told you so' eyes.

"Move!" I swatted at Deidra, who crouched frozen by the controls.

Marty grabbed an extra R4. After suiting up, we scrambled out of the cargo bay as *Titan* smoked and new flames broke out on her starboard side. Thank god for artificial grav. We raced along the padway past V-Zons and loader craft before any security men riddled us with shells. We moved as fast as our suits could carry us. Time was running out. Our chances were slim, if any. Stray gunfire nipped at our heels. One wrong shot and it would be all over in this vacuum.

I shot back at the gunners and glanced back at the dying *Titan*. Her flank was black-streaked and smoking, our remaining beryl lost forever. Our get rich schemes had gone up in flames. Maybe Marty had the right idea all along if it were just a venture for profit. Yet we were still alive—but maybe not for long.

The place was cavernous with lots of metal piping and upper walkways. Huffing and puffing for breath from the mad sprint in our suits, we made it to the first airlock and turned the silver ring to pressure lock.

The chamber pressurized. Once through, Marty was about to strip off his ape-suit but I held him back. "Keep it on, Mar. We don't know when this place is going to birdshit or the sky will fall on our heads."

He gave a grim nod. For once the bastard actually listened to me. Without arguing. A record.

A plan, Rusco, a plan. What's the use of all this running about without a plan? We were nearly at parabola #1 and its ominous stingray-shaped gun mounted far below. The thing loomed over us like a monstrous, long-necked insect from hell. Below us in a circular dugout sat eight massive crucibles of raw beryl, waiting to be ionized, polarized in vacuum, whatever the fuck they did to it here. Three ships sat parked a hundred feet away. Also the portal to the depths of space not eighty feet the other way.

Of course—we could use the gun as a weapon. Melt the other parabola and the station's hardware in the meantime. Why not?

"Quick, up into the control station," I hissed at Marty over the suit com. "We take our final stand there, in the solar tower."

"What for?" Marty gawped. "Die high up?"

"Trust me."

"I've trusted you enough already, Rusco."

"You'll have to trust me some more."

"Bullshit. You're a fucking menace." He stared at the chaos, cursing with eyes white as gunfire. Shouts and death streamed all around us. "You sure?" he grunted.

"No, but what other choice do we have?"

We ripped shells into the detail of men at the base of the solar gun. They dropped one by one. Fire tore by us, but theirs was poorly aimed. Marty was an ace shot, me no less. Between the three of us we took them down. Deidra picked up the stragglers. Damn we were a prime killing machine. Could that woman shoot. The defenders died before they got a chance to aim.

We stormed up the stairs in the vacuum-protected tower to the gun's control base. Gunfire erupted away somewhere behind us. Some fellows were mighty pissed at our illegal entry. Especially when we should be floating corpses in space. Tough shit.

We scaled the metal-gridded ladder like calves driven in a stampede. I ripped open the steel door to the control post.

A uniformed man stood gaping at a console overlooking the beryl vessels. He'd been frightened out of his mind at the chaos below. We caught him in mid op while he had been aiming the gun at crucible #4. His mouth gaped wide. "Hey, you clowns, you can't just waltz in here to a restricted area."

"Not restricted any more." I pushed him back. "Show us how to work this thing."

"You crazy? I'm not just going to—"

I rapped him hard with the end of my rifle.

"Ow! What the fuck? Who the hell are you people?"

"Get it moving pal, west, toward the end of the station. Lift that solar gun away from those loads of beryl. Now!"

"Okay, take it easy."

He was stalling so I smacked him hard again on the head. He howled.

"Don't fuck with me! Do it now or I'll blast a hole in your head."

Marty rounded on the operator with a toad's grin, his R4 tipped at the man's groin.

The man capitulated then, raised trembling hands. "No need for violence. Okay, I'm doing it." He adjusted the gun's trajectory, turning dials with trembling hands. I watched him with a hawk's glare, waiting for him to dillydally again. I eyed the sequences and noted the intensities and the degrees of shift he used. "Good, Elmer. We'll take over from here." I clubbed him hard over the ear and he fell unconscious.

Shots came up from below. "Shit, what else?" I cried. "You two take care of it."

Marty pulled Deidra along. Good thing we all had working weapons.

Marty and Deidra clambered down the stairs to the lower level. They took up positions at the cross landing. Just in time to rain fire into gunmen coming up after us. Like picking off flies.

I hesitated only a second. Any more would have been our doom.

This would be the last time this gun would ever fire for Sharki's operation. I trained it at the other parabola far across the length of the station. I kissed goodbye to the shipment on *Titan* and any other we might salvage here. Channeling and magnifying solar power thousands of times, the solar beam lashed out to melt the tripod-shaped metal base of the other gun. It disintegrated in a wall of sizzling metal and steam. The structure caught on fire then burst into flames.

The heat blast triggered more explosions—a convulsive chain reaction that ripped along the spine of the station's superstructure. I hoped Sharki was down there, getting fried.

Thetis Station started to list like a boat at sea. Artificial gravity was going to shit. We floated a few inches off the ground to our startlement, then settled back down again on the metal grates at half our weight.

I swung the gun back to zap the most aggressive of the newcomers who'd slipped through Marty and Deidra's net. I gave a grim laugh, an ugly sound at the back of my throat. Soon there'd be nothing left of this station. Nothing to stand on. If we were going to die, why not go out with a bang? A crazy smirk crawled across my face. An intoxicating feeling, this wielding of immense power like one of the titans.

I shook the daze out of my head. Zombie talk, Rusco. You're breathing gas fumes. Get with the program. There are ships down there. In a second you could be making a getaway—why fry to death on this perch?

"Time to get the hell out of here," I mumbled to myself.

I herded the other two down the stairs. "Move. Party's over." We scrambled down to the base and out across the smoking pad to one of the small carrier ships, an Alpha-messenger craft.

One of its neighbors, a V-Zon went up in flames as a nearby crucible blew, heated beyond measure by our runaway solar gun. It poured hot slag onto the ship's fuselage.

Marty howled in anguish as a bullet ripped into his left leg. His suit was finished. Heaven help him if this place ever turned to complete vacuum. Already I could hear a roar and hissing in my ears as parts of the station went flying past; shrapnel, machine parts, and out to a breach point farther down the hull's superstructure. In minutes this place would be a cold tomb. It was a straight dash to the Alpha carrier. We were only fifty feet away. But fifty feet could as well be five hundred.

I took Marty's arm. We slogged on avoiding gunfire and random debris riding the air hissing out of the station. Shells skidded around us, smashed into the nearby hull. Deidra ducked, returned fire, a wild gleam in her eye. A laugh too on her tongue. I could see the dream of survival swirling in her head, fighting against all odds against Sharki. She was a vixen gone rogue caught in a frenzy of blood lust. "Die, you shitbox station! No more a prison for me." She shrieked, laying fire every which way, taking out foes. I gave a grim laugh. Kamikaze Deidra. We reached the cargo door and were inside. I closed the hatch and breathed relief, hustled Marty along the darkened hall toward the bridge while Deidra raced ahead to get the ship started and moving as thumps and bangs echoed across the hull. Just a parked ship, nobody aboard. I reached the weapon nav and blasted the station's portal open. We surged though as bits of hot metal and loose fibrofoil fell away from our sides.

Marty slumped in a nav chair, his face pale and breath hoarse. First time I'd seem him so vulnerable.

A great ball of fire lit behind us. Thetis 3 exploded in an angry burning ball. I saw among the fragments and supercharged debris, several bright specks that might have been starships making their escape from the doomed station. But these were few and most of them ended up in cinders, engulfed in bright flames before they could get too far. Thetis 3 was no more. Just another blip in history. I felt no remorse.

The concussion knocked us sideways, zapping our impulse drive and our nav haywire. But we were far enough away from the disintegrating station that it didn't compromise our light drive for long. For once, the gods seemed to be on our side.

But I am ever skeptical of that assumption.

We surged across the black gulfs and the Varwol's green light blinked on. I jammed the hyperdrive to full, sending us across the threshold of singularity.

We sat in silence, disbelieving the stillness and safety of the light drive, staring at the impossible trails of time-light streaming from our sides.

Marty's voice came as a hoarse rasp. He was hurting, his supply of Myscol run out. I scoured the bridge, looking for some regen. It'd be a while before we could get some for him if there was none aboard. I found some in a half-stocked storage bin. I peeled off his spacesuit, slathered the smelly orange paste on his lower leg. He gave a howl, then a sigh of relief. The miracle goo was already starting to work its magic.

Whether Sharki perished down there or had escaped on one of the evac ships, I did not know. The prospect left an uneasy knot lingering in the pit of my gut. I sensed Deidra felt this unease too, though I could see in her twisted expression her burying it deep, along with her hurt from the past.

Deidra spoke in a cracked voice, "If it's any consolation, I've got a mechanic friend out on Voodries world in Aldebaran who can fix us up good with an *Alpha Explorer*. Might even trade in this junk for a better vessel."

"Good. That's the best news I've heard all day. We need a break. Marty, what do you say?"

He just waved and groaned, the sounds of longing for a hit of Myscol.

"My brain's still wondering how we're gonna stay afloat. Only a week of vacuum-packed food on this rig and we're down to our last yols."

"Rusco, you're a killjoy. We've got each other."

I looked at her and gave her a hard stare.

Her mouth got all puffy and glistening like a flower in dew. "Where you got to go so fast?" She hooked an arm around my shoulder. I looked back at her, my face deadpan. An idea warmed in my head. I suppose I could make an exception along the lines of a bit of R&R.

Marty just rolled his eyes. "Come on, really?"

"Relax, Mar. Sure as rain there's some desperate gal down on one of these scum worlds we can drop in on who'll fancy even a dog like you."

CHRIS TURNER

STARHUSTLER

BOOK II

CHRIS TURNER

(1 Sol year later)

Chapter 1

I got the transcall from Marty two days ago on Starrunner. *Meet me at Drenny's Bodega. Bring explosives.*

I was tempted to blow it off, but something in my gut told me to follow through. Business had been slow out in Veglos and the cons we had pulled up and down that wretched sector, had either blown up in our faces or been substandard. Like that smuggling op to get land mines down to the rebels on Rlenion. Three shipments, discovered at the last minute, up in flames.

Not to mention the blood-soaked debacle in the Muridon Belt before all this. Marty and I'd managed to hyper within range of Bariff's Star, escaping to some low-tech desert planet, after a series of random light hops courtesy of our wonky varwol aboard the junk freighter, Trident.

I'd quickly traded in that hauler for the much smaller *Starrunner*, from a rich but drunken caravan master. A deal if there ever was one. We'd hypered to Veglos, did our little thing there, now were on stopover at this slum planet, Brisis, waiting for the heat to die down on Veglos. We'd parted ways for a while, both of us needing a break from our own miserable company. Seems as if he was now longing for my companionship? Or else he had landed some deal worth chatting about. Somehow I suspected the latter.

Looking at the decadence and slummery of Hoath here on Brisis 9, capital of the supplier planet of all goods, I wasn't quite so sure now. A giant shanty town of neon and old glitter, a place I'd vowed never to return to, with its seedy dives, black markets, toothless hawkers and painted brides.

What was the point of it, I asked. Without one taking a chance, opportunity always made its way to the next bidder.

Maybe that's why I was in the traders' depot. Following up on the lead just come in from Marty. That or a slump. Call it what you want, a malaise of spirit, some last desperation after the last string of bad luck.

This waiting line was taking too long. Really? That many shmucks in line for firearms? Granted, the depot was the best place to go for munitions this side of the Orbego ghetto, aside from regular black market channels. But I didn't feel like getting my legs blown off today.

The eminent sociologist, J. Markel Braeth, wrote in an informal essay, that human corruption reaches its peak during times of a dark age, after war has obliterated the countryside, after the planets, once prosperous, ache for green once again. When the worlds far and near, once so proud and with such potential, cry tears of dry sand, vomit up garbage pits and every half-baked crime lord in the galaxy.

I'm inclined to disagree with Sir Braeth's statement of tomorrow. I think it can go lower.

Rusco, you moron, who cares what you think? You're just another rambler risk-taker wanting to play it loose and fast. No different than the other hustlers in what's left of the free sectors of the galaxy, those lawless regions, the pleasure domes, the ghettos, the gang-ruled cities. The difference is you pride yourself on being one step ahead of the average con, a little quicker on your toes, a little edgier, sidestepping the dangerous beast waiting around the corner. It's a dangerous assumption, one that can get you killed.

All six-foot leathery hide of me reeked of the same starveling message. Go easy on the burnt-out con today. Here's my medallion of battle scars as proof of claim. The pale purple-tinted hair trailing to shoulder hiding the torn off ear. The wicked tear-dropped curve on the left wrist from that knife fight on Tethris. The pink scarring down the right cheek where a red hot iron had pressed the wrong way and the fleshy part of ear had kind of up and disappeared. No broken bones, no implants, no prosthetics, or anything that modern flesh-regen couldn't fix, given the right amount of funds. All it said was you were lucky.

As I scrutinized today's clientele at the depot, I felt the familiar tired sigh hiss through my teeth. What was the sod in front of me going to do with those stolen bills he clutched in his purple-veined fingers? Grab the luger off the shelf, go out and rob the local diner? Kill a couple of innocent women or some old man to feed his mescal habit?

Merc Surplus was just a hop, skip and jump down the line, stocking mint-condition gas lanterns, bowie knives, lighter fluid and rope, you name it. Great kit for arsonists or hangmen. On the other end, a pawn shop and the ubiquitous recyclo-mart distributing everything from boxsprings, old leather boots, water pumps to sex toys and tire irons. This edge of the colonized worlds had gone from seedy to seediest. Technology had all but vanished on this out-of-the-way planet. But then again, where hadn't it? The last of the space wars had gutted mother nature's belly, milked her dry. Now she sported only bands of raiders savaging the free planets. Outlaws, hoodlums, scumbags, wannabes, small men carrying big guns and wanting to be big chiefs in a messed-up world. A feudal universe of settled planets, raped of their resources; burned out cities ravaged by pulse cannons, run by organized crime thugs, crazies, religionists, every known breed of gangster the criminal world could offer.

The odd resistance fighter still roamed about, sure…freedom fighters they called them, fighting against decadence and injustice, but those were few and far between, and stupid in my opinion for risking a bullet in the head or torture by flamethrower to prove a point. For what? Wearing their crispy, blood-drenched capes to the grave.

Martyrs without a cause, or hope? The slippery slope for Jet Rusco started long ago. I could have been a greater man, but instead settled on the life of a two-bit thief, trying to make ends meet, a sad vagabond, owner of a dilapidated space junker I'd won, or rather stolen from a couple of dying ruffians. Yet a part deep down in me wanted to be one of those valiant types that made a difference in this decrepit framework of humanity. I croaked out a laugh, shook my shaggy head, thinking maybe not today, Rusco, maybe not today.

The guy in front of me with the pale, haunted eyes moved off with his quivering fist clutching a handgun.

"I'll have one of those," I said across the scarred counter to the attendant poised behind the reinforced cage mesh. A lot of pulse guns and ammunition sat there, weaponry of all sorts stacked on the walls. Everything the local desperado could ever want.

The attendant flashed me a cool glance, lifted a disinterested finger to a row of black, cylindrical objects spread in a neat, tidy line.

"Yep, those ones—with the black mufflers on the ends. Mighty fine pieces," I said, trying to fake out a drawl for kicks.

"They're double-range explosives," he asserted. "Fine kick, twenty yols extra."

I flourished a hand. "Let me gauge them for weight. Two, please."

The attendant engaged the safety which ensured a ten minute lead in case of accidental detonation, passed the merchandise through the gap. Everyone knew there was no chance to steal merchandise and run. Hidden cameras worked with regular efficiency behind those reinforced panels and security gunmen posed as beggars or others traipsing about the place ready to pounce on any snatch-and-grab thieves.

I held the black cylinders in my hand, admiring the compact efficiency of their streamlined deadly potential. Juggling the canisters from hand to hand, I turned for a second, using my body to shield me from the camera, then worked my old confuse and switch gag, reaching down at an opportune time, replacing the one in my left hand with the dud concealed in my left jacket pocket. It was a ruse I'd been practicing for years. Worked every time. Oldest trick in the book.

I put on a long frown. "Actually, I'll go for the brand down, chief. These babies're a bit heavy and my pocket's a little too light."

"Told you," clucked the attendant. "Pass them back. Don't get fancy and waste my time."

I nodded and grinned and thrust them back through the hole in the cage, as if lowly equipment clerks' reprimands were the highlight of my day.

I fingered the coin-sized, scaled-down models pushed through the wire mesh, passed through twelve yols and thrust the goods in my dusty pockets as I fiddled for a home-rolled cigarette. The air was stifling and my head swam to a babel of voices. I was reaching my limit of how many shoulder jostles I could take from druggies and tough guys today. I sauntered out of the depot, whistling a tuneless jingle out of the side of my mouth. My meeting with Marty came up in the hour. A shoddy place The Bodega, but it would have to do.

As I slogged through the puddles from a recent rain toward the market, I could hear the beats of techno-music exuding from the tarped-up shanties down the way: all bass and some mid-range slurred female voice-overs in an unrecognizable mash. A glut of offworlders roamed about, a slum of small tent-like enclosures made from pieces of old rubber tires and broken vehicles. Rusty oil drums with smoking garbage burned away. Several grubby figures congregated in a huddle. An altercation broke out and knives suddenly flashed in dirty hands. Then the crash of broken glass through the grimy window of what looked a clapboard salami shop. Two ham-handed men stood arguing over who had chopped the last livers and mixed them with the pork, or some dumb thing.

As I stopped to ponder, I felt a tug at my pantleg. A mousy brown boy sat, legs splayed in the dirt and puddles, his leg missing below the knee, begging for coins. I crouched down and gave him a few of the loose yols I had, catching the dull look in the sunken, young eyes, drinking deep of the sorrow mirrored there then moving on.

My eyes wandered over him and other such sights with a familiarity that created tiny ripples in my soul. I'd had to steel myself to the suffering of others to get the jobs done that put food on the table. Only a rare glimmer of compassion did I let steal over me from time to time. The universe was what it was. Long ago I'd accepted such travesties as fate; they would continue on, regardless of what I did or didn't do.

A sickly glow permeated the sky with the sound of thunder promising more rain. I trudged through the rubble and the mud puddles, skirting wide piles of bomb debris. An air-speeder whistled past close overhead. I gave it little attention, little concerned with the comings and goings of the privileged and few. That, and the rattle of electric three-wheelers on the dingy streets whose riders wore their goggled ski-masks, racing the odd ramshackle van or lorry to the next barricaded junction.

I came to Drenny's. An eatery of fine repute, of battered brick and energetic graffiti scrawled on front, wide swoops and swirls of the lost symbols of modern vernacular. Overhead, mothers' laundry dripped and kids screamed from the balconies of squalid apartments. The city cops, aka hired mercenaries, came to this meet-place of smugglers, dope dealers and lowlifes less often than the hotter places closer to downtown. A collection of mixed sorts huddled about in drab clothing, generally trench coats and beat-up boots, sitting at tables and mumbling monosyllables or milling around at the bar. Some machines stood at the back, upright gambling units and old pinball machines, while low, distorted lounge music huffed out a muffled beat.

Marty sat over at a far table. He hunched in the dimness, bullet head and chin tipped down in the haze of blue smoke. He sat away from the hubbub and the bar. He got up and waved when he saw me. I approached with measured confidence and he took my hand with a firm grip and nodded, the faintest of grins. "Rusco, been a while. You look good."

"Could be better."

Marty patted my back with more vigor than necessary. "Attaboy! Keeping up the faith?"

I shrugged. Marty, a shock of mustard-colored hair that clung to his oiled scalp like a fish fin, was a short, heavy-boned bully with thick lips and crooked grin. But fast. Last guy who underestimated Marty lay in a shallow grave.

Marty was a good guy, well-informed but somewhat of a fanatic for odd jobs, volatile, headstrong, violent, ready to plug shells into a problem rather than think it through. Don't ever get him angry or he'd rip your head off and shove it up the next guy's ass. That's Marty. Got to know him in Rega. We'd been drinking, shooting the shit at the local casino bar, and got to musing… 'you know, like maybe we should join forces or something and capitalize on the smuggling market, a couple of delivery wise guys like us, we could be peddling and fencing weapons and contraband versus collecting the chump change we're making now.' So we got to thinking and the old gears got whirring. Now I was a little ahead of Marty in big picture planning and could play three angles at once where he could only play one, so I humored him into thinking it was all his idea—you know, the whole let the big bad dog think he's the alpha-male, pissing on every corner, while the nice little white dog keeps his head down.

"So what's this about?" I asked.

"Got something down the line. Some easy pickings on the river way in the warehouse district."

"What, those abandoned factories and chop shops?"

"Yeah, something like that. Some small time gangsters run out of there, moving stuff new and old, you know? Big stuff."

"Yeah, like what?"

He scratched at the bridge of his nose. "I don't know, this and that."

"What? You don't even know what it is we're pulling?"

He looked away with an offended glare.

"What about transpo?" I growled. I peered over with annoyance at the two deadbeats playing old retro video games in the back shadows. The noise of buzzers and beeps and their grunts and sniggers rubbed at the edge of my concentration.

"You got your ship," said Marty, "plus we can steal some local rides if need be. They've got some air speeders I've heard."

"What, like we're just going to fly in there, gun them down, and take their goods?"

"Something like that," Marty said with a grin.

I shook my head, blinking with amazement. "You're something else, Marty, you know that? I think all that gumtox you've been chewing has gotten to your head."

"Careful there, Ruskie. The old Q himself gave me this drop. And he don't drop favors like that for nothing."

"Maybe." I grunted, licking my lips. "I just like to know what I'm getting into."

"Don't be a pussy. It's half the fun not knowing everything."

"Not really, Marty. Remember the last time we winged it, was nearly the end of us working together."

"This is your chance to make it big, Rusco. A slam dunk, instead of all those cheap little gigs out in backwaters-ville. I need ride and backup and figured you'd be good for it. I'll wait point while you nose around, scoping the place out. We'll keep in contact by bug wireless. Here—" He held up a pair of little black earpieces. "These little babies are untrackable. Shortwave or something. Tape it behind your ear."

"Shortwave," I scoffed. "Why me, stuck with the dirty work?"

Marty grinned his cat-like grin. "You're the security guard, aren't you? Didn't you tell me once you did—"

"Yeah, yeah, let's skip the little Red Riding Hood story."

"You were always good with B & E. I'm a better bullshitter and better at messing up wise guys, you know it."

I looked at him in wonder, seeing where this was going.

"Relax, this is what we're going to do, Rusco. We camo our faces, go in like cats, knock out their surveillance system. Those cams they have are ancient tech like everything on this scumbucket planet. CCTV, or something like that."

"Nighttime heists are tricky, Marty." My voice wavered between the condescending and serious.

He shook his head. "There won't be a 'nighttime'. I've been staking them out. The contra-crews and loader-boys work nights. Daytime, just a dumb fuck bunch of skeleton crew guards. Sleepy types, nothing ever happens during the day in Baer's yard. We go in in broad daylight."

"And transpo? You still haven't told me what your plan is for that. What are we going to do, fly there on our pink little wings? We're going to need a van or something to go in and truck out a load."

"You kidding me? A truck parked on the side of the road is a red flag, asking for attention, conspicuous as doggy-do."

"Scooter then," I said with irritation. "We hide it somewhere in the grass and foot it the rest of the way."

"Better. From what I gather, this contraband is not needing a lot of horsepower to move it. We can always snag some wheels along the way."

"I'll think it through," I said. I bridled my doubts, clamped my jaw shut, cradling chin in my hands.

CHRIS TURNER

Chapter 2

We took an electric three-wheeler with high chopper handlebars a buddy of Marty's had stored up on the end of the old U-line in his equipment yard. I made Marty sit in the back, be the bitch for once, indicated we'd hide it in the ditch when we got closer. The wheels rolled up on the hardtop which turned to gravel as we snaked along the river. More fenced yards, larger plants, disused factories, metal-pressing mills, boatyards. Not much of anything here away from the smelly, dirty city that was Hoath. Abandoned warehouses, loading docks, crane and metal factories, food packing companies, you name it, suppliers and distributers of every manufactured product one could imagine. The river wound itself tightly alongside a service road behind those complexes, black, slimy water that back in times of older generations used to carry cargoes into town. I felt a desolate unease wash over me. The memories of old sin and dark doings lingered about these tumbledown bastions of yesteryear. Again, that nagging feeling pricked at me, of regretting I had taken on this job.

Now the river was fouled with contaminants and garbage, thick oily water that no respectable fish would be caught dead in. I looked in wonder at the sight of the makeshift shelters and wanderers dressed in tattered khaki or lumberjack shirts, with hand-made rods casting out for fish. I shuddered to think what they'd catch.

Marty tapped my shoulder and pointed at the looming warehouse. We slowed up. Beyond a fenced yard two large, gray-muzzled Behusian hounds yanked at their rusty chains by the cement block outbuilding. I didn't like the beasts' incessant yapping, so I moved away and ditched the three-wheeler, hiding it in the weeds while Marty did his best to usher me along.

We walked past that place and stared at the next yard, Baer's yard, where the docking crane lay and the chain-wired fence, and ugly looking cinder-block, prison-like warehouse with its equally rundown outbuildings.

"This is it?"

Marty opened palms in what looked like a mock apology.

"Seems kind of dumb, Baer having this kind of setup for something this big."

Marty's lips hooked in a knowing grin. "All part of the act, Rusco. Small security crew means nothing worth stealing. The bigger players don't bother. Works well, costs them less, and doesn't draw attention."

"Whatever you say, Marty." I'd only met Q once, and didn't like the man, that big shaggy mother of a criminal, with a dirty cigar hanging out of his mouth, brown teeth, b.o. and a shifty gaze.

Marty stabbed a finger over toward the far side closest to the river. "Right, we jump a ride over there."

"Okay, you can work on 'jumping a ride'. One of those air speeders?"

"I don't know, there may be something inside you can nab that's better."

I shrugged. "I'm liking this less and less, Marty. Shoddy planning, it means somebody gets killed."

"Relax, Ruskie. You always worry too much." He patted me on the back, again a little too hard. "Let's go with the flow. This is a hot lead I've privileged your ears with. We've got a few hours' lead on any other hustlers Q decides to spread the news to."

I rounded on him, my teeth bared. "So, why doesn't big Q do this thing himself, instead of pissing this lead your way?"

"Q's done with Hoathville. Too many enemies here. He'll call in his favor to me at some time. But by that time, I hope to be long gone." He gave me that moony grin I knew too well and rubbed his chin as a flicker of past dealings came and went across that swarthy face of his. "Okay, I'll let you in on a secret, Rusco. Word is 'what's going down in Baer's crib is bigger than Lwippi's spread back in '82'. Those were Q's exact words."

My eyes dulled. "Woo, think I'm going to faint with excitement."

In the end I agreed to give the scope-out a shot, though I was ready to call it quits right there. Much against my better judgment, I contemplated the wire fence, ignoring that little nagging voice in the back of my head, the one that says, you stupid horse's ass, Rusco, what are you thinking? The promise of riches to a man in a hard place though, was a hypnotic lure outweighing risk.

Baer had taken over an old welding shop. A long rectangular building—white-washed cement blocks with tall twin brick chimneys missing several pieces. Rusted metal lay ripped off the outbuildings. Some dingy cargo-holders, transports, v-gauge Cessnas with wings clipped, fly-trucks, auto-meltzers, rusty cranes, some loading docks peeked around the edges. Probably a variety of stolen goods and contraband inside, worthwhile metal parts, salvageable electronics, fuels, explosives. Baer was likely a middle man for some bigger fish up the line. Okay, I was intrigued.

One guard was way down the other end. From where we crouched by the service gate in the gravel, I could see him pacing by the wall, machine gun in hand. No dogs that I could see, fortunately. Just a single sentry.

I looked across the dark thatch of river and caught the rise and fall of heavy metal arms, moving rigs. Migrant workers toiled in the fields there, shipped in from Escaron to work those oil rigs and the strip mines. Many died there, but that was life. A source of cheap labor and cash to boot and work for them. Hard to believe, but a better place for those migrants than the war-torn planets from where they had come. Marty interrupted my reverie.

"What I figure is we take the guard down, blast the door with that dynamite I told you to bring."

"Or maybe not," I grunted. "It ain't dynamite either. Pipe down, I'm trying to think."

Marty grumbled, his fists curled.

When the guard was well down the length of the wall doing his marching soldier routine, I aimed my R4 with its muzzled silencer and took out the main camera with a single, well-aimed shot. No more sound than the buzz of an angry bee.

Marty blinked. "Why not just shoot the guard too?"

"I got something against murder."

Marty snorted. "Give me the gun."

I pulled the weapon back from him and gave him a sullen stare. "Save your groping for your boyfriend."

Marty shook his head, muttering some disparaging comment.

We checked our earpieces. We were still in good working order. Marty donned the black ski-mask; I settled for soot on my cheeks, not that either would save us if it came to a firefight.

Killing the guard early on would be bad for us. First off, Marty was all too impulsive. If he thought the guard was down, he might get some cock-eyed idea, get careless and think he could slack off and just blast his way to the spoils. I didn't feel like getting myself killed the first five minutes into our heist. Nor did I like the restless way Marty got up and started pacing from side to side. It was sloppy, and sloppiness meant disaster. More practical reasons were self-evident: cameras maybe I had missed. A dead body bleeding out on the tarmac. The other thing is that sometimes these solitary guards were wired such that if their vitals failed, it sent a signal to a command post higher up that something had gone wrong.

I was banking that nobody was checking that camera very often, if Marty's information was to be believed. Our faces were covered, so nobody could ID us. I checked the kit strapped at my waist: pry tool, custom glock, penlight, blaster, explosives, medicaments, other useful knickknacks.

I hopped the steel-wire fence, taking care not to jingle it too loudly, dropped on the tarmac on the balls of my feet.

Marty followed, noisier than a dog. The sod made me wince with the racket. I cautioned him, and he nodded with a steel-eyed glare.

I threaded my way along the weed-eaten tarmac, ducking behind a generator post and an old dray-cart then lost sight of Marty as he dipped toward the back of the main complex.

Could I get at the guard from the roof? No. Too high. Drop a rock on his head? Dumbass, if you missed... come on, Rusco, you can do better than that. Blaster? Messy and bloody, undeniably noisy.

The easiest, simplest way availed itself. Always the easiest, and the best. The man yawned. Tired from a mindless day of nothing but back and forth in the sun and the drone of air speeders and bottle flies buzzing about. He was not getting paid enough to do this gig. So what if he checked out for an hour? His guard buddy down the line would pick up the slack. Just keep on nodding off, fella. I saw the double chin drop a little lower, then the hand come to clutch at the walrus-like mustache. That's it, a little lower. Probably got hammered last night and he's yawning off the hangover after his drunken lay.

I crept up behind the sap with my weapon cocked just as Poncho lifted his hand to stifle another of those cavernous yawns. One quick chop to the back of the neck along the Vagus nerve and the man fell in a soundless heap. I snatched up the fallen guard's vintage AK—it brought a nostalgic lurch to my heart—

I frisked the unconscious body, found a key ring, jammed it into the steel door, dragged him in, heels first then closed the door behind me.

The blood pounded in my temples and I forced myself to relax. I looked out upon an unmanned, dimly-lit area. A few fluorescent lights cast a dull glow on a concrete floor that stretched far back to my left, into a haze of darkness and mystery. I paused to orient myself. A loading dock spread down to my left with the usual trappings: a ramp of gridded metal, guide bars and dormant red service light above. Across the way, a gray concrete wall loomed dotted with steel doors to other rooms. I caught the vague forms of forklifts, stacked crates, machine parts and tools spread out along the peripheries. A few weigh scales stood next to a loader.

"Guard down," I hissed into the com. "Marty, anything?"

"Some rusted out three-wheelers around the back," Marty replied. "Nothing to brag about. Going to try to juice an air cart I scouted out. Slower than hell, but serviceable. Over."

"Affirmative. Over."

Marty seemed to be dicking around. I hoped he was watching for cameras.

I dragged the unconscious guard over to the far wall and tested the steel door. Unlocked. I stuffed him into the small storeroom. He'd be out for a couple of hours at least. Enough time for me to case the joint and snatch any spoils worth snatching. Hopefully a transport van of lucrative stock or contraband in some wing or bay around the sides I could drive out through the loading bay with none the wiser. Risky, and kind of a longshot, but hey, I was groping for anything at this point, and Marty assured me there was stuff here worth stealing.

No one inside; no guards to speak of. I didn't see any cameras—yet my eye was trained for them. Still, better to err on the side of caution. I thought to flush any other guards out quickly; an old trick I'd learned over the years. Basic but effective. Didn't want any nasty surprises.

Ducking in the shadows, I gripped the pebble I had snatched earlier. I tossed it lightly over my shoulder while I hid behind a wooden crate. The clinking echo rebounded throughout the loading area. I counted the heartbeats. Nothing. Only the hum of the fluorescent lights that played dim and cold over the bare concrete floor. Okay, that was a positive sign.

I crept out of my hiding place, taking noiseless steps, the guard's AK trained ahead.

The place was a little too eerie for my tastes. Kind of a grisly vibe, as if it weren't used much and had bad things happen here, like interrogation under torture. My mind replayed the dark, brown stains on the floor where I'd dumped Poncho. Sure as hell it wasn't pigs' blood. This didn't look like an abattoir or meat packing place to me.

The first creepers of disappointment tugged at my heart. I didn't see anything here worth stealing, and my doubts grew, realizing the futility of this heist. Perhaps I was expecting too much. I saw the desolate reality of this complex. A bunch of mini forklifts, empty crates on skids materializing in the gloom. The hypnotic buzz of cheap, old, electrical wiring while the stale smell lingered in my nostrils: tar, ancient dust, old engine oil.

I continued my rummaging. More crates filled with standard stuff. Boxes of grenades packed in sawdust, foot mines, circular mine sweepers, mild contraband. Military. But nothing to make any yols from this five and dime trash. The place was veritably empty.

Wtf then? That toad-licking Q give Marty false information? Maybe Marty messed up with the details? No, he was not that incompetent.

A wasted trip unless I could spring something fast. Floors bare and clean enough to eat fried eggs off.

I tapped my earpiece. "Marty, you there?"

Nothing.

"Marty, this place is looking like a dud."

Where the hell was he? I was getting more pissed by the minute. Risking my neck out in this empty coop. I whispered harshly into the com again. Nothing. I gave another colorful curse. Maybe Marty'd gotten cold feet or bailed. Was he made?

The storehouse branched out in an L-shape, and I stayed close to the rightmost wall. Across the way, I spied an electric flatbed tucked by the wall, one of the old, four-wheel lorries, riding low on its axles with covered canvas stretching over a back bed top. I slunk over. Nothing around in the back. This could come in handy if I found anything interesting, or if Marty didn't come through with a ride. The driver door was open. I poked my head in and checked the console. Nothing that wasn't easy enough to hardwire. On a whim, I tried starting it up. Ha! The engine whirred to life.

I shut it down, creeping on back to the rightmost wall like a specter.

A door loomed on my right. Blue plate steel with patches of rust caked on the edges. Grimy glass panes granted a view inside: some squarish-rectangular, cramped room. Too dim to distinguish details, but it was crowded with crates and other shadowy objects. Worth a look-see. The door looked fragile. I tried the outer U-ring. Locked. Should I blow it open? Seemed a risk, not to mention overkill. But unless I found something worthwhile here, this trip was batting a big fat zero. Maybe... I reached into my pouch. My universal pry tool gleamed in my hand, cool to the touch and very useful; I began a hack job jimmying the lock. I kept noise to a minimum, put my shoulder into it, forced it open.

A light switch on the side tempted me, but I resisted it. Others could come roaming about.

Crates and boxes of stuff lay stacked to the side. The lids of some I pried off to see weird things, looking like artifacts. Piles of them. Old technological junk, corroded batteries, wired circuits, strange bits of electrical panels, many half destroyed. But they didn't look familiar. Could as easily've been telesat equipment for all I knew. Gutted ship parts? I poked about some more, becoming more puzzled by the second. Disappointed too. Why lock up all this junk?

A set of small crates, stacked two high, aroused my attention. One was set off from the others.

I shone my penlight in the topmost box. Three small, hand-sized objects like rings with a central disc lay in the bottom of the packed cellophane. Curiosity whetted, I reached for the first. It looked like hyperized barsol, like what they made ship hulls out of. When my fingers were about to make contact, it pulsed with peculiar iridescence, like the colors of a butterfly's wings. I'm thinking it might have been something important, the way it swirled with all those alien colors, like chameleons' scales, so I wrapped the cellophane around it, tucked it into my kit, not thinking of any consequences.

Here, by the wall, stood a pair of devices, U-shaped, with waist-high parallel plates set a few feet apart. The things were balanced on black bases. I studied those plates. Circular designs like sucker marks inscribed their insides—alien tech by the look of it—with squiggles etched between its pale ribs. A chill passed over my spine.

Something warned me that this was even more important. I dragged the first parallel-plate device out back to the flatbed. Lighter than I'd thought it'd be. Gingerly, I hefted it into the back and covered it with a tarp, then crept back to the room, thinking to grab the other one, when footsteps and the light scuff of a boot alerted me. I ducked down behind the truck's rear tires.

Two guards, wearing black and white caps pushed down over their short-cut hair, came inching up to the door from the other direction. I could see they wore black chest armor and hefted AKs with murderous ease. Truncheons bobbed at their hips. Their black boots made little noise on the concrete floor. One motioned to the other and they ducked into the room, creeping forward like weasels along the walls. One stayed low to the left, the other to the opposite wall. I could see the thinner one from the angle where I crouched.

Shit, they must have been camped up in some command room watching the sensors. Could have been an infrared beam I'd triggered, which explained why the door was so lightly guarded.

Pinned like a grasshopper, I ran through my options. If I tried to start the lorry, they'd be on me. I could storm in and waste the two, but that was risky, two against one and they looked competent. Sit tight, Rusco. No need to play the hero. Slowly, I edged toward the open door, holding my weapon and breath, feeling the nakedness of my position. Only an open swath between me and death. No protection, and they'd be searching this lorry before long.

The seconds ticked by.

I heard a grunt, then an exhalation of surprise. "Mitch, there's nobody here. Maybe mice tripped the alarm."

"Right, mice just happened to jimmy the door?"

"Yeah, that is a problem; okay, scrap that." The other grumbled.

"Hey, you been messing with this box? Something's tore through the wrap. I remember three of the phasos, now there's two. Maybe rats took one away."

"Yeah, rats took one and I came in like a Madonna, wearing them like bracelets behind your back, like I always do."

"Shut up, wise-ass. It's my neck on the line too. Baer hears about this and we're cooked—"

"Relax. Baer doesn't have to hear about it."

"Are you kidding me? We're fucked. Look—one of the amalgos is missing. Two of them were here propped by the wall, remember? Maybe some filchers are still prowling around?"

"Look around again," hissed the other. "Some fuck may be hiding in the shadows." I ducked lower, hearing shuffling and curses, boots laid against boxes and mutters. This was not looking good.

They came up near the door, breathing through their mouths. "Nothing. Let's check the warehouse."

"No, wait. What about the phasos?"

"Fuck the phasos, come on."

"I don't like leaving them, Mitch, if there're skulkers about." He grabbed one. "Baer said they're for Mong, the star lord—"

"I don't give a fuck if they're for Bork of Ork. Put it away, those things give me the shivers."

"I don't appreciate that kind of language, Mitch. Furthermore, I'll touch what I want, bitchface. We're living in a free world, aren't we?"

"You going to get stupid on me, Fario? I said leave it alone." And he grabbed at the other's arm, wrestled the thing out of his hand.

In a blinding flash of light, the thug disappeared. I stared with stupid, blank-faced amazement. I blinked, rubbing my eyes. No ray, no secret gun aimed from the ceiling, no Marty behind holding a blaster. The one named Mitch just disappeared. For a second, I thought someone had spiked the wine I'd swilled at The Bodega. I shook my head. The guy'd been holding the disc thing, juggling it like an ape in front of the other, whispering some wise guy stuff, then poof, was gone.

That could have been me holding that gizmo. I reached for my waist where I'd tucked the disc or phaso, then thought twice of it. Lucky I had covered it with cellophane. I swallowed hard.

So…some kind of weapon? I shifted from my hiding place, head feeling woozy. The nitwit who triggered it was vaporized and his buddy, Fario, was coming out of his stupor, eyes wide in shock, a wild quiver in his gunhand. I thought fast. A medley of plans shuttled through my head. Plan 1, get out of here asap and chuck the phaso, Plan 2, double back, get the other units and mount an escape, Plan 3, blast everybody and run.

Option# 2 had its appeal, considering the potential rewards. One of those phasos still sat in that box, so when blinky eye decided there was nothing to see and booted it, I could easily snatch the disc-ring plus the larger amalgo with parallel plates which looked like antennae, but wasn't. It didn't look homemade, more like some alien tech unless that script on it was some language I'd never seen before.

Rusco, focus.

I heard the other speak into his com, his hands shaking. "Sully, you there?"

The guard tapped his com. No answer.

"Damn you, Sully! Mitch's out. Fucker's dead. Gone. Vamoose. Where are you, you idiot? You're supposed to be watching the entrance. You let some nosepickers in."

Bloody hell. Fario was not giving me many options at this time, scratching his head like a monkey, then loitering too close by. That box of phasos could be worth some serious dough, if I got it to the right people. Maybe Q wasn't so deadbeat after all. But where was Marty? Why hadn't he checked in? Maybe he couldn't, without being made.

A more likely scenario—Marty had fucked up and was probably dead. As I'd be soon if I didn't do something quick.

This was getting complex so I scrapped my well-intended plans. I needed to get out of here fast before my luck ran dry. These guys would kill me for whatever was in that back room. The stuff was hot, maybe too hot given my meager resources.

Fario shifted and I sighted in for the kill, trigger finger ready to deal with him. As I was rounding the vehicle door, keeping my eyes on him, a sudden waft of air tickled my skin. Boom! My left knee exploded in pain. Another guy was over me like a bad rash, kicking away my weapon. He must have been lurking there, heard my breathing or something. Or was it Mitch reappeared back like a genie? Grinning, with his AK hoisted, poised to swing it like a club to clock my other leg, I could see the gloating look in his eyes: to have scored the intruder who had nicked the contraband. Bully was written all over that miserable face, reveling in a sense of superiority over his victim, a toy he could play with.

But stupid of any bully not to take his victim out while he had a chance.

Chapter 3

I slid out of my painful daze as the guard's weapon came swinging down. I rolled aside. The cold metal only grazed my left ribs. I grabbed the stock and wrenched him forward, at the same time ramming my right boot as hard as I could into his groin. He sagged with a high-pitched cry. While he was gasping for breath, I reached for the syringe tucked in the kit at my belt and jammed it in my left thigh. That got me howling the banshee's yell from hell with the pain stabbing me like a longbow of agony. But above the pain I was already feeling a euphoric high. Myscol, aka Devirol, was the wonder drug of the new age and made me suddenly superman. For a moment the pain fled to a far corner of the universe, but it would come back.

I saw anger and adrenaline and invincibility wash into a blur of unreality. My attacker's face went white as he doubled over, weapon clattering to the ground. I became a fire bomb—a demon juiced up on *Devirol*, the old form of the ancient speed, or some derivative. Down he went in a tumble of tired muscle as my boot connected with his skull.

I snatched up his flesh ripper, the AK—didn't want him to use it on me, if he were to recover, unlikely as that might be.

Everything ticked in slow motion. The man's drool and broken teeth spilled out of his mouth along with a trickle of blood, his quivering cheek pushed flat to the concrete. The staticky whine of voices crackled on his com.

Fuck, there was backup coming. I shook the haze out of my head. A dark spot appeared on my leg where he'd clubbed me. I staggered to the flatbed, still clutching the man's AK, wrenched open the door and started the engine. The vehicle jolted forward, past the forklifts, down the hall, straight up the middle toward the exit. The other guard, Fario from the tickle-trunk room, came barreling after me, shooting at random. I rolled down the window, angled my weapon back at him, releasing a spray of machine fire, but I couldn't aim properly. Rotten bastard had a fast leg and caught up with me as I dodged and weaved, grasping the edge of the open window, grabbed my weapon out of my hand and wrenched it backward. Grunting, trying to jam the prick with my elbow while holding the wheel, I wrenched his arm about, snapping bone. He cursed and I kept his arm locked. The machine gun clattered to the paves. I gunned the engine straight for the sheet metal wall where I knew the loading bay to be.

A strangled scream broke from the guard's lips, as the whites of his eyes mooned in horror. The bumper sheared through the bay doors as jagged metal folded him sideways, erasing his shoulder and crushing his right limb.

The shredded gatepieces clattered behind as I crashed through the sheet metal, the wheels bucking as they took the two-foot drop without hiccup in the absence of any loading ramp. I looked back in the mirror to see his palsying form sprawled on the concrete. I burst out into the pale overcast, wondering where the hell Marty was. No one in sight. A sallow glare streamed from the sky.

Sense started to come to me. What to do with that piece of tech?

The gears in my brain worked with slow precision as I hit the gravel road and headed toward Hoath. I looked for a quick solution. Take the device to my ship at the rendezvous point, several miles out from the east end of town. A no brainer, right?

No.

An abandoned warehouse came up to my left and my heart did a little tumble.

That feeling that grips you when you're forced to make a quick decision in a time of trouble. Take Path A or Path B. The path through the woods on the tried and true trail, or that unknown animal path down by the lake you've never been to. *Step right up, folks, sign your name on the dotted line in blood.* The bad feeling that had been lurking in the pit of my stomach just suddenly jerked up a notch.

"Aw, screw me!" Acid boiling to my throat, I cranked the wheel hard, front tires spitting gravel. The flatbed broke through the rickety steel gate, and I pulled up to the loading docks.

Stumbling out of the vehicle, panting, I kicked open the rusty door of the warehouse with my good leg. Cursing, I tucked my hands in my sleeves. With hands shielded, I dragged the foreign parallel-plate gadget into the gloom, dropped it into a storeroom with only bats and mice flitting about. The place smelled of dung and mildew, but I didn't care. Hadn't been used in years. I pushed the tech deeper into the shadows and covered it with some old mildewed battered skids and tarps. One brown rat with pointed snout jumped out with a baleful stare and squeaked. Knock yourself out, rodent. Get blasted to oblivion, if you like. I limped out to the flatbed and gunned the engine, churning gravel all the way.

Forget Marty. Got to get to my ship.

I drove toward the outskirts of Hoath, following the main road. I must have driven for miles before I became aware of little oncoming traffic.

Warning bells chimed in my mind. What the hell? Minutes ago, only an odd lorry had passed, probably carrying dubious cargo. I didn't know the side roads. Might have to run some detours, which was a bad thing. My leg tingled to the barest edge of feeling as the Myscol began to wear off. To drive that piece of junk into the city— was not ideal.

The flatbed rattled over the top of a hill. Ahead and below, I saw flashing lights. A blockade of some sort: steel girders, surface cars, a few air speeders and milling figures. No way! Men in uniform, hailing down traffic, and detaining and searching vehicles. My mind raced.

Baer's work? Coincidence?

Baer's boys must have called in for reinforcements—which meant I was meat if I didn't quit this scene.

I slammed on the brakes and did a full 180. An air speeder looped out after me, its airhorn piercing the stillness and scaring a flock of ducks with long spoonbill beaks. Those horseshoe-shaped air speeders looked like local law. Could Baer's reach run so deep?

I screeched down a gravelled side road. The lights flashed as an official police van lurched after me from the blockade. Now I was up shit creek. This clunker wouldn't hold up to air pursuit and souped-up cop van. In desperation, I cranked the wheel hard and ran her into the fields.

Not wise. The ground was wet and soggy with a recent rain. The engine whined at max rpm, tires spinning in the black mud. The van halted and two burly figures leaped out who looked none too pleased, grimacing through their beards. I could see their faces set and rifles in their hands. The air speeder came bearing down on me.

I bolted the doors, clutched my glock, but they smashed through the glass and hairy hands pulled me out onto the wet grass. I struggled, getting off a wild shot, but losing my grip on my gun, as it was kicked out of my grasp.

"You rotten prick," I bawled. "Pick on someone your own size."

"Funny man at two o'clock, Roy. Spike him."

I still had some juice left in me from the Myscol and I kneed the bastard in the chest just as he bent down to clobber me with his rifle. These thugs were keen on taking me alive, otherwise they would have peppered me long ago. Wrestling, I jammed his weapon in his face, breaking his nose and mashing an eye. He howled and went down in the mud, clutching at the ruin of his face. His partner reached to help him as I staggered off.

The air speeder disgorged three air guards. Husky, military boys. They looked royally pissed, a mean bunch, though nothing more than mercenaries paid to patrol and beat down whomever their employers told them to—which in this case must be Baer. I could see the blue decals with the hunting eagle on the underbelly of the craft. Not that that meant anything, the insignia of city air guards.

Rat-a-tat-tat, Three men and a rat. The rhyme worked in rhythm with the slugs that ate into the flatbed.

I wasn't going out without a fight. I pulled out a large hand-sized explosive from my waist kit. Tossed it at the air speeder. The marshals shielded themselves but I was the only one to duck in time.

Marshals and air speeder went up in a roaring flame.

I heard voices through the haze and smoke as I struggled through the wet sod.

"Nothing in the back!" cried one of the van riders. "No amalgos."

"What the fuck? Where's the amalgo? Where's that shitweasel with the bombs?"

I grinned as I hobbled away. One came loping after me through the smoke, grunting again. "Where's the bloody amalgo?"

"Up your ass, fucker. Eat shit."

A billyclub came smashing down on my head and I knew no more.

Chapter 4

I passed from world to world, from past to present, in a kaleidoscope of fact and fiction. My disembodied self hovered above the floor that dim day out working as a security guard over at Crystal Mindworks Ltd. Days when I entertained a notion of upholding some law-keeping role in society. Five thugs busting down the door, wearing masks.

The beat down of the guards, Frenzetti and Markus, my friends, slain in front of my eyes. Two shots clipping from my R9, one killing the first, point blank, the other sending a lowlife writhing on his back. A bullet grazing by my ear. Stumbling out the side alley, my ears ringing, blood pouring down my scalp. My one thought was to get out of here while others roved about, knowing that the bungling would be pinned on me as an accomplice. *Why were you the only one left after the robbery, Rusco?* Trying to start the air speeder to get out there, start fresh on a new world. Taking other softer jobs offworld, working star carrier baggage, playing bouncer, pawn shop security, construction crew, you name it, but it only got worse—the violence, the murder, the theft, always catching up to me, as if I were some beacon for it, with a dark cloud hovering over my soul, plunging me deeper into a nightmare of illusion. The drinking becoming more intense, the only way to drown the pain, until Mela at last left me.

Dreams have the uncanny knack of telling us hard dark truths about ourselves.

When that saw edge of reality surfaced, so began my slow descent down the road 'if you can't beat them, join them'. My looking for crime as a quick means to an end, flirting with its seductive narcotic, searching for the one big score that would never happen.

I came to, with the smell of sweat and machine oil in my nose. Some rough hands dragging me across the cement floor. In a dingy hall lit with fluorescent lights the familiar smell hit me. I groaned. Well, I'll be a monkey's fuckbuddy if I wasn't back in that shithole warehouse.

Then I discerned the sounds of a beat-down. A familiar voice. Quiet, child-like, mixed with thudding sounds like a metal pipe whacked on flesh. Only because it came through a steel door left slightly ajar did it sound surreal, like something out of a cartoon. The two goons thrust me in. I rolled on a bare concrete floor, blinking like the bedraggled wretch I was.

I took one look at Marty beside me and knew things had gone very wrong. His haggard face resembled a terrified mask. He mouthed words "had to scram or give away your position."

Marty sagged as a meaty fist clipped him in his well-purpled face. With two black eyes and lips messed up, it explained why I couldn't recognize that voice right away.

The man who'd clipped him turned his burning gaze upon me. I had seen wild animals in the zoo less feral and repulsive than that aberration who stood before me. Everything about the thug screamed bear. A shaggy ruff of black hair like the fur of a large predator coated head and arms. Wide sideburns covered his cheeks, his bared forearms exposed by rolled-up sleeves. Wide-spaced beady eyes and mallet fists. A mouthful of shark teeth. Easily could have been the most hideous creature I'd seen. Some modern-day mutant? Or one who'd experimented with, or OD'd on too many modern day transfigurative drugs and lost the fight?

"Welcome, Mr. Rusco," the man growled in his husky voice. "Glad you could make our little appointment."

"The pleasure is all mine." I spat blood, along with a tooth.

"You know who I am?"

"Mr. Magoo from the Metro Zoo. Dunno, don't care."

He flashed my long-nosed captor a meaningful look.

Long Nose grunted. "Busted up Floss and Bix real good. They won't be walking too soon. Vin's Air speeder took a hit. Some little incendiary he had up his sleeve. No amalgo."

The man sighed, a murmur of grave amusement. "Clown Hair, you've been a busy boy. Care to enlighten us on the whereabouts of my amalgo?"

"Dunno anything about any amalgo."

He paced the room, his lips getting cold and stiff, his teeth flashing as if ready to bite someone's head off. "That's funny. Fario, who lies with half his arm hanging off, claimed he saw one in the flatbed you crashed through my warehouse."

"Fario sounds like a man with an overactive imagination."

He jerked a thumb at Long Nose. "Clown Hair thinks he's gonna word-play his way out of this." He turned to me. "You know, one of the amalgos is no good without the other."

"Do I give a fuck?"

"You don't get it, do you?" he echoed in wonder.

"Sure, Baer," Marty slurred through a broken nose. "We do."

"Mr. Baer to you." He growled, turning his feral gaze on Marty. "Some clients of mine are going to be sorely pissed when they ask me where their amalgo is and I say, "beats me, Will, a couple of wise-guys broke in and stole it.""

"That's a hard thing to have to say," Marty wheezed. "I can understand, Mr. Baer. Rusco's just bargaining for his life is all, aren't you, Jet?"

Baer smiled and shook his head with a sad laugh. "I'll ask you again, where's the amalgo?"

One of Marty's eyes had swollen shut. "I'm just the dog-boy here, Baer. If you want to pull somebody's legs off, you're looking at the wrong guy. *Ask, Jet.*"

"Like this sack of shit's going to tell us anything?" Baer snarled.

He flashed a pistol and held it to my head. "This fuck looks as if he couldn't blow himself out of a paper bag. Last chance, Marty. You're ribbing with the wrong man, with this, 'ask Jet, shit'."

"That's rich, boss," guffawed Long Nose. He gave Marty a jab in the ribs with his truncheon that had him groaning.

"Shut up," growled Baer. "If I want you to open your mouth, I'll rattle my zipper."

I twitched, almost wanting to laugh. Marty, the faithless fucker. He was going to sell me to the dogs before long with his good-guy talk. I could see the yellow look in his eye. Fuck Marty. I'd have to rely on my own devices to live through this. The hoodlums seemed sure of themselves to have kept us unbound. They wouldn't kill me as long as I knew where their amalgo was. Torture, yes, but there was the Myscol. What was Marty's game? Was he done playing sycophant, giving up his only leverage of having something of worth they wanted? Unless, of course, Marty was being trickier still with his old good guy, bad guy routine. My mind was not thinking straight. I was in shock from the last ten hits to my skull.

Marty was stalling, always good at that, mixing fact with fiction, hopefully creating possibilities out of thin air to keep the enemy guessing and scratching his head. That it would stall Baer long enough before one of us could break out of here, was another thing. Marty wasn't looking as if he could hack too much more.

"Search him," Baer said.

"Already did. We found this little phaso on him. This big explosive too." My husky captor tossed it to Baer.

Baer nodded. "Got that. Explains the wrecked speeder. Demolitions man, are you?" he said, turning to me.

I smiled.

"Where's the amalgo? The funny little roboty-looking googad with twin parallel plates. Glows green when armed."

I tossed back my wavy dyed purple hair, trying for a gambit. Nothing to lose, right? Well, almost right. Sorry for what it cost Marty. I am sorry for that.

The Myscol, still pulsing in my veins, fueled fire to an inner strength we all have but rarely tap into. I'd taken a triple dose, something unheard of—my doctored batch, the one they had no clue I'd taken. It drew them deeper into underestimating me.

Long Nose, on a cue from his boss, stepped in to truncheon me as he had Marty. That was a mistake. My steely fist crashed into his thigh. It's as close as I could get to the brute. Left a charley horse he wouldn't forget. He buckled over with a painful rictus and my steel-toed boot caught him in the throat and that made his charley horse look like a love tap. Teeth and blood dripped on the ground with sticky white drool. Nasty scene.

Baer made his move, but I was quicker. I snatched the coin-sized explosive out of his hand, ducked in a drunken roll and tossed it right back at him, just as I armed the detonator.

The white flare caught his right side, lit him up like a candle, as he held up a hand to shield his face. Too late. The blast also caught Marty and singed half his hair and upper cheek off. Me, I was blinded for a second and my left side blood-spattered and burnt. The boss roared like a bear, clutching at his burning arm, shorn at the elbow. He'd mend it with some bio-regen, if he hurried. Doubted he had any on him at the moment.

The shaggy man staggered for the side door, coughing blood through the smoke. How he did so was beyond me; the man must not be human. I pocketed the phaso he'd dropped, grabbed Marty, and stumbled after.

I hauled Marty's sorry ass out of that burning, smoking death crib, lips curling in crazed grin at Baer's tumult. We stumbled through the gaping ruin of the loading dock. Across the tarmac we beetled like a couple of twisted scarecrows. An air speeder and two lorries stood out back of a communications tower surrounded by wire fencing. Screw the lorries. Useless against air attack. That air speeder looked like a heavenly prize, especially since it was one of Baer's.

I hopped around the other side of it with Marty all gasping and limping. The first parked vehicle shielded us from the machine gun fire that would have cut us in two. We scrambled back, ducking to the rat-a-tat-tat of stray bullets. I clawed open the speeder door, hopped in, as machine gun fire clipped the tail fins.

I pulled Marty in head down and dove behind the wheel.

Kicking the throttle full on, I veered straight up, as black smoke and pressure gauges plummeted. "Come on, baby!" I roared. "Get us out of here before old man Baer grows wings. To the air depot."

"We ain't gonna make it, Rusco," rasped Marty, caressing his soot-grimed cheek and ruined ear that oozed fluids.

I grimaced at the sight and smell of his burned flesh. "Sure we will, Marty. Shut up. Sit back and enjoy the ride. Course we'll make it."

For the first time I got a good look at Marty and shivered at what I saw. His lank mustard-colored hair was coated in slick dark fluid. His breath wheezed in and out like a terminal smoker. Coagulated blood caked the side of his head and his right arm spasmed.

"You okay?" A dumb question that I wished I hadn't asked.

He held up a quivering hand and grimaced through his pained, red-rimmed eyes. "Had better days."

"Helluva ride."

"Helluva ride. Didn't by any chance snatch up that little phaso of his before Baer was grasping for pieces of his arm?"

"Not particularly." Lies were easy to spill out of my mouth. The disc was a death curse and Marty wasn't up for what was next.

"Uh huh. Guess we could end up with nothing then after all."

"Guess so."

Marty closed his eyes and lay back his slick head against the headrest as the air speeder sputtered along, trailing a stream of ugly black smoke. The engine growled and hiccupped. It wouldn't stay airborne for long. Below us, the city came into view in all its grisly glory: broken water towers, bombed-over apartment complexes, crumbled buildings, checkerboard smokehouse slums.

"Listen, I have to set us down somewhere. We can't be caught again."

A long pause. Marty shook his head. "Ain't leaving Hoath, Rusco. You're bad luck to me. Don't want anything to do with you."

"Don't blame you, Marty. I can get you fixed up on Starrunner."

"Forget it."

"Suit yourself."

"Drop me at the nearest U-ground link," he croaked. "I'll catch a ride downtown."

"Dammit Marty, let's talk about this."

"There's nothing to say, Rusco."

I shrugged. Marty was a proud man. I couldn't blame him for despising me. The job was a cockup, we'd almost gotten killed, and in his mind, I'd screwed up and abandoned him. Perhaps that's why I had ridden solo for so long.

Marty spat out a wad of blood on the floor at his feet. I veered down over a side street on the outskirts of the Jildaree district, milling with immigrants. One of the main streets would take Marty to the old market, downtown. He could disappear in the underground like a wisp of air. Part of me hated to leave him, but it was his choice.

In his lucid moments, he'd come to see the dark cloud hovering over me, the one that had shadowed my hide for so long now. The old, painful, rat-gnawing wound in my soul that drew danger and mishap like a moth to the flame.

"So long, Jet," he muttered with a tired sigh. His crooked grin had gone cold and brittle.

As I landed in a disused equipment yard, I popped open the door and watched him ease off his seat, leaving a blood trail behind. "So long, Marty. Take care of yourself."

He limped off into the yard, catching the blinking surprise of many ragged beggars and potheads warming their hands around their fires. I opened my mouth to say something, but thought better of it. I took off into the hazy sky, doubting that despite what Marty said, the poor bastard would make it through the night.

Chapter 5

I glided down to the refueling-docking station where I had left Starrunner, a big sun-bleached yard with two mid-size control towers and four rusty hangars. Glad I'd paid my twenty yols to secure it— safe for a little while at least. Anything over two days wasn't guaranteed, neither here nor at any approved docks on this planet.

I set the stolen speeder down in a designated landing zone and hobbled up to the security guard at Hangar 3. I gave the gate security guard my most disarming smile. He gave me the once-over, frowning at my blackened and bruised appearance and tattered clothing, but after positive ID, he let me pass.

My ship, a sleek and gray Alpha 9 had a rough diamond shape at rear with ox horn-shaped prow at front—a balm for my soul. Many adventures we'd shared together. She'd gotten me out of jams before.

Several other ships were berthed nearby, from the dingiest rustbuckets this side of Vega, to a few Alpha retrofit models with double-flared ion thrusters, cigar fuselages and weapons defense to boot. I couldn't help but admire these vessels despite my haggard state, beauties in their own right in this day and age. One fine morning I'd graduate to a Kepler 350 or a Hexler 410 A2.

Stay focused, Jet.

The hatch peeled back after I fumbled the controls at the side. I'd rewired the thumbprint ID-pad to bypass the scan, in case my thumbs were less than thumbs.

I ducked into the hatch and stumbled to the bridge, fired up my eagle. I reached below the console and took a bottle, downed a chug of Astra whiskey to loosen me up. Then another. I needed something to take the edge off my agony when I started to really come down off the Myscol. I patted the console with all her lit-up sensors and the extra upgrades I'd installed over the years. A better version of the battle hound older models. Self-refueling, drawing the radiant energy from suns when she came close to one, replenishing the Radium-Cesium ion thrusters and wafer cells. It had less range on impulse power and less speed at sub-warp, but it saved me a lot of grief, and yols, in risking refueling at some redneck, outer-planetary dock.

As the sallow sky grew flat, stars tinkled at the edge of my vision. I heard whispering voices in my head over the hum of the engines as Starrunner passed through the clouds. Hoath became a faraway memory. A stab of bright light licked out from the sun Tiga then disappeared as I arched into planetary shadow, then the blackness of space.

At this point I'm wondering what the hell am I doing? Why pursue this gig, Rusco? Are you a masochist?

Smartest thing would be to get out of the Phaedra sector as fast as I could. To where? Beleron 6? Mixraen? Both planets were safe—relatively speaking. Mixraen, one of the less shabby worlds where I could get this knee looked after without being at risk of infection or some botch-up. The throbbing had receded to a dull ache but that likely wasn't going to go away soon.

Thing was, Starrunner wasn't protected from pot-shot hunters. Easy for Baer and his goons to do a hyperclasson trace on the heat signature, if they so desired. Triangulate from last vector before light speed. I'd have to jump worlds to give them the slip.

With such thoughts crowding my mind, I programmed the Varwol light drive for Mixraen, in the meantime coasting on steady impulse power toward Brisis's moon, knowing I'd have to clear planetary gravity before I could risk engaging the light drive.

I gazed with pride upon my rack of guns, from small pistol to semi-automatic RX series to Uzi to remodeled AK to modern high-blaster. A weapon for every day of the week. Even experimental ray guns at the end of the rack. But I tended to go for the older-generation guns. Call me a traditionalist.

My attention drifted back to the view in space. Several monstrous cylinders hovered before me. I eased past the now hulking derelict remnants of ancient planetary defense systems, orbiting Brisis. Their nuclear powerplants had winked out of existence ages ago, their pulse ray cannons, at one time able to destroy star cruisers, now iced and inert. Many half shorn barrels looked back at me. Though hollow and scavenged by junkers or freelancers for parts, they still sent shivers down my spine.

A blip appeared on my sensor readouts. I frowned. A bright object reeled in behind the nearest cylinder. At first I thought it was the actual derelict coming to life.

But no. Raiders! Clinging to the underside, piggy-backing off the defense probes like tics, eluding my sensors.

The klaxon rang from the overhead bulkhead and Molly's computerized voice began beating out an insistent monotone, "*Red alert. Enemy in pursuit. Pulser waves to hit in five seconds.*"

What the bloody hell! They weren't active when I flew down to this god-forsaken planet.

I activated shields and banked Starrunner in a steep dive away from the pulse beams arching my way. It gave me a few more seconds. But the impact grazed the starboard thruster and sent me in a tailspin. Shit! The Varwol couldn't engage this close to planetary gravity, so I was scuppered.

"Great, Molly. Skurgian raiders? What this time?"

"*Databanks report high probability of Skurgian origin.*"

Two more bogies popped up out of nowhere on my short range scanners. Three old, refitted craft with high stems, bullet noses and gray bodies. No match for Starrunner on a good day, but a risk now with her in a side slew. I maxed out the stabilizers and with help of the ship's computer, managed to pull her out of her tailspin. "Molly! Lock weapons on their engines, now!"

"Affirmative."

As the forerunner gained ground, I caught a glimpse of the raider's forecannon. Large and lethal. Nothing less than heat-seeking missiles, spiked cubes with wicked guiding systems. They'd pulse Starrunner to immobility, then blow me open like a tin can with one of their torpedoes, with the added bonus of being able to scavenge at their leisure with the crew dead.

My mind worked in furious calculation. Raiders as these went for the small fry like myself and left the big freighters alone—the big cargo transports moving world to world selling their ores, raw materials and contraband on less impoverished worlds than Hoath.

The Skurgian stalkers turned on an intercept course. I sent out a high-energy fareon beam, after Molly had done the math. The first enemy craft careened left too late as concentrated pulser made contact with metal, and a bright orange ball burst outside my starboard viewport.

I cheered. The lights dimmed and reserve power took a hit, and the shields took a beating upon the return fire. But the other two banked off.

I struggled to gain control of the fluctuating sensors. "T minus 10 to escape window," Molly droned. Like slow leaps into infinity, the seconds ticked by. Just as the next spiked missile came a ghost's breath away, the Varwol kicked in, and the universe slipped sideways. Colored lights dazzled my visual space, a million sparkles of bright light licked out at me from the void ahead. Then blackness. Starrunner had entered the no-zone of singularity. *Running again.* Rusco's signature.

Yet something was off. The last hit must have damaged the singularity stabilizers. My heart did a dive.

Odd thing about warp is that sound is often distorted. One's movements seemed blurred around the edges, as if reality is skewed, impinged by an external force. A human hand moves a little too late, or an extra finger appears on that hand but it's just a blur of five fingers moving at once. The mobilitor's tech corrected and tried to adjust for the time-dilation effect, but even that was never infallible and created little glitches of speech and movement. Exaggerated now with the mobilitors impaired.

"Molly, do something."

"Mobit tech at 82% and dropping. High impulse beam was sustained by shield at 40%. Compensating."

"Do what you can!"

A sudden dark thought edged my mind. I clawed at my pant's pocket. Still there. I grabbed a soft cloth and extracted the phaso and lay the disc on the bridge console with extreme care.

The object sat there in its weird way, shimmering with a dull iridescence. I eyed it as a tiger might eye a steel-rimmed trap. Something about the thing did not seem natural, or of any human world, with its unreadable script and its strange symbols writ along the curve's inner edge. Hieroglyphics? Numbers? Coordinates? I shook my head. Inscribed on the light hyperbarsol they reeked of heavy mystery. I daren't touch the script, for it looked as if it might be where the last schmuck had fingered it, and gone into hyperspace.

I shivered, moved the evil talisman into a metal strongbox I kept in the storage bulkhead. I closed the box with a loud clack and stuck it under the console. A spasm of pain rippled through my knee. My hand reached down, clutched at the bulged rent in my leather spaceman's garb that covered my quivering kneecap, aching and swollen.

The hydrophane from the Myscol was wearing off. Spidery pain crawled up my leg with a ripple effect, from shin to knee. I stumbled to the medicine cabinet, biting back curses, fingers arching for that place where I kept my stash of get-well drugs. My hands shook as I reached for the little pink bottle, the one I saved for special occasions. That I'd distilled from a home blend of morphine and dyzanol. I refrained from another shot of Myscol, knowing well the next jolt would send me into cardiac arrest. Muscle up, Jet boy.

Stomach your pain.

Fingers beaded with sweat, I stuck a wooden rod between my teeth and champed down hard.

Eyes glued to the sensors, I watched the Varwol integrity dip down to 62%. But it held. Movement was tricky in this syrupy warp and repairs impossible. As long as it didn't get below 40% before the next planet, I was okay. If it did…ship and crew would disappear into a singularity.

I cruised for hours, maybe days, enjoying the silence of deep light travel, warring with old thoughts, aware of a nagging feeling brewing at the back of my skull. Something about this situation seemed worse than past ones—a shadow zone, as if I were staring in the black pit of the unknown. I really didn't know what my next step was, something unusual for Jet Rusco. Calm, cool, phlegmatic Rusco of the dark pool of scammers and avengers, with a million cons all ready to go. To have survived them thus far, had given me a richer confidence than I deserved. A dangerous place to be. It was a bubble waiting to be burst. That grand bungle in Hoath had been the first warning; staring down death, not once but twice. It had shaken the belief in my invulnerability, got me thinking.

Thirty-five going on eighty, melting into the wasteland of middle age. I wasn't getting any younger. The creaks in my spine were getting all too loud and more frequent. The lithe pliancy, the hard muscle that had once moved fast and rattled so many heads had toned down a peg.

The warning sensor came back and Molly's shrill voice seeped into my brain like a bullet shredding chipboard.

"Systems failure. Port wing stabilizer. Varwol disengaging. T minus 6. Impulse power at 10%."

"Molly, you doom-monger! Where the hell are we?"

"Minos sector, The Orion Zone. Coordinates T56.988234—"

"Alright, nowheresville. Target the closest habitable planet."

"Affirmative. Planetary gravity field affecting compromised Varwol." She brought up the nearest planetary datasheet on the holo display. A

dusty world, of shell-shocked craters within range. Estimated indigenous population: 12,000.

"Great, okay, make for it. What is it?"

"Talyon 8A. Terraformed planet settled in the second wave of the settlers' rush, circa 2945.67.123—"

"Yeah, yeah." The fourth planet showed as a pale saffron disc in orbit around Silirus, the bright orange star dead ahead. The nearby planet's gravity was too much for the drive. The Varwol fluttered to a halt, leaving me on impulse, caught within grappling distance of Talyon's gravity. The main thrusters, already compromised, shuddered under the tidal grab, not potent enough to steer me clear.

I guided the ship as best I could down through the colorless atmosphere. Even that was rocky. Starrunner couldn't stay in the air.

I picked the straightest strip of sand I could find, between two massive mountains of what looked like monstrous garbage piles, and what looked like massive pits beyond them. I kept the nose high, tightening the straps securing me in the pilot's chair.

Starrunner's fuselage heated up to a red blur. Ship sensors warned me of further failures. I shut them off.

The ship ground its gray underbelly along the alien turf as I bashed along and watched my fragile existence flash before my eyes. No regrets, Rusco, none. Though there should have been a thousand.

The grinding of pebbles against the hull came to a screeching apex; the buffeting, rocking knocked my brain about, as I was jostled and jerked until blackness stole over my mind.

Chapter 6

I jerked up with a gasp, passing a hand over my brow. It came back crimson from a throbbing gash. Some loose object must have whacked me on the skull.

Blood dripped down my cheek. I blinked through the porthole at a giant mound of reddish-black crud and scummy earth glaring back at me. Whiplash, bruises and aching joints strobed in and out with red welts where the straps had held me. No broken bones. The ship's interior functions blinked in nominal condition. Better condition than what I expected. Emergency lights bathed a pale glow over the power console and sensors kept bleeping.

The pilot panel flashed like something out of a gamer's session and dust particles hung thick in the air. The ship was useless to me with the drive so impaired. Nor was I any ace mechanic. I counted the seconds as I drifted in and out of crash daze. I could sit there like a grinning statue, pretending none of this had ever happened, or I could get up and brave the elements. At some point I would have to, as my supplies were not inexhaustible. The sooner the better. My eyes traveled to the surplus space suit hanging from the wall. I visualized the sustenance I would have to gather up, stumbling about on an alien world. But who knew what horrors lurked out there? Sucking in another gasp of air, I hitched off my safety straps and collapsed to the metal-grated floor before groping to my knees and picking myself up to hobble across the bridge. The pain clutched at the heart of my nerve centers.

Readout showed a breathable atmosphere, a few decimals shy of 38 Celsius. Damn, hot out there. Terraformed likely centuries ago. But a bad feeling brewed in my gut. Shaking my head, I grabbed an R4 blaster, part Uzi, part modern tech, from the weapons rack close-by and opened the hatch. Dull sunlight struck my eyes. I staggered out, wincing, feeling the haze of disorientation.

Starrunner's fuselage smoked. I swayed on unsteady feet, struck by the heat wave. I closed the hatch, rolled up my sleeves, made the mistake of grazing the gleaming metal while keeping my balance. "Ouch, you fucking mother—" My wild curse fell on dead air. I shook out my hand.

A sandy lane disappeared around a bend between massive piles of twisted junk. Behind, a sandy streak where my smoking ship had skidded to an unceremonious halt. This looked like a vast human-made dump. Broken plastics, twisted metal, pipes, culverts, wires, charred wood, every bit of refuse I could imagine. An old dusty reek filled my nostrils, as if the cloud of slow decay had floated over here for generations. No rain had fallen here for what, decades? The dryness had ground decomposition to a halt. I reached out, touched a hank of metal, a lance-edged piece from the bumper of an old ground vehicle. The metal seemed little rusted for the time it had spent here.

The Veglos system and all the rest of the galaxy had gone to hell, but did I have to get marooned on a shit pile like this?

What were these giant mounds of garbage? Not just ass-wiping little dungcock heaps you see on the satellite, five and dime feeder worlds, but *giant* mounds. Miles of them. An ecological disaster. Not that it mattered much considering my plight on this forsaken world.

Sound to my left. A flicker of movement. I ducked behind a small heap of mangled wires and prosthetic robot parts, gripping my R4, my senses on high alert.

Two figures emerged, one tall, one short. They carried no weapons that I could see, only what looked like a Geiger counter held in the hands of the older, taller man. I blinked, shaking my head of the cobwebs.

"Billy," the older one croaked in an excited voice, "looks as if we've found our pot of gold. The sounder has found our fortune." His loose tan-brown desert rags drooped from neck to toe. "There, just like I said! A downed craft. Yahoo!" He slapped his thighs in glee, stabbed a finger of triumph at my ship, the place where she smoked and crackled.

The boy, no more than fifteen, jumped up and down like a sidekick, did a kind of jig like one of those crazy panhandlers I see back at Hoath.

"Careful, Billy," the man warned. "This thing could be booby-trapped." He pulled the teen away with a determined hand. He looked ready to cry.

I narrowed my brows. Whoever these halfwits were, I was at a low melting point with an itchy trigger. As the older fellow blinked and set down his metal detector on the hot sand, he gave my ship a careful inspection and reached within his rags, withdrew a tool of some sort to tinker with the outer hatch.

A small smile touched my lips. Good luck, pops, getting in that titanium-sealed—

My jaw dropped as the door slid open and the old man gave a victorious chuckle. The alarm sounded, a piercing intermittent klaxon whose lows and highs dripped with Molly's anticlimactic warning,

"Intruder alert, intruder alert!"

I cringed. So did my guests who stared around wild-eyed, as if monsters were ready to eat their brains. The old man's eyes kindled in desperation and he fiddled with the cowling trying to disable the alarm.

No luck. I gripped my R4, ready to blast these two desert rats. They'd invaded the one sacred place left to me in this big universe. Another voice called out a throaty drawl that made me pause.

"Back off, weasels! Mine first." The figured motioned the narrow bore of her rifle at them. Youngish to middle age, bowlegged, dressed in worn leathers, goggles strapped tight as protective eyeware against the sun, she was a sight to behold, legs set wide in an aggressive stance.

The old man turned with care and put a restraining arm around Billy's shoulder. Seemed the boy was keen on running out and getting himself shot. He snarled like a vicious animal, like some wolverine I'd seen on the nature holo-feed.

"Move," she ordered, roaring in a harsher voice, motioning to where a charred single mangle of metal hung out of the smaller mountain of debris.

Grumbling, the two hurried to stand beside a crumpled space cruiser, clinging out of the pile like some squashed insect.

She padded toward the open ship with a slow saunter, and I blinked, getting my senses together, then crept after her, my blaster raised.

"Back away," she growled. "I get first dibs on this crate, you bumpkins, then you can paw your way over it as much as you like. The grubs'll be coming out soon. Yes, the crazy boys, and you know what that means."

She leveled her sawed off black rod, a custom blaster, rigged with flamethrower and bayonet. Peeking into the entrance bay, she nodded in appreciation.

I frowned. What a filthy piece of work. Dirty as sin. Grime all over her skin and face and loose leather jacket and pants and shin-guards. Black, of all colors, in this stifling heat. Yet underneath the grime was a limber female, with lean muscles to boot.

Before she got the bright idea of staking out my ride, I stepped over and called out a pleasantry. "Okay, commander Tomboy, ease back real slow."

She whirled, lifted her weapon, but misfired a round that whistled inches from my ear. I shot off a slug that nicked the bayonet's end and made her think twice about another shot.

She held her hands up and let her weapon drop.

"That's smart. Kick it away," I said. She did, though with sullen reluctance which irked me, all that lioness pride.

I frisked her from chest to toe and she quivered in rancor. This one didn't like to be touched, I could tell. Couldn't blame her.

"You're wasting your time," she rasped. "When the crawlers get wind of this little ship, there'll be nothing left of it."

The old man clicked his tongue. "Nasty bit of luck, landing here on this planet."

"Shut up." I ducked into the hatch, entered the key code that shut Molly's remorseless voice off and whirled on the skinhead lady who seemed ready to make a move. "Who are these crazy boys you're talking about?"

She snorted. "You'll find out soon enough." I didn't like the sound of that or the lazy smirk curling across those lush lips, pretty ones in a former life.

"What's that supposed to mean?"

She licked her lips with a smirk. "Just wait, fly boy."

I gave her the once over. She gave me a once over, appraised my gleaming sinew and my doubtful looks.

Not that I was prejudiced or anything. Not my type. Too tomboyish—and dirty. The challenging stare, the tough girl stance, the stiff thrust of hip. A slight swagger that didn't quite fit her, and that mannish little brush cut—ouch, butch written all over. I wondered what this planet had done to her.

"My suggestion is, lose the butch raven cut," I grunted.

"What do you know?" she snarled, ducking in a crouch to grab for another weapon I'd missed strapped at her ankle under the dust-grimed black leather.

"Unh uh," I warned, motioning her up with my weapon, and she rose in slow motion from her cat-like crouch. I confiscated the weapon.

"Well, looks as if we got ourselves a regular standoff here," said the old man wistfully.

"The hell we do." I shook my head, flakes of soot dropping, leftovers from the explosion at Baer's crib. "From my position, you're looking down the end of a loaded barrel."

"Maybe," croaked the man, "but if you want to save your ship, you'll let Billy and me get it moving to safer ground." I saw his white mustache bristle and tassel of gray rooster hair twitch. A keen intelligence lurked behind those bushy brows. The boy had a mousy face and busy fingers, and looked as if he had as much brains as two hammers left out in the rain.

I jeered. "What you going to do, get on your hands and knees and carry it to safety?"

"Billy can run back and get a couple of anti gravs, can't you, Billy? The AGs'll lift it and we can propel it along with jet thrusters."

Snot-nose Billy gave an eager nod.

I blinked in new amazement. "Some joke, old man? Last I heard anti-gravs were quite large."

"Not mine," he called.

"How far away are these AGs?"

"About half mile back, though I think if you're thinking of following Billy, it's a bad idea."

"Why would I think of that?"

"Just thinking. Billy's a fast runner."

I exhaled a long breath, wiping the river of sweat from my forehead.

The woman grunted out a sardonic breezy sound that in no way improved my mood. "Well, now that we've got that all sorted, how be we set us up a table and napkins and have some tea and cookies before the mad boy's join us?"

"Thought they were the 'crazy boys'—suddenly now they're the 'mad boys'?"

"Happy to meet you too, space man. Name's Wren." She thrust out a hand.

"Mine's TK." The old man stepped forward.

I stared at the two of them—as if I were on a planet of crazies. The heat, the injuries were getting to me. "Rusco," I snapped with reluctance.

"Well, that's dandy," said Wren, rubbing her wrists and clapping her hands. The woman was all smiles and chuckles now.

The old man whispered some energetic words in the kid's ear who then beetled off down the sand path and disappeared around a curve in the nearest mound and was gone.

"Billy's a good boy. A little slow on the mark, but dependable."

"What's to stop your munchkin from bringing a posse down on me or some other unpleasant surprise?"

"Nothing. What other options you have? Not to worry, Billy doesn't do stuff like that anyway. Found him hiding under a mound. Burrowed himself deep like a cricket hunting for food. Shivering. His parents had been taken by the mad boys. He had the sense to hide under the refuse and I've taken him under my wing ever since."

"Very touching," I grunted.

My leg had started to quiver. The older man's eyes glowed with a trace of curiosity at my discomfort. I hunkered down to massage my burning knee. The blazing heat was making me sweat something awful, as if I had a bad fever. I must have sweat a cup of liquid in the last fifteen minutes. Tongue swelling up in my mouth, I rolled it over my parched lips.

Wren grinned. "What's the matter, space boy? Rat nip you in the knee?"

"Shut up, for crap sakes!" I lurched to my feet, rounded on her. I glared at the old man. "What if you get the ship skyworthy? I doubt if you're going to do any favors as a good samaritan?"

He lifted his chin and scratched his neck. "About time I got off this planet. How about transpo to Aldebaran?"

I shrugged. "We'll see."

"While you're at it," called Skinhead. "I could use a lift to the nearest transhub."

"Like I owe you something?" I turned and glowered at her.

The sun seemed to inch its way across the yellow sky like a big bad ball of fire kindling my insides. Sweat did wonders to help combat the pain. I pulled at my vest, snapping open the buttons, exposing my chest.

The day was long on this forgotten world—double the daylight I was used to.

My leg amped up again and throbbed. I crouched and sprawled in what was a patch of shade. Maybe I drowsed for a second then. My head lolled and I caught the woman creeping up on me with a fist clenched. "Back!" I grunted, motioning my weapon at her. Her slinking frame came to a standstill, and she gave me a forced, sullen grin.

All the time I expected monsters to come jumping out of the garbage and kill us all, like those mad boys they kept yapping about. I picked up on the woman's apprehension; even the old man was edgy, making me nervous with his shifty feet and eyes darting to the surrounding dungheap. No matter, we'd all just sit tight until somebody showed.

At last, Billy came skipping out of the shimmering heat waves, eyes all a-glimmer, sporting a toothy grin like a cat that's caught a fat mouse. Three rectangular-shaped objects he clutched in his tanned-brown hands.

"That was quick, Billy," congratulated the old man. "Let me see them."

The boy returned some words I couldn't understand. Mumbles, child-like baby sounds. Was he a mute?

TK took the square blocks out of his hands, dug a small hole and fixed them up under the fuselage, one at the front, two at the back. He fired up the power on one and while I hobbled over in curiosity, he rubbed his gnarled hands. "The grav-push is heli-powered, courtesy of good old Silirus."

He went around and pressed a button on each unit and they folded in a curious way as pressure rotors kicked in and the bottom gripped the sand and the top extended and clamped to the hull. It pushed up on it, like some kind of hydraulic arm. I gaped and stood in awe as the ship levitated two feet off the ground with a blue glow shining off the flattened sand and a similar glow off the underside of the AGs. Some gravo-thrust kept the tons of metal aloft. At least some advanced technology was still alive in these days of collapse. He activated some other gizmo on the side and used the remote control he'd snatched from Billy. It spurted jets of white steam from the AG's lower flanks and pushed the Starrunner down the sandy ravine like a magno train. Wren and I loped after the old man and his prize.

"Well, I'll be a son of a bitch—"

Sand dunes curled up to the edges of the mounds on either side.

"About that ride out of here...," persisted Wren. "Shit! Incoming."

We'd barely gone fifty feet when the woman dove into the sand drift. The whine of engines roared overhead.

I swore and scrambled for the nearest mini dung pile as a flash bomb flared, nearly singeing my hide and knocking me and snot-nose and the old man off our feet. Luckily the shell had missed Starrunner by a sliver and her reinforced battle plates took the shrapnel.

Two ships came angling out of the sky: lean, grey with cannons locked. I opened my mouth in a startled cry but Wren was already moving. She was skipping under my line of fire before I could do anything and jumping into the hatch. The first ship dropped down in the space between us and the mountain of crud.

I fucking knew it. Baer!

I got to my feet, dazed from the blast. I gimped along, somehow twisting my already savaged leg in the fall. My eyes stung, blinded by the bomb's flare. The second ship waited in the sky, weapons trained.

"For fuck's sake!" I was shaking my head, aiming too late before a blaster beam clipped the barrel, and I dropped it as it became sizzling hot.

The man, Baer's man, wearing helmet and blue body armor, jumped out of the hatch, pointing his blaster at me. "Easy, chief. No stupid moves. Drop the other weapon. Edge back away from the ship."

"Relax, no need to get excited." I let the mini-glock that I'd tried to snatch from my belt fall at my toes.

"Move away," he snarled. Two more emerged from the hatch to

stand at either side.

While TK and Billy scuttled sideways like crabs, my mind worked to come up with a plan.

I caught a movement out of the corner of my eye—some slinking, mummy-wrapped shape. "Dung mite!" I cried, motioning to the pile to the man's left.

He whirled and with a snarl, shot the head off some grotesque figure dressed in rags in a spray of blood and brains.

I licked my lips. "Good play, chief. Aim for the head, always the best percentage shot. Good thing I'm watching your back."

"Cut the cute talk, smart man."

"Let's cut a deal here," I wheedled. "You can see I've nothing. If I did, think I'd be hanging around with these grubbers?" I made a sweep of hand toward TK and the boy huddled in the refuse. "You go your way, I go mine. Maybe we can come to a solution."

"You're a dead man, Rusco. Baer wants you dead, and I do too for wasting Kriegs, plus a cut of the reward money on your head. Rub is, we have to bring you in alive."

"Isn't that interesting? I'm suddenly a celebrity. Worth more than Marvin K. Dicks."

"Shut up. You're a dead mother fuck—" The right front cannon of Starrunner lifted and a hell of a blast came spitting out from her barrel to fry the man on the spot.

Hot damn, that crafty skinhead knew how to shoot! I rolled as blaster fire came a hair's breadth from my throat. The two other thugs crouching by the ship, rained fire at anything that moved. Hunched like a beetle, I ran up to the pile, grabbed my weapon, emptied it on the closest merc. He crumpled with a shot-out leg just as the damned mummy people, who I guessed might be the mad boys, crawled over them like ants and the downed ship. Must have poured out from some lizard hole behind the ship. There were thuds of metal on metal, broken glass and screams as mummy flesh met thug flesh. Then followed only the harsh breathing and hillbilly grunts like some redneck rape scene out of a bad horror movie.

Misshapen men, women, or neither, it was hard to tell, came streaming from out of the garbage pits and stinking heaps from all directions, clutching black batons like truncheons, hunks of metal, any weapon they could forage out of those refuse piles. All wrapped in rags, bandaged like lepers, only their fingertips showed, clawed nails glinting through the dirty brown wraps of cloth. Snorkel masks frogged their mouths, black-rimmed goggles on the eyes. Metal caps on the skulls.

The mummy people were coming for us next, but the second ship banked in and sprayed pulse beams at them. They took care not to wipe our ship out. Red fire exploded into the mass of moving figures. Limbs and heads separated from bodies. Starrunner's rear cannon swiveled, aimed and shot the ship out of the sky.

"Yeehow!" I yelled at TK to get Starrunner moving. I could detect faint motion, for activity still stirred amongst that rubble. The sad, stark reality was if they got the ship, we were sunk.

The old man came huffing and puffing around the side of the smoking metal, hauling Billy by the arm. "Get a move on! More ships can drop on us any second."

Wren jumped out of the hatch, a fresh AK in her hand, breathless, flushed at her kills. I was warming to this lady.

"Let them come. We'll let them blow the crap out of these dunghill rats." She kicked at one of the mummy-wrapped things lying in a smouldering heap after I'd blasted it, their albino heads gleaming ghoulishly in the sun.

I winced.

"The sun eated them up," crooned the kid, all smiles, the only thing he'd said so far.

"That's right, Billy. You know it, don't you?" TK said with a sad laugh.

The mad boys seemed occupied with their spoils, rustling like rats. Two smoking ships and a trio or more of fresh corpses. Needless to say, I kept an eye out for more unexpected crazies as we jogged along Starrunner's moving flank, putting the hustle on to get the ship away from here.

We left the smoking rubble and the dead vestiges of humanity behind. Despite my gratitude for the quick bloodshed, I almost wished Wren hadn't blasted both Baer's ships out of commission. At least then there'd have been an alternative means of escape off this planet, if the old man couldn't get Starrunner operational.

Rounding a bend out of sight down another sandy corridor, TK aimed the AG jet spurts to guide us between great mounds of crud and garbage.

"How long before they catch up with us?" I asked.

"Half hour, maybe less."

I pawed at my grimy grimace.

"Don't worry, I have protection," TK said.

"It better be good."

I looked at the old man's billyclub, the firepipe he clutched in his hand that he'd pulled out from his desert cloak. "That's all you got? You're going to get killed with primitive junk like that. Stop the rig."

He did. I jumped into the hatch, motioning him to stay put. "There're weapons in the hall aft. Wait here."

A few limping strides and I was rummaging around through the spare armory rack. Old man didn't listen and came stumbling down the main aisle with wide eyes, blinking in the semi-dark of emergency light. "Wow, this ship's something else."

"I told you to stay out," I rasped, pushing him back down the hall, leveling my weapon at him.

"Sorry." He gaped. "Been a long time since I've seen an Alpha Explorer, anything remotely like the interior of a working ship."

Something about the comment made me feel compassion for the man and his plight, marooned here on this trash planet.

"She's a vintage model," I said grudgingly. "Couple of gangsters heisted it. They're no longer with us, so I took the liberty of being its ward. Renamed it Starrunner."

"A fine name."

"I thought so." I tossed him an R3A, a short-range blaster that would kill anything within a twenty yard range.

The kid came in, pointing and gibbering. I backed the two out into the hall by the hatch and gave Wren a helping hand up into the ship. I urged TK and his boy with strong words to get Starrunner moving along with full speed. I didn't need to repeat myself. This way there'd be no tracks. As long as we gave the mummy boys the slip, the scavengers couldn't follow us.

Chapter 7

We wound through sandy paths with TK and Billy guiding Starrunner. TK sat legs dangling out the hatch, looking up along the line of the hull. Wren crouched, flashing me weird, curious looks, until the mounds to either side became less massive and we arched up over a wide, well-trodden path along a ridge. The distant teeth of broken buildings spread below us down a long valley, the settlers' city: toppled towers, blasted squares, a sight all too familiar for me— some war-torn urban wasteland abandoned for generations.

We came abreast a large mound and TK halted the convoy. We climbed out while the ship hovered two feet above the baking sand. A ruined building hulked to the side, only the corner posts and a few girders showing like the ribs of a desiccated whale.

"Why're we stopping?" I asked as TK flicked off the jets, leaving a heavy silence over the desert.

"You want to circumambulate the entire planet?"

"Why here? Where's this safety you promised?"

"You're looking at it."

"This broken pile of cement blocks and pillars?" I reached for my gun, temper short, guessing that the old man was pulling a fast one on me. Wren was looking straight at me with her raven-pearl eyes glinting with something of mirth, watching what I'd do next.

"Relax." TK held up his hand. He herded me over to the ruin and got me to take a closer look at the pit yawning below. The floor had collapsed long ago, but I saw in the depression below a basement or somesuch, a section of one side which had crumbled. I stared at it for a while. What my eyes didn't first register was that it had been tarped up with clever handiwork to blend into the sand and conceal a large space behind.

I looked up at the four stone pillars and a spider-web roof framework. This place could have been a cathedral as easily as a warehouse, or some eccentric's mansion.

Scratching my head, I watched as TK worked the remote control with a wink at Billy. The propellant steamed and the antigravs guided Starrunner down into the pit.

TK clambered down a steep, crumbling staircase and I followed, gripping my gun with a ready hand. He moved over to the tarp, cranked the handle of a hidden wheel cached in the earth and up ratcheted the tarp. A huge work area burrowed within that far side of the pit.

I gave a low whistle. "Well, I'll be a damned monkey."

TK did a little bow. "You can congratulate me later, Rusco. Here, Billy, help me guide this thing in."

I stepped inside the darkened quarters, suppressing a grunt. The place projected deeply into the back of the pit. Old engines, machine parts and housing lay strewn on the sand, rotors and gears and panels, whatnots, some on workbenches and tables. The old man lit a pair of battery-powered lights near the door while Billy guided my ship over the sprawl of engine parts then let her rest by the wall. Wren scooted in before TK closed the flap. "Never can be too careful," he said with a worried grin.

I could see the desert man had built something of a garage for himself. Tables with hammers, drills, electrical gauges, hoses, cables, all salvaged from the rubbish heaps outside. Old vehicle batteries were linked together to give him the power to do his tinkering. "I charge them from solar panels rigged out back where no one can see them. From time to time I need to change them."

He motioned to a series of jigsaw cutters, pry bars and twisted pieces of metal. "I salvage whatever's useful from the dump, always more to find even as the years roll on."

"So I see. Very clever."

"Never gave up trying to get off this heap," he said wistfully.

"Some grand little shop you have here, old man."

He nodded, beaming with pride. "Never had enough of a working engine to get off this rock though. Believe me, friend, I tried." He picked up a mini pneumatic drill and smacked it on the table. "Been scavenging parts from these dumps since as long as I can remember. Still haven't given up on the mother lode. You can appreciate my excitement when I saw your Alpha coming down out of the sky."

"I bet."

He laughed at the memory. "I once got an old Rixen Eagle space probe up a hundred yards into the air before she crashed past the washboard wastes other side of these mounds. She still sits there collecting dust. Nearly killed me and Billy."

"How long to fix this thing?"

"Depends on what's broke."

"Well, I can tell you the mobilitors are in bad shape, probably dead. Less than 60% before she went down." I eyed him, checking to see if the term meant anything to him.

"Mobilitors, eh? They can be tricky."

"What isn't?"

"Let's have a look-see then." He crouched beneath the underpanel while the AGs kept Starrunner aloft. He unscrewed a panel, crawled up the conduit a ways, gave it a shifty glance. "What have we here?"

He knuckled a fist at the twin Barenium cylinders. I poked my head in and blinked. Barenium cylinders...That much I knew. About waist high. Green in a liquid medium, with a golden glow around the edges. Some unstable isotope discovered way back, the liquid masking the radiation somehow, from what I gathered.

"All gunkum to me," growled Wren, crowding over my shoulder.

"That green liquid there," he said. "Think of it as a compact potent pressure pump. When excited with photons from that light gun at the end, you've got yourself warp power to go." He waved a casual hand like a professor explaining something to a young child.

"Left one's shot. Explains why you were down to 60% integrity."

I sighed. "So, what's the damage?"

"Won't know until I look inside."

"Okay. Let's check it out."

While Wren poked around the cowling, I watched over the man's shoulder like a hawk as he hiked her up higher on the AGs and got Billy to monitor the power.

He stood back, poking an elbow in my ribs. "Oi!" give me some breathing space, will you?" I stepped back with a reluctant grunt. I didn't like anybody prodding around my ship. Especially the engines. Not to mention, I wanted to learn something in case I needed to tinker with Starrunner myself some day.

"What gets me is we're light years from Brisis. How the hell they tracked me so quickly—"

"No mystery there," interrupted TK. "Your enemies traced the residual Barenium from those leaky seals—Couldn't have had a clearer signal, active dust on the outer cowling from the burn warp, a clear heat signature. The failed mobilitors would have made even more of a dust trail. You're lucky to have gone any distance at all."

I gave my head a sober shake. "Just my luck."

"In my opinion, Rusco, you've had plenty of luck. Nine lives of it." He squinted hard at the canisters. "I can fix it at 50%. Enough to get you to a proper station."

"Better than sitting around here waiting for Baer and his bounty hunters to nab us."

TK grunted. "Let's get to it then. Show me to the bridge. I'll check the warp engine controls."

We went on board, down the main service hall lit in dim crimson by the emergency lights, past the cabins and the head into the bridge, with Billy and Wren trailing like kites in the wind.

I shuttled TK over to the pilot's chair where the console still blinked and lay bathed in the eerie glow of the emergency lights.

TK sighed. "Bring up the warp panel. These modern interfaces are a little more new-fangled than I care for."

"As you like." I hit some side bars on the keypad, showed him the utility menus and he played long fingers along the touchscreen, bringing up a menu. "*Varwol 6.0. Mezanine 3.4 kbs. Waxrin thrust gain, nominal.* There, Barenium seal. See, you're too low."

He played with the sensors and he couldn't help but notice the iridescent disc that lay three feet away below the auxiliary console. It must have flown free from the strongbox during impact. Could have been it or the box itself that hit me on the head. "What's this shimmering disc you have here on the floor?" He reached for it.

I snatched it out of the old man's hand before I remembered how dangerous the thing was, and dropped it like a red hot coal. "Nothing. Just some artifact." I lanced the old man a wary look.

He did a double take and jerked back his head. "Artifact, my eye." His eyes narrowed. "That's why those men were chasing you, right?"

"Forgot to tuck it away in the back. Kinda hard when you're crashlanding in a garbage pit." I grabbed it up with my sleeve, laid it out on the control board with care. Something told me to trust the old man, as he'd figured most of it out anyway.

"It's a small version of something else I saw back on Brisis. Some sort of weapon, I figure. Careful, it's dangerous."

He flipped it over in his gloved hands, while Wren came to stare over his shoulder, peering at it with doubt.

"Any more of these things?" he asked.

"None aboard. A larger version of something that looks quite different is locked in a safe place," I said cryptically.

"What you've got here is a phase shifter. Moves atoms around from one time or place to another. How it does it, the physics is beyond me, but I've read about them."

"Even you?" I guffawed. "Thought you were Mr. Fix-it-up and

Encyclopedia man."

"Not me," he barked, "still a long ways to go. This here's a remnant of another newfangled tech before the galaxy went to shit."

I grunted, a thoughtful murmur on my tongue. "Explains how one yobo dematerialized to nowhere-land in front of my eyes." I wondered how Baer and his idiot hirelings got it. They must have stumbled on it somewhere digging through the many crates of contraband going through their warehouse. Holding out for the highest bidder, like the vultures they were.

TK mused, "In the hands of ruthless people, this device could mean trouble."

Wren blew air out of her nose. "Don't you think we're already on the road to hell, old man? As a species we should have been stamped out long ago."

"No argument there," he laughed.

"I think that sinking ship has already sunk," I said.

"See those key codes or glyphs, bug script?" TK said. "Somehow they set a location. But they're scrambled or encoded in some cryptic language. Nothing like I've ever seen before."

"Bug, what do you mean, bug?" I croaked.

"Mentera tech, lost long ago—an old alien insect race. Rulers of the galaxy. Good luck finding a translator key."

"So it's useless?"

"I wouldn't say that. The technobrains could probably back-engineer it. Someone with the yols and the clout to organize a think tank."

"Hence your friend Baer, trying to fence it to someone," muttered Wren.

Some star lord, if I recall.

"See, I think—" I reached for the thing without thinking, and wished I hadn't, because TK had somehow armed it with his handling. As soon as I made contact—Zap. I came out in some other place, clutching that thing, blinking like an owl.

A sallow dawn greeted me, a snaky loop of smoke misting on the horizon. Cold dry air entered my lungs, very hard to breath. I clutched at my throat, gasping. Aphid-like shapes moved with slow synchrony across a steely grey sky. I saw more there than ever I cared to see in any lifetime.

The eye can only process so many things at once. I dropped to my knees, fiddling with the device, trying to get it to push me back to the world where I had come from. But nothing seemed to work and it just pulsed that eerie, iridescent glow all the stronger, like an evil eye while my lungs croaked for air. Clouds, strange life forms flitted over the horizon. Birds, aliens, far-off alien craft? I didn't know, nor cared to guess. Maybe I was hallucinating. The future, past, present? Could have been all or none. From the corner of my eye, I caught glimpses of desiccated human bodies lying about. Whatever I did next, fiddling with the script, something jarred the thing back to life.

Zap. I was back in Starrunner, peering up at the hazy forms of figures prodding me. "You okay?" Wren snapped. "You just blinked out there for a second."

"Holy crap!" I gasped. I sank lower on my knees, chucking the thing aside, as if it were radioactive. "I was out there—somewhere. Some putrid, rotten world. A ruined city. War was in the air, out there, somewhere in time. Alien wars. Strange things roved on the horizon. Decayed bodies all around, leathery skin and old bones." My voice quavered. "Maybe it was all a dream of the past."

"Easy, Rusco," said TK.

"That's nutso," scoffed Wren, shaking her head. "Either one or all of us is on some kind of drugs."

"No trip," I growled. "It was real, right down to my bursting lungs."

"Your eyes went wide and staring, as if you were a ghost, fading fast. My hand passed right through you," she said.

TK muttered, "Phase shift, to some far world. Could have been any one of the desolate planets out there."

The old man placed a hand on my arm. "Can't let this get into devils' paws like those after you."

"Like who?" sputtered Wren. "Some rich, wicked little buyer trips out to his favorite planetary resort for holidays? I'm shaking in my boots, TK."

"No, you fool! I mean, by installing one of these devices on a drone or a mechnobot, they can blast any city or space station to smithereens and come back out of it without a scratch. An army of these could—well, make ruin of what's left of the populated worlds."

Wren scoffed. "Yeah, just like these bug-like things you talk about that are now extinct. Fat lot of good this tech did them in taking over the galaxy."

"The details of the Mentera's demise are lost in time."

My trembling reverie came to an end. "Let's just keep it out of anybody's hands for now." I shuddered to think what a brute like Baer would do with it, or who he might sell it to. He'd talked about some star lord wanting to buy it. It now dawned on me what had happened to Mitch, the guard back there. The phaso seemed to work its mischief when some combination of the alien script and its surface was touched. He'd gone to one of those worlds, but without the device, he couldn't get back. I only managed to get back because I had a firm grip on it. Mitch didn't.

I couldn't help notice the hungry look in TK's eye as he studied the disc, despite his gallant words. I quickly gathered the strongbox up from under the conference table and locked up that evil, little treasure. I kept it clasped in my arms, thinking to hide it away somewhere on the ship.

Mumbling, rubbing hand on chin, I stepped back a few paces, while he rubbed his brow with a dirty cloth. "I'd better start fixing that drive. All of you, leave me alone. Sit on your thumbs, swap tales, play tiddlywinks, I don't care, just don't distract me. I need space and quiet to concentrate."

"Sure thing, pops," I said.

"Billy! Change up the batteries. Load the spares that I charged yesterday. We're going to need more juice to incite the Barenium."

I granted the old man his space. Leaving him to his tasks, I wandered through his workshop, staring in a daze at the maze of machinery. Wren was at my heels.

"So what's it like out there?" she asked. "Always dreamed about going to the planets."

"Lot of poverty and corruption. Believe me, you haven't missed much." She was all for asking a bunch of questions, but I waved her off. My mind was preoccupied with Baer's bounty hunters and if more would be on their way.

Some time later TK came to us, rubbing his oily hands with a soiled rag.

"So, I did a full scan and mustered what I could. The Barenium'll take time to settle in those canisters. I'm guessing about eight hours. We give it a try after. If it starts up first shot, we're lucky, if not, we've got ourselves a problem."

"Let's hope it starts up then." I wished it was sooner, but realized the settling was out of my hands.

We edged back out of the workshop, the bright light stinging our eyes. "So what now, professor?" I asked him, squinting under the glare. The sun looked as if it had not dipped a degree in the sky.

"Time to eat," he said. He and Billy ratcheted up the tarp. "This way." He pointed a forked hand to another place, far away from the workshop. "It's a forty hour day on this world, so it's easy to get hungry."

I could see the method in TK's madness, keeping his residence far from work, in case one of the 'mad boys' happened to stumble on his crib. He'd have a temporary place to lie low in, if that wasn't compromised too.

Chapter 8

TK had made his residence in the side of one of the dung piles, like an igloo of crud, indistinguishable from the rest of the other compost.

I stepped closer to the fifty-foot-high gummed mass, recoiling at the sudden cloying stench that hit me, but a skittering sound had me turning around wild-eyed. Aiming my blaster at two mean-looking scorpion-like knee-high crab things scuttling across the sand straight at us.

"Fuck! What are these things?" I got off a shot, but didn't do any significant damage.

TK let out a shrill whistle, his finger to lips. He slapped down my weapon before I could get the next shot off and waste it too. The creatures bobbed back, springing on their spindly, segmented legs a foot away. They hissed and clicked, barbed stingers coiling over their scaled backs. The pincers out in front looked like capable clipping machines.

"Protection," TK explained. "Come on, inside."

I realized the scorpion dung at the side of the mound was the source of the smell. Gingerly I stepped around it, eyeing the six-legged crustaceans with a wary eye. Clear translucent exoskeleton, eyes perched on stalks, armored carapace, one could see right through to the lungs pumping, heart beating, and some black red, kidney-shaped organs.

I shivered and Wren ducked in a defensive crouch, muttering some foul words under her breath.

I whirled to another sound, my blaster lifting. A mummy-like shape hobbled out of the shimmering heat waves, a walking stick in hand. Brown-wrapped rags hugged the sleek body, up to the high hood; white albino eyes shone through the black oval of a cowled face. The scorpions didn't budge.

"Relax." TK pulled down my weapon. "I know him." He lifted a hand in greeting. "Oi, Toog. Some new friends I'd like you to meet."

He introduced the wary figure to us. The newcomer was about five seven, thin, wiry like others of his kind. Only his eyes showed, white pools into nowhere. Even his hands were mitted as if he had scabies. Those eyes, as white as an egg, mesmerized me.

"Toog's been a friend for a long time. Ever since Billy caught desert fever and almost died two seasons back." My foggy, tired brain pondered on how long a Talyon year was.

"You're welcome to join us, Toog," he said. "We're just sitting down to a meal. This here's Wren and that there's Rusco."

Toog dipped his head in thanks, accepted Wren and I as equals, seeing as we were friends of TK's.

A trap door led inside the igloo of sanctuary, camouflaged to look like the other junk metal and plastics in the pile. Inside it was dark and surprisingly cool, protection at least from the mad boys.

"Toog's one of the few who fled from the crawlers, searching other ways. He's one of the good ones, Rusco. You've nothing to fear." He glanced at my clenched fists on my assault rifle.

To my relief the house pets stayed outside.

"Raised those dervishes from babies. I fed them, tamed them and watered their backs. Now they're loyal to me, as long as I keep feeding them."

"What do you feed them?" asked Wren.

"Dead meat. Anything I can catch. I look for the condors or buzzards circling overhead. Anywhere they're circling means fresh meat is about. Sometimes they sight a sick crawler wandered off to die or some fresh carrion. Rest of the time I hunt whatever I can for food with my bow."

I nodded as if nothing could be more natural.

The floor was fine white sand, the ceiling beamed with girders; the walls, dried mud, making it cool and dry inside, and a relief to my pounding head. Billy went running over to a shelf of pots to gulp water from a beat-up bucket. I saw the old man kept a crude, fire-stoked stove complete with chimney. Buckets of water ranged around, dozens of them; a chest of junk for fuel, elsewhere a few potted cacti, some low cots. Spartan but serviceable. A mystery where TK got water.

He motioned us to a low steel table with woven place mats in the middle of the room. While we sat around it, the old man fired up the pot-iron stove, rustled up some food, banging various pots and before long he served us a piping-hot soup of green vegetables and some crunchy brown sticks.

I dove in, famished. Munching away, I lifted my spoon to him. "This is not half bad, TK. What is it?"

"The green stuff's cactus, high in trace minerals and nutrients. The desert insects, those brown sticks you're shoveling in by the forkful, are common to this region, easy to catch and super high in protein."

I dropped my utensil on the plate, coughed, and my mouth hung open.

Wren smirked. "What's the matter, Rusco? There're more in the pot where that came from. Grasshopper is a novelty on Talyon."

Loosing a sigh, I studied my company. Toog with his quiet, diminutive movements, never taking a mouthful too swiftly, Wren, her challenging stare, as if everything was wrong in the world, and TK, a glint of amusement in his gray eyes, watching us as if we were all a study in social experiment.

TK read my mind about the next question about the water. "Don't worry. I have to manufacture my own liquids. I have a rig further down. I call it the hydrophon." He grinned. "My back's not what it used to be in the old days so I rig up the AGs and get Billy to help me haul a barrow of filled buckets to this place."

I nodded. "Seems as if you have everything worked out. Except maybe the bloodthirsty scorps and the zombie mummies lurking about your doorstep."

"Them…well, I have my ways of keeping them at bay. Xig and Xag, those two brutes outside, help me with that. They've killed many wandering crawly boys who've come nosing around. If word got out me and Billy were holed up here…" He let the idea hang in dead air.

"So you've survived," I said. "I'd count that as impressive. Was there ever a better yesterday?"

"Dezran City used to be a self-supporting community. A bunch of us used to live in scattered settlements. Along the foot of the desert ridge, not like the big metropolises you see on the settled planets. Talyon was different, had a fresh start, even though it served as the recycling center of the solar system. Then they came and burned up the town."

"Who's 'they'?"

"Some glory-seeking warlords out to make a name for themselves. Heard this place was fair game, rich in mining, beryllium and other elements, and laid waste to the city."

"Sounds like any of a dozen lowlifes I know."

TK shrugged. "The strongest of us banded together and we became fighters. In the end, ultimately refugees, living hand to mouth. Many of us drank poison water, I don't know what else: some became the mutants you saw out there. Messed up their heads, burned their skin, deformed their bodies. That's why they're all wrapped up in rags. Used to be human, but they went—feral, let's say. If you saw them—" he shuddered and cast a sharp look at Toog.

Toog stirred and spoke in a lisp. I caught a flash of harelip beneath the cowl as if his teeth were set the wrong way. "Some genetics company had been brewing toxic bio-mixtures. They got mixed up in the water supply when the outlaws were blasting the place all up."

TK loosed a choked growl. "That and the toxic waste dump burning and smoldering and seeping scum into the water table. Don't forget that, Toog. A toxic jury-rigged slurry, a disaster waiting to happen, courtesy of the growing recycle piles!"

"Where did all this junk come from?" I asked.

"Shipped in from innumerable planets. All the worlds far and near used Talyon as their dumping grounds. For generations and generations. That all ended when the wars started."

I drummed my knuckles on the table. "So how come you guys aren't all twisted up like our mummy friends out there—no offense to our friend Toog here?"

TK held up a glass bottle of pills, liquid capsules on the table. "Quizanine. Methyl basene—plus a smidge of isopropyl alcohol."

"Well, aren't you the clever one," I marveled.

"I pride myself in knowing things."

"I can see that." I frowned and turned to Wren. "What about you?"

"What would you like to know?"

"Why didn't you turn into one of our mummy friends?"

"Lucky, I guess. Always added a bit of vinegar from fermented cactus to my water."

TK laughed at the notion. "Some of us are just resistant to the effects."

Wren shrugged, apparently not in the mood for arguing with the old man.

"Family?" I turned to her. "How have you been surviving?"

"Dodge and blast, nothing else. My crib's hidden far away. On the other side of the pits. I saw your ship come down. Then I came to look. My rod's been keeping me alive, no thanks to you, losing it out there somewhere in the sand. Built it myself."

"Treat that new piece at your waist as your new improved 'rod'. You still haven't explained how—"

"Nothing much different from TK's story," she said in a harsh voice. "My family was killed, my daughter too."

"Sorry to hear that."

"Don't be. You didn't know her from Eve. Bad shit happens to good people. Happens all the time. I got over it."

I could see that Wren hadn't and probably never would. But I was no grief therapist and so I moved on. "If we get my ship running again, I'm inviting you all out for a ride—you too, skinhead." I shadow-boxed her playfully on the shoulder. Her body remained rigid. My sudden act of charity was not just in good nature. A little bit of self-preservation was mixed in with a whole lot of scheming. "I could use a resourceful bunch of entrepreneurs like you."

TK swigged down a gulp of water.

"So, you've never made it off this rock?"

"Nope." He shrugged. "I've been off and traveled at lot in my younger days before the space docks and starships were wiped out and communication towers destroyed. A few rogue ships have dropped out of the sky over the years, but on seeing nothing here but desert ruin and mummy freaks they speed off in a hell of a hurry."

"Nobody's come to this planet since I've been a girl," croaked Wren in a faraway voice. "Even then the memory is dim. I remember a silver, cigar-shaped craft angling down in the plain once, before it became another toxic waste dump. I watched from one of the recycle hills." Her eyes clouded over. "They landed, let out a bunch of people—prisoners, I reckoned, with their arms bound behind their backs. Three tried to make a run for it, and the captors blasted them in cold blood." She shivered. "The rest they let live. Then they flew off."

"What happened to the survivors?" I asked.

"Dunno, I scrambled away, fast as I could, being just a little kid. When I came back, they were gone. Sand dervishes must have got them."

I stared in grim silence. "And you, Toog?"

"I kill mad boys as easily as TK here. Sometimes they hunt me, but I lure them to my special place—where an army of dervishes nest. They feed nicely that day." He gave a snorting exclamation. "Was just checking on TK here, seeing that he's feeding his pets properly."

"And was I?" TK asked with a crooked grin.

"Seemed so."

"A good trick," I said. "Letting the dervishes control your mad boys. Surprises me you'd kill your own kind though."

Toog grunted, the first real emotion I'd heard from him. "I owe them nothing. They killed my family, ground them up, ate them for stew. Made me one of them. But I escaped. Now I kill them on sight."

"You're one against an army," I pointed out.

"Doesn't matter."

"I admire your spirit, Toog. All of you. Just think you're on the wrong world."

"What world isn't 'wrong'?" grunted TK.

"I invite you to come with us, Toog."

He stared at me a long time. "No, this is the only home I've known. Call it sentimental, but I've a kinship here. There are others like me, like TK and Billy."

"Knock yourself out." I shrugged. But in those eyes I saw the sadness of generations, as I had seen so many times on many worlds. Worlds ripped apart by senseless violence, and privation, sunk in the deepest mire of decadence.

While TK and Wren went off with Billy and Toog to fetch water and look out for more mad boys crawling about, I drifted off in the opposite direction to the repair shop, my Uzi slung over a shoulder, thinking it better to be closer to my ship. I followed what I remembered of the route we took, wiping my brow in the baking sun. No number of nervous glances over my shoulder allayed my suspicion that those damn sand crabs weren't following me.

The ruins came in sight and I heaved myself down on a sand drift at the edge of the pit. The merciless sun beat down on my head and my mind wandered on how I'd always wanted a tan.

I lay the Uzi on my lap in case a mad boy decided to make a move. It was a good compact submachine gun, modified to fire a heat-swath plus bullets, frying anything within a twenty yard range. Lumo, infrared scope for night fight and laser lock, cool smooth barrel, compact hand stock—I liked the lighter feel, its quickness to slide off the shoulder and into the hands.

The throb in my knee had receded to a dull ache, that or I'd gotten used to it. Nevertheless, I up-ended the last of the pain pill-bottle I'd pulled from Starrunner into my gullet. Seemed I was about due for another dose. I glanced down at the pit: a stark, baking hole with crumbling earth on all sides. No soul would ever guess a hidden workshop lurked down in that abyss holding a Class A starship and stocked with tools.

I shook my head with an amazed grin, hardly aware that I was starting to doze off.

I awoke to the drop of something in my lap, a black-leathered figure crouching before me with a wry smile.

"Must have drifted off."

"Dangerous place to do that," Wren admonished, dropping the handful of pebbles she'd been tossing.

I gave a careless grunt, rose to my undignified half crouch, squinting in the obnoxious glare.

"Boring over there hauling water," she bantered. "Thought I'd bug you instead." She squinted down at me. "You serious about taking me with you, if the old man fixes the ship?"

"Why not? I'm generally not a liar. There're things to discuss first. Like business. Not just a free ride here; work to be done."

"Like what?"

"Let's cross that bridge when the time comes."

A stiff silence came over us and I could see her pouty frown moving across her fine lips, so it prompted me to mellow somewhat.

"Listen, I'm sorry for what I said back there."

"About what?"

"About saying you had a butch cut."

She laughed. "Well, it's kinda true, isn't it? Though I'm no butch."

"Think you'd look a lot prettier with a whole head of hair though, instead of a few bristles like a porcupine. Not that you aren't pretty. Just saying."

"Opinion noted," she said dryly. "This brush cut is more for practical reasons than anything. It's cooler on the skull."

"Those leathers sure aren't."

"They're for protection, Rusco. In case I run into some dervishes. Their pincers are deadly."

Voices drifted from down the path and a scuffling of moving figures.

TK, Billy, and the mummy-ish Toog came trundling up the hot sand, with the old man wearing a worried frown. His two scorpion friends scuttled at his heels.

"Bad news," he said. "Mad boys are on the prowl. Saw 'em skulking up the ridge farther on. This is the closest they've come to this area." He gave a brusque flourish. "Let's get into the workshop."

"Don't need to convince me."

We were hardly down the crude stair and moving across the pit when a ghost of motion caught my eye.

I gave a choked cry, shielded my eyes from the sun's glare up top the pit.

TK lifted his head, swearing a wicked curse. "Into the workshop!"

Shapes came prowling around the edge and began to drop at our feet. Crapola! Our tracks must have led them right here.

"Get down!" I hissed.

Too late. I blasted one as they threw metal spikes at us and I lunged in the same motion. Another tried to gut stab me with a chunk of metal. I whirled, grabbed my knife from my belt, and slashed it soundly across the chest. Steel ripped up to its chin.

Dark blood sprayed over my open shirt and a white pulpy face fell flat at my feet. I kicked away the grotesque corpse.

More malformed shapes gathered in numbers. Wren crouched in attack, fired a spray of bullets into the faces of swaying, reaching mad boys. "Die, you bitches!" she cried. Billy uttered some Neanderthal sound and scrambled back behind the old man.

I tossed Toog the extra weapon in my belt. He opened fire with a bloodthirstiness that seemed uncharacteristic of his mild manner.

Limbs parted and mummy shapes rolled in the sand with mewling sobs. Fresh blood dripped on the sand.

Silence. Heat. The shimmer of an unnatural stillness. The cry of a carrion bird echoed overhead.

Swarms of crazies crawled everywhere, peeking over the rim like feral spectators. I lifted my weapon and opened fire, peppering any I saw. Somehow the presence of Starrunner had lured these ghouls here. And somehow the old man had known they would come.

Hordes of them dropped down on us like monkeys, only the whites of their eyes showing in ghostly, blotched faces partially hidden under brown, cowled hoods.

TK's two sand dervishes scuttled down the path after the cloth-wrapped zombies, their stingers raised. A pincer clipped out to clamp on a brown-garbed leg, then a stinger fell and arched into a rag-garbed neck.

I blasted two between the eyes but a slinking shape crawling at my legs got hold of my weapon and yanked it out of my grasp. "Motherfucker." I pulled my knife out, only to reel as a chunk of pipe came angling for my skull. I dodged back, but the thing ended up thunking on my shoulder. I cried out in pain. Wren was yelling at the top of her lungs. She blasted mummy flesh left, right and center.

Shoots of agony rippled up my arm, but I recovered, grabbed my spare glock, slashed out with its butt end and kicked the gnashing scavenger away in the fleshy part of the gut, before blasting open its skull.

"Get to the ship," I cried.

TK and Billy fought in a wild muddle of bodies. Wise thing that I had given the old man that R3A, else he and his world would have come to an abrupt end.

I slashed a hole in the tarp, pulled aside the burlap and raced through the maze of machine parts with Wren, TK and Billy staggering at my heels.

Toog was too far away. The man was doomed unless he cleared a path. I saw the head of one of the dervishes squashed by a giant rock. Brown shapes pounced on it like bobcats and pulled off its legs and ripped it apart with their bare hands, metal weapons in their clawed fingers. Like the ghouls they were, they stuck the fleshy pieces in burlap sacks and carried them away.

I reached Starrunner and thrust open the port hatch. Pushing Wren through, I yanked TK in last who had shoved Billy in before him and jammed the door shut just as a mass of flesh thudded against the plated metal. One of the scumbitches rolled in with us and Wren stomped its neck and face. I shook the blood out of my hair, scrambled to the bridge. I got the thrusters warmed up, praying to god that those deep space engines would fire—at least, the impulse drive.

Wren raced to the weapons console and aimed the starboard cannon still operating under auxiliary power.

The clunks of weapons into the metal hull and thuds against the port glass caused me to wince.

"Bloody hell! They're going to break the glass!"

I reached for the thruster impulse to give it max juice, but TK reached to pull my hand away. "It's too early to task the ship. The Barenium hasn't settled yet. Sudden acceleration will—"

"Fuck it! We either get out of here, or those mummy fiends of yours bust through the glass and we're dead." I forced the lever up.

Wren cried, "He's right! Hundreds of them out there. They won't stop at a few blaster shots."

Billy stared wild-eyed, holding his head, whimpering like a child. Menacing shapes clustered at the windows.

TK ground his teeth with a fatalistic groan.

I gunned the engines. The impulse drive made an unwholesome

growl, but fired up. Starrunner's curved prow broke through the top of the low ceiling, raining crumbling earth down and scattering tools and benches while hordes of mad boys clung to the fuselage like bloodsuckers.

"Woohee! That's what I want to hear, baby." I cranked the thrusters.

I wasn't worried about finesse now. Those leachy-ghouls wouldn't last long once Starrunner got going. *If she got going.*

I cleared the pit and circled back, watching the crawlers fall to their doom. I reamed a generous spray of pulse blasts on those stinking vermin, grinding my teeth in vindication, hoping to give Toog a fighting chance, if he were still alive. Saw no sign of him. Only those hooded creepos parceling up their own dead for the evening stew. I lifted off into the bright sky, a grumble of exultation in my throat. I was glad to see the end of Talyon…or at least I hoped it was the end.

Chapter 9

The Barenium held. After clearing Talyon's gravity we jumped to warp. The nearest shelter was the outpost at Skeller's Run, a massive space station in the Wizrin sector on the far edge of Orion. Not a first pick for me, the space station, but it would do for now. We needed supplies, particularly water.

TK paced back and forth on the bridge in a huff, face contorted at the risk of the compromised Barenium. "The liquid's not settled. Besides, they're still going to trace you."

"Right. Have to get that fixed."

He shook his head and threw his hands in the air.

"Okay, Beleron then," I said, "but first things first. We make it to the outpost. Go and play cribbage with Billy or something. You're making me nervous with all your pacing. We've got time to burn aboard this ship."

TK didn't budge. Wren occasioned to bump her hip against me as I was swiveling to check the log coordinates on the nav. I turned to cast her an inquiring glance. Her cheeky smile culminated in a lush rise of black brows. It intrigued but also irked me at the same time. I ordered her to scrub down in the shower. On the next stop, our second priority would be to get her some proper clothes. She didn't seem to appreciate the hint, and stormed off.

"Molly, get us info on the next destination."

"Orbital station, class D. Captive of gas giant Orves. Inception 2362. Fueling and supply center for inner, terraformed worlds Megal and Vylnos."

TK's mouth dropped. "Molly?"

"It's as good a name as any," I growled. "My first girl if you want to know. You've got a problem with that?"

"No, but—"

"Good, then check out the landing protocol on the station, if you want to make yourself useful. See who's on duty, what they're looking for, and on guard against. Sometimes these stations can be funny about deep space cruisers coming in out of nowhere, with skeleton crews and ones without papers."

TK grumbled and tapped some holo keys on the data console. It was something Molly could have told me in an instant, but I needed to keep TK busy. At the moment the man was a nuisance. Judging from his hobbies down on his home world, his mind was too fertile to be idle for any length of time.

"A certain Roga Flann is the designated contraband checker," TK muttered.

"And?"

"They seem to be particularly intolerant of bombs and peddlers hassling clientele in transit."

"Good. Keep digging, TK. What's Flann's official's game? Credentials, past history. There's more info lurking about on what they're looking for. Not that we're carrying anything illicit, but sometimes these officials try to pull a scam where they plant stuff on an incoming ship like ours then shake the captain down for yols, a bribe not to report us."

"How's me digging for stuff going to help if—"

"Just do it," I grunted.

He clamped his mouth shut and set to work. Billy was moving at his side like a spider. Damn, that munchkin, shadowing the old man like a leech. The kid couldn't sit still. Another source of frustration for me.

Seemed we'd been flying forever. The Varwol disengaged and the course coordinates finally became a reality. The ship lurched, bucked like a crotchety old mule. The slow corkscrew out of warp had minimal hiccups, I suppose.

In the viewport, the station loomed—a gigantic figure-eight with hundreds of birthing docks, bays and pods, with untold shield meshes, solar panels, tracking stations. My jaw dropped. Hundreds of ships passed in and out of the ring. So many? Another unexpected sight, these masses of ships converging on the space station. "What in—?" I wheezed.

TK grumbled, "Looks like a mass run on the station."

"Something must have gone wrong on one of the nearby worlds. Look at those space junkers and tramp freighters. I sense desperation here. They're ready to fall apart."

"Should we try somewhere else?" Wren asked.

"No, we need supplies. Some news wouldn't hurt at this point."

I eased Starrunner through the bee-like swarm of traffic. We approached the far side of the station. From what I could see it was going to be slim pickings for berthing docks. Lucky to see two free stalls. I made contact with the ground personnel.

An officious voice resonated over the com. "Alpha Explorer XU6, proceed to reserve dock A2. Berthing will be restricted to two hours."

"Two hours?" I croaked. "That's not nearly enough time to either piss or shit—"

"Sir, we do not appreciate vulgarities. The station is under high volume. Do you wish to cancel your reservation?"

"No," I growled. "But—okay, book it." I cut the connection.

"Like a mass exodus," said Wren, her eyes glowing in wonder.

"Never seen so many ships in my life," mused TK.

True, every space vessel in the vicinity seemed to be seeking refuge.

"Seems we picked a bad time to dock. Okay, we'll touch down, get our supplies and move on."

Light seeped through the cracks as the circular gate opened and I docked Starrunner in berth A2-983. A snug fit but workable. Deep in the mooring bay, robot arms secured the prow. The hatch closed behind us and the chamber pressurized. I took my small hand weapon disguised as a small pen, and tossed a like model to Wren.

"Machine guns aren't allowed, for obvious reasons."

We de-boarded and I attached the water cable from the utility wall to Starrunner's underbelly. After I'd inserted ten yols in the dispenser, the green light came on and with a grunt of satisfaction, I could hear water flowing into Starrunner's bare tanks.

"Let's hit the observation decks, since we have such a brief time. The water'll shut off on its own."

TK nodded and herded Billy down the wide hall. Wren looked about with wonder, smelling much better after her shower. Her eyes flashed on the polished chrome railings, imitation marble floors, small potted trees and dust-free cleanliness. "This is a snazzy station." Seemed all these sights were new to her.

"Not really. Skeller Station's been around for centuries. But it's improved over the years. Megal's a rich world; they can afford to pay for some luxury."

"Why so far out from Megal though?" TK asked, as if to no one in particular. His eyes wandered past the glass over Orves, the gas giant, looming below. Our orbit was hundreds of thousands of miles out, yet still the giant planet arched below us like a monstrous white and red banded egg.

I shrugged. "Tradition? Who knows? Probably its ore-rich moons were the first mining interest before the inner planets were settled. I think they were more interested in mining rights than terraforming the inner worlds. Over time the place became a resort stop. You'd have to ask the builders, but they're four hundred years in the grave."

"I'll pass, thanks," said TK.

We passed the first checkpoints, me sliding through with my breezy confidence. *No, sirs, we came directly from Wiesen in Cassiopeia. No sirs, no illicit drugs or firearms. These are a couple of travelers I picked up on the ride roster en route to Alphanor. We're more interested in getting repairs than any layovers. Thank you, sirs.'*

All kinds of outworlders milled about, from those with hair piled up on their heads like donuts, to those in trim, tight space jumpers: pilots, shuttle monkeys, cargo couriers. Some were in worse shape than others. A babel of sound hummed in the background, making conversation difficult.

From the port window, a security docker ship, squat and unsightly like a gray bloated toad, floated with ominous import. Such a ship would be looking to maintain law and order—shakedown any runners peddling contraband or out to leverage any of the station's business. Skeller's Run would not be an easy place to work scams.

I tapped a tall outworlder on the shoulder, carrying a parcel in one hand and a paneled, cameo briefcase. He looked like an Arkadian on official business caught in an inordinately busy rush. At any rate, someone who knew what was going on. "What's up, chief?" I asked. "Why the hubbub?"

He turned a high forehead to me crowned with a sculpted drift of tan-colored hair. "Haven't you heard? Ah, you just came in, didn't you? Megal's been attacked. Some rogue bandit just declared war and flew in with his stealth craft and took over the planet."

I blinked. "Planetary defenses?"

"Minimal and antiquated. This Mong's got state-of-the-art equipment, and know-how."

"Who?" I croaked.

"Mong."

I frowned, recalling that name. "Why attack the space station? Didn't they just nab a world?"

"Out of the way. Easy spoils." The man's eyes darted to the destination boards, as if distracted. "He's taking ships and men, everything. Laying waste, crippling any offenses, moving on."

TK mused, "That sounds like a tried and true formula, repeated throughout history, like the Vandal hordes and Blitzkrieg of Earth's early history."

"Another petty warlord come to make life miserable for everyone," the man spat. "Just another power-monger rising from the ashes of doom."

"Mong," I grunted. "So, that bastard changed his name, did he?"

"What do you mean?" the outworlder demanded.

"I knew a Ging or a Gong on Hazzerot planet—the scum planet of the universe. Raged bloody murder and mayhem there, tore it to pieces. Drank human blood from the victims' skulls."

"That sounds like a bit of hokum to me," said the outworlder.

"You mean old wives' tales?" hissed Wren. "Try visiting Talyon some time."

"Yeah, tell that to the victims' families," I said.

TK pulled at his whiskers. "I seem to recall a legend of a degenerate warlord out of old Earth history savaging the lands, a Googis Khem. Took over half the ancient world before he was killed."

"That's Genghis Khan," I corrected him.

"So maybe this Mong guy takes after him?" asked Wren.

The outworlder shrugged. "No doubt he's a role model."

"Haven't had the grace to meet the man," I said with a low mutter. "Hope I never do."

"Let's just get our stuff and go," Wren asserted. She wrung her hands, clutched her sides and flashed impatient looks.

"What else do we need here?" asked TK.

"Just packaged goods. Dry packs, meals of any sort, add water and you have instant nutrients. Here." I tossed over some thirty yols and motioned him to the confectionary section to get the supplies. Billy hopped after him, his ferret-dark eyes blinking in adoration. I shook my head. It's as if I'd given his mentor a 'prize of the year'.

I directed Wren to the clothing shop, passed her a handful of credits. I further noted it would be taken out of her share when work was divvied up and the spoils came in. She trotted off with a haughty air and came back from the change rooms a new woman. Leathers hugged her slim hide like a sleek leopard with a fit pleasing to any eye. I wished I could get a real wig for her or something to cover up that blasted bald crown...

In fact... I shuttled her to the hair salon down the way and tossed a thick black wig into the basket at the sales counter.

"That'll be three yols," the attendant said.

"What's that for?" Wren demanded suspiciously.

I smirked. "Nothing, really, just part of my plan. Relax, all good."

Moving onward deeper within the terminus, we came to a giant rotating rotunda milling with people. A high dome spread overhead with reinforced glass that overlooked a lovely view to the stars. Service shops, eateries, hair stylists, outerwear, everything the casual, weary traveler could want, young or old, rich or poor. Step right up, folks. There was even an executive pad on the upper level like a casino royale, stocked with fancy restaurants, shave and a haircut, shoe-shining parlors, rent a courtesan by the minute. My mind reeled with the cons I could pull up there. But I reined myself in. Not the time or place. Keep your imaginative skull on hold, Rusco.

This was like something out of time, from an older generation before the slums and ghettos had edged over the bloodied city ruins.

Meanwhile Wren and I hustled over to the general section for a last minute stop, some Devirol to make more of my homebrew. TK pulled Billy along and scoped out the dry goods. This section of the Run, a giant circular revolving wheel with port windows every fifty feet, was unusually busy with traffic. All kinds from the surrounding sectors.

I bumped shoulders with a lot of impatient folk from duty officers to transients, all milling about and talking a lot of hokum in loud voices. I caught snippets of conversation that were not entirely of reassuring nature. Drought on this world, killings on that world, planetary genocide. Gang takeover. Refugees from Megal, merchants from Vylnos, down and out speculators from any of the mining worlds and prospectors scoping out asteroids, uncharted moons, any chunk of rock that could churn out a dime. Any number of garden-variety drifters and hopefuls looking for a new life on a new world. I heard them all, like the buzz of angry bees, haggling over prices of basic commodities like soup, drypak, underwear, which seemed to have escalated in the sudden demand created by the exodus. A tense expectancy hung in the air; a flurry of desperation that made everyone edgy, like a massive feedback loop, the threat of scarcity and the fragile security of their lives.

"Let's get out of here," Wren muttered, after I'd paid for the two bottles I needed. "The vibes are terrible."

"Agreed."

"What's that glass bottle? Little bit of a garden cocktail?"

"Something like that." I cast her a chilly grin before I surged ahead.

Suddenly there came a low drone, pulsing through the air like an air siren out from an audio-net nightmare. Eyes darted up, dull whispers broke from dry lips.

A security monitor next to me spoke in a clipped whisper. "Advance armada—Early distant warning. They'll be coming out of warp in two minutes."

The monitor's partner spat out a curse. "Shit, they're already here. Why?"

TK mumbled, grabbing my shoulder. "Bad idea to berth here, Rusco, bad idea." He shook his gray head.

I snatched at Wren's arm. "Let's get back to the ship."

Out the porthole I saw the docking security ship take a turn and bank away, her weapons lights streaming on her foredeck.

That was not good.

Orange lights winked over the shops and service counters. A robot voice pealed over the loudspeaker: *"Amber alert. All dockers aboard Skeller's Run report to emergency bay. Lockdown in process. All docking bays from A1-T3 will be closed in T minus 2 minutes. All boarders proceed to emergency support bay. Repeat, report to emergency bay."*

"Jesus, can you believe it?" I bawled.

The attack came in less than two minutes.

Several stealth raiders came out of warp like banshees and flanked the station. Long beetle-like prows with glass eyes surveyed the station with predatory menace. Their tapered purple-grey hulls pulsed with malignant energy.

The emergency alert was as useless as tits on a bull.

A group of frightened souls snarled curses at the vanguard. White fingers gripped wrists; pale-faces goggled at what faced them.

The battle cruisers came arching into view. The lead craft glowed an ominous grey with triangular nose and bulkheads racked on an octagonal rear body like a souped up war freighter. The *Galaga*.

"Holy mother of god—" a bystander cried. "That's Mong's devil ship. Enough firepower there to wipe out half of Veglos."

More and more of that name 'Mong'. It tinkled in the back of my mind like a shaman's death rattle. *Hoath*. That two-bit guard. He'd dropped the name. Some star lord or mega star-mogul.

A black-bearded man, clutching a bag of drypak meals, crowded close to the glass. The man looked like a pilot, judging from the eagle logo on his blue spacer uniform. "He's an ugly brute. Some kind of cult leader. Whatever the case, you don't want to mess with him."

"Founded the Temple of Tirith on *Ciros*, I heard," croaked another. "Priest, nomad, witch-hunter, warlord, jack of every trade. With some weird kind of powers to boot."

"Like what?" I snarled, whirling on him.

"Don't know, like moving stuff with his mind. Weird shit like that."

"That's all crap," I scoffed. "He's just a flesh-eating shitter like the rest of us." But somehow I knew not, and my greatest fears were realized, remembering the tales of blood and rapine that Ging fellow on Hazzerot had committed. But it had been so long ago.

"Maybe, but that's what I've heard," said the outworlder. "Whatever, you don't want to mess with him."

Seems as if I already had, if Baer was mixed up with him—and I had provoked him by rifling his secret stash and blowing off his arm.

I moved off with a grunt, feeling a tremor of sick unease crawling up my gut.

"Rusco, we should—"

I waved TK off.

Without warning all hell broke loose. It seemed any

communications' parley had failed. The wasps surged in with amazing dexterity, making retaliation impossible.

The security docker opened fire but stood no chance against so many enemies. The attackers pounded it to chipboard, its shields blinking red before dying.

The security vessel and companion ships rocked under the firepower. The enemy looped around them like blackflies circling a wounded deer, peppering them with rays, penetrating shields and shearing cannons.

The flagship blew the main security docker ship to dust. That gray-bloated pig with antennae, towers and cannons was no more.

TK paled. "They just nuked the main security vessel."

"No kidding," I growled. "The thing's really just show and glitter. A sitting duck for those smaller spitfires. See?"

The wasps roared over the last of the defenders, taking out crafts, military and civilian.

"Why? What's their purpose?" cried Wren. "Why take a station when they can have a planet?"

I shifted uncomfortably. "For show, kicks, greed? Teach the refugees there's no safe place to hide?"

I stood in helpless awe as the invaders employed that blitzkrieg technique TK'd mentioned. It was devastatingly effective.

"Get to Starrunner, before it's too late," I mumbled.

The first smart bombs struck the upper decks of the Run, rocking the floor under our boots and knocking us off our feet.

Screams rose from all quarters. Metal crumpled around us, glass shattered, and smoke rose in a shower of sparks, spraying me with debris.

I picked myself up and ran with Wren down the littered terminus, picking my way through the stampede, against the flow.

Pandemonium hit the rotunda. Most tried to scramble for the main avenue to the emergency bay—a mistake, and soon it was a clot of writhing, fighting hordes, crammed against themselves like lemmings.

I grabbed Wren and pushed TK forward. "Back to the ship—"

"But they said—"

I waved him off. "Forget it. Follow my lead if you want to live."

I ran right into a checkpoint station guard crouching, holding an R2 at my chest. "Get back. You can't go in there!" he bawled. "Lock down."

One thing I hated was protocol during life and death situations. I pretended to bow my head in submission, then upended him in the chops with an elbow, knocking him flat on his ass. I kicked the weapon out of his reach and lifted my pen blaster.

His buddy crouched and aimed for my head.

Wren lifted her pen and blew the man's head off without a second's hesitation.

I blinked. "Let's go."

We raced past the checkpoint for the A2 dock where Starrunner berthed; fortunately she hadn't been destroyed, only trembling to explosive rumbles and flecked with silver metal plates fallen from the ceiling. Smoke curled from down the hall and cries of the dying reverberated with sparks raging and metal beams crashing down.

The docking arm still hung clamped to our bow. I swore and jerked open the hatch, raced for the bridge, got the engine running. The others were not far behind me. I pulled Starrunner out, breaking off the docking struts and the arm. The water connection severed, sending pipe and water spewing like a fire hose. Sparks flew where pieces were still attached. I turned the cannon and blasted a hole in the stubborn berth gate. I gunned the engines and she ripped through the jagged opening and under impulse power shot up on a ninety degree angle straight out of there. Pulse rays tore across our beam and flared around us like firecrackers with enemy ships on our tail. Bug-shaped marauders with two wings fore and aft, like two ice picks end to end.

Odd sounds streamed from Billy's mouth in a disturbing manner. Wren, flush-faced and grimacing, manned the starboard guns.

"The hostiles are coming too close for comfort," yelled TK.

"Quit blabbing and start shooting! Do I need to coach you? Is there no compliance in this universe?"

"You been praying to the wrong gods, Rusco," gibed Wren. "Maybe you should quit squawking."

I whirled on the old man whose arms were trembling. "TK, man the auxiliary starboard guns. Wren, you take the port. We're going to have ourselves a dogfight before this is all over."

"We've got multiple bogies on our tail," she called.

"The manuals are in the console, if you need them," I said.

"Warp out of here," she cried.

"Can't. That's a gas giant down there in case you didn't notice. Gravity galore. I have to clear another 100k miles away before I can even think about Varwol."

"He's right," TK groaned.

Wren stared in disbelief. "Why is this happening? How could we have warped in within orbital distance—"

"Shut up. Fire!"

Other ships burst from their stalls, some of them hopelessly damaged and catching fire in the process. I winced as they became incendiaries, ripe prey for the enemy stealth ships bearing down on them. Some tried to jump to warp too soon and became stretched discs miles long before they shimmered blue and winked out of existence forever. I saw a Vega 6 ultra light cruiser go up in flames, drowned in pulse fire. Others followed suit. Fat pulse beams whipped so close to Starrunner they almost tagged her flanks as the black and grey starfleas bombarded us with every weapon they had. All I could do was urge every ounce of speed out of Starrunner before I could trigger the Varwol.

I pondered the motive of any man to unleash such wholesale slaughter. Target: all the refugees from that doomed planet. Truly a vengeful bastard in the extreme, this Mong character. On the chance it was the same Mong I'd heard dropped on Hoath, we'd better be wary. My thoughts were interrupted as a larger, blue wasp-enemy came vaulting out of the ether with fareons locked. What were the chances it was the same Mong?

"Molly, give me live feed and max juice."

"Affirmative."

The holo display came up. A target zoomed in and possible missile trajectories for intercept. I targeted it and smashed it broadside on the rear thrusters, near the heat-sink. "Die, fucker." But my mouth sagged. The wasp-like fuselage flared in a red aureole then faded down to standard gray. I whacked my fist on the weapons console. "Why don't you die, fucker?" I launched another fareon. Now those stealthguard cannons were aiming straight at us. No wonder those bee-stinging, bitch-faced flydirts had defeated an entire planet. "Molly, we'd better be getting out of here pretty damn fast!"

"Affirmative. ETA T-1:36 before Varwol can engage."

"That's an awfully long road to hell. Molly. Snap it up!"

I whirled on Wren. "Give that bitch your best shot. If we combine blasts, maybe our attacks can penetrate those crypto-shields."

"10-4! On the count of three. Three—two—one. Now!"

Our blasts coordinated at the same point, a four-foot square on the underbelly of the approaching, offensive craft. The thing glowed for several seconds, one baleful crimson, then began to flame around the edges. My mouth quivered for a second, then curled in triumph. "Hot damn! Wallow in oblivion, you bandit shitweasel—"

Fareon beams came arching from the two attacking ships at the flaming ship's heel which I dodged as other escaping craft died in our rear sights. Shields held but upper panels began to smoke and the Varwol was beginning to shiver and kick in.

Maybe, just maybe. Multiple beams arced out across the gulfs, but Starrunner blinked out in a haze of nothingness as the Varwol, miracle of science, kicked in.

Chapter 10

We all took a time out, and celebrated over a bottle of gin I had tucked in the forward bulkhead I called the 'back hamper'. Starrunner was off to the Norios belt or some never-never land, and I hoped to hell the Barenium would hold. After the backslapping and congratulations were over and Billy had finished his powdered milk and munched his synthetic cookies, we sat down for a fireside chat at the circular conference table on the bridge. "I see the Varwol's already degraded 2.5%."

"Sad thing that," muttered TK.

"We survived this round, but next time might not be so pretty. I'm not saying that was a typical day in the life of an honest crook, but if you're running with me, it's not going to be easy."

Wren shrugged her sinewy shoulders. "All the same to me, dads. I've been dodging mad boys and dervishes most of my life, so this just felt like home." She adjusted her Uzi on her shoulder at a better angle.

"First of all, I'm not dads, and it's not grey hair, it's purple, in case you didn't notice."

She reached across the tinted tabletop and patted my hand, as if to console my feelings. "There, there, Rusco, just horsing around. Don't take it the wrong way."

It was a nice addition, even if it was a touch condescending.

"Forget it, Wren. None taken. Now, way I see it, we can run scams and cons up and down the populated worlds, starting with the most prosperous planets. I got one in mind now, where we play tag team at the rich dives and the casinos, looking for manageable marks. We showboat them around, give them a good time, make ourselves out as easy marks, then take them for all they're worth."

Wren shrugged. "It sounds easy, but I got a better idea. Why not fake a shipwreck, set up a distress signal, and let them come to us, then we nab their ship and goods."

TK muttered, rubbing his chin, "It has potential, but too many variables and violent possibilities. I don't have that many years left in my old bones and don't feel like cutting them short, lying in a pool of blood."

"Good luck with that, old man." I chuckled. "If you're running with bad boys, blood there'll be. Tell you what, we can always let you off at Beta Aquilae or the nearest hub."

The old man gave a withering grimace. "Billy and I'll stay on here, I think."

"Good choice. But I tend to agree with your rejection of the shipwreck plan. Wren, as much as I like your idea, I'll have to downvote it. Let's stick to plan A."

She shrugged, gave a surly scowl. "All the same to me, Rusco. Go for it."

"On another note, Starrunner's due for an overhaul. New stabilizers, Barenium seals, whatever. You contribute your share and we're all fine. I've facilitated your escape and I'll put in for the bulk of repairs. After that we share in the spoils."

TK blinked and growled, "I can live with that, Rusco, but I'd rather you pay me hard yols for the repairs I do, and give me a garage, diagnostic equipment and tools."

I smiled. "See, there's the rub, TK." I put my arm around his shoulders. "Things like hangar space and tools, cost money."

"Why not dump this silly crate and buy a whole new kit?" grunted Wren.

I stared at her for a moment. "How do you figure that? You think quality spacecraft are just lying about, waiting to be plucked from trees?"

"Steal one."

"Something unethical about that," I said, in my most deadpan voice.

TK snorted.

These rubes didn't appreciate a good joke. "I need to take a nap, sleep off these wounds. Knock yourself out, the bridge is yours.

"Wait!" cried TK. "Let's talk more about these heists. If you're serious, why not start on Vasel or Perseus? Lot of trade up there, or at least was, when I was touring."

"Perseus is a high draw," I admitted. "I've heard ripe business goes on up there. Some money to milk at least."

"Another place comes to mind is Skguron."

"With Skurgian raiders coming up your ass out of every nook and cranny in hyperspace. I think not."

"Scrap it then. Perseus, it is."

"We'll talk about it more later." I yawned. "Plenty of water in the dispenser and dry food in the paks, and some more cheap gin under the bulkhead, if you need a kick."

"Thanks, dads," said Wren with unveiled sarcasm. "That's a great package, the dry meal included."

"Don't mention it," I said, tipping my head in salute.

Exhaustion had more than taken its toll. After showing Wren and TK to their quarters in the spare cabins, I thought to hit my bunk. But first I locked the controls on autopilot for Beleron, with only a key code that I knew. Didn't trust them farther than I could spit. Yet.

I flopped down on my hard foam, locking the door tightly by remote. I caught some restless sleep, but awoke in a cold sweat some hours later, feeling the gnarling pain in my knee, a gnawing ache which was like a saw penetrating to the bone.

I descended to the hold, checking things over, sauntered back up the service hall where I saw the bridge lights on. Wren had already retired, but as I approached, I caught TK snooping by the controls, rummaging for something. He seemed to be fiddling with the auxiliary panel. It looked as if he were searching for booze, but on second glance, he pretended to tie his boot lace. Then I got suspicious with his head snapping up like that with a stupid grin, fingers tapping some keystrokes into the data console.

"Says here packed Barenium will hold up 50% longer, Jet, if it's nazolene-pressed vs raw-treated. You know what era your Barenium's from?"

"Not rightly, TK. Wasn't given the proper maintenance papers by the lowlifes I snatched the ship from."

"I can imagine that. Well, seems as if we should make some effort to track those papers down, shouldn't we? I was searching for them in the utility cabinets below when you startled me—"

"They aren't there." I curled up my lip. It might have been a legitimate story but I thought not. TK was slier than he looked. Seemed he had pulled up some info on the free data stream via holo net. Kits which included diagrams, well-marked-up color-coded map, step-by-step instructions with two young, vivacious birdies giving a servicing tutorial on the finer points of Barenium and handling fresh product in vacuum sealed canisters. Nice girls. Pretty looking, but it looked much like a cute trick to sidestep me, and a feint to cover his real intentions.

"Bridge is off limits while I'm not here," I muttered in a cold voice.

"I thought you said to make ourselves—"

"I said no bridge access. New rules." I'd have to make a point of moving that strongbox with the phaso to a more secure location. The last hungry look I saw on the old man's face had that wild, eager edge that stuck in my mind. The phaso was already hidden well in the forward bulkhead, but one could never be too sure.

* * *

We skipped Beleron and docked at Zanzadeer, known for its mech shops and abundant ship parts. Also gambling houses, party houseboats, rave depots, plenty to placate the varied vices of humankind: sex sports, needle games, you name it, they had it. I opted to kill two birds with one stone, repairs and profit. Not the best place to dock for a leisurely layover. Lots of mishaps reported on Zanzadeer: missing bodies, child abductions, random blast attacks, but we couldn't be choosy with Starrunner acting up as she was.

The repairs were complex, items that even TK couldn't fix, despite his protestations to the contrary. Without a proper garage, his skills were limited. But he said he'd look over the mechanics' work after they were done to check for shoddy service. I nodded, muting my skepticism of honest-dealers. Meanwhile, we needed funds. I was sadly lacking, after shelling out for the supplies, and it was not as if any of the hangers-on aboard, my new crew, had a yol to share between them.

"We need to go out on the town and rustle up some coin."

"Anything in mind?" asked Wren.

I nodded, worried my lip. "We work the gaming boats on Lake Yoe first. Follow my lead, stay low and alert, and you two may learn something."

"Yes, Captain Ruskie," said Wren with a cynical salute.

No mention of the phase-distorter from TK, though I knew it was on his mind. Billy was useless to us so he stayed back on the ship. I just hoped the halfwit wouldn't trash the place. I'd disabled all the controls, and left him with some crude magazines to pore over, unbeknownst to TK, but one couldn't be too sure.

After scanning the ship's database for loopholes in the Zanzadeer gambling systems, I discovered we needed some updated props; new games were in play on the boats. I went to work on some loaded die and some fancy cards. Been a while since I'd been to this planet so I had to refresh my memory. My mind worked over the endless scams I could pitch: the spinners, the loopers, the big sting. In that way my brain was like a computer. I could soak up cons like sponges water: spin a mark's mind up so tight, he's wanting to get scammed. Or, the big lie, the loopers, the ones almost impossible to believe, but the reward so high that the mark can't resist.

A simple con came to mind: Me and Wren'd work the game houses along the wharf, a husband-wife team, 'Emmie and Hamber', newly-weds, playing the amorous duffers.

Wren, determined and proficient, played the part a little closer to the mark than I expected, but if it earned us credence among the big players, I was game. All the flighty little moves she contrived, the touches, the pets and kisses, pecks on the cheek at the right moment, seemed credible enough. Been five years since I'd worked that scam. Did it with my ex-girl, Katie, back on Kalsinar, but that had ended on a bad note when she got roughed up; it'd soured any attempt on my part to revive it. I was superstitious that way—no raising of old ghosts. But now was not the time for superstition, or to sabotage this venture, seeing as we needed funds so I could get Starrunner back in space.

I was surprised to see Wren wearing a black skirt, tight-pressed that showed her upper curves well, all dolled up, very sexy; she cleaned up well, in my opinion. She must have bought that garment back at the station. The butchy, skinhead look would never fly, so I pulled out the wig and plopped it on her head. "There, black, just as you like." I patted it down roughly. "Matches everything else on your hide."

She groused about it, but only a little. I turned her to the mirror and told her she looked beautiful. With a reluctant grunt, she accepted the wig.

With my last instructions to the mechanics, telling them we'd pay them later, we took a tram from the service garage into the glitter and glitz of centertown. The place made Hoath look like a complete scumhole. But the crumbled buildings, gang-graffiti and blackened, shell-torn smokestacks rising beyond the old quarters demonstrated otherwise and still lurked around the edges as we got closer. Much was hidden in Zanzadeer city.

We scouted out several joints, me and TK in disguise, and

separately, so as not to attract any outriders by association. We came up with a system, different than others, for the games had changed as I had remembered them, and so had the management. One thing about the con business, never make any assumptions. Do your research, check your facts, figures, plans, and recheck them at least three times before committing. Something I'd failed badly at back in Hoath, trusting Marty with the particulars, and almost getting the two of us killed.

Yoe was a shallow lake and a bunch of entrepreneurs had got together and formed the novel idea of setting their gambling houses up on the water. A flotilla of fun. Dancing, music, the works, house games like Monster, Juju, Bluewrack, and names like Barney J's Lil' Ole Boathouse and Iggy's Pop, and my favorite—Popcorn. Goofy names, but Zanzadeer was a goofy place. Disarm the sheep, separate them of their money. Only moneyed folk could afford these floating mini-palaces, but they were here in this town, as I had discovered early on in my prior visits. The organized crime leaders, the ones with the private guards and the refitted space yachts all dressed in mahogany and marble complete with private bars and waitresses, made it a dangerous arena, but a lucrative one for the clever artist. I'd overcome my fears of fencing with the big boys long ago. All a matter of confidence, a mind over matter thing. If I stripped every vibe of doubt and radiated confidence, there was nothing I couldn't do. Such a mindset overrode fear mechanisms which got even the best cons killed. Even in the toughest situations I could worm my way out. I used to get juiced up on Myscol before a swindle in my younger years, to build up enough nerve, but I got over that kid's ploy when I realized it was a losing battle, a battle of addiction that I'd never win. So, I sucked it up, took a deep breath, visualized how it was all going to go down and practiced my affirmation, and my mantras. Most importantly, tried to work with competent players in the game. Now TK and Wren were untested, and I assumed had no experience with real scams, though that Wren was a mean one on her feet, but so far they had shown promise. Let's hope my instincts were correct about them.

After scrutinizing several games on various boats, TK the mathematician, ran the numbers and figured out a workable system. We put our heads together to select the best possible outcomes.

The house had rigged Juju, so that was out of the question. But Bluewrack and Monster had potential. They were group, not house games and promise for some tidy profit. Of course, we'd need a point-scout. That's where TK came in who'd agreed to devise hand signals.

The ten-sided dice were new to me, geared to throw off sharks who had already polished their scams.

"Seed the aces," TK said. "Half the die are loaded. We insert our own in play. At drop fifteen we play full out and win, then drop back, lose a little so they don't get suspicious."

"Okay, old man, we play one against the other. I'll engineer a way to signal so nobody figures it out and pulls the alarm on us. As I see it, the house will always win in the long run, but short term gains are possible. The more players, the more likelihood of a gain. It's a matter of getting out at the right time."

"We're on board then. Let's establish a coordinated plan of exit."

"Right."

"How's your Bluewrack?" I grinned at Wren.

She shrugged. "Never played it, but I became proficient at something like it back when I used to trounce my brothers."

"Oh, yeah? It'll have to do. I needn't remind you that the stakes are high here—broken legs and fingers are not uncommon. Fates get worse than that for cheaters."

"Don't sweat it, I've got it under control."

I didn't like the nonchalance in her voice, considering the stakes of the enterprise; it could get ugly very quickly.

We practiced several rounds on the bridge with my own weighted die and marked cards. I coached Wren on the finer points of the game, when to toss and when to roll a losing hand and when to go for the jugular. She learned fast. Like she said, she seemed to have experience with the game before.

"Throw them without getting intimidated. Get them to land a certain way. You dig your nail in the three-spot on the heavy side and the magnets kick in and the dice'll fall the other way."

"Not bad, Rusco. Some clever rigging here."

I shrugged. "I've used these scams before, engineered a way to peer in on other's hands, putting a reflective strip of polyeselon, a reflective bit of glass, on the opposite wall where I sat and kept chatting to divert my opponents."

TK shook his head. "Risky. If they caught you—"

"They're not looking for it, don't you see?" I said. "Without a point man or some nondescript posing as an innocent spectator, they're looking for other things."

"I don't know," said TK. "The strip sounds easy for a roving eye to pick up."

"What I did was photograph the wall pattern prior to playing and mock up some reflecto-pad to follow its blend. I'd brush against the wall, elbow the pad sticky side out when no one was looking. Voila. Stuck there like an invisible stamp. The thing's thin, so there's no visible evidence, and it's slightly convex to show a wide view."

"Don't see how that would show you anything."

"I wore a kind of contact lens to pick up the faint reflection."

TK shook his head. "I'm just glad we're not using a scam like that. I can blend in easy enough, a sad alcoholic wanting a piece of the action but no yols to play."

"Good, simpler's better. BJ's is busy, lots of players there. Small timers too, so it won't be as hot."

"Any idea of how long we'll be out on the floor?"

"As long as the tables are dealing, we work up some stash, then we skip to the next boat. Or I give you the signal to cut for the night."

I saw TK's hesitation. "Any hint of anything going sour, we bail, agreed?"

Grumbles. Shrugs. Looked as if we were on track.

Chapter 11

We were finally ready to deal and I picked BJ's to start. The place was popular, busy, a buzz of pleasant excitement in the air. Bright lights lit up the back that hurt the eyes, made you feel tired and radiated a lot of heat, leaving a lot of hot sweaty residue on the skin. Geared to get you to make impulsive moves to release that excess discomfort, blow your money while munching complimentary nuts and salted tidbits at the tables so you'd feel thirstier and drink more of the local brew. Slot machines jingled to the side; group games progressed toward the front. Live band at the back, playing an upbeat techno-jazz with juicy electro frills unfamiliar to my ear. The clink of glasses caught my attention, the titter of women's voices as they watched the big players toss glittering die or spread fan-colored cards in front of their faces, hoping for the big win. The hustlers latched on to the winners, blinked in derision at the losers.

Wren and I wended our way to the happening section while TK stayed back. The alpha dog at the head table of four had at least two guys working for him, or watching out for him. I could tell by the subtle eye movements and stiffening of shoulders. I earmarked that information.

We sat down at the Bluewrack table, in between two of the foremost gamblers, Wren as Emmie, all smiles and giggles, looking a little tipsy, but as sober as a shark, me on her other side. I was a different story, not so easily able to fake drunkenness, despite the local juice giving me a flushed face and a fuzzy skull. I had an uncanny knack of keeping my thoughts coherent, even though my body language might show the influence of drink.

Sitting aside Wren, I gave the players my most disarming smile and nod. I'd slicked back my long hair like an old hipster and had it knotted in a ponytail so it didn't look so beatnik. That look wasn't going to fly at these highbrow tables. I'd lost most of the purple tint but let a few of the violet traces show through, figured it might make me look more like a groovy, middle-aged trendster, momma's rich boy, making his second attempt at life with a new bride swinging on his arm.

The game was a combo of dice and cards, iridescent pieces which showed up like magic tricks, and danger to boot, dazzling the eyes.

We'd rehearsed our signals. Blink twice for a move to up the ante. Once, plus a pause to fold. We'd switch it up to a parting of lips and scratch of jowl, then back to the double-blink when TK'd take a swig of his local liquor and lick his chops.

The boats or overhauled barges were packed really close together along the shore and lit up with bright neon. Red, yellow and white light streamed across the dark waters. Fireworks arched across the lake—faraway festivities were in the works.

Other pleasure boats plied the water like gaudy floating birthday cakes. The waters were dense with salts and minerals and gave greater buoyancy to the gambling houses. The draw on these flat-bottomed boats was a whopping twenty-six inches. Not much speed. They could pull in at three knots, slow as turtles, but why go fast when you're making yols by the minute? Better to keep the fat fish aboard slapping their chips onto the tables.

All the while I kept a wary eye out for trouble. Those hard faces around us, laughing and wisecracking, were the faces of killers. Violent repercussions could be the result of one failed gambit, should one be caught. We'd be thrown to the monster moonrays, feral eels that haunted the salty waters. Heard horror stories of cons weighted at the ankles and thrust into the deeper water, while the gangsters watched the disappearing act from the comfort of their yachts, eating surf and turf and sipping martinis.

Wren, who looked less suspicious, would clock up most of the wins, while I'd sit back on my thumbs and tank hands and blame it on wifey. Wife and Hubby team. Rich and spoiled from moneyed families who had struck out on the ill-fated expedition of marriage, then made the naïve mistake of wasting their yols on these nice gentlemen.

It was important to give the right cues, not to set anyone's suspicions off. I was reading these guys as best I could while Emmie chattered on about nothing. She was doing well; one would never know the woman was a cold-blooded killer. Fatty, directly opposite me, with the dimpled cheeks and airbrushed hair, was all smiles amid peanut eating and shell cracking. Munching away with his quail-ass grin while he won hand after hand. Pissed me off. But it was part of the act.

Patience, Rusco. Keep losing.

The skinny one with the black suit and dour looks paid me no heed but managed a nod and grunt from time to time to his crony. No less crafty, I could tell. The older one was harder to read. Salt and pepper hair, serious type but not so serious. A blank, bulldog face with strong lines on the upper cheeks, sometimes crinkling in a smug grimace; other times he'd drop a line of philosophic rhetoric straight from Goethe. Because he was the boss, he was the most dangerous of the lot. They called him Elmer. What kind of jackleg name was that? Either it was a gag, or I was missing something. Still, I gave Elmer his due respect and played the happy hubby, drinking more than my share, wincing with every gasp of the local swamp water laced with distilled spirits, twice as potent as normal alcohol. I let the flush rise to my cheeks, a healthy pink—the gambler's flush they called it—pulled at the sweaty fabric on my collar, made a half-hearted smile and little coo at my beloved wife—who the others seemed to dig, despite the horrid wig job. Amused me, while my brain worked overtime trying to figure out how to stall the game and lose some more.

TK was doing his part, wandering about to different tables, chatting, letting us play out our tricks and hands, so it didn't look as if he was feeding us any information. Also letting us lose a lot while he was there, to create a negative association with his presence. A clever diversion.

That tingling feeling between my shoulder blades told me that our window of opportunity was closing fast. Time to cash out. Emmie had accumulated a good stash on the last hand. I'd lost the next round deliberately, and badly, though I had put in small bids.

"I told you not to lead with that flush!" I yelled at her.

"Sorry," she giggled. "I'm not thinking straight, dearie. Must be these highballs. They're stronger than what I'm used to."

Layering it on a little thick perhaps, but it got some chuckles from our card crew. Husband and wife team, wife stricken with a case of the tipsy giggles and an excess of yols.

I threw down the dice in a huff of disgust. "Emmie, I'm out, need a break. You'd better come too. You've won quite a bit."

"Nothing doing, Hamber, I'm just warming up."

"Beginner's luck," I grumbled at her with unfeigned jealousy. "We're not inexhaustible, you know."

"Hush, dear," she cooed, "I'm just getting into the game! Don't be a prig. I'm sure these nice gentlemen'll go easy on me—if I start to lose."

One of the shark eyes leaned in with an oily, but genial tip of the head. "To keep your charm in the game, madam, is our modest pleasure. It's Lemmy here you have to worry about." He nudged the man next to him in the ribs and gave a harsh guffaw. "We still have to earn back some of the yols you've taken from us."

Real rib ticklers, these sharks.

The faint, seaweedy smell continued to ooze off the dark water, drifting in the window, making me feel slightly ill.

When Wren played coy at leaving the game, I made a scene,

pretending to get in a drunken huff and stalked off to the bar.

Weaving a little as I walked, for effect, I could hear Wren murmur some gracious, bubble-headed words, giving a whole spiel of effusive apologies for her disgruntled husband whom she felt *compelled* to nursemaid from his griefs—the big sullen, drunken baby—while promising to return to the game asap. TK edged slowly toward the other games in progress closer to the exit.

Good girl, cash out your chips, hit the ladies' room, then make a beeline to the back door while those sods await your return.

Drink in hand, I pushed through the double doors and hit the deck, glad of the fresh air. The sky was dark, starless; the air cool and musky. The shots of the local spirits, clouds of nicotine and the bebop beat had started to eat away at my skull.

I counted the moments, listening to the laughter and the revelry and disco beats carry on across the water from the other boats. Wren came out, her cheeks flushed.

"You got the yols?" I grunted.

"Nice job, Rusco. Seems your scheme worked."

"Where?"

"Right here." She tapped the inside of her thigh where she had taped it.

"Peachy."

A good act, but maybe not good enough. The door flapped opened.

Elmer tripped over with a grim smile. "Hey, girlie, game's still rolling. Well, what's this? Hubby and dollface taking a little timeout by the water? Charming." Elmer, with a smile that'd kill a grouper, slapped an arm around my shoulder.

"Just came out for some fresh air, Elmer. Be back in in a sec when I get my second wind."

"Don't rush. You don't look so good, Hamber."

"Think I ate some bad fish."

His head bobbed as he smiled. "You know what, I think you guys are a bunch of shamsters. Funny how I take a dislike to scammers, on account that I live here. Own a legitimate business, have some genuine friends. Makes me and my chums look bad. All the stories you jokers'd tell of how you conned a couple of the local fish." He laughed and TK took the unfortunate moment to breeze out of the swinging doors and give a gasping breath. Catching wind of the little gathering, he turned to hustle back in.

"Wait up, gramps." Elmer snapped his fingers. A couple of his thugs, all murder and glares, intercepted and pushed TK back to the rail in our direction. Elmer moved over to TK and threw an arm over his shoulder, as he had done to me. "I like you, gramps. Very slick of you in there, giving signals like that as if you were swatting away flies. Nice gig. These two I don't like, especially Hammy here with all his glib talk." His boot shot out and kicked me in the bad knee, as if he'd known it was my weak spot. I went down, crouching in agony. "Smarts, doesn't it, Hammy?" He laughed. "Suck it up, you pussy. Doesn't look good in front of the missus." He grabbed Wren by the hair and pulled her down to his crotch with his other hand rubbing his knuckles hard across her wig. The piece dropped off to show her skin head.

"My, my, surprises by the minute. Didn't know you went in for baldies, Hammy."

I was groaning, cursing myself for my stupidity. Fucker'd taken me by surprise. Innocent old uncle Elmer, a thug who'd whack you with a tire iron before you could blink and you'd still be wondering what hit you.

"Don't want no trouble here," TK stammered, looking as if he'd seen a ghost and was going to piss his pants.

"Oh, no trouble, gramps, just a small misunderstanding. See, we're going to go back into the gambling house and continue our game. We'll let you join for free."

I got to my feet, swaying, pretending a show of drunken bravado, as Wren struggled in Elmer's grip and I took a half-assed swing at Grease Hair to his side, making it easy for him to block. He gave a clown's laugh and pushed me into his henchmen while I flailed away like a jackass. He thought I was an easy takedown and grabbed the cuff of my sportman's jacket. Mistake #1. Never leave yourself open to attack, against even the dorkiest, most ham-handed drunk. One small tap on the throat or other sensitive area and the stars are spinning in your head. Then up comes the knee into the nose, pushing back the bone and cartilage into the brain. Then it's lights out…which is exactly what happened. One step inside the left leg and I was all over Lemmy with a chop to the neck for added measure.

I heaved the limp body over the rail, wincing at the splashing and flapping going on as something large and gurgling did their work. Elmer grimaced and licked his chops. Luckily the music was loud, or there'd be more fuss. But scattered couples were coming out to catch the next houseboat and watch the free show. I like putting on a show as much as the next wiseass, but all facts considered, things were not looking too good for us. We were in poor disguise and on a foreign world. Anything could escalate into bloodshed.

Wren gurgled out a throaty cry and kicked Elmer in the groin while I sprang to toe-tangle with the other fellow. She dropped to grab her concealed gun taped on the inside of her black-skirted thigh as TK pushed through the gathering crowd to get to the boarding dock. Wise and heroic move, TK. Leave your team behind while you make your escape.

I stumbled after the old coward, cursing and grumbling and hopped the rail as he did, making a flying leap over to the next boat, but my midriff struck hard against the hull, knocking the wind out of me. Meanwhile feral critters thrashed below. The alcohol gurgled up in my throat. TK was spryer than I imagined, the wispy-haired codger, fingers clutching the varnished wood just as Wren vaulted over and grasped at a higher point along the rail.

Quick, neat, but we weren't out the frying pan yet. We had to skip this houseboat in case more of Elmer's goons noticed the boss's absence. That second boat was angling to shore.

As soon as it bumped against the pier, we were off, tramping our way through the red light district and the back alleys, avoiding the downtown tram stops, in case Elmer's thugs had eyes on them. I had to fry some enterprising vagrants who jumped out at us, looking for spare coins. Hell would freeze over before I'd let all that work go to waste while almost getting killed, only to get sacked by some grubby backalley punks.

We doubled back toward the lake on a zigzagging course and caught an air taxi farther up the line back to the repair shop. As we flew away from the boats, I let out a sigh of relief, knowing we had escaped a deadly scenario relatively unharmed.

Billy, turns out, had gotten himself in a bit of trouble, locking himself out of the loo, running back and forth not knowing what to do until he had finally wet himself. Was a while before one of the mechanics heard him banging on the hatch and had let him out. A sorry sight.

We got Billy cleaned up and squared up with the repairmen. Back on Starrunner, I took a bit of Myscol to help with my reinjured knee. The familiar tingly warm feeling overshadowed the throbbing agony as my eyes glazed over. Okay for now, but that leg was taking a beating. I'd have to see some doctor. Wren, who had been eyeing me with more than appraisal as the night wore on, took advantage of the success of our little venture to attempt some familiarity of flesh. She leaned in, brushing against me to snake her arm about my waist, a gesture so intimate as to feel almost passion-driven. Her voice dropped in a husky murmur, "Well, hubby, a good night's work, let's do it again real soon."

I leaned in on my good leg with only slightly less languid intent. "Tigress, you're being a naughty puss. Let the law of thuggery prevail. While the heat's on, lie low."

TK chose to blunder in on us like an ox at that moment. "I don't like this town, or their greasy games."

I blurted out an oath. "You and me both."

She slumped, turning away in frustration that the moment had been spoiled. "You know, you two are real wussies."

I shrugged. I could see that Wren was hedging for Miss Prickly of the Year award. TK and I moved off to the bridge.

We'd just about broken even after dispensing the funds for repairs, coming out a few hundred yols ahead. Not bad, but not good either. Split three ways, that wasn't much. Well, strictly speaking, I took 60%, considering it was my ship and I was doing them a favor, saving all our asses by getting out of Dodge twice now.

The rear fin stabilizer was working so we couldn't burn up or wobble ourselves to death upon reentry. The warp drive was still an issue, the Barenium canister still with a hairpin leak, but it was an old part that couldn't be replaced too easily, the lead mechanic had told us. "We can put it on order, but a used part like that would be only 85% operational."

I slapped my fist down on the nav console at the memory as we warped out to Baile's planet, somewhere far away in Yanadar.

TK growled, "I know I should have monitored those greased monkeys better. I don't believe the drive was 'irreparable'."

"Good luck hanging around Zanzadeer while Uncle Elmer is on the rampage," Wren groused. "We should've killed him and all his thugs while we had the chance."

I waved a hand. "Don't get too trigger happy. Do no good anyway. His business associate rats'd still come out of the culverts and get us. This is the problem with being a traveling huckster, Wren. No time to do fix-it-up jobs. One chance, and it's vamoose. We'd better suck up our losses and move on. Bigger fish await in the pond across the way."

I felt glad to be away from Zanzadeer and the boats.

Wren caught up with me in the hall as I was stumbling my way to my cabin. She pressed her mouth hard against mine. I was surprised, for she was up front to a fault, but she was a tomboy after all. Pretty no-nonsense and a convincing one at that, despite my initial non-interest in her. It didn't feel proper to resist.

Back in her cabin, our clothes quickly became unpeeled and after the inevitable, 'Ew, what happened to your ear?' we were right down to business.

The woman had a luxuriant figure when stripped of her hunter's-gauge black leathers. I suppose our first joining was fated. The cabin vibrated to the sounds of our lovemaking. A long sweaty dance of push and pull that had both of us gasping and sucking in the same lungfuls of air. It seemed Wren had always wanted to get it on with me. Okay, I'd bite. I couldn't admit to the same, but I humored her all the same. It took the edge off the loneliness of a con-artist's existence, with no hope for tomorrow.

I awoke some hours later to a tangle of limbs. Her soft breathing on my left shoulder, a warm breast pressed to my chest. I rolled over and my lightly purple-tinted hair brushed her neck like a horsehair fan. Her long legs twitched, a moan pattered in her throat. The memory of some horror of the past? I rumbled out a lion's roar and squeezed her tightly and ran my tongue along her neck which prompted a murmur of escalated breath.

She seemed amused by the animal roar and gave me a playful slap. "Enough, tiger. Let's sleep it off. Plenty more time to play bride and groom in the days ahead."

Chapter 12

We'd been scamming up and down the Zaion worlds for a few weeks now and after several false starts, began to turn a profit. We'd finally repaired the Barenium leak and equipped the landing shuttle on Starrunner with extra space suits. I'd got my knee looked after at the local regen clinic on Gainor, one of the six habitable, terraformed worlds. Some regen—not cheap, and a loving pat on the leg by the stony-eyed medic. After scouting down a new-old Barenium cylinder on Gainor, I gave a praise to the good Kazoo that I no longer had to worry about Baer tracking us. As for the blood-hungry pirate Mong, we'd keep an eye out for him. The man had discovered a superior form of armor or shield technology that had given him a significant edge over his enemies.

I walked onto the bridge to catch TK and Wren glued to the holo screen. The free store planetary press was having a field day with the latest sensation—always a new goldmine of cheery information. The face that stared back at me with those eyes black as charred coal had me cringing.

The broadcast came over the public channel—Mong, in all his glory and ceremonial garb, black-braided ponytails and leather shoulderpiece. His cheeks flushed a ruddy bronze, but that face was set as serene as an avatar.

"Citizens and people of Questra! Surrender your government, your ships and your wealth, or I will unleash a rain of fire that will send you to hell!"

The image cut out and the screen panned back to the announcer. "And that is the latest ultimatum from warmonger, Kaibus Mong, known as the 'star lord' or the 'dark lord of death'. His latest conquest on Megal orbiting Tiran's star turned the landscape into a fiery, feudal wasteland. Will 'Questra', another of the inner planets, suffer the same fate? No one has come to offer aid to either Megal or Questra. Experts say that nearby governments and planetary United Nations are reluctant to defy Mong, fearing retaliation with his blitzkrieg tactics."

"Turn that fucker off, please," I ordered.

TK hit the switch. "See, this renegade Mong is bad news, Rusco. Doesn't look as if he's going to let a few petty worlds satisfy his greed."

"No kidding." The transmission had cast a shadow over my mood. "No different than Genghis Khan, from what I gathered from history. Snatching up territories as if they were candy for the taking." I shook my head. "No matter. Nothing we can do except keep a wide berth."

I finally decided to quit Gainor and scout out crime leads in my old haunts on Tarsus, the second innermost planet. The gigs we were pulling out in the hinterlands were but two-bit shams, raking in a few yols, mere milk money, in retrospect. But they were stepping stones to test out my team, iron out the wrinkles, so to speak, see where TK and Wren's weaknesses lay and how we could improve upon them. Wren was always too impulsive, a natural hothead, but brave and for the most part, unquestioning. TK, on the other hand, was a cautious worrier and a slightly lazy sort. But smart, and his input on cons, particularly timing and logistics, had given me an edge. Even that caper down on Zanzadeer had been a cockup, truthfully, a little bit too convoluted for my ragamuffin recruits. Had almost blown up in our faces. Not that I was Captain Gohimbo or anything. TK and Wren were rising in my estimation and I felt I could trust them with some bigger fish to fry. After purchasing some explosives down on

Gainor with the gambling money from Zanzadeer, I decided to reach a little higher.

An old acquaintance of mine in Haifor City gave us our first genuine break. A Gigor Knox aka 'Blinky', who worked as the concierge at the Big Apple Hotel was my lead. He was a middle man up to his ears in larceny and schemes, from black market to sex trade. A contract job had come up through the grapevine, orchestrated by a certain gangster, the Dancing Slugger, Pazarol.

At the hotel and after a few words of catch up, Blinky took me aside. "I can hook you up for a meet down with Pazzy, kind of an open house." He spread his arms wide, and I saw brown rotten teeth rooted there in his grin.

"Sure," I said. "Whatever you say, Blinky. Just looking for a few opportunities here."

"That's the spirit, JR. That's why I like you." He patted my back with his ham-like hand.

Risky, making the contact with Pazarol, knowing the man was on a par with Baer from what I'd heard. A faint watery voice, a very distant one, told me to back off. But not a loud enough voice for me to take heed.

I did my research and checked out his modus operandi. A jack-of-all trades: arms, clothing, slaves, mercenaries for hire, anything that he could use to turn a profit, which in these days of gang-run, war-torn cities, was mostly contraband.

The gas cloud in the holo view coalesced and morphed into whatever 3D stimulus the ship's computer willed of it. The holo image, drawn from the public free-store, showed a series of dingy warehouses in a seedy industrial neighborhood with broken antennae prickling its rusty roof and decaying load lifters scattered in the yard with flat balloon tires. Inside, the secret cam, highlighting bootlegged clips from the free-store darknet, revealed some old sewing equipment. Outside, a wider pan revealed a few aging dumpsters and cargo ships. Junkers. Didn't think they would fly. A good front.

"You coming with me?" I muttered at Wren.

She shrugged. "Why not? We can go down together, but no wig this time."

I smiled. "Suit yourself."

TK grunted, "I'll stay put with Billy."

"As you wish. Keep an eye on our progress. We'll be wired for sound and video. If things go sour, that little red button'll glow. Hit the override sequence, fire up Starrunner and blast that piece of shit warehouse to shreds. Then I'll know my death was avenged. I'm not planning on Pazarol being that much of a shyster—but one can never be too sure... In the meantime, put that big brain of yours to work devising new and wonderful scams."

"I'll do that," he agreed with a laugh.

Keep old TK busy, out of mischief.

Those holo data dumps, part of the free store, came in handy. Someone had told me that far world data was updated by a simple file-sharing algorithm, courtesy of the ships' computers that came into proximity of a star system. Every time a ship made the Varwol leap, the local network of a new world would collect any updated info and merge it with its own local database while uploading new data to the ship's computer. Hence the system stayed current. Ingenious, but not 100% real time. Of course, worlds like Wren's on Talyon would get nothing of this, having no traffic to speak of nor any network infrastructure.

I met Pazarol and his gang down in his crib out in Tarsus in the decrepit town of Belgen, liking none of it from the get-go. I hoped to hell TK and Billy came through if there was trouble. Wren seemed indifferent to the meet, as if she were immune to danger. I think the days of violent terror she'd lived through in early years, with sand dervishes and mad boys had made her immune to fear.

I landed neatly in the service yard and debarked. As the engines wound down, the wide gated shutter of tin fluttered up and eight men of a standard merc detail jumped out and escorted Wren and me inside. A large echoey warehouse was busy with motion, tall upright machines and long low vats, looking like stitching and dyeing equipment to me, and some robot assembly machinery stamping out circuits. Pazarol met me with a meaty hand, a big rubicund man with a gleaming pate and a fuzz of blond hair at the back. He wore a starchly-ironed blue plaid suit, polished black shoes, gaudy necktie, all smelling of cigar smoke. Protruding buck teeth dominated his face, goatee hanging from a snub chin. I had no reason to dislike the man on first meeting, but nonetheless I did.

He motioned to his assembly plant with what could have been a gesture of pride. "This is my side business," he said, spreading a sweaty palm at the production line of boys and young women working fingers to bone to manufacture heavy clothing and boots, others fastening bolts and small latches to what looked like equipment scanners of some sort.

"You mean, 'front'?"

"Sure, whatever you want to call it, Rusco. Why argue over details?"

"No reason." A half dozen gunmen idled by, toying with their remodeled Uzis, lazy yawns on their thick lips, evincing casual interest, sleeping lions, but I knew better. I could sense they were wire alert, their lazy, easy steps too light, their sleek bodies too toned, their quick fingers too close to the triggers. To Pazarol's side, two of his men seemed to be paying more attention to the banter, one tall, swarthy, and sleazy looking with short greased hair; the other shorter, stockier, with down-turned brows and slicked back grey mullet and wearing small round glasses.

"A man needs a legitimate business in this world," asserted Pazarol, "otherwise he's got nothing, right? A few scams giving him a bit of bread now and then. His heist money always running low; no investments, nothing to fall back on, and the wolves, the opportunists, the terrorists, the hired government guard, whatever's left of them, coming out of the woodwork like termites, asking awkward questions."

I just smiled.

"Something tells me you never really got a business going

yourself, did you, Rusco?...you should try it."

"On the to-do list, Mr. Pazarol, earmarked for a rainy day."

"That's good!" He wheezed, slapped me on the back. A bad smoker's cough. I'd give him five years, no more.

I wondered when he'd broach particulars about the job. This was his game, feeling out his new personnel, gauging the reactions, sparring with bullshit, testing reflexes, even though he was doing all the talking.

"Hire 'em cheap, work 'em hard," he went on. "Rusco, that's my credo. Watch and learn. No labor costs here. Look at these patsies. They're a bunch of dumb, happy freaks. I give 'em room and board—for the price of protection."

It was a sweatshop in the worst of ways. I saw frightened eyes, young boys, battered women with bruised cheeks or a blackened eye, the cocky guards walking about with Uzis, cracking jokes, ogling the prettier women.

"Get out your lumo pen, Rusco!" Pazarol laughed. "I'll let you take notes for a limited time, no extra charge."

I clenched my teeth, a part of me vowing to come back to this dumphole and free every one of those slave laborers. Blow Pazarol's enterprise to kingdom come. "What's this they're making? Looks like army clothes."

"Boots and combat fatigues. Guerilla outerwear for all sorts. High demand for merchandise like this in these times. A lot of traditional guerrillas, aka war thugs, are doing assaults on land."

"No doubt." I moved over and hefted a boot on a rack. Brown leather, durable, super light. Fast for runners in the bush, swamps or other onerous terrain.

"There's an extra kick in those babies, for sure." Pazarol shook out his fingers, bragging. "A barb with nerve toxin stub on the toe. One kick to exposed flesh and the victim is paralyzed, dies in twenty seconds."

"Nice." I set the boot down, wincing. He picked up a pair of fresh fatigues a nervous woman had sewn a battery pack to and motioned to the hand-sized circuit box wired to the back collar.

"This khaki blends into whatever environment a combat soldier is in. Brown bush, grey concrete, red sunset, don't matter. A phosphoro-gluten plant-based resin coats the inside surface. This doohickey on the back, a black box, sends the signal down to the plant membranes or whatever, telling it what form to take. Right down to the color, texture. Big seller. The rage these days. Touch it. It's realistic."

"I'll pass. Seems impressive though."

"Ah, a cautious man."

I offered no comment.

"I'll throw in a pair for you as a freebie, my token of appreciation and good faith. What size? Oh, you look about a ten." He grabbed a new suit off the storage rack and plunged it too into my hands." He eyed me, seeing how I'd react.

"Who's this lovely young lad you got here? Hiding behind your skirts like a bashful choir boy."

"This here's Wren—as in the bird."

"A mighty fine bird, that. Got her all dressed up like an army brat and what, with a fuck-boy cut? Surprises me, Rusco. Didn't peg you going for that. I'm liking what I see. Got to get me a fuck-boy."

"Very funny," I said and Wren growled her contempt. In spite of the rudeness of the remark, I let a dog snicker of grin brush my face. *Get on Paz's good side. It'll give you an edge in this fencing. Let Wren get a little sore, no harm.* Dressed in khakis and looking as unlady-like as possible, Wren was well, Wren.

"How 'bout it, sister?" He motioned to the fatigues. "You want a pair?"

"No, thanks," she said. "Might make me too sexy in front of your boys and give them some unwelcome ideas."

He snuffled out a laugh. "A good wit on her, Rusco. I like her. Better hang on to her. She's a good one."

"That she is."

His expression turned serious in a second.

"They're a trigger happy bunch of bitches down in the desert where you'll be going—desert mongrels, primitives holed up on a hot planet too long. So don't go getting any ideas to wise-guy them or do a double-cross. You'll guard the shipment, make sure things go smooth as olive oil. They'll string your nuts up on their voodoo-crossed banyans faster than you can spit prune pits out your ass, if you get on their bad side."

"I'll keep that in mind."

"Take Raez here with you. I want him and Gris to report all operations direct."

I looked over at the shifty man with the cold grin on his face. "No deal. Don't know him from Adam."

"Tough titty. Either Raez goes with you or no deal and you can walk and we'll never cross paths again. A one time offer."

I chewed my lip, pretending to hem and haw over it. I studied Raez, with the slicked-back hair, thin nose and beefy cheeks, wondering how I could dislike the man even more than Pazarol, without him having opened his mouth. The wide stance, the 'I don't-give-a-fuck' attitude conveyed through the animal eyes, the challenging, bad-boy posture, it was a subliminal code of 'screw with me and you die' I'd picked up from experience. I ought to discuss it with TK and Wren, my partners, but there was no time. If I waffled here, Pazarol would look elsewhere and the deal would disintegrate, and a part of me vied to play longer. I gave a slow nod.

"Wise choice, Rusco. Now, more facts of life: Grisheimer, aka Gris, will be called in to run the main freighter and oversee a team of my own boys—hand picked." He motioned to the older shiftless fellow with penetrating owl-like eyes, the slack jowl, gangly limbs, but no less violent a man than Raez—the kind that would slit your throat and ask questions later for less reason than a dirty look. "He'll act as navigator on the Urgon, the freighter out back, and backup for the handling, pick up and drop of the cargo. In case things go ape and you fuck up, Rusco, Gris will carry out the rest of the plan."

I could see Pazarol was a prudent man, an arranger, despite his fat, friendly airs. He liked to cover his bases, though with an arrogance and pride that stank up the air from here to Perseus. Nor did I like the idea of 'brother' Raez hobgobbling about my ship with his foul breath polluting the air. Something odd about the man, and something odd about this job in general; it seemed off from the start. Raez's greasy look, Paz's all too easy gestures and his quick impulse to fast-track this job and dish out roles without any discussion at all. A wiser man would listen to advice and input from the players, and never take on a fresh hireling so readily, at least without a test. Perhaps that was in the works. I got the crazy idea Paz'd gotten wind of something I wasn't aware of. So my first warning was triggered. "You still haven't told me what it is we're carrying or where it is to be transported."

"We fly Urgon from Besi 6 to Jasmel, plus your ship to guard. It's enough to transfer the product. Fareon beam replacements, extended range, kills starfleas dead. That and raw Beryllium crystal needed to manufacture the beams. Need you to pick up raw product in Gizren on Besi then deliver that plus a full load of the replacement parts to Jasmel. I got me some full fareon beams in the back for shipment to the same source. But that's another story."

I stifled a grimace. *How's it feel, Rusco, to be giving your friendly neighborhood warlord like Mong a helping hand in the arm's race? Maybe it could have been you down on Megal when the bombs dropped?* The automatic voice rattled in my head: *Well, if it isn't you, it's some other slimeball playing delivery boy.*

Yet somehow these circular kind of reasonings didn't soothe me. More than ever I wished I'd never walked into Pazarol's warehouse.

"Sounds pretty heavy. What's in it for me?"

"You'd be looking at 10 Gs if everything works out. As for risk, plenty of raiders out there. Those are lawless territories. We'll need firepower to keep our investment protected. The ore freighter can move at impulse power only, sub warp, no more. It's more than she was made for, but will move her from Besi 6 to Jasmel space in a week or more."

"Skurgian raiders always find a hole."

He chuckled. "As for the split, it's a three-way deal. The Tanza boys at Gizren'll take their cut plus a few bribes along the way. I take mine, and you get yours."

"So, why don't you do this yourself?" I asked. "You seem to have capable men. What do you need me for?"

"That's the complex part, Rusco, nothing's ever straightforward. I got other business commitments going on. My team's maybe not so savvy in foreign affairs. Blinky says you're competent. You wouldn't be here if I didn't trust him and his good word."

"Sure, and what's the real reason?"

He looked at me for a second, wearing a feral scowl, gripping his goatee. "I need a shamster down there to grease the wheels and make this work. Dammit! I don't trust those Tanza boys—always fighting and scrapping amongst each other like a pack of wild dogs. Stringing each other up in banyans and letting the buzzards gnaw at them. This's a rush job here. We need the crystals right now to make fareon boosters. Or this buyer, a certain 'Dark Angel', will go elsewhere. I don't want to lose this deal. As I've said, you've got a reputation. So I took Blinky's recommendation to heart."

"I'm flattered."

"Don't be. Just get the job done and everybody's good, and maybe there's more where that came from."

"Let's cross that bridge when the time comes."

"Don't get cocky, Rusco. You're wanted by a dozen agencies and cartels around the galaxy. Men who'll have you snuffed out for a yol if they catch up with you. On lists galore." He snuffled a laugh. "A bounty hunter's dream. Your reputation precedes you—grand larceny, willful destruction of property, first degree murder, assault, border jumping, explosives, on and on." His face took on a brighter cast. "What I'm saying, Rusco, you're my kind of shyster. Welcome to the club." He patted my arm.

Somehow I was not liking being on Pazarol's 'good' side. The man was a slimy *douchebag*, even slimier than the lower echelon of thugs I sometimes did business with.

"The Tanza boys won't just take a simple cash deal. They'll want to escort the load too, or some fool thing like that. I want you to thwart them, if possible. It just muddies the pie. Convince them otherwise. I don't care just as long as the shipment makes it on time and in one piece."

"I'm mulling it over, Pazarol."

He gave me a cold inspection. I'd seen less predatory looks on steel-fanged viper fish.

"Tell me more about the product," I asked.

"Fresh tech, a quarter price. Fresh off the black market. Double the range, fareon state-of-the-art. Got a bunch of the devices here."

"Do I get one?"

"If you say pretty please and suck my dick." He looked around, enjoying the snickers of his henchmen. "For you I might swing a deal, with that lady friend thrown in on the side. One of the boys at the other end might equip you with a choicer one, once you've got the job done."

I shafted him a glare much like a wolf before it leaps in to rend the rabbit.

"Just kidding, Rusco. Wipe that murderous grimace off your face. Geez, you're a humorless man. This client I've got a deal with'll take the crystals and enhanced beams without fuss. An up and coming space bully. Thinks he's Captain Jojo, going to take over the universe."

"One of those at every transhub."

"You betcha. Keeps us in business." He laughed it off, a sour, hacking cough. "Wants raw crystal as well to manufacture his own weaponry. I shake my head, say, 'I can do it for you cheaper' and he says, 'no, I want to manage the trade myself'. I say, 'Okay, I can deal, half in advance', he says, 'Fine'. First rule of business, Rusco, is please the customer. Clichéd, but true. A sale is a sale." He looked at me with a cock-eyed grin.

I didn't know why he was telling me all this. I think it's one of those good guy ploys: let the new guy in town think he's more important than he is, some bigger part of the overall picture, then he'll work harder for you, stay loyal.

Pazarol's harsh voice tipped me out of my musing. "Okay, that's out of the way. What's your plan of operation?"

It was too late to back out. That time'd passed an hour ago. Suddenly I didn't want to deal any more.

"We'll go in as negotiators, me, Wren, Raez, pack weapons and explosives, in case things get ugly. We don't want things going haywire."

"Whatever, just as long as you don't damage my product."

"What do you think I am, an amateur?"

"Just so we're on the same page," he grumbled. He patted my arm a second time. He put his mouth close to my ear, spoke in a confiding whisper. "Take care, Ruski. On the off chance you sidewind me, I might become one of those mean-ass bounty hunters after your hide."

"We wouldn't want that, would we?"

Chapter 13

Back on the bridge, things were escalating. Wren was all over me about what went down in pig Pazarol's crib, even though I assured her it was all just show. We'd suffered another close scrape under impulse power by what I guessed were Baer's bounty hunters: two ships we'd barely evaded before a jump to hyperspace'd saved our hides. Why was Baer riding our asses so closely? Then again, I had blown off the guy's arm.

"Those bastards are everywhere at once," I muttered under my breath.

"And why shouldn't they be?" Wren growled. "Either they must have tracked us prior to the last repairs, or the Barenium's still leaking."

"Maybe somebody tipped them off," suggested TK.

Wren waved a hand. "If you hadn't brought that piece of shit microchip bad luck aboard, we'd be in none of this mess."

"That again?" I groaned. Shaking my head, I wished I'd never let them in on that tech. What one didn't know, couldn't hurt him, right? A shuffle of boot sounded behind me. I turned, scowling to see Raez hovering there like a ghoul. "What do you want?"

"I just wanted to check if we were good with the transshipment. We're going in tandem, right—or you going solo? Think you should put me on lead. Wren as backup, you to man the ship. What do you think, Rusco?" He gave her a lascivious look.

My fists clenched in an involuntary ball. "We already discussed that, *Raez*. I go in with Wren, you're backup. You keep your mouth shut. Remember, you're only here as a courtesy."

"Just wanted to double check."

Yeah, double check my ass. Any bit of eavesdropping you can do, you'll do, you piece of shit. I flashed Wren a warning glance, but she didn't seem to pick up on it.

Raez was one of those weasely types, slicked-back hair, thin jaw, who hangs out as a lurker, the smiling, grinning predator who looks for any trusting person or piece of interesting dirt that he can dig up, one that can be useful. I feared his sleazy habit would spill over into his work.

I had to put this apprehension aside. This was business and once the deal was over, I'd set the bastard down on the nearest transhub and be done with it. "Okay, let's go through the motions again. I don't want any margin of error."

Within moments, Raez sighed and threw down the map I'd drawn out painstakingly by hand. "Listen, we pick up the merchandise from this Gizren place on Besi, at what, 08:00? Why's it so hard? Dolgra or Dogface, and his Tanza boys'll be there with heavy guns, wanting insurance and money up front. We move in, take it aboard, guide the freighter, do whatever the hell those monkeys want done. If we get our jobs done, nobody gets hurt and everything rolls like a greased wheel."

"Yeah, exactly, if everyone gets their jobs done." I leveled him a stare.

"And what're you insinuating?"

"Exactly what it sounds like. It means let's study the map another time, and a hundredth time if we have to. I don't want any screw ups on this."

"Alright already. Don't get your tubes in a knot."

"Up yours, Raez. I'm sick of your wise-assing about. Either you up your game, or I ship you back to daddy Paz. Let him cater to your moods."

The others tensed.

Raez glared at me for a time, his mouth working in a mincy little line. He did his huffy routine, shifting from foot to foot, quivering and looking all mean, as if he were some big shot mobster. Then as I stared him down, daring him to go further, he backed down like a coward. It wasn't a subtle thing, just a change of psycho-physical energy in the air palpable to all. One I knew well. One of which I seemed to be in more command. He settled down in a snit, shook out his grease-slicked hair. But I could tell his nose was out of joint on this one and he'd be looking for some way to gain face. Let the man sulk, for fuck's sake. What did I care?

* * *

Besi 6 was a sparsely-populated, impoverished world closest to the sun Jesra. The biggest city, Tyaan, had more outdoor markets than any in the solar system, the bazaar capital of the solar system, but the rest of the planet was just scattered villages in a dry, windswept sandbath.

Because of its poverty, Besi had been spared the scars and gutting of war like the multi-citied worlds. But there were some heavy players with goods to sell and hustles to go. We were going straight into the heart of the wild, trigger-happy western tribes that spanned the arid gulches, the parched, baking wasteland.

Pazarol had mentioned the dominant tribe, the Gedra, known to extort the smaller clans of their exports, which they called 'protection fees' or some kind of fool tax for being in their territory. The Tanza of Gizren, of course, refused to pay, so I hoped we didn't have trouble with any of them this day.

Starrunner and Urgon rode low over the dust-cloaked valley. It was wide and swept with low dunes of fine, white sand. To the side snaked a ridge of pale red outcrops and black-flecked rock. On the other side, a long, thin lake, or what looked like a body of dark, greasy water, lurked. Probably caked with alien salt and poisons of high concentration.

Urgon landed at the base of the ridge where a group of rusted tin outbuildings clustered and what seemed an abandoned oil rig. But I kept Starrunner back, closer to the oily water for reasons I attributed to pure instinct. Two ships parked off to the other side of the rig: a sleek silver Sphinx, and a grey Markest, both looking in good working order.

The engines wound down and Wren and I jumped down in the stifling heat to meet the sellers, with Raez trotting at our heels. Wren carried the funds Pazarol had given us in a black bag. Raez seemed quick to make a show of the armed bulge at his hip, the R4, as if he were a real cowboy. I forbore comment on that.

The Urgon's loading hatch dropped and Grisheimer, efficient as a bulldog, clumped out with two of his heavily-armed men to stand at either side. Their AKs gleamed in the sun while the pilot stayed on the bridge, keeping the ship online in case a quick getaway was necessary.

Eight Tanza guards stood loitering about the rig, carrying a mix of submachine guns and semi-automatics; a few might have been women among that motley lot. Hard to tell from this distance. Their hair was tied up in flat brown fur caps, and no help either the baggy clothes that hid a lot of telltales. Rake-thin desert types, bronzed skin, yellow-bleached hair from decades of sun.

The steel-mill trestle-thing poked up from a low mound in the sand, like some twisted grasshopper of an earlier age. The gears worked, and a grinding, back-grating whir of an engine at high rpms brought a giant, metal, pear-shaped gourd up on heavy chains. An operator worked a side lever; chains and clamps tipped the thing lengthwise into a massive lode cart, dumping the raw, small blue crystals in without ceremony.

Some of the miners did not look good—pale, haggard and hacking with dry, rasping coughs. I only guessed the beryllium or whatever derivative of it they mined, was not the healthiest of substances. They started up the six-wheeled tractor that hauled the massive lode cart.

I caught a fleeting glimpse of the dark stuff as it tumbled into the loader, sending shrill echoes up the rugged ridge. A rare mineral combo of emerald, beryllium, quartz, and something else. Whatever the case, it didn't look too stable. I was glad the smugglers' freighter would be carrying it, and not my ship. Maybe I'd take a rain check on the 'enhanced' fareon beam for now.

The Tanza crew met Wren, me, and Raez at the foot of the loader, as the freighter's engine, noisy in age and construction, ramped down and its four landing struts sank deeper into the sand. Grisheimer signaled for the man inside to shorten the ramp to facilitate the cargo transfer.

Hardened, blunt-nosed men worked the ore cart's hatch to get the stuff dropped inside.

"These thugs look like regular guerillas." I whispered, indicating the foremost gunmen, wrapped in their tan, camel hides, roped at the waist, each with an Uzi slung over a shoulder, another gripped in hand.

Wren snorted. "More like the local terror guard hired to keep the crystal from getting snatched."

"And? You got a problem with that?" snarled Raez. "What universe do you subscribe to, woman?"

"Shut up, both of you," I hissed. "They're coming closer."

The young chief met us, waving in gruff, blunt manner. "Welcome. I didn't expect you on time. I'm Dolgra. On Besi, nobody is on time."

"Well, we are," I grunted. "My name's Rusco."

I couldn't help but notice the patch of trees, three stubby ones, on which hung grungy patches of blackened flesh of what had once been human.

The chief peered to where I was looking. "Those are ones who thought to betray our interests. Reminders of doom, a powerful incentive for obedience on Besi."

"No doubt."

Dolgra seemed smaller than the other tribesmen, lighter boned and with a face that at first glance seemed feminine: the fine nose, the soft eyes, the delicate lashes, all were testament to a misconceived gender. But on deeper inspection the layers of sinew on his oiled biceps and forearms showed muscle that'd been amassed after years of hard discipline. One of his dog-faced men pulled off his cap to wipe his sweaty brow and I saw darker hair underneath. So, they were not all fair. Many were lank-limbed with shaved chins, and there was a curious slant to their eyes, wide-spaced like oxen, but their skin and bodies were as lean as greyhounds and toughened from generations of stinking hot sun.

"You have all the Beryllium crystal?"

The chief held up a hand. "Here... Wait, you fools!" he yelled up at his loading men, then faced us. "You have the money?"

Smoke from a nearby village curled farther down the valley. I guessed they lived up in the rugged hills. The 80k yols they were due, and the 120k later when the buyer paid out, would be nothing less than a small fortune. I jerked my head to the bag Wren clutched. "In there. All 80k yols."

"Good. Let me see."

"I unzipped the leather bag and held it up for the chief's inspection.

His emerald eyes twinkled with greed. He curled a finger in beckoning. "Pass it over."

"First load up the merchandise," I insisted.

The chief shrugged. He gave a brief signal to his men. The loader jerked forward.

I frowned. There were only five hulking bins sitting tucked away to the side that looked anything like a stash of valuable ore. "Is this all of it?" I demanded. I'd expected more.

The chief scowled and fluttered his fingers. "There were complications. My workers are this minute digging out the last of the beryllium crystal." He motioned to his other loader and his men began tractoring the five heaping carts into Urgon's hold.

Raez's mouth quivered in slack-jawed anger. "Is this a joke, Dolgra? We had an agreement."

Dolgra showed a line of brown teeth. "Couldn't be helped. You're getting the goods at a fair price, so consider yourself lucky. Be patient."

"Patient?" Raez cried, flinging a hand down at his bulging hip. "We're running on a tight deadline here. If this deal goes south because of your incompetence—"

"Relax," I growled at Raez, grabbing his arm while lancing him a warning glare.

Raez grunted and wrenched his arm free. "Don't patronize me, asshole. Lay hands on me again, Rusco, and you'll regret it. These fucking grease balls are trying to dick us around, don't you see it? Pazarol is going to be eating monkey nuts for breakfast when—"

"Shut the hell up," I hissed. I turned to Dolgra, showing my most amiable face. "How long for the rest of the shipment? Two hours, maybe four?"

He shrugged. "Probably longer."

I wagged my head. "Well, nothing we can do about it. We kick back and relax."

"What do you mean, 'kick back and relax'?" uttered Raez. "No we can't just 'kick back and relax', you lamebrain. Paz said—"

"I don't give a flying fuck what 'Paz' said," I rasped. "Things are never optimal, Raez. Paz should have allowed for some contingencies."

"And he didn't." The thug's hand went for his R4. The clink of metal sounded all around as Dolgra's men trained barrels on us.

I held up my hands, smiling like a cornered cat. "Okay…let's all calm down. No need for violence." *Shit, this is going badly. That pissbrain, Raez. No wonder Paz-ass couldn't trust his own men to handle this.*

"Control your dog, Mr. Rusco," said Dolgra, "otherwise, there'll be blood on the sand today."

I glared at Raez. "You heard the man."

A whine of engines came screeching out of the sky. Two V-Zon cruisers arched down armed to the teeth with glinting armor. I shook my head in dismay. *What else could go wrong?*

"Who are they?" Wren croaked.

"Gedra." Dolgra swore. "They'll want a cut." He whirled on his aide beside him. "Vespie, I thought you said we were clean? Didn't you scout out the area?"

"They must have slipped underneath our radar, chief. Cloakers."

"That's unacceptable!"

"How much do they want?" I asked.

"Probably 30% which is the usual Gedra tax."

"No fucking way, Dole-face," Raez snorted. "Stall them, or kill them. It's up to you, or this deal's off."

Weapons came up, half on the approaching ships, the others cocked on Raez and me. Dolgra scowled, face curling in an indecisive snarl. "The deal stands, or you'll be strung in those trees minus two arms."

"See, I told you so," whined Raez. "While these morons were out sunbathing by the lake, we could've loaded up and been out of here. Now what's your plan, Rusco? You going to leap around, do a rain dance or something?"

"Shut up, I'm thinking."

"Think fast, because—"

The first Gedra ship landed nearby kicking up dust; four armored men stormed out, clutching rifles and home-grown grenades in fists that were big, ugly, olive-colored weapons, the size of melons.

The first man spoke in a guttural accent, "This is most irregular, Dolgra. You know Chief Jzrend's policy. Report all goods to the central authority—or...."

"I can pay next time, Avloz. Not this time."

"Famous excuses." The Gedra smiled and gave his head a sad shake. "No deal. Make that 40% cut this time, for insolence and wasting our time."

I approached with a breezy confidence. "No need to bat heads, gentlemen." I hefted the bag of yols. Putting on my most disarming smile, I let my words spew out in typical Rusco fashion. "I bet you boys are getting what, a tenth of a percent of your shakedown? if that, even if you are on salary? Let's sweeten the pot." Let a competitor think he's getting a better deal, he'll be all for it, and think you're on his side.

But there was no chance to explore that angle.

Raez whipped out his R4 and sprayed bullets into the midst, taking off the head of the first Gedra. The others in his troupe fired, dropping two of Dolgra's guards.

Weapons exploded from all sides. Grenades launched in the air. I ducked. Reached out to pull Wren back. Shrapnel tore at the closest Gedra and skimmed off Starrunner's back plates. Lucky that I'd set her down farther away.

Another grenade landed closer to our payload and the flames licked out at the Urgon. Grisheimer was yelling, "Shit! Back to the ship!"

I spoke harsh words into the com as I ran, "TK, get Starrunner running!" Grisheimer's man got Urgon airborne, even as metal was flying by me. I caught a glimpse of Dolgra scrambling for the silver Sphinx, dodging bullets all the way. Some of his men caught lead and fell like flies.

TK already had the hatch open as Wren and I zigzagged along, dodging shells and firing back over our shoulders.

One of the Gedra air guard flew over us, raining bullets and spraying death. I hunched, crouching behind a dune, my AK trained on some movement to my right. Wren and Raez fell in behind, sucking in labored breaths. The leather on my right arm was torn and blood flowed. Raez had an ugly slash across his left cheek from shrapnel that had grazed him. Good. All of us were soot-covered from the blast.

"You idiot, sabotaging our venture?" I wheezed at the acrid stench. "Whose side are you on?"

"None, from where I'm looking," Wren spat, blood curling from her lip.

Raez spat. "I at least, had the guts to do what neither of you chickenshits did—blast those bitches away."

I lifted a fist. "I could have smoothed it out, fed them a line and given those messenger boys some baksheesh and it would have ended smoothly."

"You think? I highly doubt that given the size of the load they'd—"

"Quit bitching and let's get to the ship," Wren cried.

An opening presented itself. The crouching Gedra were concentrating on the Urgon, raking it with fire.

I grinned. "Lick your wounds later, Raez. Let's shake a leg, get back to the ship, if you want to live."

"I don't take orders from you." Raez lifted his barrel, my eyes darting to a furtive movement several paces away. An enemy creeping up behind my back. For a second there, I thought Raez was going to cap me. Instead he blew the stalker's eyes out.

The Gedra desert men stepped out from behind the sand dunes, spraying fire. That rat-a-tat of enemy fire was a hollow echo of nightmare to me. I knew one day one of those slugs would catch me in the wrong place and it would be all over. Would it be today?

I shook off the pending image. The second enemy ship was in the air, taking sporadic shots at our freighter which nicked the underbelly's cowling. I cringed, my heart lurching. If that ship went down…but obviously they just wanted to paralyze Urgon and spare the expensive cargo. Metal plates fell off her stern.

We came staggering up Starrunner's ramp, as I smashed the hatch button closed. TK got us airborne. How that rat-bastard Raez, huffing at our heels, had managed to survive the shells and bullets and flames mystified me. He'd done some kind of crouching dance, half snaking his way through fire flares and managed to avoid the onslaught. I raced to the bridge, took the controls, and swept TK out of the way. Raez came stumbling in, trailing blood, gaping at the viewport like some dumb animal.

As soon as I had wrested the controls from TK, I veered us about in a desperate hairpin. Wren stayed at the weapons console, sighted on the closest Gedra ship and blasted it to pieces.

Dolgra's T-Arathron Sphinx came looping after us, a silver, glittering T-bone shape with modern engines, souped up forward thrusters, like the old rad-rockets of the first generation. We still hadn't paid the chief Dolgra, so I guessed he'd be pissed. Going to be a shitload of angry parties before this was all over.

Wren aimed her Uzi at Raez. "You stupid ass, you have some gall. What were you trying to pull down there?"

"Things got a little out hand, bitch, no big deal. Mind your manners. Nothing that can't be fixed."

"Fixed? What shit are you pulling? The devil's got new horns, with you wasting Gedra, now the deal's shot to hell."

"No it isn't. We can salvage it," I said. "No thanks to Raez here."

Raez bowed, flashed a cheeky grin. "Cap'n, I am duly sorry and hope you'll accept my humblest apologies."

My fists turned white. "That smug shit isn't going to work here, Raez. It comes out of your share—or Pazarol's."

Raez shrugged. "Kind of like the minnow telling the shark to go bring him some fresh mackerel." He spat a wad on the metal tiles. "Big P ain't going to like that."

"Tough titty on big P," Wren roared.

Chapter 14

We escaped Besi 6's gravity and the freighter limped along, its starboard flank smoking. Dogra's lightweight Ultra dogged us, weaving in and out, weapons spraying fire.

"Rusco," Dolgra's voice screamed over the com. "I want my yols."

"You'll get it," I grumbled. "You expected me to waltz over there and hand it to you in the middle of a firefight?"

"If this is a doublecross—"

"Relax. Let's plan on a rendezvous somewhere nearby once we clear Gizren's gravity. Say Mora-Vaille, on the way to the dropoff point. You wanted to play escort, so this'll work out for you."

"One condition—" Dolgra's wheezing voice played over the com. "Two of my men go aboard Urgon to ensure safe passage and fair play."

"Fine by me."

"Like hell it's fine!" Raez shook his greasy head as he came crowding behind me, breathing down my neck. "That wasn't the deal."

"It is now," I barked at him. "Get back and let me handle this."

"Gris will never allow it." The man glared about like a wolf, shafting me a venomous look. His gaze shifted to TK, clacking away at the keys. "What're you looking at, old codger?"

TK turned, brows raised.

"Yeah, you—the one who looks like head librarian around here."

TK's lips pressed in a firm line. "Quaint, very quaint."

"Cap'n Jet put you up as a charity case?" He laughed at his own quip. No laughter came back. "Oi..! Are you guys just a bunch of stiffs?"

"No, we just have a higher bar for humor," said Wren.

I wondered if I should be worried about Raez walking around freely with that piece at his hip. I moved over to him. "Hand over your weapon."

"Say what?"

"You heard me. No loaded firearms on my ship."

He scowled down at my R4. "What about your piece then, and hers?"

"I'm the captain and she's the first mate."

Wren covered him while I held out my hand. With reluctance he unstrapped it and tossed it over.

I locked the guns from the weapons rack in the forward bulkhead with Raez's and motioned him back. "I'll show you to your quarters." And here my mouth slackened in a smirk. There being no spare private cabins, I took Raez to the most grimy, cluttered space by the hold with a rat-chewed mattress and rusty pipes rattling on the wall. I threw a couple of old dusty shipping blankets at him. It'd have to do, and I owed this miserable troublemaker nothing. "Head's in the fore, not pretty in there, but I'm sure you'll manage." I left him seething and grumbling in the dimness, then I made my way back to the bridge.

While Starrunner and Urgon had made some distance from Besi 6, we set out for the outer planets with four-fifths of our shipment. I looked over at Wren while the darkening feeling churned in the pit of my stomach. The old maxim of what doesn't feel right, ain't right thundered like a storm. Of course, Gris had refused to let Dolgra's men board Urgon so I ended up parking at the space station orbiting Mora to give Dolgra his yols while Urgon sped ahead at subwarp.

As I charted our course to catch up, while checking and

rechecking our rendezvous with Jasmel, something gnawed at me. I knew we'd never make that destination. Why? Call it the voice of intuition that speaks in the dead of night when one wakes in a lucid moment. Everything was in order, and yet that disturbing hunch beamed like a hooker's red light. Things had been barely smoothed over with Pazarol an hour ago! Raez had done his best to highlight how botched our job had been under my direction and we possessed only a portion of our cargo. I explained to Pazarol how it was impossible to go back to Gizren and get the rest of our freight without incurring casualties and risking the rest of the shipment. The Gedra would cap our asses and we'd have nothing to show for it, without less than an army to cut through that rat swarm.

Long story short, the deal would proceed as planned, but with a third less payout. Okay, I could run with that, as this was our highest paying gig thus far, even split three ways, and I didn't want to jeopardize it. Raez didn't seem to care much at the lesser payout; he seemed to be in it for the kicks. A strange sentiment—but a hell of a lot more interesting than hobgoblining around that gloomy warehouse on Tarsus.

I stayed on the bridge. The others had gone off to their quarters, and my tired eyes were seeing fuzzy shapes while the ship stayed steady on Molly's autopilot.

As I was making for my cabin while we kept up with Urgon, I heard voices down the corridor. Wren's husky voice was raised, an audible murmur.

I crept down the passage, paused before the next corridor, my jaw set.

"How about it, Fox?" came a familiar weasely voice. "What's say you and me slip between the sheets, keep each other warm? I know you and the cap may have something going, but no worries. He isn't about to hear it from me and I won't ruin your gig."

I caught the pregnant pause, then guessed Wren, for a second, had considered the sleazy offer and had almost given in.

Then I heard her stony hiss. "Buzz, off, creep. I don't like your smell or your oily smile."

I smiled at that. Raez put up a fuss and spewed a bunch of spuriously offensive words, like 'sloe-eyed bitch', and 'pissy dike', so I stepped in, putting on a look of innocent concern.

"Everything all right here? Wren, you okay?"

Raez's face lit up in a mocking grin. "No worries, cappie. Me and the bosomy lady were just getting to know each other better, weren't we, Wren? I like to get under the skin of the people I'm working with." The man's patronizing, piss-licking grin made me want to plow him.

Raez was one of those ungracious, low-class weasels who hung out at the casinos looking for easy lays—not that there was anything wrong with that—I'd done a few myself. Those feel-good-about-yourself screws, but there was a way to do it, with a certain modicum of class. Everything in this schmuck's aura spoke of loutishness. A regular wise guy with some black and white around the edges. Irritant Raez, egging for a rude awakening. This little soap opera reminded me of some cornball vid back in that ancient earth collection I used to watch when having nothing better to do.

Raez put up a bit of a fuss, me muscling into his game, but it wasn't anything I couldn't handle. He stomped off with a bruised cheek and some ruffled pride to his hidey hole.

I followed Wren back to her cabin, keeping an eye on the lady. "Anything you'd like to tell me?"

"No."

In the end we had a little nightcap, featuring some gin she'd snuck from the hamper. "Didn't think you'd mind, Ruskie, one bottle missing."

I shrugged. "What do you think of our unwanted guest, Mr. Raez?"

"A bottom feeder." She grimaced. "I've known sleaze bags like him before. Think he's trouble."

"Agreed. He almost got us killed."

She snuffled out a noncommittal sound.

"So you think we should—"

"Forget that rat, let's think about us." She crept closer and undid her tight leather then my shirt, her lashes fluttering, full lips parted in a breathless purr.

"Good plan," I murmured.

Wren's tomboyish energy was more feral feline tonight and I had trouble keeping up with her. After a rousing interlude, I stumbled back to my cabin, a bit bowlegged. On contact with the hard foam, I sighed and went to sleep.

I awoke in the middle of the night, victim of a bad dream. Aliens, or some sort of freaks—those shoulder-high walking mantises that TK had described so eloquently—walked unseen. Mixed with that terrifying glimpse I'd seen out on the journey to nowhere with the phaso, it was a lethal combination. I shivered and shook off the memory, sitting up on my bed, wiping my dry eyes. A cold sweat had broken out around my neck. That bad feeling resurfaced, that larger-than-life feeling that something vastly unpleasant was brewing. It seemed contagious. I reached for my bottle of redneck Black Bull gin stashed under the bed and chug-a-lugged. Made my gut sour. Winced. Took another swig. That didn't go down well either. My gut was burning.

I donned my brown captain's leathers and did my patrol rounds, making for the bridge. The console lights burned brightly and I caught the old man hunched over one of the command tables, deep in concentration. Billy was at his side, making little grunting sounds like a curious chimp.

TK jerked up and gave me a guilty look. "Hey, Jet. How's the night watch?"

"What the hell are you doing?" I cried.

"Relax. Just checking out the inscriptions on this device."

My jaw dropped when I saw what he was working on and the iridescent flash of a familiar disc. "You sneaking bastard. I told you to leave that thing alone—"

"Couldn't. Managed to trace some info on the central free store,

Mentera lore, and figured I could backtrace some of the coordinates and test it out some."

"Are you fucking insane? That thing's deadly."

"No worries, I've got it all under control."

"You think? I don't give a piss in the wind what you're thinking. Put it back."

"Just another few minutes, Jet. I've almost got a handle on it—"

I pulled my sleeve over my hand and swept the shimmering disc off the table, away from his grasping hand before he could tweezer it with those rods he held.

All the time Billy's watching and getting more agitated, blinking with his googly eyes, moving from side to side like an adder, wringing his wrists and making funny little sounds in the back of his throat.

The kid reached over and grabbed at that spinning top as if it were some toy. The old man cried out. TK lunged to stop him, but it was too late. Some combination of buttons and coordinates the boy touched and he was gone in a crackling haze of dusty color. The disc rolled, spun to a stop, glaring up at us like an evil eye.

The old man's mouth worked in a rictus but no sound came out.

I swore. "I'm locking this destructo up."

"Look at what you've done!" He clutched at his hair.

"You're the bright one brought it out," I stormed. "I told you the thing was dangerous."

He looked at me with shock then began rooting through the bulkheads, rummaging through hatches, searching for Billy like a madman before he dropped to his knees. "No! He's got to be here somewhere!" The halfwit's disappearance was tearing him apart.

I rounded up the strongbox underneath the sensor panel and used my sleeve to put the phaso in there. I locked the lid.

"We've got to get him back!" TK's pathetic wail raised my hackles.

"Fat chance," I gusted. "Move away. Nothing you can do." I knew I should have hid that strongbox better, remembering the eager glint in TK's eye when I locked up that nasty little device, but it had slipped my mind.

I heard bootfall behind me. I whirled to behold *Raez*. Great timing to stroll in. How long had the slug been there eavesdropping?

He gave a low whistle. "A little love squabble? Where's the kid?"

"What do you care?" I growled.

Raez stared at TK hard, hand pressed to his mouth. "Granddad, you gone and done something to him? You dirty old man."

"Shut the fuck up," TK snarled.

I didn't know how much Raez knew or didn't know, but I could only guess it would do us no good. More than ever I wanted to knock that bastard the hell off my ship.

"Where's Billy?" cried Wren, crowding in behind Raez. *Where'd she come from? Was this party night on the Starrunner?*

"Dead," I growled.

"A joke, right? What do you mean 'dead'?" she croaked.

"What part of 'dead' don't you get?"

She looked around in disbelief.

"I told the old man not to mess with the phaso, but what does he do—he goes and starts fucking with it."

"That's not possible—" she frowned, a choked gurgle in her throat.

She saw TK's red eyes, tear-stained face and knew the truth. Unfortunate that Raez had heard all of this. In my anger I couldn't stop the flood of heated words. But he didn't seem to know what we were talking about.

"Some kind of explosives we talking here?" he asked.

"None of your business. It's over and done."

I locked the controls on the bridge and left the others staring there as I took the silver box to my cabin. I was afraid to keep the phaso on my person in case I inadvertently triggered it as Billy had.

What to do with the cursed thing? Part of me wanted to chuck it out in space, forget it ever existed. But it could be money, lots of it. The thing needed a new hiding spot, and my cabin was not the place—it was the first place anybody'd look to steal it.

* * *

No mention of the phase-distorter-shifter or Billy's sad, mysterious disappearance the next morning. No sign of Baer and his ugly goats zooming in on us at our sub-warp vector. The phaso was a sinister episode better left forgotten.

TK took me aside later in the corridor leading to the cabins and spoke in a distraught voice, "I'm still concerned about Billy. Dammit, Rusco, I think he may be still alive. How be I take a quick peek at the phaso and—"

"N-O." I grunted. "Forget it, Billy's lost. A few moments out there, and the kid's toast, let alone a few hours. Believe me, I saw the place."

"You don't know that, Rusco. We've no idea where Billy ended up. Maybe he ended up on some deserted island or in some abandoned city, calling for help."

"Maybe, but I doubt it. Unless the phaso coordinates were reset. Without a manual, we'll never know how the thing works, and without having it on him, he can never leave."

"But I can go there."

I stared at the man with awe, seeing the genuine expression of a fatherly love for a long lost son presumed dead. "Forget it, TK. The thing's jinxed. Anyone who touches it, dies." And I could see the glowering resentment in his eyes, those gray eyes that looked at me with fathomless despair and loathing and under the influence of the instruments working in his sawmill of a mind—and I didn't like what I saw.

Chapter 15

It was going to be a long trip to Jasmel. The whole mishap with Billy had me rattled. Maybe I should have tried right then to go in after the kid, or some such insane scheme, but the moment had passed. Water under the bridge. You're a real hero, Rusco. Proud of yourself? Saving an old man from sacrificing himself. What was going to go down next? Three edgy crew members, and Dolgra champing at the bit with Gris incommunicative, whom I didn't trust farther than I could spit.

As I was doing my hall rounds, I went to check on the phaso, something bugging me again. I reached the panel bulkhead where I'd hidden it in the small hallway leading to the utility room, then opened the strongbox. All seemed in order. I shook my head. Paranoia. It played tricks on the brain. I packed up the kit, made doubly sure the box was locked with a combo only I knew and walked away with a weary yawn to my cabin. Wren was watching the bridge; I could count on her. It was time to turn in, get some shut-eye.

I paused. Raez was staring at me, his ugly face catching the dim light from down the hall.

"What do you want?" I growled.

He lifted his hand in greeting. "Out for a little stroll, Rusco. I get insomnia on small space craft. Suffer from it all the time."

"Get back to your cabin. We're keeping strict curfew here.

Besides, this area is off limits to all but personnel."

"Oh, and spank my wee bottom, Cap'n. Gonna tuck me into bed too for a good night's sleep?"

"Don't get cute with me, Raez. My ship, I make the rules." I lifted my blaster, trusting the scoundrel less than ever.

He held up his hands. "Okay, Cap'n, I'm hurrying. Don't shoot me. I'm allergic to gunfire."

I saw him skip back to his grungy little cubbyhole and returned to my own digs, doing badly at falling asleep, wondering if I should call on Wren to help me relax. A bit of night play could do wonders for the soul.

But not tonight. That disturbing feeling kept nagging me, even with all my precautions. I rustled on some clothes and staggered down the hall into the bath of dim blue light.

I opened the strongbox. The phaso was missing. *That fucker. Raez, you're a dead man.*

I stalked to the hold looking for him.

He stood by the emergency escape vehicle, fiddling with the hatch as if he meant to take it somewhere. Like over to Urgon. We were nearing Jasmel at the cusp of the asteroid belt and it would be an easy jaunt for a thief on impulse power to get there or over to Urgon.

He was speaking in a low monotone to someone in his ear communicator. Must have hid that device on him.

When he caught sight of me, he cut the connection as if in apology, while reaching for his left hip for a small concealed weapon. I put a bullet through his brain. He dropped like a stone, eyes staring up like glassy pearls. I kicked the body over, turned him about. Discovered the phaso in his black waist belt. Rotten bastard. I had to smile at the irony. The thief calling the beggar a thief. My smile didn't last long.

I ripped off Raez's ear communicator, figured it would be useful down the road. Raez was about to jump ship and take the emergency vessel when we were close to a drop point. How he planned to accomplish this without getting his head blown off, or blasted by Starrunner's fareon beams was beyond me. It kind of insulted my intelligence. But then, Raez was not the brightest bulb in the box. Yet this was the same guy who had stolen the phaso right out from under my eyes and was minutes away from his getaway. I needed a new hiding spot for the damn thing. I began bagging Raez's corpse to jettison it out in the garbage hatch, all the while formulating a story to feed Wren and TK. He was stealing our share? *No, what share?* We got in a fight. He turned into a wise guy, and pulled a gun on me? *Better. Yeah, closer to the truth, maybe I'll stick with that.*

I got the body in the garbage compactor and released the load out to space. Relief. No evidence. Bye bye, Raez.

I'd make some enemies with Pazarol when he got wind. The fat fuck deserved it though. Had he put Raez up to it? The schemer'd be cut out of his share. I'd steal his shipment and double bag the profits, provided his goons didn't hunt me down and pepper us full of holes. There was still the problem of Gris out there in the freighter. A tricky business getting rid of him. The longer we stayed in this system, the more likelihood Pazarol'd catch up and deal with us, for double-timing him and murdering his man. Rusco, you're making enemies like flies. *Can't help it, captain, just who I am.*

I snapped out my reverie. Okay, stop daydreaming and start thinking. Wake up the others and tell them what happened.

We assembled at the bridge, TK groggy and Wren wiping her eyes. "You what?"

"You heard me, Raez caught a bullet, on account of he kind of pulled a weapon on me and was taking Messenger for a ride."

TK groaned, his face in his palms. "Now what? We're dead when Pazarol finds out."

"Not necessarily. Let me think—A longshot, but are you up for a blastfest?"

Wren shrugged. "When haven't I been?"

"If I can figure out how to spin this…" I rubbed my chin, mumbling, letting the ideas run through my crooked mind. "Okay, how's this?" I turned to TK. "Pull up as much data as you can on Urgon, the floor layouts, the sentry posts, weapons deployment, everything you got." What I had in mind, was risky. I didn't like keeping TK back on Starrunner, especially after the disappearance of Billy, but I had no choice. The few I could trust were getting fewer.

Wren caught wind of what I was planning and glowed with enthusiasm. "Take Dolgra along for the ride. We'll need backup."

"Good idea."

I contacted the Tanza crew. "Is this a secure line?"

"I've flipped it to encrypt secure," said Dolgra. "What is it?"

"Raez's meat. Fucker tried to kill me. Trying to make off with the escape pod, so I had to smoke him."

A wheezing groan came over the com. "Why would he do something stupid like that?"

"Who knows what that devious fuckwad was up to? I suggest if we want to save our hides, we either scram, or take over Urgon. Personally I like the second option, as it gives us the flexibility of selling the cargo on our own terms."

There was a long pause. "What do you need from me?"

"Get over here so you can help us take down Gris. We take the shuttle over, fake them out, and kill the crew."

"What, are you berserkers?" Dolgra barked.

"Any other ideas?"

"How do I know you won't scuttle me and take me out like you did Raez?"

"You don't. But who do you trust—me or Pazarol?"

"No contest. Okay, how many men do we need?"

"Wren, me and two of your guys."

"That's all?" He spat out a harsh croak. "Rusco, you're a bold bastard. Well, you only live once."

I cut the channel and called up Urgon on Raez's ear com.

"Gris, it's Raez here." I disguised my voice.

Silence, then a hard-edged mutter. "You got the piece? Did Rusco cause any trouble?"

"I'm heading over in the pod now. Rusco went out like a lamb. He doesn't know a thing. I've some interesting merchandise—think you and Paz might like it. Turn off the video and cut this channel when we're done, in case our boy is on the wire."

"10-4."

I grinned my sour grin. "Let's have ourselves a little rendezvous, Wren. Give a little surprise to our 'partners-in-crime'."

I paused. *Raez...* I tried to understand the man's game. The fuck could pretend he got tired staking out Starrunner and that the old man could be pinned with the theft of the phaso if anything were found out. He'd lie low on Urgon, use it as a shielded fortress to protect his ass and sit tight, keep both prizes, the fareon tech and the phaso. Not a bad plan, but desperate, and flawed. Leaving me a live unknown was as stupid a mistake as he could ever make. Glad I confiscated his R4. Should've checked him more carefully for that concealed pistol. He must have cached it in his boot. No wonder he so easily relinquished his weapon earlier.

I glanced at the clock. 04:07. We had time. Raez wouldn't be checking with anyone on Tarsus anytime soon. I faked a call to summon Dolgra over and piggy-back for refueling, keeping the communication on open channel. This way Gris could overhear.

When Dolgra's ship did dock on ours, Dolgra and two of his men came aboard, armed to the hilts.

We entered the Messenger and reviewed our plans. "Four men we're going to have to take down quickly," I whispered in a raspy voice. We all stared grimly at each other like wolves before the hunt. "Pazarol's going to get wise pretty soon, but if we can take over the freighter quickly, we can be off before Paz can do anything about it."

Dolgra peeled back his black mask. His nose twitched in a grimace. "It's risky, Rusco. About even odds man-for-man in a blast-out, but we have the bonus of surprise."

I remembered Raez and the murderous look on his face which reflected the murderous schemes in his twisted mind. "This big crime business is ugly, Dolgra—risky and ugly."

The Urgon transport carrier grew large as we approached. It dwarfed our vessel like a grey toad floating in space. The monster's hatch opened, mouthing an unpleasant grin. I guided Messenger in with technical ease. "On my signal."

The hatch closed, a dull clink reverberating through layers of steel. I deliberately kept the landing dock lights in our area dim. I hoped to hell this hare-brained scheme worked. The point of return had passed. Four sets of eyes looked on as the cold metal grates of Urgon's docking platform materialized and the landing chamber re-pressurized from vacuum. We crouched, weapons gripped. Only a pool of pale light shone through the port windows from Urgon's teal dockyard. I could see the whites of Wren's and Dolgra's men's eyes gleaming in the half murk.

The hatch peeled back and we hugged the walls of our own vessel, keeping back in the shadows. Gris's first man strode in, the proverbial unsuspecting lamb. "Raez, about time you showed—What the fuck—?"

The man exploded in a fountain of blood as Dolgra's men lay bullets into him, head and chest peppered with R4 fire. He flopped like a puppet to the metal grates. Wren and I burst through, kicking the mangled body aside while I crashed a shoulder into his henchman only a few feet away. But the man's Uzi came up and got off a blast, triggering the ship's alarm.

Shit. I twisted and kicked the weapon aside while Wren stomped on the man's larynx.

Two down. How many more to go?

They'd be watching, closed-circuit video. I aimed my barrel and knocked out the sensor light poised high on the far wall. There could be more. Better to assume Gris had eyes on us; he was the most dangerous of the lot. I could tell by that efficient wastage of Gedra flesh down on Gizren.

Soon blasts raged from around the hallway. Two more came in ducking around the corners, well-trained and fast. How many more of the ferrets manned this freighter? I cursed myself for not querying

Paz more about the infrastructure of his ship and its manpower. A mistake that could cost us our lives.

While Gris's men bore down on us, Dolgra ducked around the side of the pod, motioning his men to sneak out and cover him.

Blasts raked the hallway, blue and green beams, pinning us down in the docking area. *Not good.*

"Wren, you fake them out, and I'll try to blow Gris's boys to kingdom come," I whispered. She nodded. I looked to Dolgra. "Now!" I lobbed a hunk of broken pipe fallen from the ceiling at the closest of the men down the hall.

Blue fire came spitting to blast the metal to a pulp. Wren pushed off in a crouching run. She rolled for cover behind a white-paneled wall, aiming a stream of fire at the wall for added subterfuge. *Good girl.* I chose to pepper the place where the other man lurked, my gunfire eating away at the wall. Showers of sparks and metallic rubble covered the wretch. He cried out in pain, a shot catching him high up on the shoulder. The smoke and dust masked my rush for an instant, so I ran through, bold as brass. Dolgra, swift as an ocelot, ran close on my heels. It was now or never. I caught a glimpse of a dark form lurking in the smoke and sprayed it with fire, hoping I could snag even the slightest of body hits. Return fire spat back at me, but I rolled on my belly, moving like a fish out of water. I heard a painful cry and hiss of anger as my assailant fell over. My lips curled in a triumphant grin.

I caught a glimpse of Gris. No mistaking that salt and pepper grey, the ends of the hair trailing at the back. It was a fine mullet for a man of his age, but he had on a gas mask and that alerted me.

The man was good, a cold-blooded killer. Deadly. I saw Dolgra's man, Yeir, lying face down in a smoking heap, blood pooling around his inert form.

A clink of metal sounded in front of me. My head shot around, eyes blinking as a silver cylinder, six inches in length rolled a few feet away. Smoking gray coils rose from its core. My eyes started to burn.

"Tear gas. Get back!" My throat contracted in a wheezing rasp.

This was something I hadn't expected.

Dolgra, Wren and I staggered back into the pod. A rain of blue fire came ripping into the shuttle, decimating our only defenses.

Lolling on the rubble-strewn floor, I clawed for the utility panel in the forward bulkhead. Through the clouds of dust, I motioned Wren to grab the masks inside. I sprayed the entrance with fire so that some bright light didn't march in and waste us right there. She and I snatched masks from the bulkhead. Wren tossed extras to Dolgra and others. I lay low, urging Dolgra's two henchmen to curb their wretched, muffled yells.

I knew they'd be advancing through dusty clouds in the murk, protected by masks and breathing tubes. They'd keep low, their weapons aimed to kill anything that moved. Gris, the crafty bastard, knew his assault techniques. Perhaps I'd underestimated his cunning.

More was yet to play out. Gris was about to move in and waste us, but I held Dolgra back, made a small hand signal indicating I would draw them out and he would storm in and kill them. He gave a grim nod and patted me on the shoulder, wishing me luck.

I grabbed a piece of ruined pipe at my feet, knowing I had perhaps seconds to live. The blood pounded in my ears. In a rolling twist, I tossed it out as I frog-hopped along the edge of the shuttle's wall, blasting the grey cloud before me. I heard a cry of anguish, the pad of desperate feet behind me. Dolgra and Wren scrambled forward, taking advantage of the confusion.

My last barrage of blasts must have charred Gris's right side and he stumbled out, like some wounded animal, cursing in the open air, dropping to his knees.

I seized the man's shoulders and jerked him around, gun trained.

Gris croaked, "You fucking popsicle-brain, Rusco. When Paz hears—he'll kill—"

Dolgra jumped in and peppered the man full of holes. "That's for Yeir." The man's last act of contempt. Grisheimer sank in a heap of charred, limp bones.

Silence. Even the alarm had blown itself out.

The ship was ours.

We stripped the bodies of their communicators and weapons. I helped Dolgra drag Gris and the others to the jettison hatch, disposing of the bodies in a brief whoosh of vacuum. Though I had no personal quarrel with any of these thugs, I felt no remorse in seeing any of them go. Too many lowlifes in this universe. The rational part of my brain said it was a cleansing.

Dolgra suffered a broken finger, Wren a scraped elbow, me, my usual battery of cuts and bruises while rolling and shielding my head from falling debris. All in all we were lucky to have survived, but not so lucky, Yeir and Dolgra's other man, Benzit.

Wren looked around with contempt. "Raez or Gris's going dark will signify something went wrong and one or both of them are dead. We're screwed."

I made a low sound. "If we can hide the ship or TK can reprogram the tracking beams, we can be in the clear."

"Where'll we do that?"

"We backtrack, hide the load on Phoros, that large asteroid on the fringe of the belt. No one will look for it there. Once the dust settles, we'll take Urgon elsewhere to sell the product, maybe one of the outer planets. Shouldn't be hard, if this stuff is hot."

"It'll take weeks to get there."

"So? At least we get paid and blow Pazarol off."

Dolgra shrugged. "We ensure that our payload is intact first."

"Agreed." We marched down the companionway to the lower levels, Wren tagging my heels. It was a goldmine of goods: five heaping lodecarts full of crystal and a thousand cylindrical rods, fareon beam enhancers, stacked in upright racks a few inches apart. Even if we didn't fence those tons of Beryllium crystal, the fareon beams were worth millions, and I'd be a fool if I was going to pawn it off on Paz's warlord on Jasmel—

"I'm staying to guard our investment," Dolgra grunted. "I'll radio my ship to have them drop me off a couple of men. Send along this TK fellow of yours to do the tracking alterations."

"Stand by."

I flew Wren back on the Messenger to fetch TK so he could pilot Urgon to Phoros and work his magic on reprogramming the flight plan and the tracking chips.

The Urgon was one of those old freighters that needed to refuel so we charted out Elphi Alpha II, the next planet away. I worked with TK all day to get the Urgon's flight path reprogrammed and disable the home beacons. Then TK and I flew back on Messenger to Starrunner, with a promise to rendezvous with Dolgra and his men on Phoros within a week. I'd quietly informed Dolgra not to get too adventurous, that I'd taken precautions against doublecrossing, and he could expect a big kaboom if he failed to show for the next meet with Urgon. I was a paranoid man. As with Raez who had ill-timed his getaway, he had not counted on my extreme paranoia. It had spelled his doom...

Chapter 16

We landed on the outskirts of the capital city Desia on Elphi Alpha II. I needed to get away from my crew. The twists and turns had rattled my nerves, not to mention the bloodshed. TK was gloomy as death with the absence of Billy, absorbed in his own private melancholy. Wren had gotten weird, distant, sullen, but mostly whiny as if pleased with nothing and becoming something of a live-in wife with her high demands between the sheets, cramping my bachelor's style as if we were in some committed relationship after only a few screws. Which kind of astounded me, considering we were hardly soul mates, just a couple of waifs trucking along the harsh road of life, blasting people to death and stealing. My old adage rebounded back on me: Don't mix coital experiences with the hired help.

So, I cooked up some lie to run to port on Desia to get supplies for our next heist. I'd lay over for a day or so, with some cock-and-bull story about needing to scout out the terrain, research what other side scams we could rustle up while on layover. Which wasn't far from the truth.

"I want to tag along too," insisted Wren. "Like you, I need to get off this crate."

"Not today. Find your own entertainment, Wren. Remember we leave at oh-twelve hundred tomorrow."

"Fine, sure." She packed up some gear and left, taking the local air tube into town. TK opted to stay behind. Predictable. *Good luck finding that phaso, pops.*

I disabled the main drive by pulling out a special circuit, the orbigon, or something like that, something even TK couldn't easily figure out. I didn't trust the old man who'd been giving me evil looks ever since Billy had vanished. Either way, I didn't have time to ponder his next move.

There were things to do. Water tanks, new purifier, frozen meal packs: microwaveable, several yummy flavors, including synthetic chicken, fish, stripped steak, liver, no salt. Loaded with nutrients, also synthetic. Of course, scurvy was a bit of a concern out in deep space. Like the old mariners of the ancient Earth, back when humans had first explored the new worlds and faced down the formidable sea beasts, they had suffered. Loved those old classics yarns, *Moby Dick* and *Gulliver's Travels.*

We spiked our drinks with Vit C liquid drops and threw in supplements whenever we could get them: kiwi fruit, apples, genetically engineered and modified. I kind of wondered at the long term effects. Humans hadn't died off as of yet, it seemed. Other things to worry about. Like when the next blood-toothed warlord was going to plug a bomb on our ass.

Okay, Rusco, off topic.

Lack of sunlight was a problem too. To solve that, I had a lamp room installed early on in Starrunner to sunbathe in and soak up rays. Throw on the oil, lay back with the old eye patch, the dark glasses. Hence, my bronzed look. A worthwhile investment. Also a hot tub installed, but rarely used, water being a scarce resource on such a small starship as Starrunner. If I really wanted to impress though, the tub came in handy...

I treated myself to an evening at the hotel Medusa in downtown Desia. Looking forward to something other than protein powder and microwaved patty dinners with TK and Wren's doom and gloom scenarios about the state of the galaxy and their communal trials on Talyon, that garbage pit of a world they'd holed up on for so long.

Looking forward to bright lights and space to move around in. Some upbeat human contact.

In the glass lounge I kicked back at the bar and sipped my dry gin. Quite a selection of highbrows here, some fine fillies too. In laced tops and tight skirts, black and white, modular hair styles. The men wore executive type suits. Clean cut, ran the syndicates, the food production and transpo systems of the new age—at least before the gangsters got to them, bombarded them with naphtha. Then there was the run of regular shysters and crime jojos, but fancy ones with classy, gold cufflinks and tailor-made suits. It was a high end place with multiple security webs and high-voltage fencing staked about, electro-grids and a hundred yols cover entrance. We'd made some dough on our prior cons, so I could afford it. The latest in techno music played, live bands with tables and dance. I set my creaking back down in a soft sofa and loosed a whistling breath, trying to release the cobwebs from my head and ease my joints.

But still the old brain buzzed. Many cons and scams worked their course. Outside of the fat wallets to pickpocket, not a lot to move on. I could scavenge the games table in the next room, but there were limits to what I could do solo. My hound ears picked up snatches of conversation, of this merger and that merger, the need for under-the-table investment—gangster money. Wouldn't be too hard to work up some con here, build some contacts with thin bread down the line. Make some friends, rub shoulders with the moneyed players and leverage them with a kick in the ass later.

Give it a rest, Rusco. Is this your day off or what? I grabbed another drink, a tall tuber at the bar.

I chatted up the young brunette sitting two stools down, who intrigued me—Raquel—with long legs and enigmatic smile that was a compelling lure, classic lines to the face, even though the face was a little too lean for my tastes. Seems she was game, while being coy at the same time. They were always like that. I gave the hint of money, dropped some yols on a fancy dinner and some local champagne, which springboarded the rental of the cheapest room in the hotel. Sir, what is your budget? 100 yols? Hmnn, our feature suites are 500 yol rooms, but that's clearly unaffordable. But we have them as cheap as 80. I blinked. The 80 yol room, please, for a night. Another 80 yols. Yeah, it was adding up, but I was worth it.

She moved to the rhythm and thrusts of the moment that had a way of turning me on in a unique way. I roused her higher by not giving into her climax. Was the sex good? Better than average, I'd say. I had a lighter spring to my step, a bit of kick in my bones, a spice in my blood, eyes a little dreamier by the end of it, and my voice a little lower. Our slow gallop to the finish line had moved in synch with the sounds of the alley below from the open window, and the sleazier hotels that ranged appallingly close: a blend of low level techno pop, the sound of breaking glass, wide gas holo screens playing loud movies, a woman's scream, followed by a man's laughter.

My brain spun. Spent and lathered, I lay back in the damp blankets, blinking, contemplating life at this moment. For all its glamor, it was one of those low moments, Raquel's sighing breath, the warm air playing across my bare chest, her slender white fingers on my scarred arm, knowing she would soon age and be forgotten, my own sad ass chased across the galaxy by crime scum, whipped at the heels by fatal impulse, still hoping to be some hero at the end of the day. What a pathetic dream. At least I'd rid the universe of one Raez, and if I had my choice, I'd include Pazarol, Baer and Mong on that list. My implausible excuses for rationalizing my own criminality were like an overused mantra. When I was young, I wanted to be a rocket engineer, build ships, the best that could fly. Then came the gangs and the beat downs and the drugs and rock and roll, and my parents wiped out in a single strike by a warlord's cannon in our humble neighborhood on Jaunus 8. Me scavenging the streets with no family, no friends, driven like all the other poor refugees to some tarped-up camp, starving, hollow-eyed, wondering where to go from here. What a pipe dream. Where did the dream of young Jet Rusco go? The dream about his little rocket engines and do-gooding. Blown away in some ugly tale where the ogre swallows all and stamps out all thoughts of philanthropy.

I dreamed somebody was rapping at the door.

Figuring it was some room service personnel, I staggered half nude to the door. I opened the door, my jaw dropping. Wren? She caught a glimpse of a tangle of naked arms and legs in the white, disheveled sheets, and slapped my face. Cursed like there was no tomorrow.

I awoke to damp sheets.

Just a guilt-ridden dream. I was gone and back on Starrunner before dawn's light with my packs full of supplies on a world with less daylight than what I was used to. Raquel, I'd left a note for and was managing to forget her, as she, no doubt, me.

Wren was all coos and giggles on the bridge, digging through the yummies I'd brought: the protein packs, the flavored meats. Granted, I would too, living off lizards and grasshoppers for so many years.

I watched the mainscreen holo-vid. This maniac Mong again, conducting a cult ceremony. Seems he was all the rage with his planetary takeovers and promises of liberation. He had a murderous dark hero look, emancipating worlds of their oppressive gang control and abject slummery. Some ambitious journalist had done a human interest story on him. Was this mongrel everywhere at once? Gave me the creeps. A big hulking ape of a man with a fatherly face. A flat-topped, amber hat padded his oversized crown. The brute had some power, sure, to have all those people under his thumb. Look at them—tragic sheep, chanting his name, bowing and praising the works of Mong. He stood tall before the colonnaded temple giving a lecture to thousands, maybe tens of thousands, surrounded by a ring of devotees dressed in blue and gold robes with half shaved heads but for a crop of chicken hair sticking up on top. With a slew of thousands more out in the field, holding their hands up in mindless abandon and chanting some Ciros thing—*long live Ciros, long live Ciros, the fortress of Mong! Fortress of Mong!*

TK snapped me out of my reverie. "Ciros is the name of the temple," he explained.

"How would you know?"

"Because they just said."

"Thanks." I turned the set off and told them we had work to do. Starting with an idea I had for our next heist.

"TK, scour the free data store for buyers of cutting edge, high end arms. First we need to unload our cargo. Outfits, organizations, anyone who'll pay premium for Class A hardware. Go as high as you can and dark as you dare, on the Free Store. There're enough low-ballers out there as it is. Don't make contact with anybody," I warned him, "just compile a list. Anywhere but Jasmel. I'll go through your list later and pick the ones I think are good matches."

"Sure enough, sounds easy."

I turned to Wren. "I scoped out some impound shops down Elphi Alpha. A goldmine of hardware there for the picking: ships, shuttles, probes, drones, the works. All arriving illegally, carrying contraband, gangsters caught by local police, mercs, shakedowns, that kind of thing. One branch is city-owned, just a regional office, so it's light on security."

"What's your angle?" she asked.

"We go in, collecting a worthwhile hulk for transfer to a chop shop, bag the ship for our own and sell it cheap for quick yols."

"Sounds promising." Although her voice was doubtful. "What's the risk?"

"Minimal, if we play it right. Good news is, I'll be doing the initial scout, the run ahead and the main con. You help with the packaging and back me up if necessary."

"Whatever you say, Cap'n."

"Atta girl." That's what I liked about Wren, no fuss, no trouble during business. If only all women could be so cooperative.

We'd go in with papers, pretending to be all official and scam us some hefty hardware for half-decent resale. Outfits like city impound send the ships there anyway, at least the seized vessels the bosses didn't commandeer for their own uses. Better we get the money than some other shyster.

The con operated on the loophole that these shops all kept paper copies of their records. Known fact: Breaking into a secure digital system would be much harder and not worth the risk.

The next day I staked out the joint, The RAI: Regional Airspace Impound. I was at the office depot a few days before the heist. Low security there, easy to slip past the sensors. I'd worked on these types of shops before.

I made sure my face was covered by a mask and disabled any cameras in ready sight I could find. Rifled the office while the staff was off duty, photographed the hundreds of letterheads of certain important acquisition forms, serial numbers of impounded crafts and particulars, studied both the names of the impound officers, owners, managers of the local office and those of the local businesses to whom they supplied parts. I hid out in the file room, eavesdropping on the clerks when they arrived in the morning the following day, heard a few names dropped, then listened keenly for more names when transcalls came through: Benzie Krai, Kata Layne, jotted a few down, recorded the rest on my little black recorder. Found out who presided over whom and whose authority made the difference. Tedious work, but necessary. It was enough to bluff my way through two days later, when I came in, all important and business-like, deliberately arriving early in the morning, plopping my forged papers on the wicket counter and dropping the right combination of names I'd memorized the night before.

"Who are you again?" the attendant asked, all squinty-eyed.

"Juss Rambo. Over at Militia Distributing. Seems here that Mr. Kata Layne authorized this requisition. I'll be taking the J-Zen cruiser to Meik's strip yard, parts and wholesale."

"This is irregular, sir. I should get Mr. Layne personally on the line to confirm."

"You can do that," I said with a frown, "but Layne might get upset—no, pissed if you bother him at this hour. The other day he sent me over here to get this job done quickly. Seems as if something slipped through the main branch's wire and now Mr. Layne's weighing on us. There's his signature at the bottom."

"Yes, sir, I see it is. One moment please." The clerk frowned, scrutinized the papers, the seals, signatures and serial number, and scratched his initials on several pages, then fiddled with some files in the back cabinet. Finally he ripped off some yellow pieces of paper and passed me two with a pink slip. "Go ahead, Mr. Rambo. The impound yard is down the way to your left."

"I know, been here before."

The attendant gave a curt nod.

And that was that. A brief moment of nailbiting on the odd chance that sleepy pencil neck decided to call my bluff and summon the big boss Layne. Secret here is to look important and gruff and as confident as possible. Any bit of doubt or hesitation on the con's part and the deal floats south. But I'd planned for that, recalling the hardware under my brown leathers, fingering my blaster and the grenade tucked in my waist pouch. Although that route could get ugly very quickly.

Couldn't work the same scam twice at the same place. No, no. Once they found out they'd been conned, they'd be up to their armpits in security. Somebody's neck would be on the line. I pitied the poor soul to work a scam similar to mine.

I radioed Starrunner in over the impound yard and, while TK hovered overhead, Wren jumped down. After a few moments with a yardman and a flash of pink papers, we attached the four towlines to the vehicle in question and boarded Starrunner, hauling the hulk away. It was a lighter job than her load limit, within her horsepower capabilities. Her impulse engines whirred in a high scream and we carried the J-Zen off across the smoggy skyline and on to the next city, dropped her at Regzie's WR, one of the black market warehouses on the east end of town. 5G cash yols, no question asked. A quick job. We took off into the wild blue yonder, with the blackness of space curling around Starrunner as Elphi Alpha faded behind us like a dwindling star.

Chapter 17

TK came through with the compiled list. After a quick review I whittled it down to four possibles. The third was promising, a certain Vee Hars. Said he'd pay cash for everything, especially the manufactured, enhanced weapons. The crystal he'd take as a favor. "Meet us in three days in the capital of Myx on the nearby world of Trellian. Volgrim Enterprises, north end of the city."

Time to rendezvous with Dolgra on Urgon. I varwoled into orbit around Phoros, radioed Dolgra, told him we'd be there in minutes. Dolgra confirmed. I took TK over in the shuttle, where he set up the flight path and we shuttled back.

Next stop Trellian.

A day to arrive at Myx City and some more time to find the drop point. That's a long time on a starship. A man's mind can wander into stray territory. As mine did. Something about the whole affair with Pazarol still rankled. I'd had to kill Raez; Gris was casualty damage, scumbags without question, that was not a problem. But another loose end, some stone left unturned, I couldn't figure it out. The puzzle left me staring up at the plated ceiling, lying in my hard bunk that night in wordless dismay, wondering what wolf was waiting around the next corner. Not even the lusty affections of Wren could assuage that.

I jolted up, knowing there was going to be trouble with that phaso. I whipped on my clothes and staggered down to the hold. There in my workshop, near Raez's former cubby hole, I set about making a clever imitation of it with the materials I had aboard and my budding artistic talent. To foil any eager searchers, I used extra varnish and colored lead tinsel to give it that shiny, iridescent look. I felt better when it was done. I inserted the fake in the strongbox and put it back in the forward bulkhead where it had been and hid the real phaso in a place no one would find it—in the conduit leading to the engine core, the Barenium chambers, taped to the inner wall. Maybe not the safest place for it, but at least out of TK's reach, or anyone else who might be searching. I could trust nobody.

Trellian came up on our sights and we bore down on the single, prominent continent. Starrunner flew over rich woodland—gigantic, three hundred-foot trees with plumed tops like ostrich tails. Beyond the outriders of Myx's towers we coasted where a long patch of industrial lots stretched within the forest confines.

We landed in Volgrim's yard, Urgon first and Starrunner after, spraying up dust and specks of dirt from the grainy tarmac. The sky was overcast and the air slightly muggy. Even these outer worlds seemed to have been terraformed long ago with thick atmospheres to make them habitable. Their air generators had been running for decades to keep the planet warm, in addition to thousands of geothermal stations set up around the globe to pipe heat from the planet's crust into the air. Major acreage of forests had been planted to supply ready oxygen.

Two battered, rusty buildings stood in the foreground, with flat, rectangular roofs. A gravel pit loomed in the back, with several large freighters and smaller range vehicles huddled in the landing yard out front. It looked dead as a graveyard, could as easily have been a gravel yard, or some construction depot. Dolgra's men stayed back to watchdog the shipment while Wren, Dolgra and I debarked to meet Vee Hars and his associates and consummate the transaction. I relished closure on this deal. I packed extra weapons—R4, R3, some explosives—while ensuring Wren and I were carrying trackers that

TK could monitor steadily from Starrunner. I wasn't taking any chances. That bad feeling had not abated, even after hiding the phaso in a safe place, so I started to wonder if it was something else that had my imagination piqued.

I motioned to Dolgra. "There, at two o'clock." The equipment yard was bare but for oil drums, fork lifts and some metal skids piled with crates. Four figures came out of the first set of ugly, rust-coated double-doors on the warehouse.

Hars was a medium-boned man of no great stature. A woman kept his stride, wearing a hardhat and two other men in coveralls trailed behind. I sized them up in a second—a set of trade business professionals, black market operators, possibly, but clean. So, why the worry?

"Rusco? Hars, here," the man said, husky of chest, short of leg, and held out a pink hand. "These are my colleagues: Deen, Faber and Lozane." I gave them a salute and they all nodded.

"Pleasure, Hars. My crew, Dolgra and Wren."

Hars tipped his head. "You have my merchandise?"

"In the Urgon over there." I pointed. "Ready for transport."

"Good, let's move it out then. I've got a busy day and there are lots more things to do. There's a spot set out in the warehouse."

"Not so fast," I called. "Where's our yols?"

"Relax, you'll get them, Rusco." He frowned, fingering his jaw at the delay. "All two million of it. Fresh credits."

"Then let's go get them, shall we?"

He shook his head. "Let me take a look first at the merchandise."

"Fair enough. Follow me." I set out at a brisk pace, Wren behind me, Dolgra to my side, forcing Hars and his gang to keep up to my impatient stride. Normally all this would have been formal, a simultaneous transfer at a more leisure location. But these guys seemed a bit overcautious, even amateur—

My thoughts came to a grinding halt at a deep rumbling sound from the sky. My hand went to my weapons belt. I looked up. Three ships streaked out of the clouds like dive bombers. An XT-5 warship, then a white-gray service freighter, and then one of those grey Markests I'd seen on Talyon, looking suspiciously like one of Baer's.

I swore. Guns from the XT-5 trained on us, reminiscent of the ships I'd seen in raids on civilian territories.

Hars's eyes darted up in sudden terror. "What the hell?—Rusco are you playing us?"

"They're aiming at me as much as you, Hars! Get down!"

He ducked, but too late. Fareon blasts set fire to the oil drums nearby and hot gases licked out at us like chemical bombs. Flames lit the tarmac and sent us flying. I pulled Wren to my side to shield her.

Two bullets slammed between Hars' eyes and he sagged like a rag doll. One of his henchmen went to his knees, blood spraying from his chest. The other, I gather, the woman, was running, but she didn't get far.

A vulpine howl rattled in Wren's throat. Dolgra had a slug in his leg. All this happened so fast, my reflexes could hardly keep up with the unreality of it all.

Starrunner and Urgon were rising in the air. Pulse blasts slammed from the Warhawk, then flashed down to disable our ships' electrical circuits for brief instants. The two ships clunked down on the tarmac like dead weights.

I saw the Warkhawk blast the rear thrusters and struts off Urgon. Armed men stormed out of the Warkhawk and blew the hatch and boarded Urgon. I don't know whether they killed Dolgra's men that instant or took them prisoners. Warhawk crew members were moving crystal out of the freighter on a big load lifter to their freighter. They weren't taking any chances of their cash cow flying away.

Wren was firing rounds into the cloud of smoke, but not getting much action. I was reaching for my grenade pin.

The Warhawk wasn't even on the ground when a dozen men in khaki fatigues jumped out of the hatch, spraying us with fire. We crawled on our bellies like worms, Dolgra moaning in pain. A paralyzer-slug zapped my shoulder. I convulsed, cursing. I looked up to see five grim faces peering down at me with weapons trained on us all. Boots flicked out and kicked the weapons out of our hands. Rough hands seized us and dragged us into the warehouse.

I felt my shell-shocked grip on reality fading. More figures disembarked from the Markest and in my horror, I thought to see big P leisurely making his way down the tarmac with three of his ape-armed escorts.

One of our captors threw a bag over my head while others dragged Wren and Dolgra down the dim-lit hall. I couldn't figure it out. I easily expected we'd all be taken aboard P's bandit cruiser and that would be the end of us. Truncheons slapped down on my neck; my shoulder spasmed and I groaned in pain. Thuds, blows, curses. Wren's wild cries, Dolgra's murmurs of agony—all came in a wild orgy—the opening and slamming of doors, heated arguing of voices, muttered yells, pitched insults. More blunt objects wracked against my body, and I was forced onto a cold, cement floor. Hands seized me by the hair and arms and thrust me into a hard-backed chair. They bound my forearms with twine to the armrests, roped my calves to the leg-rests. The whimpers of my team faded to a primal keening. Only the harsh mutters of violent men accompanied the scuff of booted feet.

The bag was removed from my head, and I gulped in lungfuls of air. The paralyzer was fading and I reeled to the throes of a splitting headache, my face all puffy and my arms throbbing something awful. I struggled in vain to free myself from that chair in that bare storeroom with no windows.

I recognized the hairy face that leered over me, but it was not who I expected it to be.

"Déjà vu, eh, Rusco?" came Baer's gruff voice. "Wipe that purple grin off your face. Hope your trip wasn't too painful?"

The shadowy figure donned a pair of heavy work gloves, blue-grey industrial grade with raspy edges and steel knit weave, and patted my cheek with a rough caress as if those mitts were made for handling asbestos. His arm seemed to be repaired, assuming he had either some wicked miracle glue or hardcore flesh regen. How about a mechno-arm?

He nodded to the three of his goons with AKs at their belt. "I paid Pazarol to pass you off to us. Or we wouldn't be having this conversation. He wanted to kill you outright. But that would have been a waste of time and useless for our purposes. We still have unfinished business, Rusco, don't you remember?"

"What do you want?"

His bushy brows shot up in inquiry. "I assumed that'd be obvious. We got the phaso, thank you very much. But where's my amalgo? Seems as if Lugi couldn't find it on your ship."

I wondered how long it would take them to figure out I didn't have the amalgo and the phaso was a dud. Wren sprawled on the floor, a sorry sight, coming to with a groggy shake of her head. She was stripped near naked. Dolgra was at her side, splayed in shameless abandon, out cold. I took one look at the two of them and I knew that the jig was up. We were dead regardless of what we did or said.

That sneaky bastard Raez must have bugged the Starrunner before he'd died. How else could that maggot-spawn Paz, in cahoots with Baer, have known so much about our movements? I cursed myself for my carelessness, neglecting to sweep for bugs after I wasted that slime ball.

My mind worked at any desperate plan at all. Needed to figure a way out of this, otherwise we were dead.

Struggle was useless. They'd strapped me in tight. I hated my impotence, but gave my hosts my most defiant look.

Baer grunted in disgust. "What about you, black beauty?" He turned and back-ended Wren with the heel of his boot. "Know anything about a shiny disc, glittering all colors, size of your hand that can take you to faraway places? What about my big horseshoe gadget, like a wonder magnet, something you may have seen in a haute moderne living room?"

She looked away, shook her purpled face, looking as if she was going to vomit.

"Thought so."

Had they gotten to TK? Maybe he was sprawled in another room, getting his face plastered all over the wall.

With cat-like strength, Dolgra shot up and clawed at the nearest thug, bringing him down in a crashing heap. Thumbs caught in his eye. He cried out in pain as fingers worked and he kicked Dolgra off him. The other two pinned Dolgra's arms and began clubbing him.

The one rubbing at his face swore. "That miserable catclawer. Fucked up my eye."

"Whine somewhere else," cried Baer. "Get that trash out of here. I need to have a one-on-one with Rusco."

He peered with critical appraisal at Wren. "And this bitch is a bit mannish for my tastes, so remove her too." He motioned to one of his henchmen who gave an anticipatory growl.

"A woman's a woman, boss." The bald-headed thug grabbed Wren by the ears and hauled her up and dragged her out by what had grown of her hair. Wren kicked and screamed all the way.

Baer shrugged. "Nasty piece of work, Rusco. Such company you keep. Now, I might just let you live, albeit it painfully, if you'll tell me where the amalgo is?"

"What amalgo?"

He gave a weary sigh. "We have to do this the hard way?" He nodded to his other man; they cut my right arm bonds and forced open my palm flat. I struggled but Baer shoved a coin-sized object in it, while the other thug closed and tied my fingers around it.

I protested in horror when I saw what that silver thing was and what they planned to do. On a nod, all three left the room and whispered in anticipation amongst themselves.

"I always repay any favors done to me." Baer gave a last look. He closed the door while I counted the seconds.

Kaboom.

The blast came from far away in my mind as my ears adjusted to the shock, and my fingers were gone in a second and the hand with it. Blood and flesh kicked up in my face. Then the agony came in mountainous waves.

Red hot gallons of it. A minute, two days, a year? How much time passed? I don't know.

I remember a figure larger than life lumbering into that room. Could have been an avatar, a dark angel, some figment of my distorted imagination. He was big, his shoulders so wide, hawk eyes so dark and bright at the same time. The man wore a long, wine-colored trenchcoat, with white stripes down the middle and golden eagles off to the side. His hair was thick and black as buffalo fur and trailed past the middle of his back. The eyes, sightless as a blind crow's eyes, penetrated into my soul, windows into new universes. But the presence of the man was what awed and stunned me most, despite my pain. He made Baer look like a mangy rat. Those ageless eyes scrutinized me as a raptor might bore into a helpless rabbit, but then his eyes went soft and gentle, as if he were trying to coax the truth out of an errant child.

"You've wandered far from the truth, haven't you, child? Empty your soul, become one with the universe."

I must be in heaven, dreaming a benevolent dream. My hand had ceased to throb, just a warm jelly feeling there.

"Yes, the pain is not that crippling, is it?" he asked. "Doesn't last, like all things in this transient world."

His voice changed as he muttered something to Baer who had clumped in, "So this is your darkhorse, the one who's been causing me so much trouble and giving you merry chase?"

With my eyes adjusting to the pink mist of pain, I recognized that face!—*Mong*. The holo screen…I croaked a hang-man's curse.

"Yes, you know me, don't you?" the warlord jeered with a grotesque grin. "You have something of mine. A very important item. Tell us about it, and I'll make sure the pain goes away. Forever."

I shook my blood-stained head, coming in and out of delirium.

He exhaled a sad laugh. "That phaso's nothing but a cheap imitation. You expecting to pawn it off on somebody in a quick sale?" He gave a spitting growl. "Good luck." In impatient, cruel pantomime, he reached in his trenchcoat and pulled out a green vial, which he opened and flicked the caustic liquid on my stump of a wrist. The fires of agony bit into my flesh. The severed nerves reanimated. A good reminder of the pain to come.

Yet Mong's promise of pain meant the end of me, a bullet to the brain or worse. I'd hold out and die. They'd never get the amalgo, those fucking scavengers.

As if reading my mind, Mong grinned and pulled a pick-hook out of his grab-bag of tricks and approached me from behind. He jabbed it into my stub of a wrist bone and proceeded to carve out the marrow.

I howled in misery, croaking out a rasp as a lunatic might make, hoping for the oblivion of unconsciousness. The warlord paused, his eyes blinking in expectation, his presence a still of death. As he leaned forward, I could not help but cringe—the man was built like a tank, an iron killing machine, a mountain of muscle.

Baer muttered, "The girl might give us a location, Mong. Hold up. Right now Branx and Madler are working her over for the truth, loosening her up, if you know what I mean."

"Fool! I don't care what your slackwit goons are doing to the bitch. I want my merchandise."

"Alright, hold your horses." Baer held up his hand. "I'm working on her. If you hadn't been so impulsive and brought the Megalians to their knees so early, I'd have caught up with this Rusco scum long ago on Skeller's Reach—"

Mong's patience wore thin and his hand flicked out. I blinked as the air went cold and dark. An invisible force seemed to lift Baer up by the throat and slam him against the wall. The thug gurgled, coughed, snorted, his eyes bulging like a frog's. His hairy face went beet red. Mong thundered out a curse. "You stupid bungler! You were the shipping agent. Your job was to secure those Mentera techs back in Hoath. You didn't. The amalgamators were highest priority. It's been weeks since you promised them."

"I—know, M-Mong. S-sure," Baer croaked, his voice a high-pitched twang. His feet dangled inches from the bare floor. "Just a minor detail. Rusco'll be squawking like a hen before long."

"I don't see him squawking like a hen." Mong released the thug with whatever voodoo powers he had, and the hate-mongering Baer fell to his knees, clawing at his throat, like a drowning man.

A prolonged howl came from the adjoining room, a thin wail of helplessness like the cry of a tortured animal. It could have easily been Wren's or Dolgra's, and I shuddered. A lament that might come from my own throat soon enough. Mong seemed to pay no heed.

"I came here on a call that I would get results and my tech in my hand. My devotees are waiting for me on Z-Mezarath—you know that, to rally them to the true path." He thrust a finger high. "One day my religion will spread throughout the galaxy, as popular as the Christ savior of old." His voice had risen to a self-righteous pitch.

"Sure, Mong, sure. You know I'm your staunchest supporter."

"Shut up. That's enough of your fatuous words for one day."

A beeper rang on the warlord's communicator. He snatched at it. "What?" he growled. His face darkened.

"Unacceptable, Ry-yin! Fix it." He cut the connection. "Is there no end to incompetence?" He exhaled a dark breath. "The war on Questra is going badly, Baer. I must go. See that this worm talks or you'll be the next in that chair."

The star lord's contemptuous glance brushed me a warlock's hex as he made for the exit. "A mere flesh baby," he chided in contempt, shaking his head. "A few bruises, a missing hand, and some bodily discomfort and the weakling mewls like a newborn child."

I wanted to fling out an insult but my tongue could form no words, only gurgles.

"If you experienced the primal initiations on my home planet, Rusco, you'd be laughing right now—a man of iron, daring me to bring on more." He gave a final shake of his leonine head and flung open the door. "You are not worthy of my teachings."

He strode out and Baer flinched, his burning bearish eyes raking me with sinister fervor. He reached out with his prosthetic hand to squeeze my stump of a wrist, the exposed bone and purple flesh. The dirty, rough glove reached high, maybe to pour gasoline on the raw wound, I couldn't tell. My eyes circled up in agony, even as blackness overcame me.

CHRIS TURNER

Chapter 18

I drifted in and out of consciousness, stirred by some distant blast, a thunder clap, or it could have been a faraway mountain exploding. It was all the same.

Wren was beside me, slapping my cheeks, yelling in my ear.

She unstrapped my arms and legs. *No, Wren was dead.* Her scratched, bloodied face gleamed with sweat and blackened soot and grime. Her leathers were torn, but a wild look blazed in her eye, the other swollen nearly shut, as if she'd been to hell and back. Good old Wren! She had come back.

"TK came through, Rusco. If you want to live, let's hurry."

I struggled, hobbling like an eighty year old. Gunfire and blasts echoed down the hall. I was limping with Wren's supporting arm around my waist down the rubble-strewn corridors, the rat-darkened places, doubled over in pain. More booms resounded from the cracked concrete above and the crumpled steel.

It seemed a million miles we staggered, half dragging ourselves along, my head snapping sideways, peering in horror into one of the nearby storerooms. The door was half ajar. I caught a quick glimpse of Dolgra sprawled there, head pulled back, eyes glazed up in terror. The muscular olive skin body lay half stripped, half naked, the small, petal shaped breasts exposed high on the sun-browned chest. I knew that, despite the denial of my instincts on first meeting, she had been a woman, dressed up in costume and posing as a man, jousting, fighting in a world ruled by males, trying to survive and rise up the ranks in a world ruled by iron fists. Metal picks stuck up her arms and pincushioned her ribs like a sewing-box voodoo doll. I couldn't look away, let alone imagine the last minutes of her agony. I grimaced and forced my feet on, vowing that I would avenge that brave woman's sacrifice, if I ever got out of this misery alive. Which didn't look very likely with half an arm, and the ceiling crumbling over our heads. Bomb fire threatened to kill us all.

Even in my daze, I couldn't help but realize that Dolgra's defiance to the end had saved both Wren and me, or at least delayed having our throats cut in ruthless spite.

Wren kicked open the steel door at the end of the hall. We stumbled into the harsh light on the tarmac, my eyes adjusting to the white sunlight as it shafted through a rent in the clouds. I heard the blast of pulse fire, then the roar of engines. Fareon beams sighted on the warehouse roof. Another licked out at the diving Markest and the ship buckled in flames. Its grey bulk crashed into the warehouse. Right on target, TK! Starrunner burst through a cloud of fire and landed beside us, smoking. I looked up to see two of Mong's auxiliary warships screaming in, which he'd left to safeguard the cargo. We were screwed. Wren pushed me through the open hatch, yelling commands. TK lifted off at full impulse, miraculously dodging the sprays of fire left by fareons, even as Wren got the hatch closing. Our reserve shields took major hits. I could hear Molly's voice caterwauling: *"Danger! Warning. Shields at 4%. Structural overload. Expected hull implosion in T minus 30 seconds."*

I shook my head in despair, staggering to the bridge, the ship rocking to TK's clever maneuvering.

The sensors were off the charts. Starrunner was toast. I looked over at Wren, my eyes vacant.

Wren seized the controls and spat fareon fury at the Warkhawk in pursuit. The vessel lit up in red but did not explode.

She gave a wild start. "Aw, fuck it!"

Her hand reached for the Varwol initiate. "No!" TK jerked

forward to stop her, but too late. Starrunner's warp engaged. We tumbled end over end in a funland of blinding multicolored light. Mong's ships in immediate pursuit stretched out like pancakes, then flared.

I heard banging like unholy drums, the deafening peals of hell ogres, as if the gongs of oblivion were out there to reduce us to atoms.

Inconceivable forces arced from Varwol to Trellian gravity. Conflicting time and gravitational forces wreaked havoc on the continuum. Our bones were slowly popping from our joints, stretching to infinity. Wren, moving in slow-motion, released the Varwol, her face a rictus of agony. The ship dropped back to impulse, slewing sideways like some rogue comet caught in a collision of 3D and 4D realities. We floated in another realm, one with a black sky drawn like a curtain with pale stars, an eerie globe with craters below us. The ship idled; we blinked as raw agony throbbed all over but we were alive, as the sensors went quiet.

Were we in the same system? In a different time? No. My right hand was still gone. The agony was still there, of course, if not worse.

TK leaned over and vomited. He lifted himself up, pale as a ghost. He flicked some dials, pulled up a 3D visual. "We're orbiting Feldris," he coughed, a trickle of blood seeping at the corner of his mouth. My slow brain made sense of the name. We'd made Trellian's moon in the few light seconds we'd been in marred, warped-up no man's land.

In other circumstances we would have been stretched to nothingness, at the mercy of infathomable physics.

None of Mong's ships showed on our sensors. I hoped they'd all been blown to space dust, entered the horizon of oblivion, but somehow I doubted that. How long would it take our pursuers, if any there were, to pinpoint our coordinates?

I slumped back in the co-pilot's chair, holding my mangled stump under an armpit. The cloth Wren had wrapped around it staunched the blood. I motioned to her to bring the Myscol from the cabinet and every damn painkiller there. She brought down a dozen glass pill bottles. I downed them at once like a starving man. I chased them down with what was left of the whiskey. Wren gobbled a few herself while TK felt too sick to eat anything.

"Get us out of here," I growled at Wren.

"We've got to get you to a surgeon."

"I don't know where the nearest black market op shop is," I croaked hoarsely, "certainly not on that crater below us." My voice, reedy and faraway, sounded alien to my ear.

"Molly," I coughed. "Op shop's nearest to, to—where the hell are we?"

"Feldris."

"Feldris!" I gasped.

"Affirmative. Delta sector. Malron, Malron City on Gainor."

"How long?" I cried.

"Four hours, three minutes, on impulse."

"On Varwol, you silly girl."

"Varwol at 1% light speed capability makes it two hours."

"Set the course."

TK set the coordinates and engaged the drive, what was left of it, and we were in the unreality of sub warp. I looked up through bleary eyes, my arm quivering, my legs spasming, and waves of nausea assaulting my shattered nerves.

Wren looked at me from a bruised face and through a blackened, swollen eye, but with a vindictive gleam and blood on the bowie knife belted at her side.

I could tell the way TK was shivering, it was the bravest thing he ever did, coming back with Starrunner and blasting our enemies.

He saw my incredulous look and gestured. "I hid in the hold, under the mattress and moldy blankets you gave Raez. They searched the ship, eight of them, looking for crew. Didn't find any."

"The phaso?"

"I'm afraid they got it. If it was in that strongbox you hid, it's gone." He bit his bloody lip. "Wren's locator was dead. I knew you were in trouble. But yours was still active."

So, the fact that they had not damaged my locator had saved our hides. It was still plastered to my blood-sprayed jacket, weaved into the fabric to look like a button. I flashed Wren what might have been a grateful, questioning stare.

She grinned. "You saved me from that sorry planet of Talyon, so the least I could do is save your hide."

"You did well. I don't know how you did it, but you pulled it off."

Her shoulders twitched in a shrug. "Those cretins underestimated me, as does every lout, and they all died. I must thank you, TK. Those fareons you showered made them think twice and I grabbed the first scum's knife and cut off his balls. Then I got his gun. Small payback for the pains those lowlifes've caused us."

I flinched and got Wren to bring the metal tin labeled 'regen' from the overhead bulkhead. I got her to smear a generous dose on my throbbing stump. I cried out in agony as the thick orange paste made contact with the exposed bone and the nerve ends. But the glopping goo did its work. A stinging pain, like pepper spray applied to an open wound, then a sizzling of flesh, as it cauterized the flesh and bone. Then came a flood of warm, tingling sensations, as small bits of tissue rebuilt themselves, and I was in heaven—momentarily.

The flesh-regen was good for rebuilding small tissues like a missing ear, damaged tongue or even major skin damage, but not, I knew, for regenerating bones. Ligaments or complex nerve tissue would need a level of regen I did not have. But the orange paste would keep the tissue primed if there was any hope for a new hand—which I seriously doubted at this point.

I began to drift away, my eyes dilating, swinging back in my skull like a church bell, with the loss of blood and Wren slapping my face. She began mouthing words, anything that would keep me from fading into non-existence. I remember a garbled story, out of sync with the words coming from her lips. She was probably trying to keep me from succumbing to shock and bleeding out, despite the regen.

"Stay with us, Rusco, you stupid sod." *Slap, slap.* I blinked. "Think of my daughter before you think of dying. I lost Kela and I was a broken, empty doll. No purpose or direction. The manner of her death messed me up most, Rusco, brought me nightmares every sleepless night. I tucked myself into some safe harbor, away from them, away from harm, knowing that those scumlord sadists were out there hiding in the shadows with their machetes and ships and guns, waiting to rape and torture and wring every bit of goodness out of me and everybody else—my kin and friends. So, I hid like a feral animal, just like what we're doing now, and went back into a deep, dark place, like the sand dervishes, hiding under rock, dunghill, every piece of broken metal, a dirty, scavenging castaway killing anything that threatened us with my sawed-off rod. Once when the thing refused to fire, I used it to beat off two grimy, hooded lowlifes with lust and murder on their minds. Another time four had tried to gang rape me, pulled off all my clothes, bloodied me up, broke my fingers. This one never healed right—" She held up her left hand and in my delirium, I saw how the index finger had been twisted and crooked. But I knew that already, didn't I?

"They failed, Rusco. Not too far off from what the scum tried to do to me today in that storeroom, but they got a surprise."

Her voice faded in and out, as we neared Gainor and she took our earnings from the stash box where I kept the phaso and I mouthed the combination in her ears, not TK's, as I didn't trust the man despite his recent heroics...

I sat there, my mind hallucinating as if I were on psychedelics with the regen and the Myscol.

The next series of events passed in a dream, with a strange bliss punctuated by snippets of conversations and figures I knew must be medics. Concerned faces peered at me. Men and women dressed in white coats, objects of whimsy and perplexity. Echoes of endless speculation and questions arrowed at me. I blinked like a dumb mule, opened my mouth, unable to fire up my vocal chords.

When I came out of the anesthetic, I realized Wren had taken me to some black market shop. A raw ache trickled down my right side. Fingertips alienated from fingers, fingers alienated from hand, hand alienated from wrist, alternating from a dull numbness to rabid agony.

I grunted, rolled over with a curse.

"Careful, sir," the female attendant said. "The circuits will need time to adjust to the nerve signals. I know it is disorienting." I looked down at my duck hand and flexed the mechanical fingers. Pain, lots of it; the effort to get them to flutter, even the minutest, was staggering.

"Therapy will be in-depth and intense," she said. "Two weeks you should have most of your motor control back, but not strength. We installed a Trinbal T4 circuit limber in your wrist. It was within your budget." The orderly's remark seemed to be almost an afterthought.

I flashed Wren a sallow grin. Step right up, kids—JR, mechno man coming through!

I got back to the Starrunner, and we made for the nearby world. I didn't know which one nor did I care. So began the first day of a long series on a road to depression. The worst had finally caught up to me. Maimed for life.

But now was not the time for self pity. I gathered TK and we scoured the bridge. At last we found that tracking bug hidden under the console. Like a tiny black parasite. Raez'd taken a panel off. It was a clever plant; TK's previous searches for the phaso had not found the tracker. I motioned the old man's hand away when he reached to pull it off and destroy it. "No!" A part of me was still Jet Rusco, the cunning fox that never gave up. I knew that miserable device would come in handy one day. "Can you disable it?"

"Probably."

"Do it then."

TK complied without a grumble. An hour later it was done and I took the bug and locked it away in my cabin.

Looking down at my mechno hand, I admired the fake covering of human skin, a hue slightly lighter than my own, the fingers stronger than my fleshy ones, but not my own. Feeling something of dead and wooden weight there.

And with it came the raging urge to strip off my old identity, become the fierce torrent, the unstoppable rush of what I was to become. The old Jet Rusco was gone, kaput. A vengeful one birthed—an avenger to destroy every scumbag crime lord I could get my hands on, starting with Pazarol, Baer and that mad fuck, Mong, who had caused so many senseless miseries and the deaths of so many people. I didn't care who died, who lived, or who got mangled up, or if I got robot parts to replace my whole body. Those fuckers were going down.

We'd lost our payout and our cargo, and our shields were whittled to about zero—as our Varwol.

These details I noted and considered, as we limped along to the next planet, though I was barely there in essence, going through the motions like some sock puppet powered by a clown master. I felt half a man, as if my manhood had been shunted. Biomech Rusco, suffering from implant stress disorder. Mech organ rejection.

Whatever the fuck.

I didn't care and I had to snap out of this downward spiral.

Chapter 19

After repairing the Varwol on Gainor, I pushed TK away from the controls and set the course for Merius, the asteroid belt. To a place on the fringe where I remembered Deros the dwarf planet shone with its greenish tinge around its edges.

"Rusco? Are you out of your mind?" TK gasped.

"They fucked with the wrong asshole."

"What're you scheming?"

"Lure those scumbags into a trap they'll wish they'd never sprung."

"How?" TK's mouth twitched. "I don't like that murderous look in your eyes, Rusco. I've seen it in you before and I don't want anything to do with it."

"Tough shit. Get used to it, TK. There's a reckoning to be had."

"With big bad Baer?" he guffawed. "What have you got to bargain with? The phaso's gone. Remember, they got it?"

"Yeah, too bad about that."

He flashed me a perplexed look. "You don't sound too broken up about it." His eyes widened. "Wait, you still got it?"

"Whatever gave you that idea?"

"You're a tricky bastard, Rusco." He slapped me on the back, his lips working in a grin. I pulled away, not liking his overly familiar back slaps.

It was a full scale war I waged now on Baer and Pazarol. Unfair of me to ensnare TK and Wren in it, but I was committed and I knew I'd need their help. Bounty hunters had no doubt been alerted, with a larger price on my head and all our miserable hides. Our ship, bugged, a magnet for slaughter and yet I planned to push the red card a little further.

Time to install the tracker back in the ship. As I tinkered under the console with wires I'd ripped out two weeks ago, TK's jaw went slack.

"What in hell are you doing?"

"Installing the bug back in the transcom, what's it look like?"

"Are you crazy?" He reached down to pull the device out.

I slapped his hand away and told him to back off. "It stays on." I flashed him a dangerous look.

"What do you mean, it stays on?"

"Listen, can you jumpstart this thing, TK, so we can monitor it, where it transmits?"

He blinked, gave me a dazed inspection. "I can, sure. But why? There's a risk you'll tip them off by sending static down the line."

"Just want to know the message is getting through and it's received. A lot depends on this working, like our lives."

He gave me a lip-chewing appraisal when I told him more of my plan. "I can do that."

"I'm banking that they won't kill us, without getting their precious phaso back."

Misinformation. Misdirection. We'll lead the flies to the spider's web. A ghoulish smirk played across my lips. I looked down and flexed my robot hand. Pulling myself to my feet, I recalled all the forsaken derelicts of this solar system floating out in space and an old memory stirred: Belisar One, Primary Ore Station near Deros, the largest of the dwarf planets in the asteroid belt. I tapped some keypads and it came up in the holo field. "There!" I zoomed in and we studied the floor plans. "It's still intact. We can probably rig the place without suits, if the air generators are still operational."

TK muttered under his breath.

I summoned Wren to the bridge and told her the basics of my plan. "The phaso and amalgo are the imaginary bait we use to seed the dropoff point. Some fictional buyer while our gangster friends are listening on the wire. They come running to seize the cargo, but a little surprise awaits them. Simple."

"Sounds doable." She grinned.

"And dangerous," TK snarled. "I don't think it's survivable, Rusco, given the firepower they had on Trellian."

"I wasn't asking you. Now can you study the upper floor plan and map out entrances and exits? It's vast. We need a confined area to work from."

The Varwol kicked out and got us to Deros, a misshapen would-be planet, looming brown and grey under distant Jesra's weak light. On the near side hung Belisar station, an old derelict fish-spine station with multiple bays and landing docks stemming from the main vertebrae—one of those giant outposts left over from yesteryear—a monster of the past no longer operational. Had the works: artificial gravity, ore processing equipment, massive storage, redistribution.

The station grew closer as Starrunner's impulse engines guided us in to its central core, a desolate hulk, which had survived massive wars, now dark and dead. Life support systems? Unlikely. Air, heat, emergency lights, I hoped, if we could activate them.

We approached the top, diamond-shaped crown and landed in a still-open port—Bay D-2. I tried various radio signals hoping to trigger the hatch behind. One of the common bands worked. The hatch closed behind us and sealed the depressurization chamber, letting the air flood back up. A green light showed on the inner wall. So...some of the systems were still online after all these years—incredible. A power source was still connected, solar, I deduced from the array of panels deployed on the station's superstructure.

I got out with Wren, wearing a light mask and suit. At the back of the landing pad, double doors led to a command bay that had been looted over the years. Many ore bins and sorting stations that it overlooked on a lower level caught my attention. A perfect ambush zone. We could stage an explosive web of horrors for our guests. Blow those bastards out of the sky.

Wren and I worked for hours installing explosive packs and trip wires that I'd picked up on Gainor, booby trapping the place nicely. The artificial grav docks were still functional, a definite plus, otherwise we'd be floating off our feet. Heating and air systems had automatically kicked in with our presence. When it was done, we had two sets of fireworks installed in the command bay, fore and aft. All exits were wired to the touch of a button. Both Wren and I would carry remote detonators.

I'd even rigged Starrunner to explode should the worse-case scenario occur, we got boarded, then we'd all go up in a cloud of smoke. Let's hope it didn't come to that. TK's bulging eyes blinked when he saw what we were doing and what I was planning.

"Why don't we just zoom off to a faraway star system? Do we have to be so dramatic?" His voice was a low plaintive mutter.

I snorted. "And have the next ice man waiting around to jab us with a pick? Gotta nip these moguls in the bud, TK, buddy. Do you want to live running in fear for the rest of your days?"

"No, but you're not considering all the risks."

"Trust me. This is the minimum risk. Once we get rid of our bugbears, we're free to roam the galaxy, working our scams."

Wren mumbled her agreement. "I'm fed up with being shadowed by murderous scum."

TK sighed and threw his hands up in the air. The man looked gray and worn around the edges. Arolin, a martial arts expert, once told me the color of a man reflects his aura when his number is up. I think TK was feeling a bit of that. That slight quivering in the left wrist, the nervous tic of eye, the quick labored breathing and grey pallor of face. Perhaps the scrape back on Trellian had been too much, or maybe Billy's death had got to him, or my hand being shot off. Whatever, he looked as gray as a ghost, and I guessed he was on his way to cracking.

I set Starrunner on a course for Elphi Alpha's airspace to stage the call, far away from Deros. I made sure that we were out of warp and the tracker was active and we were speaking within range of its pickup. I had my friend Loue on Elphi Alpha play an imaginary script, rehearsed in advance on an encrypted line. I didn't want to give Baer and his mongrel brood a lot of time to plan an attack on us, so I only gave them two hours lead time.

"Loue? Meet us at the upper dock D-2 on Belisar...yeah, that's the one, the abandoned ore hub orbiting Deros...Yes, that's two hours on the nose, not a minute later or sooner. Don't worry, I'll have both phaso and amalgo ready and waiting for you....Price, an even 40. Any fuckups, or no shows, and the price goes up 50%... Believe me, I've had enough hassles with these pieces of shit and I'll be glad to get rid of them...that cockroach Baer's almost cooked me twice. After this deal I'm going on a long ride to Pegasus or Ramses or whatever...Yeah, bittersweet memories." I cut the line and saw the activating circuit light in yellow and knew the message had gotten through, to whoever, wherever. The signal piggybacked off our own transcom and would be sent through encrypted and unencrypted channels.

"It's done," I said and moved away from the pickup range.

Wren remarked, "Let's just hope they don't seize the opportunity to blast us out of the sky."

"Don't worry, Wren. We'll get our payback."

A particularly dark legend surrounded Belisar station, one of alien origin lost in time. Strange and inexplicable artifacts found down there on the dwarf planet: a squid-like intelligent warlord race, Zakro or Zipri or something, extinct now, whose only legacy was scattered bones with fanned, herring-bone spines turning up on the odd world or two. Made me shiver. All the mine charters came through Belisar at one time, the mining deeds for every jackleg asteroid, no matter how small. But some unknown scourge had infected the dwarf planet, an epidemic or parasite of some sort, made its way into the mined ore and the station had been closed.

"You should be more worried about Mong than Baer," said TK, interrupting my reverie, "at least from what you describe of the man while you were strapped in that chair. If it were me, I'd turn tail and never look back."

"That's you, not me. As I said, TK, there's no bucking necessity." Still I recalled that frightful face of the star lord and his hulking presence and shivered. Mong was a red herring who was impossible to read.

TK's bright bird-like voice chirped. "Mong's lust for the alien tech exceeds what you'd expect from a power monger of his sort. He could have empires, planets, wealth and power beyond measure! Yet he's chasing us all over the galaxy for a tiny piece of hardware. Ever think of that? Something to consider before you leap into the lion's jaws."

I shrugged and focused on the last minute details of the operation. Yet TK's voice had infected me with a bug that had my brain spinning. I pored over all the words I had ever heard from Mong and the news reports on him. So what drove the megalomaniac? Galactic dominion, yes. But why was the amalgo so important to him? Some men, or quasi-humans, desired power over all other beings. Mong was different. He wanted respect also—to be perceived as the next messiah. Go a peg deeper, Rusco. Was the man really that deluded into thinking that he was actually helping the human race by taking over their planets? A poignant snippet came to mind, *"They do not know what they want. A unified community and existence, free of warring bandits, free from slums. I will give it to them, Baer. Through hell or high water, I will give it to them."* Vivid was the crusader's manifesto I'd overheard back in that torture room on Trellian...

It seemed that Baer was no crueler or kinder than this master. But Baer was only a peon, a simple minion in the larger scheme of a grander visionary; Mong could have modelled himself on the warlord Genghis Khan, throwing in a twist of the cultist. No matter. The beast was after me, to the death. As was Baer. I'd robbed him of his limb, true, as he had mine. Now we were even, and one of us had to die…

I reviewed my strategies and could find no flaw. Starrunner's shields were low, so I'd spared no expense in replenishing my ship's defenses with a heavy duty Rexar 3 magno-electrovolt mesh, knowing one day the device might save my hide—like the present. Wren was grinning like a cat; TK was shitting bricks. As I punched the hyperdrive to get to Belisar, I wondered what ball I'd started rolling by the simple act of turning on that tracker.

The red lights glowed on the overhead panel, signaling our arrival at Deros as the Varwol cut out.

Asteroid belt, Merius, spread behind us and Deros station loomed below, a half billion miles from Jesra.

From what I had gathered of its operation, all ore and crystals, including Barenium, amassed from the nearby moons, asteroids and space rock, had been collected here for transshipment to neighboring worlds.

If this plan worked, the reapers would come knocking soon.

The camouflaged suit hung still there on the peg by the weapons rack, along with the poison-tipped boots Pazarol had given me. I looked at the garb and cast them a sour grin: Pazarol's gift might come in handy.

I murmured to Wren, "They'll probably try to ambush us when we get settled into the drop point. Let's be ready." I adjusted the straps on the AK custom blaster slung over my shoulder, and the pouch containing the grenades.

"You don't know that," hissed TK, his face grim.

"Your point?"

Wren interceded. "I'm surprised they haven't tried to blow us up already."

"Until Mong and his monkeys get their alien tech, they'll keep us alive. That's what I've been banking on this whole time."

As we came within docking distance of the station, I made out more details: immeasurably long superstructure, shaped like a fish vertebrae with scores of side wings extending ninety degrees outward.

The upper tiers of the main hub spread out like a honeycomb: rows for small craft like ours to dock in. Below that, larger octagonal ports spread, gray and sealed now, as they had been for centuries, since the large freighters had come to dock and transfer their payloads. An impressive piece of architecture all said and done. Belisar sprawled like a fantastic ark, the single portal open to the landing bay, just as we had left it. Already our scanners had picked up one bogey on our tail, too far away to do any damage, but proof that the bait had been nibbled. We'd hole up in the mining station before long, ready our explosives and wait for armageddon.

No sooner had we reached docking distance with upper deck loading bay D-2 than a sudden blue blip flashed across the starboard viewport. A black ship vaulted out of nowhere. Wtf? A stealth ship? Drone? It was shaped like a manta ray and had that sleek, streamlined look of new tech and black death, some harbinger of doom. Either way, it had slipped under our radar. A blue beam of destruction came flaring out of its fuselage, one of those long-range fareon rays. With horror, I realized my well-oiled plans were becoming unglued from the onset. Our enemies had timed their strike with just enough force to incapacitate us, rather than destroy us.

Our shields buckled; the ship rocked, sending us in a tailspin as we slewed into the landing port. I jammed the forward thrusters to compensate and save us from colliding with the side of the docking bay. Starrunner ran high up into the open landing bay.

Starrunner spun down on her side, trailing sparks from her underbelly, smoking from her midsection. *What can go wrong, will go wrong*, the universal law of consequences. Molly's voice crackled through the gloom. *"Critical meltdown of engine core. Ship's Barenium unstable."*

At the edge of my vision, the viewscreen showed impending disaster. Baer's ship and her companion vessel, a stealth V-Ray, glided in through the hatch before we could manually trigger the portal closed. *Shit.*

I snapped out of my daze. We were sitting ducks in this smoking coffin. "Out! Now!"

Wren and TK scrambled through the smoke, grabbing R4s and masks and coughing, staggered to the port hatch. The sealed landing dock re-pressurized automatically and I cranked the hatch wheel upon seeing the green lamp blink on the far wall. But it would only turn half way, and I had to kick it several times before it would loosen. We were in a bad place, trapped between the ship's stern and our protective enclave while enemies roved about. The booby-trapped command area with all my careful snares was the only safe area for us at the moment. My synthetic fingers clenched the detonators with tingling desperation.

I did not set any off.

We forced our way through the cold but warming air, toward the double revolving safety doors of the command area. I ran up to the exit, my steel-tipped boots clanking on the grates.

Wren and I dove for the command room, TK lagging behind, puffing for air, his breath coming out in steamy gasps. I got off a few shots, but I wasn't going to trade ammo with the vague figures emerging from both ships and become instant space fodder.

"Into the command bay! Quickly," I hissed. "Let them fall prey to our traps."

"If we don't have a ship," cried TK, "what good will it do?"

I waved a hand. "Messenger shuttle may still by salvageable." *Better to give them hope than futility.*

"We don't have time—"

"Shut up and move!" I cried.

Wren herded the old man on, grumbling for him to tough it up. "We go to plan, TK. Think 'plan'."

I could see the terror writ in the old man's eyes. Under that dim swath of emergency lights, his broken, defeated look mirrored the inevitable, the shadow of looming death.

"Use minimum fire," I barked. "Draw them out with the explosives. Don't give away our positions."

I looked back and Baer and two dozen of his men were pouring out of the first vessel with laser-guided AKs—remodeled blasters with stun capability. Swift, capable men, garbed in loose black fatigues, like modern ninjas, dark skull caps tucked over their ears. I knew in an instant those killers meant to capture us and torture us for the information leading to the amalgo. I was under no illusion that this round of torture would make the last look like a kindergarten picnic. Under no circumstance must any of us get captured.

A group of five of them branched off to search Starrunner. *Good, keep them busy.* The rest moved in after us.

Chapter 20

My eyes dilated, adjusting to the murk. The command area of Belisar One was a rubble-strewn sprawl just as we'd left it. A pool of blue-black shadows with lots of places to hide showed itself, rigged with enough booby traps to kill an elephant and several lions thrown in. The place had been looted by bandits over the decades, as evidenced by the hodgepodge of overturned consoles, smashed component boxes, spilled circuits with wires showing. The pillars that supported the honeycombed ceiling had whole sections eaten out of them. By machine gun fire. Wedges were cut out as if drunken bandits had aimed a thousand shots and chewed holes into the walls. At least the idiots had left the port door alone.

The light was so dim as to make it difficult to see. Only a faint ambient bluish glow spilled from the windows overlooking the interior of the station.

I motioned to TK and Wren, urging them to the side wall to duck behind the random wastage while I staggered in a bent-kneed crouch over to the opposite wall to lure the others out and activate the explosives. Good thing the heating and air systems had powered on during our last mission, eliminating the need for suits. I made quick time to the back corner where the paneled glass looked into the interior: a place of silence, brooding and mystery. Below, the lower level showed massive ore bins, sorting stations and holding pods. A vast tangle of machinery, piping, docking stations, catwalks and inky depressions lurked in those confines. The emergency lights dimmed, then cut out. The unearthly blue glow flickered back on again, so recently activated by human presence after many decades.

Despite what I'd told TK about Starrunner, I felt sick at the loss of her. In her state she was of little use. We were marooned here—like castaways, stuck out in nowhere with no hope of rescue or little chance of making repairs. I thrust that anxiety out of my mind.

A dozen and a half enemy, lean and silent as weasels, came slinking in low on a wide sweep of the area. Their laser sights gave away their position while ours remained dark. We had an advantage, but they had the superior numbers.

I signaled Wren with my silent communicator: lie low. The plan was for me to draw them out, pick off stragglers with explosives, and rely on the camo qualities of my guerrilla suit to keep them at bay.

I chucked a piece of broken circuitry toward the first plant of explosives by the lower level ore carts. Several green laser sights lanced to the spot and eager figures split up to investigate.

My sweat-beaded face curled in a cold grin. I saw a line of them moving toward the sound. *Fools.* My body tingled with expectation. Imminent slaughter was moments away.

Just as the pack was within blasting distance of the far wall, I pinched my thumb on the detonator. Flesh and sinew erupted in a crimson mash. The force took out six of them, shredding them like ripe carrots in a blender. Bloody shreds of arms, legs and torsos sprayed in the immediate vicinity.

Baer's voice rumbled over the flames. "Fan out, you stupid fools! That fuck Rusco's got the place rigged! He wasn't so dumb after all. Flush him out. Quickly. Now!"

"But boss—"

"Shut the fuck up! What am I paying you for, blockhead? Move!" He thrust the man forward. "Don't cluster in too tight and let him take you down."

I pressed the left detonator. *Kabam.* Another bright blast took out four more of the black-masked bastards, leaving a gaping hole in the ore bins and tangle of machinery below. Bright fire licked out at me as I sprang from one hiding place to another behind an overturned console. *Keep them moving.* Make them think there was a rat's nest of snipers and ambushers around them.

I winced. Shit, they were rounding on Wren. Someone must have sighted a flicker of movement. That idiot TK panicked, for he began shooting a spray into the fray. I told the fuck not to fire! Except in an emergency as it gave away location.

A howling cry rose above the mayhem. Another black enemy fell on a knee, shin shattered by the shells.

Wren joined in the firefight. Two more gunmen groaned in anguish and fell face down in the rubble.

We were down to four plus change.

But three of them started firing, and like a death squad, rained a fury of inescapable green at Wren and TK. They were smart, those stalkers; they took out the pillar where Wren and TK had dug in and the ceiling collapsed on them. A ton of metal came crashing down and I heard Wren's sharp cry echo in peaked anguish. The girders folded like a tent around them, offering them some small cocoon—I hoped. All I could see was a dull gleam of metal where she was. I swore silently and acted without hesitation. The explosion had left her pinned behind a mangled ceiling panel.

TK must have managed to wiggle free for I could hear his hoarse grunts and curses. I could vaguely make out a dark outline moving along the shadowy backdrop of the side wall. His or an enemy's?

I scooted closer. Like a thief in the dark, I kept low. My itchy fingers hovered over the last of the detonators. But the enemy was nowhere in my sights, nowhere near my kill zone.

I think the last four heard Wren. I set off the last explosive, only serving as a costly diversion, and while they staggered back, wondering what next booby trap they'd step into, I raced forward, struggling to cover the area to their left side. She was gasping and cursing and banging on the metal that covered her.

I rapped hard, hissing at her to quiet down. I grabbed an old machine tool, a hammer or something, caked with eons of dust and launched it somewhere behind them. One of the stalkers whirled around at the clatter of metal and loosed a shot. I launched out like a cat to a new defensive position, but was forced to dodge around and confuse them before I could come back to her.

"Sh," I hissed at her, trying to imagine the terror she felt trapped under that mangled mess. "Stay silent, you hurt?"

"Pinned, can't get out," her muffled voice came back. "Left arm is throbbing."

I whispered, "Wren, listen to me. Stay put, no noise. Don't try to move. I'll get you out—but not now." I couldn't peel the metal back around her without alerting those fucks to my position.

They were returning. Shit! This was not going well. I backed off, my head in a quandary, a high buzzing in my ear.

"The old subterfuge trick," Baer called out in the murk. "Nice job, Rusco. I expected more from you. Disappointing that you let your arm get blown up like mine. We're two peas in a pod, you and me, two fools in a stew pot."

That's it, you dumb fuck. Keep talking. Draw yourself out like a fat fool and use up your energy.

An assassin had positioned himself between Baer and the tangle of metal. Now he was moving closer. Before long he'd clue in to where Wren was, trapped and helpless.

I slunk away, hoping to draw him away. No luck. The bugger kept sidling closer, weapon trained at the fallen mass of metal. Where the hell was TK? Why wasn't the twit helping?

I sidewinded back and snuck up behind him while the gunman was focused on the debris, weapon aimed at the fallen ceiling. I hoped to neutralize him while he was preparing to take out the two of us whom he thought cowered behind that mound.

I dove at this hulking figure, meaning to kick him in the groin with my poison-tipped boot to avoid firing and giving away my position. But the stalker heard the crunch of glass under my boot and pivoted. I ducked, missing by a hair his stun beam, wrapped my arms about his waist and brought him crashing to the ground. I knocked his weapon away. The man was exceedingly strong and he bent me backward to the point I could feel my spine creaking under the pressure. I pummeled him with my fists and in a mad tangle of arms and legs, we grappled and hooked, grunted and cursed. My hard right lashed out and I caught him with my elbow in his teeth. He loosed a garbled cry. I scrambled to my feet, kicked out a foot while rising, and grazed him high on the thigh. He went down with a howl, shivering for an instant and was dead within seconds. An impressive fast-acting poison. I staggered over the body, panting as I saw his glassy eyes stare up. No time to get Wren. I stumbled away from the booted feet coming closer to my position as they set scarlet sights upon me—scarlet meant moderate to lethal.

Peeow. Peeow. Bright laser fire licked past my ribs, shredding consoles and metal.

I couldn't find my weapon in the dim light. Fuck it. I'd lost it.

I saw the dead man's firearm, a long fat rod of dark length in the shadows. I dove for it, snatching up his modified AK, then rolled flat to fire on the last moving shapes in the dark. But the damn thing jammed. I threw it away in disgust. Laser lines were sighting on me. With a hissing curse, I scrambled crab-wise for cover. *Rat-a-tat-tat.* A death rattle for heart-pumping Rusco. Terror raged at my heels, shredding everything around me. Those were no stun rays. They were real shelled bullets.

"Rusco, give it up," shouted Baer. "You're a dead man. You've no ship and your explosives can't last forever." His panting voice rose above the shell chatter. "Tell you what—give me the phaso, and I'll call it even—"

"Phaso? Why didn't you say so?" I called.

Restless rumblings came from the huddle, like a nest of rats from where I counted three, with weapons cocked, laser sights trained in my direction. I ducked, held my breath behind a mound of shredded tin. Wished I was the invisible man right now.

Baer held up a hand to the others to hold their fire. He advanced like a hairy beast.

"Tell me where it is, Rusco."

"If you really want it, Baer, it's in the conduit leading to the Barenium cylinders in my ship. I hid it there, taped it to the silver metal siding for safe-keeping. Go ahead and check—it's out of harm's reach, and the hands of even my own crew."

"More like a trap," he jeered.

"Believe what you want. Send one of your crew members to check." I ducked down, inching away from there to another overturned console a few yards away.

I hoped they'd fall for the lure as I'd bomb-rigged that conduit. It would mean one or two less thugs for me to kill.

How everything was going to shit right now. It would kill Starrunner's Barenium drive for good but better that than dying here at the hands of these cutthroats. A gamble. I hadn't counted on both TK and Wren being neutralized so soon.

One of them left on quiet feet; I could feel a lightening of presence. It was about the same time I noticed some other dark figure trail after him with a hobbling gait. TK? Where was that sneaky fuck going? Maybe he was going to take down the errand boy. I hoped so.

My explosives were done. I'd been reaching for a fallen hunk of metal a yard away from my defensive position. It lay in open sight, but I was afraid that if they saw the small movement, they'd blow my hand off. And I wasn't about to let that happen again.

I tried to keep Baer talking. Fortunately Wren had made herself quieter than a church mouse. *Make the Baer blunder.* The man had a gun, I didn't. A distinct disadvantage in this miserable situation so any winning trick was a good one. I'd grab onto it like a drowning man grasped for straws.

"I'm not sweet on the phaso, truth be told, Rusco," said Baer. "Just tell us where the amalgo is, and we'll be out of your hair."

Just like that, you slimebitch, as if we were old pals? I grinned. "The amalgo's a little trickier, Baer. Truth be told, it isn't here, hate to tell you. I put it somewhere safe. Thought you'd like that."

He chuckled. "I do, and that's good to hear. For a second, I thought you might have gone and done something stupid like destroy it to spite me. After that unfortunate incident back on Trellian."

"No, nothing like that, Baer. I got better things to do with my time than play the spiteful bitch."

"Haw haw. You'll have to tell me where it is sometime. I got a short temper with this one at the moment."

To my right came a shuffle of feet. I could hear two of them. Flanking me like foxes at the henhouse, moving inch by inch, expecting that I had another detonator to trigger, but I'd drawn my last card.

"Tell your gophers to stay back," I croaked. "Otherwise I'll blow them up like the rest of your tainted meat."

Baer nodded, signaled the two to stop. "So, what do we do now?" he said. "Seems as if we're at a stalemate."

I let the seconds pass. I was running out of options. Just when I was about to do something desperate, I detected a hint of motion back near the landing dock entrance.

TK, the mysterious sod, was slinking by the side wall. The crystal ring clutched in his trembling hand; it radiated that queer iridescent glow that had always mesmerized me. What was the fool up to? Maybe he thought to use the phaso as a bargaining chip? To save his own hide? Why had he left Wren, though? Seemed cowardly in my opinion. I couldn't quite figure it.

The dark animal shape of Baer lunged out of the shadows and intercepted him, speaking low in his ear. "The phase-shifter or I blow your cock off, asshole."

TK whirled, looking as surprised as I'd been. "Stay back or I nuke it," he rasped, twisting on his hips. He jammed his weapon down at the phaso.

"Go ahead, blast it, you muttonhead, you die next."

TK's eyes flicked away, a trickle of anxiety running down his hollow cheeks.

"Don't be stupid, TK," I warned him. "Give him the phaso. Or we all die."

"Shut up, Rusco. We're all dead anyway!" He turned, scowling at me like a fishwife. "You let Billy die. I owe you nothing. You left him out there, you bastard."

"Think again. Billy's dead and you can't save him."

"We might have saved him," he whimpered. The old man was all choked up. "He might have gotten away." He lifted his gun hand to wipe at his running nose.

A moment of distraction that allowed Baer to put a ruby ray between his eyes. TK dropped like a strawman, the phaso rolling out of his hand like a pinwheel. One of Baer's goons reached to snatch it up then disappeared in a haze of multicolored light. The idiot hadn't grabbed it properly, so he winked out of existence much as had Billy and Mitch, unaware of the alien device's potential.

Baer swore as I jumped up and hurled the bar in my hand like a boomerang. Didn't care who I hit. Just that it hit. I clocked the first thug in the neck. He fell choking in his own blood with a crushed windpipe. At the same time, I scuttled out like a crab, grabbed the phaso with my sleeve, and was up and running to the next place of protection. I dove behind a component box just before Baer's fire could eat away at me.

He cursed and I heard muffled cries coming from Wren, still trapped underneath that wretched panel, maybe injured or maybe not. She kicked and cursed, lashed out at the metal. *Shut up, you stupid woman.* Christ, she had a foul tongue.

"Nice move, Rusco. I'm guessing you're right out of explosives by now by the look of that little missile you cast. Makes my job a lot easier."

The bear-man moved forward, emptying fire into the scraps of metal that shielded me and I cried out in pain as a hot flare grazed my side, singeing leather and drawing blood.

"Feel like talking now?" he grunted. "I know you're still there. I can smell your dirty hide. Once I get you, I'm going to cut off your head, then take your squealing bitch back for a ride she'll never forget."

I crouched, my heart beating, counting the moments. *Come on, Rusco, think.*

"Just you and me," laughed Baer. "Your geriatric mechanic is down, but I guess you saw that, didn't you? Sure you did. The girl? Well, she ain't sounding as if she's too available right now." He laughed, an acidy hyena chuckle. "Why don't you just come out like a good boy, and we can settle this like men, instead of rustling around in the dark, shitting in the corners like mice?"

'That's a nice idea for someone with a gun."

"It is what it is, Rusco. Not leaving here until I have your head on a platter. Part of the deal I made with Mong. Either your head or mine. Mong gave me the choice, a month to track your miserable hide down and deliver the phaso. Said he'd make a captain of me in his army, with all the material perks of war."

"That's a nice deal, Baer. Congratulations." *Three down, only one black bear to go.*

My prosthetic hand twitched. A bad time for it to act up. Control it, Rusco. It reached out and clutched the smooth, cool surface of the phaso, my last card.

"You've been duped by a charlatan with psi power, Baer. Parlor tricks that a well-timed hit from a blaster can end in a second."

"You're wrong there," Baer grunted, loosing another spray of fire as he moved closer. "I've seen Mong employ telekinetic powers that you wouldn't believe. Got 'em through his meditation on dark gods, that black religion or whatever he dabbles in. You don't know the power of the man."

"I could give a shit about his powers, if he sucked Adam's dick. Give me a gun and I'll put a bullet in the lizard's brain."

"Tsk, tsk. Now that's no way to badmouth somebody who isn't here to defend himself. Didn't your mother teach you manners? Think Mong would have something to say about that fly-away tongue of yours. Shame on you, Rusco. Plan on getting me back that little phaso. If I don't, the star lord's death warrant awaits."

"You've already mentioned that, Baer. Going Alzheimer on me?"

Hearing my labored breathing, he strode in with a leisurely gait. "Mong told me all about that phaso. The Mentera were stupid enough in how they employed the technology. They could have ruled the universe, and almost did, but lost it at the end. Now they're only passing memories. Mong and I'll not make the same mistake."

Famous last words, reptile brain. All the while I'd been edging around his left side, inching on my stomach like an eel, leaving a small trail of blood and slime behind me. Wren chose that instant to whimper and as Baer turned his ugly head and muttered, "That's right, bitch, you'd better—" I lurched up.

"Peekaboo." I lobbed the phaso at him and he swatted out a hairy hand to block it, or grab it? It amounted to the same. As I dove sideways in a desperate roll, he blinked out of existence, flicked out to nowhere land like his buddy and Mitch and Billy before him. I shuttled forward, snatched up the dead gunman's AK and did a wide sweep, expecting a host of criminals to come at me all at once. They didn't. I loosed a spray of fire and a wolfish howl all around me in a half moon. Heart beating, I stumbled to the place where the phaso was and where Baer had last blinked out, as warily as a wolf who approaches a steel-ringed trap.

I stooped to pick up the glimmering disc with my sleeve and pocketed it. I grinned from ear to ear, familiar Rusco now, raw, crinkly grin. "Okay, good, everything's good," I assured myself. I staggered over to the tented hump of metal where Wren lay trapped and began pulling the sheets back. I had to use the full force of my dwindling strength, legs braced, while the aches crawled up my arms. Wren's obvious distress gave me added haste.

"Okay, kiddo, we're clear." Grunting, with anguished efforts and the augmented strength of my mechano-hand, I pried back the last of the metal and dragged her to her feet. She was a dusty mess, all stooped and haggard, limping and bedraggled, but her dark eyes burned with a fierce light. A dark crust of blood caked her left forearm. She shook her slim body out, blinking. Her right hand massaged the small of her back where I'd guessed she'd lain for too long on her bulky R4.

"Took you long enough," she groused. She looked around, scooping up her weapon from the cramped cubbyhole. "They all dead?"

"Dead."

"Baer?"

"Dead."

"Good." She snuffled out a grunt of satisfaction. "All's fair in love and war. So we've won?"

"I'd say so, outside of having no Starrunner."

Wren swore. "Let's go take a look. TK might be able to work some magic on it. Where is the old complainer?"

"I regret to say TK's no longer with us."

She gave her head a sad, wistful shake. "The man had a death wish right from the start. I almost felt he'd expected to join Billy one way or the other today."

"Those were my very same feelings."

She scowled. "Let's get to the ship then."

She held me tight, and I winced at the pressure of her trembling body, warm and a relief. "Thank you, Jet. You protected me when I thought I was done. You're a good man."

I grunted, not versed in any displays of emotion.

"Rusco, you're quivering and all shot up." She wiped away the blood smear off her hand.

"What about you? That nasty cut on your arm isn't looking too good. Mine could have been worse."

She lifted up my leathers, ignoring her own gash, and tore a strip off her own jacket and wrapped it around my ribs. "We need to get that wound cleaned up. You're going to have a nasty scar there."

"Nothing new." I shrugged, taking only shallow breaths. "Looks as if we both need some patching up."

We limped back to the landing dock.

Starrunner still smoked and crackled as we drew near. Molly's voice, a low garbled robo staccato, rang out from the interior: *"Warning, warning... Barenium irrecoverable leak..."*

"Yeah, I know, Molly."

The computer voice trailed out and died.

I blinked. Starrunner looked crippled beyond repair. I kicked my boot at her hull in despair. I winced at my futile action. "Sorry, Molly. Wherever you are." I ran a caressing finger across the smooth smoking curve of her right wing. Maybe it was time to retire her. The old Rusco too—the one before the mechno hand, and let a new Rusco surface.

"Weeping for your old girlfriend?" she muttered.

"Sort of."

"Sorry to hear, Rusco. She was a good ship to you, I know. She took you places. She brought you to me, and TK and Billy."

"You don't seem too broken up by her demise, considering she's our ride out of here." I clutched my side where the brown leather and makeshift tourniquet bulged and grimaced.

She looked at me with puzzlement. Her gaze shifted to the stealth ship. "What about that one there?"

"Worth a try."

We advanced with caution. The ship was a black sleek killing machine, that manta-ray stealth V. I kept low, weapon ready, in case there were others aboard.

There weren't. No movement, no life. I forced my way through the hatch. Kindly, the crew had left it open. None of the thugs had expected to lose this fight and resort to defending their ship.

We made our way to the bridge. Immaculate. The stealth V was a beauty with state-of-the-art weaponry, compact design, chrome, posh leather seats. Mong must have lent it to the dead Baer, rest his black soul. It would have trackers aboard, and that was a problem. We no longer had TK's expertise to help us out with that. We'd have to make our getaway quickly then ditch the vessel first chance we got.

One more loose end to attend to. I jumped out and dragged two hulks of the shrapneled bodies over to Starrunner and lay them beside her open, smoking hatch. I was worried the Barenium might blow, given Molly's last shrill warning, but risk was risk. I clambered in through the companionways, grabbing some personal effects, regen and the last bottle of whiskey from my smoked-out cabin. I coughed, edged back out in a hurry and dropped my gold watch on one of the charred remains. I aimed my blaster and blackened the remains some more, disfiguring the watch just enough so it could still be recognized. I grabbed Wren's hand and tore off the ring that she still wore on her index finger. She protested, uttering no small number of profane words, but I ignored them. I put the ring on one of the corpse's finger, nearly gagging from the state of the body. I made sure this one was messier than the last, and not easily recognizable as a male versus a female body. TK was next, dragged his sorry hide out, and placed it by the others, face down, what was left of it anyways. Dragged some more pieces of human torsos over to make it look more grisly and authentic. A thrum of voices ran through my head: Where's Baer and the rest of the bodies? Who knows? Where's the stealth ship? Oh, Baer and one or more of his thugs must have gone rogue and stolen it, took the phaso. Rusco and crew? Ha. You're looking at them.

It was a sorrowful business, but anything that'd keep that killer Mong off my tail and make him believe we were dead, was worth the effort.

A sour taste flooded my mouth, surfacing from throat to palate, that bad bit of bile that comes from deep down as I mulled over the sordid events of the day. Up till the end it would remain a mystery to me what exactly TK's motives were. I could only guess that he had some crazy scheme up his sleeve to try to rescue Billy or something. I was sorry he had to die, that the old man had to go and get himself killed, but he did it all under his own free will. For now, I'd give him the benefit of the doubt that he'd come back to help us.

We climbed aboard the stealth V and I slathered the last of the regen on Wren's long gash, wiping the excess on my own ribs. I familiarized myself with the bridge controls while I invited her to take over the weapons console. I never looked back, doubted I'd ever seen Starrunner again.

Chapter 21

Maybe not whole, but I was alive and had one last piece of unfinished business to carry out. The prosthetic started to feel like a part of me, more natural. Maybe I was just getting used to the lack of sensations in my right fingers? I had this mechanized hand on the end of my wrist, something that used to be flesh and bone.

The ship crossed the gulfs back to Elphi Alpha. Returning in good time, our first priority was to ditch this stealth craft. We traded our state-of-the-art vehicle for *Bantam*, an Alpha-Omega Beamer similar to my own Explorer. Regzie's WR, whom we'd done business with during the impound scam, was happy to oblige. He and his associates gave us an extra bonus in change—15k yols, citing our current track record of good business relations. I convinced them to throw in a bunch of tools and ship accessories on the side.

"A mighty fine piece of hardware you have there, Mr. Rambo. Any more trades you'd like to propose, bring 'em our way."

"Sure, I'll do that."

It was time to give Jesra and her brood of planets a rest and let Baer and his men's ghosts lie. I took the Beamer on a direct course toward the inner planets, Tarsus.

"Where now?" Wren asked from across the bridge's conference table. A pang of worry flicked across those dark-shadowed eyes.

When I didn't reply, she grew more restless. "Rusco, don't do anything stupid. That fucker Mong will break your legs and pluck out your eyebrows."

"Don't worry, Wren, nothing so dramatic. If I want dear old Mong dead, I'll leave the heavy lifting to Batman."

"Very funny, but seriously, why not let sleeping dogs—"

"Relax." I outlined my plan to her. The fact that Pazarol was still alive was a loose end that couldn't be tolerated. "Dollars to donuts, Mong'll contract Pazarol to be my next executioner." I grimaced, recalling Pazzy's last promise of playing bounty hunter.

Wren shook her head in dim frustration. "Does it ever end?" She rubbed her eyes, heaving a sigh.

We came in smooth and low over the north end of the shell-shocked industrial zone that marked Belgen's business section. Buzzing the haggard clumps of trees, we left Bantam just under a half mile away in an abandoned yard, not far from Pazzy's crib. Close enough to make a mad dash if we needed to, far enough away that our landing would draw no undue attention. I cut the engines, grabbed my gear, the arsenal of weaponry and snips to cut the wire fence guarding the lot, then we'd have an exit hole readily accessible when the time came to hoof it out of there. It'd be nip and tuck. I had a remote control for the ship. I could run and operate Bantam in limited scope in case we needed the fury of her guns if the situation got desperate. I hoped to hell not.

I drew in a deep breath, inhaling the pungent odor of ozone, tar and something else—a far-off reek of petrochemicals lacing the air from some tall, grimed smokestacks farther down the way. A smoky glow lit up the early evening haze.

I convinced myself the main goal of our expedition was a rescue mission, of the workers whom I'd seen so bruised and mistreated. If Pazarol was there and just happened to get in the way, well, too bad. Right, Rusco, who are you kidding?

I slowed up, my determined stride coming to a halt at the sight of the crumbling line of the brick warehouse. Wren paused at my side, limber and relaxed, as if we were just staking out a kid's birthday party. She had recovered nicely from her scrape at Belisar, given the regen and the efficient muscle machine she was. Those years on Talyon had sure toughened her up, surviving those scuttling dervishes and creepo mad boys. They'd blooded her like a SEAL, ironically made her ideal for the purposes I had in mind. Her loyalty was without question. We were like two peas in a pod. I grinned. Bonnie and Clyde, victims of violent disaster, lost family and trauma at an early age.

We moved with low-crouching strides, noiseless, straight toward the warehouse, through the tall, dry prickle-weeds and past the broken crates and skids, the old disused machinery.

The front and side exits we needed to secure. The guards were all inside. The cameras would pose a problem.

There'd be no grand entrance, no bombs or glitter. Just a stealth op, my specialty—the lives in there needed protection and a more delicate touch than the hack and slash fireflares I was used to. Dressed in my ragged camo suit and Wren in her black Kevlar gear, we slunk in like cats, our Uzis and R4s slung on our shoulders, the backup weaponry snug at our belts. I hunched just out of the view of the first overhead camera and aimed my disrupter at it, a thin black rod, bulbed at the end to shoot out a black net of spidery film. The sticky gel covered the lens and would dissolve in three minutes, giving us time to plant our explosives and move on. The lens would revert back to its original state. Enabling the cameras again was a key component in our undetected break-in. *Just a brief outage, Ned. Must have been a technical glitch.*

Wren did the same to the side cam. All this in prep for our exit, if exit there'd be. The tricky part would be getting the workers out, the young women and boys I remembered vividly with their bruised cheeks and blackened, despairing eyes. There was an ample margin of knuckle-gnawing in this excursion. A hair's separation from death. Many things could go wrong.

We crouched before the last side entrance, wasting no time. A part of me knew this venture was insane, but I couldn't back out now. Not if I wanted to sleep easy at night. It was one follow-up promise I'd made to myself. Might even take down Paz in the doing.

The high rusty door was an emergency exit and looked to have been little used. I applied some putty to the cracks around the edges and alongside the metal ring and wired the pulse cylinder. I hoped the door wasn't under alarm. We turned and the silent blast jerked the door ajar.

It wasn't wired. Good thing, otherwise Plan B would have come into effect, and that was a hell of lot messier.

Pazarol's men were nowhere in sight. They were confident, these thugs, as evidenced by their cocksure posturing and loose-limbed gunwielding. Nobody would try to burgle the very place they called home.

Such conceit was a fortunate occurrence. I knew the workers lived there and it was off shift for the guards, having scoped out their movements in advance. Many of them had left, so only a skeleton detail remained.

We crouched, breathless, in a cramped foyer stacked with row upon row of shelves of old junk and open boxes of dusty uniforms and boots—rejects.

The sewing machines had mostly settled down for the day and I set out for the back of the warehouse, motioning Wren to get to the workers' stations fast and move the women and boys back toward the side exit we'd breached. Hers was the harder job, I knew, convincing the laborers not to panic, bolt or raise an alarm. Her presence as a woman would command more trust and compliance. I hoped. If not, Plan C.

Keeping low and out of sight, I threaded my way through the many aisles of random equipment where the victims' daily chores were ever the same: hunched on benches before long tables, cutting, dyeing, sewing the electronic components into fabric, pressing, working the tall, upright mantis-like machines to pump out Paz's guerrilla wear. I dodged the sound of a guard's coarse laugh and the murmur of nearby voices, finally to crouch before the fat, double heating pipes running length-wise three feet above the ground at the back of the sweatshop. I'd seen them in the floor layout and memorized the specs back when TK and I'd scoped the joint. Typical rectangular warehouse, complete with storage areas at the sides. I set my canister of gas down underneath them and armed it for thirty seconds. I pressed the mask over my face. The hiss grew as I beetled away, for soon it'd blow and the funland of hell would begin. We'd have seven minutes before the toxic gas spread throughout the compound and rendered the air unbreathable.

When I heard a distinct pop behind me as the canister released, I knew the die was cast. I scrambled back the way I'd come.

Gray clouds of hot steam hissed from the piping area, simulating a burst pipe, obscuring the view. This mix had tear gas in it for added effect. We'd have to get the workers out with speed, otherwise they'd choke to death.

I heard shouts to my right and the thuds of booted feet of big Paz's guards, converging from their diverse locations. They'd be wondering what was up: a main pipe rupture or thinking the worst, some spontaneous fire. I snuck off in the opposite direction, keeping low between the lanes of dyeing equipment and the presses, blending in with the shadows. Confuse and misdirect; that was the name of the game, for as long as possible while Wren and I got the workers out.

I ran nose to nose with Pazarol and a few of his boys before long in the cleaning area on the way back to join up with Wren: a blur of dark suits, mustachios, Uzi blasters, foul tempers and tongues. I pegged off the first of his entourage, a bewildered bodyguard, his mouth wide and gaping, before answering fire sent me spinning under a worktable.

Shots ricocheted off the shiny metal. I found myself pinned down before the dye vats. One beam nearly clipped me and I jerked away from a whoosh of green fire that nearly grazed my Adam's apple. Both far too perilously close. Feet scrabbled around me. I shouldered in behind a large vat of toxic green dye, the chemical reek making my eyes water and my throat seize up. My mask had jiggled loose. I fumbled to secure it and shook out the chemical sting from my eyes. The gunmen weren't equipped with masks, so I sent green dye pouring their way by blasting out the bottom far side of the vat. Soon they were reeling on the ground as the fumes from the dye stung their noses and throats while the more toxic billows of steam crept up on them like snakes through the aisles.

So began a shooting spree in a wild free-for-all that the gambler in me knew was bad odds at five to one. Yet gradually big Paz's gunmen started to cough and reel back, snarling and cursing.

I slipped out of my hiding spot, my mask snug on my nose now. I picked them off one by one so there'd be no blasting us in the back while we were making our escape.

Pazarol, the fat fuck, lolled in the curling swirls of mist, wiping his eyes, drooling and spitting curses all the way. So, he was here. Bonus. Someone had thrown him a mask, the strap still dangling in his pudgy hands. I kicked the weapon out of his grip and beat him down to the ground with the end of my blaster. I looked down at him with little love.

His priceless expression was one of white-faced surprise. Rusco, a grinning pumpkin man returned from the grave.

"It can't be! You're dead!" he choked and sputtered, as if he'd been struck in the head. Wish I could frame that image and pin it on my cabin wall. "I saw you hauled off by Baer," he croaked. "Then that Mong striding down the hall."

He lunged up at me between phlegmy drools, spitting out blood. "Is that cropped he-bitch woman of yours alive too?" he gasped. "Should've plowed her while I had the chance."

"Would have thought this little exchange had given you more humility."

"Fuck off, dogshit asshole. I hope you and that broad get wasted—"

I finished him off with a single shot. He lay still, with a gaping, smoking hole in his forehead. Good riddance. Couldn't stand the man.

A death was a death, and this was no less gruesome, though more like putting a rabid hound out of its misery. But the cost of taking a life always stirred the hairs on the back of my neck.

I caught up with Wren. She and the others were hustling toward the east wall, the workers frightened out of their wits at the echoes of gunfire blasting away and the hint of white steam floating ever closer toward them. "Out the side door!" I grunted. "This area'll be gassed out in minutes."

A group of fifty of them looked at me with dilated eyes of terror. "Who are you?" they cried.

"Pazarol's nemesis. Get moving! This is your lucky day. I've a ship waiting." Blinking in astonishment, they stumbled on trembling legs and I bunted them toward the side exit. Wren sighed with relief at the sight of me, alive and whole.

Some of them were too frightened to take action and stood immobile. Others gaped like fish, cowering behind the rows of khaki wear they had toiled so hard to produce. I gave a croak of frustration. "Do you want to stay here enslaved, victims of these scumlords?" A lean, hollow-cheeked woman with dark circles under her eyes visibly trembled. She wrapped her bruised arms around her chest, gave a choked sob and a call of action to the others. Then took to her heels after Wren. Some I had to leave behind, blinking in the dim emergency light as the alarms rang. So be it. I joined in the mad scramble, prodding the others from behind down the main corridor, blaster in hand. When more rats with foul teeth came out to play, I stayed back as their rounds clipped out toward us, and rolled under equipment tables, using the gathering smoke as a screen through which I shot at will. Tools and instruments skidded off tables; khaki fatigues lined up on hangers shredded around us to the rat-tat-tat of gunfire. Wren was somewhere ahead of us, gesticulating with her R4, herding the mob forward through the double doors, three and four abreast so undernourished they were.

It was a wild rush. Desperate figures burst out into the damp air onto the weed-ridden tarmac, the grey light of dusk hitting us, and the smell of chemicals in our noses. Down the service yard, past rusty forklifts. Again I had to drop back as five others came out of the emergency exit we'd booby-trapped, staggering like strawmen in a gale. I fired shots back at them.

I hit the detonator switch. All disappeared in a cloud of white flames as their charred limbs flew, severed from torsos.

More stumbled out of the side door closer to the back. This time caustic smoke billowed out at their heels like sidewinders' tails. I jammed down the detonator. It didn't fire. "Fucking hell!" The canister was a dud. I threw the useless thing away.

They chased after us. Gunmen rained fire like cannons. Two women fell, shot in the back. I cried out in dismay. A tousle-haired boy tripped and crashed to his knees, sobbing. I winced and hauled the featherweight up on his feet, urging him to run like he'd never before. Like panicked sheep, they all ran after Wren through the weeds and cracked tarmac toward the distant fenced yard. I thought some would expire from sheer exhaustion and terror before they made it to the hold. They kept apace each other, some women gripping boys' hands.

I stayed back, kneeling, pegging off those who came within range. Blaster fire kicked up. One caught me in the left foot and I cursed, felt a zinging burning sensation in my toe. *Shit, this was not progressing well.*

"Move your asses!" Wren cried, swatting at them with the flat of her gun. She crowded them forth, through the fence toward the ship, herding them in the direction of the hold like cattle at a roundup.

When the last worker was in the ship, I came hobbling, sucking in lungfuls of air. I closed the hatch. All were secured and Wren already had Bantam circling in the air. I raced to the bridge, used the remote to fire her front cannons, bright lasers which licked at the snipers retreating in haste back to the compound. I grimaced in triumph as bodies fell.

I scanned the ground. Some survivors piled into the dormant X-R Rover craft sitting out in Pazarol's dilapidated yard. The V-winged tri-fighter whisked up at us, fareon beams pouring out, catching our shields, but Wren was pounding them with our own pulse beams. We were already well ahead, engaged, and I maxed Bantam's impulse out to the twin moons, past the atmosphere and out into space. The go indicator flashed yellow and free of Tarsus's gravity, the Varwol engaged. The universe slipped sideways. Stars, light flashes, multicolored beams sheared on impossible angles that bent in wrong places and made no sense to any waking eye.

We were off to the stars, and I could only breathe a gasp of relief.

* * *

I came down into the hold, limping with Wren at my side. There they all crouched in a miserable huddle, murmuring and sniffling like lost orphans, some in shock. The women held each other like frightened sisters, consoling each other and some of the younger boys. Wish I'd had a rescue like this when the bombs and pulse beams were going off and dropping on us during my teens. I let the memories slide by, shaking loose those frightful, estranged years of a lost youth. I blinked, emotionally spent, such feelings suppressed for decades now.

I'd take these victims to a far off world and let them start fresh, give them a second chance like Wren. They deserved it. The boy I had set right came hesitantly forward, touched my mechno hand. He smiled. I placed my good hand over his with a startled glance.

I felt a stir tingle in my breast. Seeing those grateful, teary-eyed faces affected me. A wave of something memorable and wholesome blossomed in the depraved chaos of this world for a change. It was a spark of some miniscule change. So much different from the killing and the violence, the cons and blowing everything to shit. It had been so long since I had experienced anything comparable.

Wren came beside me and curled an arm about my waist. She flashed me her lopsided grin.

I thought of that tech hid in the warehouse north of Hoath and a derisive rumble caught in my throat. Let Mong search the universe for it. The bastard'd never find it and I'd never go back to retrieve it.

The phaso I'd keep as a souvenir to remind me of what I had

lost. But the other half of the amalgamator would sit there and rot in the darkness. No place for that evil caricature of bug-alien engineering in a human world. I thought of Billy's demise and TK's grief-stricken face before he died. It sent chills down my spine. No less that harrowing glimpse I'd caught out in nowhere land when I touched the phaso. All together, it had cost me my hand and taken a year off my life, or more. But it had given me something else—a sense of purpose. A spur that had driven me to liberate these downtrodden people, whom I never would have met or helped otherwise.

Somehow I knew there'd be more victims squirming like worms on the hooks of evil scumbags like Baer, Pazarol and the fanatic Mong.

I gave a gusty sigh and swung back to the bridge with Wren. "Going all maudlin on us, Rusco? Need to step up your game, I think." I croaked out a laugh and drew nearer to my companion-in-arms, a crooked grin pasted on my haggard face and my eyes agleam. "Wren, you ever hear of Xerxes station out in Perseus?"

"No, should I?"

"Well, it's remote, certainly off the radar of the big moguls. Far from Mong, far from terror. Easy pickings. We could work ourselves a master con. Dress you up real pretty. Minimum risk. That boy shows plenty of promise too."

"Leave the boy out of it. But I'm game."

STARVENGER

BOOK III

Chapter 1

I drove the loaded flatbed with an itchy foot on the accelerator. I cursed every pile of rubbly shit that made me deke around and waste more time. Bad enough to have to maneuver through a war zone than to drive this claptrap two-ton shipment in to the rebel dropoff point. Why hadn't I allowed myself more time?

Hindsight, Rusco. Everything's easy in hindsight.

Many times I'd have to tell myself the same thing. This road was blocked like the last, sprawled with some building that'd caved, spreading across the pavement like a broken tower of Babel. The city was a shambles. Courtesy of dear old Mong, our friendly neighborhood warlord, Star Lord, whatever the hell, who had torn through every nook and cranny of this metropolis. Made an example of this rebel city with his Warhawks. The insurgents would certainly like our precious cargo, that tickletrunk of fiery, feral goodies in the back, everything a diehard, red-eyed rebel could ever want to use against a hated enemy—RPGs, land mines, R4s, death-dealing fire flares. Only problem was, I wondered if they'd still be there. We were late to dropoff with all this backtracking and I'd already been running far behind on the long haul from Uziles in *Veglos* where we loaded the stuff. Not to mention nursing a very bad feeling about this gig in the first place.

Too late to back out now. Too much invested. You're up to your neck, Rusco. You've a reputation to keep. Backing out has its price.

Wren was at my side in the truck's cab, calm as the quiet before storm, her shiny dark hair grown back from its ugly baldness when I had met her. Could smell the faint odor of her sweat. Three blond youngbloods hunched in the back behind us, breathing down my neck. A trio of hothead punks I'd brought in on short notice. Breaking them in. Good training for their lot. Blest had potential, but Klane, well, dunno about Klane. Could go either way—something off with his logic. Tager, worth a chance, but I'd dump him if he messed up.

Sweat beaded under my brow, the grey showing to the discerning eye. I tossed back my faddish, purple-dyed pony tail kept tied as a nostalgic gimmick while I still had hair. I stretched my six foot frame in that cramped cabin, tired and yawning from the long space flight across the black gulfs, stewing over these zany last minute plans.

I looked around the terrain and shook my head. Too many worlds like this one, blown to shit. Wartorn prizes of space thugs and warlords, captains of disaster and ragged-eared dogs fighting over graveyard bones in a planet-wide slurry. The few pristine worlds left would be sodomized by warlords and gangsters before the decade was up. I knew it in my heart. The rest had fallen into corruption, decay, death. I'd grown up into it and it was no different now than it was say, ten years ago. If anything, worse.

Enough doom and gloom, Rusco. Get on with the program.

After a brief recap of our plans, I screeched the tires to a halt on the warehouse asphalt and ordered my new recruits out. Wren sauntered out like a lioness, slinging her R4 rifle over her lean, sinewy shoulder.

I squinted around in the opaque light. The sullen sky did not improve what I saw. A rectangular shitbox of a warehouse, steel refab beams leaning on drunken angles. The lot, strewn with crumbled concrete, was no better than the rest of the city: a write-off. Some wrecked vehicles and lift loaders to the side, nothing now but mangled junk fallen to the fire of warships. An overturned jeep sprawled with bent wheels and a jerry-rigged flamethrower mounted on overhead bars. Made to look like an abandoned base, I guessed.

Ten to one there were assault vehicles tucked inside just waiting to burst out and wreak havoc. To the other side lurked a tangled thicket that backed out onto another yard and some open land beyond, here at the western edge of the city. Broken light-posts teetered around the lot's perimeter. Remarkably, one tall one still stood and its yellow lamp burned feebly by the warehouse door where some activity caught my eye.

Two sets of explosives I carried hidden in my breast armor, coin-size, not easily detectable. In case things went awry. Any arms dealer would have them. We wore fatigues, dirty grey and green-black, padded. All of us wore Kevlar vests underneath. "You know the drill," I grunted at them. "No embellishments. Everything to plan." I stared at Klane who'd already shown a tendency to waver from orders.

They growled at that. Two of them gave nods. These recruits still gave me cause for worry. Wren I needn't worry about. She was an asset: wiry, statuesque, a gutsy brunette. We'd worked together before and she'd gotten me out of a lot of jams. Big ones. Like the one where we were shipwrecked on Talyon when Baer and his thugs had pinned us down. We knew each other. I'd fight to the end for Wren.

Two armed men stepped out of the doorway and motioned us to a rusted side entrance while others poked the back of the truck with their rifles, lifting a flap to peer in with oily smiles. They didn't disarm us but I noticed they kept their sawed-off R4s well-trained on us— probably in case we were agents of Mong. The detail escorted us none too gently into the half bombed warehouse, down a stale-aired hallway reeking of kerosene and old cheese. From there, to a dim backroom with a rat-eaten table and two bulbs burning overhead.

The nearest man jumped up from a stool: Froy, our contact. He turned about with a scowl, impatient, surly, a half-chewed beedi leaning out of his tar-gummed mouth. "You're late."

"Yeah, well, it's a fucking far way from Veglos," I said. "We were told this is the place and that we should bring no others and here we are."

Froy grunted, unimpressed.

The man was cloaked in ragged brown fatigues, frayed at the edges, hair askew. He'd suffered multiple wounds recently, judging by the hackjob on his khakis. Looked as if he hadn't bathed in weeks. Pearly eyes were round saucers into nowhere as he blinked at us. I'd seen eyes like that on wartorn mongrels before. The enlarged whites gleamed—the mark of the *invinco* addict and crack hashish user if I've ever seen one, mixed with Myscol OD, floating in his blood. With nothing to lose, these war types remained volatile to the end. A chip on their shoulders as big as an anvil and an axe to grind. I looked at him in casual disinterest, hoping to disarm him. It failed. The situation would require careful maneuvering.

His henchmen who'd escorted us from the flatbed shifted, and one inclined his head with a flick of eyes. "They came in on a truck, Froy."

"A truck? You check it?"

"It's got the stuff."

"Good." Froy nodded, momentarily appeased, but still wound as tight as a prowling tiger. "I thought you were coming in on a ship, Rusco." His voice was low, sinister.

"Plans change."

"Yeah, and so does the price, smart guy. I just dropped it. Bad for you. Market's low today, as is my mood."

Klane surged forward. "What do you mean, dropped?" The gunman choked, licking his lips, gripping his R4.

Froy turned to him. "What does 'price dropped' mean to you, kid? You deaf or something?"

"Relax. Cool it," I said, clutching at his elbow.

The idiot wriggled out of my grip. "Less profit for us, Rusco. We've got to get a profit out of this."

Froy gave a sour laugh. "Profit? Kiss your boss's ass for profit. This is wartime."

I suddenly felt a noticeable dip in our security here. The hothead lout, Klane, was all elbows and knees, clacking teeth, as if Santa Claus had denied him a toy. Too worried about losing his share of the spoils, dumbfuck. Made a move too fast which spooked Froy's nearest boy. The gunman's barrel came up and Klane took this as a threat and whirled his piece about, another stupid move. He had the butt end braced in his gut like a gangster. The clack of fire nearly killed our ears in that tiny place. Klane's innards spilled over the floor and his head exploded in a crimson mash like a melon bursting.

I jerked back, a warm sickness swarming my gut. "What the fuck—" I ducked, wiping the putrid slime of Klane's brains off my camos. "You stupid dipshit, Froy. Why the hell did you do that?"

"Get them to shut up, Garr." Froy stabbed out a fist at his men. "Bind these fuckers. Pissed me off enough today, and it's been a bad day. We won't be paying anybody anything today, Rusco. Mong's up our ass. My cousin and his brother, Joely, are jelly. They wouldn't have been corpses today if you bags of shit had showed up on time…if we had your RPGs in our hands and used them to cut down those pinkos. Cost us too many lives today. Too many valuable lives."

In any other scenario, we would be toast. But Wren and I had already acted. I pulled the pin on one of my coin-size bombs and chucked it at Froy's three minions. We dove for the exit just as gunfire raked the air where we'd been. Blest and Tager, likewise lucky, saved their heads from being shot off. We raced down the hallway, a motley misfit of four, me, lifting my weapon, blowing out the hanging bulbs. Wren bowled over a surprised guard at the door while we burst through the rusted exit and raced for the flatbed.

The seconds passed like hours in a nightmare. The first piff-paff of shells came spraying at us and I flung myself to my stomach, breathing tarmac. One of the goons came coughing out of the smoke, shooting blind. I pulled out the second flash bomb, and chucked it. Three of them disappeared in a cloud of smoke and blood splatter. Not before the first one had riddled our ride's tires to useless shreds. No getting away on this rig or retrieving the cargo.

"Fuck!" I breathed. "Out of here." I gave back covering fire while I pushed Wren and the other two toward the tangled thicket breasting the lot. "Move!"

We ran with fire flare eating at the foliage around us.

Blest's sweat-laced face was wide-eyed with terror, a curse on his lips. "Screw you, Rusco! I didn't sign up for this shit."

"What did you sign up for then? Tiddlywinks? Get your ass moving."

We struggled through the brambles, getting pricked like divers in a school of blowfish. The least of our concerns. More rebels must have buzzed out of the warehouse and swarmed after us while I felt the riffle of shots at my feet and a whizz over my ear. One grazed my thigh; not enough to damage me, but it hurt like hell. Bee stings soaked in vinegar.

"Fucking hot-headed rebels fueled up on rage, having their city sacked." Seems as if they'd forgotten who their friends were.

Chapter 2

A hail of fire blizzarded over our heads. We broke out of the scorched thicket, hopped the next yard and raced down a gravel path with the intent to loop back toward the city closer to where my ship was hidden. Froy's goons were somewhere behind us, shooting away. I caught muffled echoes of boot on gravel, stray shots, shouts.

Keep moving. That's your middle name, Rusco. Another botch up. How many more there going to be? I should kill you myself, put you out of your misery. The shell shock of the last blast had spun my head sideways. I did a quick scan.

Wren was in good shape. Tager had taken a minor hit, his left forearm grazed. Blest was ruffled but seemed okay.

Me, some cuts and scrapes and bruises here and there, nothing I couldn't handle, a wicked ache in my left thigh.

I shrugged, fingered my compact R4. Always liked the snug feel of the wooden stock in my hand and how it slipped so easily into killing mode. One of the older models. Trustworthy. The black, fast-action carbine sported an energy-pulse with good range and accuracy and unlimited shell action.

This wasn't what I had planned. But is there anything that is?

We rounded a curve in the road in a direction I roughly estimated led to our parked craft. I studied the ruined city below. Ugly as a mummy's crypt. I grimaced. I'd give Froy's screwball rebels dibs for spunk. So far they'd survived this hell. I'd promised them arms at a decent price because I have a hard on for that bastard Mong—well, okay, I like the money and the smell of it and I too have to eat. Getting too old for this shit.

We hustled down the slope into what was once a main boulevard in that concrete jungle of shattered shapes, keeping our heads down, our guns aimed in front, and alternating rearguard. We crossed the main street, past broken, burned-out vehicles. The rank smell of soot and charred flesh filled our nostrils. Our boots crunched over rubble. We passed a small pile of blown-out stone in the center of the street, something that used to be a monument. I could see the toppled marble head with a crown or coronet, some heroic figure of the past, with the eyes bullet-holed out.

Maybe not such a good idea to play hide and seek here with my ship so far away now from the drop site. I'd landed it five miles at the edge of the city in case of treachery. Treachery we got, but now *Bantam*, my Alpha-Omega Beamer, wasn't here to help us out of this madness.

The instant they'd wasted Klane, we were running on borrowed time.

The biggest problem was how to get back to Bantam without getting our heads blown off. Froy's thugs seemed farther behind us than five minutes ago. With some luck, some more of these cross-alleys would help us lose them. But that tactic could backfire at any instant.

"Loop around past the old section," I directed, "more shelter there and less chance of getting bottled up in a narrow alley."

"Mines?" Tager croaked.

"We look for signs and watch our steps." I shrugged. Wren cast me a fugitive glance which I ignored.

Why was everything so dark on this miserable world? Was this a solar eclipse? Only a creepy, leaden light from Ramus's sun. No, there was Arkades poking through the clouds like a timid widow. This world was downright eerie. Another dumbass decision to risk a quick venture on a backward planet. I ran through the rubble, breath rasping, clutching at the burning ache in my leg. No time to apply regen. Unless I wanted to get a pulse-burst in my guts. Wren labored at my side, breathing heavily like a winded mare. Blest ran a few paces behind, thin, wiry, the whites of his eyes darting back and forth from the broken structures ahead to the moving shadows behind. Tager, squat, burly, lumbersome brought up the rear, giving covering fire when he could, huffing and puffing like the Billy Goats Gruff. Was he trying to be a hero? The fool was lagging and going to get himself tagged. I dropped back. "Get up ahead, Tager. I'll take over as rearguard."

A rumble rolled across the sky. An enemy ship? Moving fast. Question was, what enemy, Mong or Froy's rebels? Likely Mong, the Star Lord.

I ducked. Shellfire rained at our sides. *Rat-a-tat.* The nightmare echo of my sweaty dreams.

"Get Noss the fuck over here," gusted Blest.

My fingers itched to do it, and call up our shipmate. But I held back, feeling a tingle in my wrist and hearing a little creak in the left finger of my prosthetic hand.

"Oh, for Christ sakes," cursed Blest, "I'll call him myself."

"Can't. They'll trace it. Then alert their scouts. If that's who I think it is, Warhawks'll blow Bantam out of the sky. I can't chance losing that ship."

"He's right," grunted Wren. "Noss is neither tactician nor marksman. They'll make mincemeat out of him."

"Then we're screwed," cried Blest. "So what do we do?"

"Do what we're doing. Come hell or high water, we get to Noss and the ship."

"You should have had a backup plan, Rusco."

"Right, like it was obvious to guess that our business partners would be so kind as to turn wolf on us. What's with you?"

Blest bleated something unintelligible.

"Speaking of which, weren't you the one gave the all-clear after radar-scouting out the city and telling me Mong's forces were gone?"

Blest licked his lips. "They must have come back."

"No, you dickhead, you didn't look hard enough and they were hunkered down somewhere, tucked away like bugs. I should have done the scan myself."

The arguing was doing us no good. Blest had fucked up. I had fucked up. Klane had fucked up, and then he paid the price with his life. I wiped my sweaty brow then rubbed my eyes. All adrenalin and rage and frustration thrown in for fun. A lethal, toxic mix that needed an outlet. But now we needed to move on and concentrate on surviving.

Supposed to have been only a simple drop off, for shit's sake. A hundred crates of R4s and various land mines and fire snares. Everything set up by our contact Romos and his gang of scumbags. Nice bunch of people to work with.

It's never simple, Rusco, you should know that, you dreamer.

If that idiot Klane hadn't shot off his mouth, we wouldn't be in this jam. Didn't he know that shortchange was part of the whole package? I'd allowed for it, factored in the slippage, that's why I charged 20% more. Something I'd been expecting. I should have briefed Klane better though. Hindsight. All this fled through my mind as we ran. Move on, Rusco, the boat is leaving the dock.

Some brief gunfire flashed from the side, startling us as we scooted across a vehicle-sprawled square. Tager dropped as a slug slammed him high in the shoulder. He gave a hound's yelp as another smacked into his temple. I looked back, saw blood gushing from his mouth. No saving Tager now.

With a choked gurgle, Blest dropped down behind an alley's corner.

"What are you doing? Blest, get up, you fool!"

He ignored me.

Two figures burst into the square, one covering the foreground while another offered covering fire.

Blest's R4 spat out a vengeful burst.

The figure flopped like a ragdoll. Wren tagged the other.

"Nailed the bastard," croaked Blest.

"What do you want, a kiss?" I hissed. "Pipe down, there may be more of them."

Wren mumbled, "Good shot." She touched Blest's arm and he gave her a terse nod, working his lips and struggling on ahead.

A sour wave of nausea hit me. I pushed on through the empty streets, shaking my head like a dog, herding myself along.

I stared down at the gash in my leathered thigh. More blood was trickling where the shell had grazed me. My nine lives were running out.

The distant rumble of ship's engines coursed above. Closer now. Much closer. Made more menacing by the low cloud cover. The explosion in the warehouse must have alerted Mong's imperial scouts.

The endless maze of streets was disorienting. More and more squares with shelled fountains, toppled statues and broken buildings and fly-ridden bodies, young, old, short, fat. Death did not discriminate. At one time it looked as if this city had been built in an elegant baroque, the style probably deliberately copied from Earth by some high class types, but with cathedrals dedicated to a new, modern-day savior.

Stone bridges ran over the canals; blown out now, so we had to wade through rank, brown-scummed water. Grey sluggish streams dotted with bloated bodies; animals too, what looked like kangaroos crossed with mastiffs.

These insurgents, I knew the type, had their noses ground in the mud too often. They'd been fighting this guerrilla war for months now. Turned red devils into savages. I hadn't realized how far they'd regressed until I snatched a look at Froy back there. I caught a flutter of movement in the arched ruin of a church.

Swore it was Froy, cloaked in his ragged brown khakis, loping like a tiger. Wild eyes gleamed with a special something of vindictive madness. The squad was far enough away for me not to be shitting bricks. He and his goons'd lost sight of the cause, chasing us like

323

rabbits. I mean, who in their right mind would go after their supplier? Were we their enemy, or Mong? I looked over and saw the Warhawk T-wing roving the sky in the low-scudding cloud, the roar of its heavy engines polluting the desolate silence over the doomed city, drowning out the raucous croaks of strange, oversized crows. The ship's homely green and brown prow thrust out like the beak of a bird of prey.

A sudden sound broke behind me.

I aimed behind me and shot a spray of death. A rebel with full beard and a fuckboy cut fell clutching his leg as one of my fire bursts hit home, knocking the feet from under him. His two lithe partners hopped over him like gazelles.

We ducked into a culvert that curved under a shell-pitted road. Puddles of water pooled at our feet, the echo of our boots sloshing through stagnant water. We scrambled out the other end then down another ruined alley, our breaths hissing in our throats, lungs pumping.

Still another mile or two to the ship, if my bearings were correct. Everything looked the same in this wreck of a city. Piles of rubble and dead bodies feasted on by carrion birds. Feral kangaroo creatures foraging for scraps and rooting amongst the dead. I kicked one of them out of the way that snapped and growled at me, defending its turf like a guard-dog of the dead. Most of the people who'd survived this holocaust had fled, but there was the odd hobo or old coot hanging around.

We'd taken a wrong turn and gotten jammed up in a dead-end alley. Shelled buildings rose to either side, the windows blown out. We were just about to backtrack when a ragged transient lurched out, scared out of his wits. A bottle of whiskey or rubbing alcohol lay clutched in his hands. "Don't shoot me, misters, don't shoot—"

The cry died in my throat as he staggered for a few steps then exploded in scarlet spray, his head blown clean off. I winced as the corpse fell in a ragged heap, the head pumpkin jelly. I flung myself to the ground behind a rubbled heap. I pulled Wren with me. Blest dove the other way into the shelter of a debris pile, broken dolls and a human foot.

A voice called out from the silent rubble, "You're a dead man, Rusco."

Froy.

The sound of my name bounced off the battered walls.

"Kill my men, will you?" he taunted. "We've got the arms. You've lost your payout."

"You killed my man first, Froy."

"Your boy was out of line," Froy called. "What I want is your ship, and you can throw in the woman as a bonus. Come out with her and I may spare your asses. We'll take your little raven tail for a ride or two." He chuckled, a sleazy echo answered by one of his henchmen.

I ground my teeth. Yes, they'd turned into savages.

I tried to make sense of it. Distorted perceptions. Any stab at a perceived enemy made a logical target. Too many loved ones snatched away in too brief a time. Too many pent-up hopes shot down in flames. Froy, half-baked on *invinco*, a hair-trigger finger on anything that moved, friend or foe. Now his goons' communal libidos were jacked up to rapacious pitch—maybe some god-awful side effect of the *invinco*.

"We've got to keep that bastard talking," I muttered at my two team members.

Wren gave a fierce nod. Blest gazed at me with resignation, his belly hugging the damp dirt. His curly blond hair was covered with dust and a blood smear to the side where he'd bashed his head on something.

The first pangs of desperation crawled over me. I called Noss on the com. Things were desperate. No answer. Where the fuck was Noss? Deserted? Stolen my ship? Sorry bugger'd get a rude surprise if he tried to leave this planet's gravity without authorization. I'd rigged something up to deter all such adventurous forays from pilots who didn't know how to disarm the sequence. The electro-force would kill him if it kicked in and would bathe his world in hell.

My red eyes roved above the cracks of the apartments and blackened stone where Mong's forces had taken out a whole block. Monstrous crows, a threesome, or what looked like a threesome, flapped out of the gaping windows, their dissonant croaks echoing down the alley of shell-blasted stone.

"I'll sit tight, draw them in," I wheezed. "You go up there, Wren, sniper them down."

She tensed. "They'll kill you. Why sacrifice yourself?"

I shrugged, gave my usual clown's grimace of a smile. "We're already dead, Wren. Trapped here. Go!" I slapped her on the back. She shook her head, her lip downturned.

Shots echoed from up the alley. Covering fire ricocheted as her weapon leaped out while they tried to pepper her.

I crouched, whipping out shots, laying into the moving figures with everything I had. Blest picked up on her cue and beetled down the alley to purchase a sniper position.

I debated taking the building on the right versus closing in after her. I risked a peek past the crumble. I saw four bogies in black suits, heavy-set, crabbing forward from pile of debris to debris. High-powered R4s. They must have taken them off the flatbed.

The gunmen blasted my shell hump of refuge with heavy fire. Enough to rattle my teeth. I pinched my eyes shut, and prayed not one of them would see me.

Fire flashed from overhead. Two of the enemy went down. I took the opportunity to poke my R4 out and spray anything in sight. One burst caught the closest not twenty feet away, tagging him in the shin and he hobbled with a curse. I heard the *rat-tat-tat* above me and Wren blasted the other bitchdog to kingdom come.

More were crawling out of the woodwork. How many of them were there? These last bastards were not so easy. Froy'd survived this long and he knew where we were and what our capabilities were. He might have even known that I was injured.

Come up with a winning plan, Rusco, or you're dead. This Froy fucker's mean as a snake and will gutshot you in an instant.

While Wren sprayed her next volley, I took a risky, stumbling dash, hoping my boots wouldn't crunch too loudly on the crumble. Fire nipped at my ankles and I dove into a jagged opening on the other side of the alley, just in time as shells nearly ripped off my heels. I edged my way up a ruined stair, my heart pumping, keeping my head down.

My breath came in ragged gasps. Some loss of blood. Enough to throw me off my game.

Klane was an idiot. You're running on borrowed time. What if they have more backup?

So you gun them down.

I squinted hard, thrust out the voices from my head and shook my reeling skull. *If Wren dies…*

She won't die. Keep moving.

Chapter 3

Through a broken window, I saw her, moving low, on the second floor of the building on the other side of the alley. Others'd be coming up the stairs after us now. A risky move, but I knew Froy's type. All risk and bravado and a sureness in himself that would make a leopard weep. He had to be juiced, on pure *invinco*—that would give a man enough courage—or a death wish—

Gunfire raked us from below, peppering the window where Wren had last hunkered down. Clouds of dust and plaster rose. Silence. No movement from within. I felt a sick dismay rising up from the pit of my stomach. I poked my head up to look out my window. A part of me sagged in despair. I forced myself to keep moving, telling myself she was still alive while dread haunted me with every step.

I shook my head in shame and mounted some more stairs and crept along an office of broken tables and water dispensers and whatnot when the *rat-a-tat* of fire nearly deafened me, ripping into the wall beside me. "Hold up! Weapon down." The harsh voice lashed out at me.

I slowly held up my gun, not daring to turn around. Think fast, Rusco. Stall them. It's your only hope.

"If it's me you're after, you've done it, Froy, let the girl go free."

"Turn around, slowly, Rusco. Kick the weapon away."

I did as Froy ordered and saw he had his piece leveled point blank, his face a livid mask of contempt. Another rebel was fast booting up the stairs.

"Where is she?" the newcomer barked. "The bitch killed Brex."

Froy's white ferret eyes darted about the room. "How many more of you rats are hiding here?" he shouted at me.

"I think you killed the rest of them," I said.

"You'll wish you'd joined them, Rusco. Move!" He rapped me with his gun. "Now it'll go the worse for you. Those RPGs could have given my team cover and saved our asses."

"If you'd been using them now instead of chasing me, maybe you could have blown up some of your real enemies."

The distant roar of an enemy ship echoed above and Froy's head turned in a shiver of fear. I likened it to a squirrel that's got dogs on both sides of him.

The rebel gripped his weapon with instinctive reflex and twisted the barrel to the window. "Shut up."

He motioned to the others, three more mounting the stairs. "Take this bugger to base. I have special uses for him. The rest of you, ferret out the woman."

They nodded.

I made as if to stall.

"Move!" Froy rapped the butt end of his rifle into the back of my skull. Stars flashed in multicolor. I massaged the lump growing there. My only hope was that Wren and Blest had the sense to keep away and get to Noss and the ship. If she were still alive.

Despair gnawed at my gut.

Rusco, you're not thinking fast enough. I walked, as slowly as I could, with the gunman prodding me along. All your fancy footwork isn't going to amount to jack shit if you don't come up with something quickly. Look for an opportunity. Use your wits!

"If it's arms you want," I began, "I can get you as many as you want, Froy. Shitloads, discounted, no end to them. You name your price. Free, if you give me enough time."

"Too late for that, asshole," he spat. "This war's lost. Writing's on the wall. We're all dead."

"What the fuck are you on about?" cried his husky crony who guarded me. He turned on Froy. "You loco? I say we waste this bastard, close his gibbering mouth forever then use his girl and take those arms he brought and blow—"

Froy waved him off with a bitter snarl. "Quiet down, Garr. For months we've been fighting this dogged war. Mong's got black magic on his side—stealth wizardry and weaponry. Armor that doesn't crack, missiles that never miss, military intelligence beyond our scope. How else could his few ships have neutralized our entire air force? We only dodge like rats from one filthy hole to another."

Sense at last. I licked the blood off my lip. Froy must be coming down off his ride. The edge peeling off his belligerent hide. For the first time, I glimpsed the flicker of madness seep out of his haggard face.

"Some say he's the devil," jeered another of the gunmen, "an angel of fate."

"I say he's a rotten scumbag," said Garr, "one who desperately needs a bullet in his brain."

"Maybe so, but how long can we keep dodging him like weasels?" probed Froy. "We've been fighting this war with not one break yet. We'll all be martyrs. One of the few worlds that fight back—the rest of the pussies capitulate and become puppet regimes of Mong's feudal state—like lapdogs to a bull terrier. He's making an example of us. Look! Our beautiful city, once an oasis amongst the stars, is now pigs' swill!" He waved a fanatical arm, spitting fire at the wall, chewing it full of holes. "Palm trees ripped to shreds, fountains and gardens blown sky high! Public squares blasted, schools destroyed, women and children killed in cold blood in the streets, destroyed by that madman." He kicked at the plaster on the ground.

His comrades had no answer; Garr's tongue licked out to wipe at his dirty lip, followed by a sudden slap of hand on my face while the rage boiled in his leonine skull.

We were back in the alley under the weight of the looming buildings and their gutshot decay. No sign of Wren. A few men came loping up from the debris.

"Nothing," said one.

A darker rumble came from the sky. Eyes looked up. To a looming mass, turtle-green with a nose of mottled color. It was all menace, some fantastic monster as it tilted toward us. Before the first red flares came spearing from its port wing, I dove for cover. A bullet sheared through the thigh of the man next to me. I saw the flicker of pain register in his face and a barrel reaching from the second story window. I recognized the arm movement at once. Wren! So, she'd survived. Been playing possum. More fire laid in behind us. Blest came charging up the alley like a mad bull, all kamikaze, spreading fire in Froy's direction.

Mong's ship bore down on us, the pilot now recognizing the source of the blast back at the warehouse.

An odd thing happened, as if time warped. The ship slewed sideways, as if racked by gunfire from the side.

I strained my eyes upward. The ship pulsed green as a missile hit it broadside. For a few seconds it wavered as if it would drop out of the sky. But it didn't. The Warhawk turned and sent a red arc of fury toward the city in the direction of Froy's rebel base. A deafening boom rocked the air.

"Fools!" Froy croaked, clutching at his hair. "They need to launch triple RPGs at a single point to pierce those shields and armor—Aie!" His anguished voice rose above the roar of engines as some shrapnel caught his left leg in a cloud of fire. Black smoke mushroomed over the tops of the ruined buildings. I guessed the rebel base was no more. The massive army-grey bird of prey swung its nose toward us again.

In the cloud of dust, Garr lifted his R3 to plug me full of holes.

"Wait!" Froy choked on his own spit. He lay sprawled there amidst the chaos of men's screams, grimacing in pain, but lucid now, clutching his ruined leg. "Rusco, run while you can. Mong's taken enough sacrifices today. We don't need more. Get away from here, you stupid idiot!—before I change my mind."

I tipped my head. "Peace be with you, Froy. We'll see each other in hell." I half staggered from the shock concussions.

I limped off and heard Froy's savage groan as Garr and two of his last men dragged him to shelter. "Rusco!" he called back. "You see what war does to a man? Makes us no better than beasts! Killers and rapists. So far down the rabbit hole we go, we don't know who we are any more."

In a moment of lucidity, Froy had spoken truth. His last words evoked a sad memory in my brain. How far had I gone, with my morals twisted like pretzels and my long-running policy of turning a blind eye to the suffering of the universe? Hustling here, grubbing there, without a second thought of tomorrow or the consequences of my actions.

The gunmen dragged Froy off, cussing and screaming, his ruined leg beyond repair if he didn't get some regen soon.

Wren came stumbling up out of the building, her rifle cocked. She was ready to shoot anything that moved. Crouching, she moved in from pile to pile. Another deep rumble shook the sky. I turned. The Warhawk had edged in, banking sharply, its shields taking some of the damage of the RPG hit. But now another ebon shape rose over the crumbled buildings. It appeared out of the sky like a magic trick and for an instant a flicker of hope rose. Fire lashed out from its port guns and hammered the Warhawk in her rear flank, wresting wide its lethal fire, sending the grey streak smashing into the building next to us and crumbling it to ruin.

The building overhead exploded, sending a fresh spray down on us.

"Down!" I shrieked, covering my head pelted with bits of mortar and stone, my throat hoarse as the shockwaves rang through my bones.

Blest was panting beside me, his face nicked, his arms cut and a wild confused look in his eyes.

A whine of engines came out of nowhere. A hulking brown fuselage with an hourglass figure came swirling out of the dust to land in the square not fifty feet away. *Bantam*! Noss couldn't have been a more joyous sight. He must have heard my signal. Shoddy of me to have ever badmouthed him. Dust pooled at our feet and stung our eyes and lungs.

We coughed and stumbled out of the billowing cloud toward the giant black curve of the smoking hull where Bantam had taken fire. The cargo hatch slid open. We piled in and the engines gunned as the hatch slid back. We were thrown to the far side as the sudden g's accelerated us skyward. Noss was efficient; he'd gotten us this far. If there had been two of those bastard Warhawks though, we'd be goners now.

Return fire chipped against our starboard armor. I shuddered at the damage to our shields. I shook out the haze and stumbled down the companionway to the bridge. Wren was at my back. Soon she overtook me; Blest was still in shock, staggering somewhere in the hallway behind.

I took the helm and slapped Noss on the back. "Good man!" He gave me a curt acknowledgement and flung back his head of brown curls. He ceded the weapon's helm to Wren.

She worked the controls, lashing out at the Warhawk which was fast looming up on our viewport.

The holo grid showed black-green silent death stalking us. Auto-guided missiles blipped bright red on the most vulnerable areas of our hull; Wren fixed her own targets mid-wing near the power cells and the reactor on the bogey's weapon's port.

Torpedoes flew out of our wing cannons. They smashed harmlessly against the enemy craft's shields and heavy armor. I cursed, maxed out Bantam's impulse power, took us straight up toward the twin moons of this sorry world, away from our low wide arc that skimmed over the remains of Resus and the nearby sea.

We couldn't warp out in the planet's gravitational field. Not without risking structural overload.

Nerve-wracking seconds passed. Shields dimmed to 5%. The hull shuddered to surface blasts, then another. Shit, the next hit would finish us. Wren's lips parted in a gasp. The enemy missile launched, loomed on the viewport, coming up on our rear at gut-wrenching speed. A half second to impact. I felt that faint flutter of life flashing by before my eyes as we cleared planetary gravity. The Varwol light drive clicked in. Bantam's hull became a non-entity. Space-time collapsed—or whatever contradiction the physics people call it, for an object cannot be in two places at one time. In a half-light second we were thrown down the wormhole, unreachable by any Warhawk fire.

Through the slipstream of hyperdrive we passed like insignificant ants within an ethereal world. I saw Wren and Blest as they moved puppet-like on a screen out of a cartoon. As the nightmare slowly washed away from my mind, I thought of Froy and his doomed cause. Despite the man's madness, his unexpected turnaround had surprised me. It helped me better understand him and his people and others like him, terrorized by Mong and his military machine around the Veglos sector. The warmonger was a menace. He must be stopped.

But how? It looked as if no force in this universe could stop the man. Small time arms traders like me could hardly scratch a dent in his growing empire.

Chapter 4

My body ached from the bruises back on Resus. Staring at the silent controls and its maze of blinking lights, I marveled at the machinery that took us those light years and beyond, away from the dust-rubbled planet.

A hollow pang stuck at the back of my throat. The loss of Tager and Klane could not be brushed off. A sick feeling pressed at my insides, knowing the obscene thousands of yols I now owed my long-time seller, Gretch, from that failed arms' shipment. I'd promised him his share the first chance I got. Though he'd warned me of the risk of COD. Now he'd be breathing fire about the botched deferred payment and out for blood. Ready to set his enforcers on me.

We slid through the ethers like greased eels and I reflected on the wonder it was to be alive. The three of us had survived Froy's manic persecutions—though we all should have been dead. That said, I wouldn't be going anywhere near Uziles in Veglos nor Gretch for that matter.

A voice intruded on my bleak speculations.

"What now, Rusco?" Wren murmured. She turned, shook out her dusty hair and let out a long sigh. Studying the holo image of the vast star cluster of the Veglos sector, she looked a figure of enchantment. Noss stared at the panorama too, gloomily, drumming his thin, pale fingers on the console, as if watching the stars with an air of fatality. Blest, beside him, oblivious to the others, picked at the mole on his left cheek.

I needed regen badly. I reached a shaky hand for the emergency kit in the forward bulkhead just as the orange light flickered on the transcall unit—I knew instinctively it must be a message from Gretch. I turned the unit off.

First things first. We needed to ease out of the stupor of battle so I held back on the regen, cracking out the Binny's Gin instead and the Black Dog Whiskey. I poured stiff rounds for all of us and pushed the shot glasses before our team of heroes gathered around the communal table on the bridge.

I poured Blest a double dose. Seems as if our bully boy needed it. All bleary-eyed and bruised and sullen, he looked like an alley cat come out of the rain after fending off a pack of wild dogs.

He lifted his glass, inclined his head at Noss, asked him why he'd come when he did.

Noss swallowed a mouthful of Black Dog. "I saw your beacon. More than far enough away from where you should have been. The Warhawk was taking crossfire from the warehouse. Figured it was the only chance to get you out alive."

"Lucky you did," I grunted.

"Took you long enough," Blest said. With a shake of head, he cursed under his breath.

"Get off it, Blest," I growled. "We all should be dead, you included." He shut up when both Wren and I glared at him.

"Klane was an idiot." Wren muttered. "Shot off his mouth after they tried to shortchange us. We'd maybe still be whole and with loot in our fingers if he hadn't gone south."

I gave a wincing grimace. So what was to be learned from this wasted exercise? The futility of war? The dumb luck of a crew of misfits? Considering my bad luck of the past, I'd been expecting disaster.

I sighed. We'd have to lay low for a while. The other bad news— Mong's bounty hunters would be after me. They wanted those pieces of alien tech bad. The little phaso disc I had on board, plus the larger,

U-shaped amalgo I'd hid on Brisis 9 months ago. Both transporter devices sent animate and inanimate matter to other dimensions like a souped-up warp drive, so it seemed. Mong and his war ghouls had a reputation for persistence. They had placed an outrageous price on the return of such tech, inspiring certain desperate individuals to thrust an ice pick in my brain. Space hound Rusco was a marked man. I had a hunch, an almost certain one, Mong'd be tipped off after the Froy incident. If we could have wasted that Warhawk...but it didn't happen. Mong's goons would soon ferret out the rebels responsible for harboring fugitives. Then they'd interrogate Froy and his roughboys until they squawked like pigeons the name of Rusco, the details of our ship and the drop off, with all the willingness of vultures pecking at fresh roadkill. I winced at the bite of the gin sloshing down my throat. This caper was never supposed to end like this.

I applied regen paste on sensitive areas, the sticky stuff causing me to wince. Wren came to assist. She pulled up my leather pantleg and rubbed in a wad on the red, raised sore where the bullet had grazed my flesh. I could feel the skin stitching over. My supply of miracle glue was getting low, in need of replenishing. Another task on the to-do list. Once we got some money together, I'd get a whole box of the stuff.

I dipped my fingers in the jar to apply some salve to Wren's shoulder but she declined.

"I'll be okay." She waved my ministrations away then passed the jar to Blest.

"We need to go where the goods are," I said.

"Yeah, like really?" said Blest. "What goods would those be?—and where do you get the idea finding jobs is as easy as picking apples off a tree?"

"Stuff isn't going to come floating to us." My eyes stared at a faraway place in the endless panorama of stars that glowed in the viewport. "We need to go out and find them."

Blest sighed.

"We've got to keep moving," I reiterated. "We can't let a little setback stall us out."

"How about a little setback featuring two broken legs and a cracked back?"

"Hold on, that's not the kind of—"

"Tager and Klane dead and you want to flirt with more disaster?"

"No, to stay alive and keep our heads above water. Keep a cash flow going."

"It's madness," protested Blest.

"It's a mad world out there."

Wren touched the young man's arm. "We need to stay in the game."

Blest loosed a bitter laugh. "You too, Wren? I thought you had more sense than him." He glared at me. "I only listen to her. Not you. If she weren't here—"

I grinned. "What? You'd chicken-whip me, Blessie? Give me a big whooping? Good thing we have her."

Blest shrugged. The conversation was fast losing its conviviality.

"We lost big time on that last job," I said absently. "Paid a lot of money and got nothing back. Two dead. Damn it."

I let the words sink in. "So, needless to say, we have to amp up our game. We'll get stocked up—food, water, and maintenance at the next hub. O two hundred. I'll see what I can do to rig up some new angles on a gig. Always something out there, if we look hard enough, keep our eyes and wits about us."

Blest peered at me between his dark lids. "Seems you're always flying by the seat of your pants, Rusco."

"And so?"

"Just wondering when you're going to nosedive and get us all killed. I'd like to have some advance warning about my death."

"This isn't a ma and pa rig. If you want to go somewhere else, Blest, we'll let you off at the next hub. You can find your fortunes elsewhere."

The others looked at him with mouths set. A tense silence

ensued.

Blest just cracked his knuckles and shrugged. "I'll stick around for a bit, Rusco."

"I thought you would."

I picked at my teeth. Blest wasn't a team player. Surprised he didn't get busted up back there. Klane was just plain foolish, a dumb fuck extraordinaire. We were close to nailing that deal and he had to go and foul up the nest and get himself killed. But then, that had been said too many times already, so maybe I should just drop it.

Chapter 5

On an inspiration, I searched through the free store—the spacefarer's planetary-wide network of information. I checked some ledgers and current events and set the course for Badinis Major. According to the register there, a space station orbited the productive world of Gistron, rich in Beryl and other minerals useful for drives and ship hulls. Gistron station had escaped the long arm of Mong's domination—thankfully. Apparently an auction was in the works on the station—for used and vintage star cruisers. Interesting. Likely it would draw a well-to-do crowd that I could work some angle on. If not, vie for the ships themselves at least. I expected a mix of the usual space prospectors, entrepreneurs looking for easy pickings, the ubiquitous greaseballs, hangers on and con artists. My kind of crowd.

We turned in to our respective cabins and slept the sleep of the dead. We took turns to watch the helm. I instructed them to wake me in case of a contingency, no matter how minor. Not much could happen while we were in the slipstream cocoon of warp—or could it?

Bantam auto-kicked out of Varwol and I heard the tiny whir of engines. The thrum of power circuits booted up as they now returned us to the dimension of reality.

The space station loomed up in the viewport, a gigantic ring with docking berths on the inside of the ring. Gistron was one of the few places not ravaged by space thugs—her lattice of interconnected girders and spirals were a product of earlier generations, built in days of opulence. How old—a hundred, two-hundred years? Mong and his crew had not got to this part of the galaxy yet.

The planet Gistron Delta hung below, a small maroon disc, gleaming like a rheumy eye.

Wren studied me, as if trying to guess what went on behind that brow of mine. Good luck with that. Desert tanned, lithe as a country cat, she stood tall, back ramrod-straight, with a pride and toughness that had always been earned rather than role-played. She always gave me something else to admire about her. Younger than me, with good pizazz, knew how to handle herself in tough situations. Wish every one of my crew was like her. No hint of our bedroom antics in the workfield. On the job it was all business. A bonus on these long excursions—voyages to nowhere looking for paradise, or was it salvation?

She fiddled with the stock of her R4. "I don't even know why we're docking here, Rusco."

"There's always an angle to run at the auctions. You'll see."

We approached Gistron station with fake registration: Bantam registered to an asteroid mining speculator, entrepreneur, unmarried, one Jorry Rambo, a favorite pseudonym. I'd had the holo-disc with Rambo's registry doctored up to look pretty, with a clean bill of health, and a history of fake stops at various ports, times and stamps, courtesy of a man in Hzadn who owed me a favor.

I paged station control on a general hailing frequency. A young-old face with blue eyes appeared on the viewscreen.

"What'll it be?" the face said.

"Berth for one mid-range craft," I replied. "Crew, maintenance and cleanup."

"Premium berths are going at 400 yols."

"What, a week?"

"No, a day."

I gave a croak of disgust. "Highway robbery. You have anything cheaper?"

"Down the end, there are lower-end berthings, going for 180. For limited time. 12 hour max."

I grunted. "Okay, but it's still very high."

I saw his lip move in irritation. He gave me a distracted shrug.

"Busy today," I muttered. "It's like a circus fairground here. What's up?"

"Holse and Detran are hosting an auction. Starships galore. Wholesale."

"You don't say?" I looked on in feigned interest, my eyes traveling to the roster of sleek, grey silver hulls neatly arranged on the far side of the ring. "Nice vehicular lines. Those some of the ships up for sale?"

"Uh huh."

"I might want to bid on one myself."

He regarded us with a dubious grunt, then scratched his cheek. "If you get the proper clearance maybe. But I'll warn you it's a minimum 600 to enter a qualifying bid, refundable on purchase of a ship."

I whistled a low note. "That's a mighty steep entry point, chief. Still, if it fetches us a decent ship—"

"It discourages sharpers."

"How far will a man go to get a good starship?"

He shrugged, clearly not engaged. "You look like you're doing pretty good with your own craft, Rambo. Why buy another? You not pleased with what you got? What is it, an early Bantam?"

I nodded. "Big on the horsepower, lean on the energy."

"Go down to central to get your badge, though I warn you, if you want to bid, there'll be some serious players."

We berthed on the farther side of the docking ring amidst somewhat dodgier-looking vessels than those on display. The automatic air lock connected to our cargo port; we passed through, strode down the hall and passed customs, though I took a disguise kit with me and another two of those hide-saving explosives that could pass easily as coins. Needless to say, no weapons were allowed beyond the checkpoint. Rectangular artificial-grav units, regularly spaced around the station and emitting their characteristic low hum, kept us walking on our feet at expected Earth g levels.

A large open-air rotunda buzzed with activity. A milling crowd flushed with pre-auction excitement, jostled for position. As did we, in its main restaurant-bar, enlivened by the noisy rattle and hum of slot machines and video games set up to the sides. Glass ports overlooked the docking station where thirty some odd starships were moored. Wren and the others grabbed seats with me around the curved bar, complete with vid screens showing sports and news. A place to scout the scene, relax. I picked an area to the left and center of the bandstand, ideal for people-watching as it offered an unobstructed view of every movement. Banners and flags pinned on the high wall behind the bandstand and over the glass observatory fluttered in the air-circulator's draft.

We nursed our drinks; Noss, poor boy, ordered a cold glass of milk, on account of his ulcerated stomach due to stress. Blest chewed a mouthful of peanuts then shoveled a handful of crackers down his maw too before downing his two shotglasses of rum straight up. I looked at him in amusement, but couldn't see anything worth salvaging, or softening in that lackluster gaze of his. Eyes two pissholes in the snow. A rosy nose, like a drunk's. Comical with that mop of dirty blond hair, but a sullen stare like a teenage rebel. I knew he had more brains than what most credited him for. Not my usual recruit, but such are the woes of running a ship on a tight delivery schedule. Wren sat back in silence, her shiny vibrancy and health the epitome of cheer—at least next to Blest.

My brain gave critical scrutiny to the clientele. A mix of sorts, but somehow the partners, Detran and Holse, had attracted a stable breed of middle-incomers and well-off business-people searching for their next pleasure craft. Maybe one to upgrade their current vessel in need of an overhaul.

Loud talk, breezy smiles, energetic drinking—all marked a definite pleasure-cruise atmosphere. Men with women on their arms, pointing at this ship or that, the women cooing with delight at the sleek lines and chromium glitter, and the man lifting eyebrows at the luxury while secretly licking his lips at the cost.

A haven for hustlers too, from the two bit con with the shifty eyes and greasy smile and overused clichés, to the higher end player who will invent his own stories and likely instruct his assistants to bid against the competition, not unlike a ploy I imagined Detran had going for himself in an effort to inflate prices.

Where was my angle? Something was here. Just had to find it. Had to keep my crew busy too, keep their teeth chewing on something. The last run had nearly put us over the edge. Blest had become more of an annoyance than ever. May have to get rid of him. Though his heroics had surprised me back in the alley.

A big man with a loud voice came bragging about his luck at the space casino in Vega. A crew of cronies at a nearby table gathered about to listen. He was getting a little tight on the Black Dog, a few too many highballs light on the rocks.

"Boys," he said, just shy of slurring his words, "you stick around with me, and you'll go places. Give you shares in pickings that you won't find anyplace else."

The bald idler beside him, maybe his business partner, grinned ear to ear. "Now, Sal, don't you go shooting your mouth off."

Jolly boys, out for a romping time away from wifey and the kids and the haze of their humdrum lives. Living it up with big talk and big drink. Didn't doubt they had all the money in the world to buy one of those space yachts parked out there but not the brains to keep it. How hard would it be to lift one of those suckers off old Sal or one of his buddies?

"I'm going to take a little walk," I said at last, depressed by it all. "You folks settle in, mingle with the gentry."

I drifted over to the end of the rotunda, gazing at the mixed bag of folk and their garish dress, and the antiquated slot machines they played on to idle away the time, half listening in on random conversations with an amused grin. Out of the corner of my eye, I saw a big man dip into an exit. He looked important, wouldn't be surprised if it were Detran or Holse himself. On a whim, I followed him, down a wide stairwell to a service bay where some maintenance crew or what could have been the big boy organizers themselves and their lackeys were preparing a kind of pre-bidding lounge. A lower level, a mini version of upstairs with large picture windows granting a view of the vintage offerings on the docking ring.

Yep, Detran, all right. I caught the drop of the name 'Halley D'. At any rate, looked as if the two partners were setting up their wheel and deal spectacle to a few VIP customers in advance. I pushed a colored hair net over my head to make my purple streak more silver, then wiped skin cream on both cheeks to create a look paler than I really was.

Detran, even from a distance, I didn't like from the start. Swarthy, long-boned with sandy walrus mustache and big, fleshy lips, a match for his mouth and ego. Something off about him, his ophidian mannerisms, like when a certain song plays on the radio that makes your skin run cold, so did this man's strident tone offend me.

I did a subtle hop and skip and bounded in behind some crates of decorations and accessories being offloaded onto their starships. To make them look prettier? Every gimmick counted. I scootched in closer to listen in on what they were saying.

I heard Detran, who had been smiling all the time and murmuring to his crony with the grey-beard, blow air out of his cheeks. "Not bad for a day's work, Lew. Unlucky for those SOBs out in deep space who lost their ships." Detran gave a sour guffaw, one that had a mean and hollow ring to it. I caught some muffled words then of him bragging about how he had grabbed the ships out from under those about to be boarded after one of the Star Lord's blitzkrieg rampages. The corpses he had jettisoned into space. He turned to his two henchman, covered in grease. "Hurry up, you bums. What's taking you so long? These showboats aren't going to sell themselves. Remember, what we don't sell in the auction, we ship to the wrecking yards, piece by piece."

"What about these X2s?" one lackey inquired. "Sure you want to unload them, Hal? If we wait, we could get a better price on consignment at one of the local shops."

"Cost us too much." Detran's sneer widened. "We unload as much as we can. Plus, I have other reasons."

The hired hand seemed to grunt at that, but clearly disliked the decision. "As you like, Hal."

There came hurried footsteps. Someone approached, wheezing. "Hal, problem on pier 14. *The Lady Lou*. Some grifter trying to make off with the audio board."

He clicked his tongue. "What the flaming hell—Come! Holse, you too." He swept off to investigate with his entourage.

Wren hunched up beside me, apparently having overheard the latter part. I raised my brows, for I hadn't even heard her.

"Seems as if that lout Detran hardly deserves the fruits of his haul."

"No kidding." I gave the ships parked outside the glass a once-over then I got a sudden idea. Caution is not usually my greatest virtue, but when an idea sparks, I'm like a kid in a candy store. "Maybe this ticket is our next easy way to cheat penury."

"How? You thinking of conning an unsuspecting playboy out of a starship?"

"Why not?" I smiled. "Kinda like stealing from the rich and giving to the poor."

"Well, if it were my pick, Jet—I'd choose that newer, silver Starburst over there." She pointed to a stream-lined space yacht with smooth, seashell contours and high, curved bow.

I gave a slow nod. "On first glance it'd be my pick. But I have another in mind…"

Chapter 6

We returned to the bar and the subdued company of Blest and Noss. Blest stared, practically comatose. Noss, ever the ordinary man, flicked back his short brown hair, looked out from a bland face with pale blue eyes. The glare of the vid screens flashed lurid news in front of us. Thankfully the volume was lowered to allow some upbeat pop music to take precedence, but I could still read the subtext:

"The warlord from Hazzerot continues to exert his threat of terror over the free colonies. When will the madman stop? Here's live footage of the scene at Bajor's square."

The reporter's voice spoke quickly and somewhat garbled over the muted noise of battle. I saw shells dropping, towers toppling, kids fleeing with family members, the odd blood-streaked pet in tow. I gritted my teeth.

The camera went blank. There was a solemn pause, a flashing picture then static.

"That's all we've got, viewers. Our cameraman and news anchor, Jerle Tomas, are presumed dead on Bajor."

I reached to turn the set off.

"Hey," cried one of the jolly boys from the nearby table. "I was watching that."

"Tough break, chief," I said, changing the channel. "We don't need any more doom and gloom to cheer our little world. Let's watch some mindless soaps, or Dustin BeeJee yodeling along to a sing-along."

"You'd deny the threat of Mong?" the man rasped.

"Don't deny anything, chief. Just don't want to hear that bastard's name, is all." That was the truth. I grew ill at hearing the lunatic Mong's name, remembering well how he and Baer had blown off my hand from the wrist down. The warlord's captain, Baer, was a hole in the ground—I saw to it myself. The details came back to me in painful waves, how Wren had managed to get me out of that death hangar on Trellian with TK and get to a regen shop. Only by a hair. Then by hairs again, managing to get me this robot, mechanical right hand that was now my albatross and a killing machine.

The blowhard Sal came shambling up, rolling up his sleeves as if to make something of the news thing. Blest, with no love for bluster or Mong, stood up to face the drunk. "You, Mr. Fancypants, can go suck—"

Eyes turned in our direction.

I shouldered Blest aside, inserting myself between him and the flustered Sal. "Language, Blest, language," I hissed. "A respectful environment here, no need to draw any undue attention to ourselves."

"I hear you, Rambo. That lowlife Mong's ship almost killed us and made ghosts of us all."

"Let's not get into the eschatological points about this."

"Do you even know…" He looked at me sideways, lowered his voice, "Do you even know what that means?" He shook his head in disgust. Sal seemed to have shrunk at the sight of something crazy in Blest's eyes because he ducked back to his table.

So far my double-speak had kept Blest's brain busy. I liked it that way. I liked the boy's spunk, but he was a constant irritant. I cleared my throat. "Wren, what do you think about our prospects here?"

Her eyes made a casual sweep. "Good to fair."

"Yeah, why do you say that?"

"That mark over there, for example, he's carrying a wad of cash and low on luck. Get a few more in him, he'll be only too willing to lick salt from your palm."

I nodded. "Not bad. But what about baldy over there? He's looking mighty ripe."

"Yeah, but risky with the dead stare and the constant swiping of nose with a twitching hand. Might try something desperate. Don't like the turn of cheek either or the way he lifts his upper lip in a leer at the young woman behind. It's as if he's a lecher feeling plucky away from his wife."

Blest glared. "What the fuck are you two talking about?"

"Relax, Blest," I said. "Just a little game Wren and I play, not to worry. We talk shop when we're bored. How about we order some food and talk about cheerier things?"

"Yeah, with what money, Mr. Rambo?" quipped Blest. "The Sir Jorry compassion fund?"

"It's on me, kid."

Noss licked his lips and grinned. "Sure, steaks are fine, medium rare, please, with fries on the side."

Wren signaled the barman. Blest and she ordered barbecued *varamein*, apparently a big game delicacy on Gistron. Blest requested another rum.

"Rambo, you're not ordering," Wren said, cocking her head. She flashed me one of those wry looks with the dark lashes.

Lips parted, I let out a near silent belch. "Later, not feeling so good, Wrensy." I stood up to make for the restroom down the hall.

I felt one of those gut aches coming on. As quickly as possible, I hustled without looking like a complete clown. Sitting down on the can, I tried to void. Nothing. Only cramps. Too much stress. A frequent happening, ever since Mong and his cretins had blown off my hand. I settled down and felt the wires and machinery loosen inside then a sharp pain rip through my guts followed by a loud plunk in the water. I closed my eyes, let them glaze up in agony.

The door cricked open. Footsteps. A familiar voice. Detran?

"Sh—" A stern cough. "Don't be talking too loud."

Something caused me to lift myself off the seat, feet straddling the rim, even while half way through a dump. I felt a familiar tingle of the hustle in my bones and I held my breath. The new arrivals couldn't see my legs under the stall.

"Quiet down," I heard the other say then a shuffling of feet. "Nobody here, Lew, you know the deal." It was Detran's voice that hissed.

I smiled. Careless of those two to assume the stalls were empty without checking them. I'd seen it happen before.

"What about our little problem?" said Lew.

"What problem?" A pause. "Ain't no problem that I know of."

"Come on, you've skimped big this time round, Hal, now we've got eyes on us. When those fools find out you've rigged the ships to look good and they haven't got anything worth having, someone's going to blow. We'll get reported."

Detran laughed, an outright guffaw. "Report us to who? They'll never know. Little dumb tweety birds pecking around the dunghill for a bit of feed. These pigeons'll have no clue who they're running with, Lew, or what they're running—Myscol XR, Magoo's magical formula, toting it around the universe for us. Haha. It's in demand in practically every port. Tourists, laypeople, the odd wealthy middleman, take your pick."

I gave an unpleasant grin. So, scammer Detran was drug-running on the side. While ripping off the ignorant spacefarer, the man got his kicks and mega yols running Myscol to all ports of the galaxy. Nice scene.

Something didn't add up. I frowned, listened with perked ears, hoping my groaning guts would stay quiet.

"They'll take what I give them, Lew. Traders' rations, Squatters' rights, Governors' Law." Detran laughed. "Once an item's sold, it's sold. No law around here's gonna hold out to some fine print. We'll be long gone, rounding up more ships and more suckers to sell them too. Universe's full of suckers, Lew. Junkers, derelicts, impounded craft, especially with that warmonger Mongo or Bongo, whatever the hell his name is, on the loose."

"So, you didn't hear then? Maybe you aren't worried, Hal, but there's an RSA agent out there, posing as some bidder. Already checked out *The Alastar.* Targa spotted him. Remembered him from a job back on Jajaran."

Detran swore. "That fouls things up. Why the fuck didn't you tell me right off?"

"Thought Targa informed you."

"He didn't. You say this RSA person scouted *Alastar* already?"

"Targa says dogs were on board sniffing around shortly after the RSA left."

"Jesus, Lew! Lucky we didn't have any stash there. Somebody must have tipped somebody off."

"Still so sure of your little plan?"

"The only one of those ships worth anything is *Alastar.* It'll go for plenty. Vintage. Transfer the contraband off the other rigs to *Alastar. Mistress Luella, Flyboy,* the rest of them. Mr. RSA won't suspect at all. We'll stall out *Alastar's* sale, put her off the list if we have to, so the scam doesn't get out from under us."

"Security's locked down all the ships' ports—auction protocol."

Detran hissed. "So, go in the back door. Get it fixed."

"Hard to muck around when there's nosy patrols crawling around the station. They've got ear coms, networks galore, cameras."

"I don't care, just get it done." A pause. "Wait, Lew." I heard some beeps as somebody fumbled for something in his breast pocket. Maybe a mini-com or tablet as Detran pulled up some data. "Here's the code. 661XA. Override the main nav and unlock the control board on *Alastar,* loosen any hatches you need to stash stuff away. The code'll give you the nav."

Another patron came into the washroom. There were sounds of running water and the two conspirators coughed, shuffled their feet, cleared their throats and left without a further word.

I pieced it all together. So, Detran'd sell the ships to tourists and magnates as pleasure craft, hopping the worlds on vacation while his lackeys stashed the drugs on board. The tourists who'd get past borders and checkpoints, would be prime cash cows, being low suspects on the list for contraband. He'd get his boys somehow on the other end to sneak the stuff off their ships and sell it on the streets.

I waited some minutes before I finished my business. Been holding the rest in too long now. I strode out of the loo, pondering Detran's greasy scheme for more than a few minutes, half my brain taking in the auction ships on the nearby ring and the busy flush of activity at the lounge. It'd be hit and miss as some of Detran's unwitting stooges would not pay out. But when others did, the profits would make up for the losses. I rubbed my chin, pretending to take personal interest in a vintage cruiser with wide tail fins and beaklike prow, *The Starbird*. To ensure he got the right dupes at auction time, I guessed he'd probably bid them out with plants giving fake bids, if they weren't the types he was looking for. A slick scheme. I wouldn't have thought the oaf had the brains to put this together, but then again, it must have been his slimy partner behind it all, Lew, or whatever the fuck he called him.

If I could get *The Alastar* out from under them, I'd get two for one—a ship and a viable product. Sell the Myscol myself on the black market. Maybe even find the need to use some myself.

Chapter 7

I approached our part of the bar where Noss was trying to enliven Blest with a joke and failing.

"New plans," I whispered, "we're going after that old bird there, the one with tinsel color and queenly look."

Blest was all ears. "Oh, yeah, how? You suddenly got a quarter of million yols?"

Noss laughed.

"Better. What I want you to do is get cleaned up—in disguise to bid against any others and stall out the process. I need you and Noss on the floor."

"What are you planning to do?" Blest asked, squinting from Wren to me in suspicion.

"Give a little surprise to Mr. Halley Detran and his accomplice then jack his ride."

Noss's lips curled in amusement. Blest just shook his head.

"One missing piece." I frowned, snatching a glance down at the beady-eyed attendant by the cargo hatch to *Alastar*. "I don't want to be on the register, even with credentials as fake as Jorry Rambo. Ties me to the ship. Puts me on a list of suspects to crosscheck. So, that means going in incognito."

Blest scoffed. "You'll never do it."

"Never say never. What I need is that turnkey ring on Detran's belt. I've watched him, he punches little buttons and enters numbers into it. It's a kind of security register, I think, helps him keep tabs on his merchandise. If I have it, more credence when I try to con my way aboard *Alastar*. Prevents me having to strongarm any of his lackeys if things go sour."

"How are you going to get it?" said Blest. "He just going to give it to you?"

"What are you, Mr. Pessimist?" I jeered.

Wren winked. "Leave that to me."

I raised an eyebrow.

Wren lifted herself off her barstool with a suggestive movement of female magic. "I used to handle braggarts like Detran on Talyon," she explained. "Had lots of experience fending off mouth breathing cretins when I was younger. I know his type, plus I'm a better dissembler than you think."

"If you want to try, give it a shot." I shrugged. "I'd try my hand at some dissembling, but I don't want Hally Detran to have any reason to get a whiff of my ugly hide."

Wren grinned. "Wait here." I idled at a nearby table while she planned her approach.

One of the RSA people came bustling by Detran who was watchdogging *The Lady Lou*, and I saw him go red in the face. "You people couldn't have picked a worst damn time to come nosing around my ships," he rasped.

"Sorry, sir. Just a routine check."

"Routine check, my ass. It's called personal harassment."

"Step aside, sir."

Wren moved forward. At the last instant, she contrived to trip on the half steps leading up to the glass observatory and accidentally spilled her drink on Detran. She clasped him in a firm hug, making sure to give him a generous dose of her breasts. Meanwhile her hands worked like spiders around his back to get the key ring off him and slip it under her own belt.

"My mistake, omigod! My bad, sir, sorry, sorry!"

"You stupid cow!" he yelled. "What kind of a klutz are you?"

When he got a better look at her, he licked his lips and stammered, "I mean—"

"No, it was my fault, sir, really. Here, let me wipe that gunk off your coat! Sorry. I really am. I feel terrible!" She lifted her head with grief-stricken eyes and peered up into his flustered face. Snatching a kerchief from her pocket, she scrubbed at his chest, all the while flashing doe-eyes at him and holding his wrist and touching his shoulder.

"Well, I guess it was an honest mistake," he grumbled at last.

"That's mighty kind of you, sir."

He frowned with a half nod. "These half steps are something of a liability anyways. Don't know why the idiot management positioned them here where decent folk can trip over them!" He paused, scrutinizing her with more interest. "Maybe you can make it up to me, doll. Stick around after the auction and we can both have a little nightcap, indulge in a drink or two at the bar, revel in how much money I made."

She winked at Detran. "That would suit me fine, mister. I love to hear how much money a handsome man like you can spend on a lonely girl like me."

That got him grinning. "It's a date then."

Wren disappeared into the crowd, did a round around the rotunda and hurried back to *Bantam* as I had instructed her. I followed a few minutes later and slouched at the *Bantam's* bridge's conference table.

"Clod," she muttered under her breath.

"No better kinds. Let's hope he doesn't get wise too soon. The others didn't come yet?"

She shook her head.

I rubbed my chin in speculation. "Gotta keep him and Blest out of trouble."

Noss and Blest arrived a quarter of an hour later, carrying a bag each of duty free water pipes and Black Dog whiskey.

I rooted around Bantam's utility bin and pulled out a strange hand-sized contraption with a magnetic stamp, feeder cable and small suction plugs. I called it the *spider*. "We just need the drive codes and this little baby can override the main nav system. Wonderful device. Works on the older models. Tricky part will be to con the guards."

"And how on Neptune are you going to get that eyesore through security?" complained Blest.

"Easy, an external pacemaker. Monitors blood. See." I hooked it up to my arm by a cable and a little red light beeped at a regular interval.

Blest shook his head and threw up his hands. "Rusco, one of these days your grand schemes are going to blow up in your face."

"Until then, let's celebrate." I poured drinks for them all.

* * *

I put on my best disguise, a blue uniform, black tie, greyed my hair, wrapped it up in a bun and hid it under a white maintenance inspector's cap. "How do I look?" I posed, did a ballerina's twirl.

"Hokey." Wren pursed her lips.

"Good. All the better. Won't take much to fool those sleepy sallys on watch. Like the one by *The Alastar*. He's practically sprawled out on the floor from boredom."

"Which might mean he'll take an active interest in you when he sees how dopey you look."

I laughed. "Nah. I fit right in with this crowd."

"You think?"

Blest drew me aside. "Why not get Noss or me to sneak aboard and fly that ship?"

"You're not up for that kind of theft, Blest. Plus, if security checks the roster, they'll see one of us missing and it'll give them cause for suspicion. Don't want any paper trails."

I pulled away from him and made my way back to the restaurant, passing easily through security. The attendant at the open cargo bay to *Alastar* just stared at me. Sure enough, he held out a hand blocking me with his R3. "Hold it."

"Inspection, sir," I said. "I'm with Gistron security, contracted by

Secure-A1, LLU #4155, and we have to check the drive codes, for the usual stolen goods. Halley Detran gave me this chit." I held up the red tablet, the master passkey. "You can check it out with him if you want."

The monitor shrugged, grumbled and waved a hand. "Go on. Don't bother any potential buyers though in *The Alastar*. Tough enough as it is to sell a starship these days. Scares them away. People might think there's something wrong with our ships."

"Not to worry. I'll be discreet."

And discreet I'd be. I put on the deadpan look of a security inspector. "If everything checks, I'll be out in no time."

He turned away.

I entered *The Alastar's* cargo hatch and made my way into the inner service bay. A series of halls branched out to various areas of the ship. I took the main one toward *Alastar's* bridge. The ship was roomy enough and built with class. High-ceiling, pleasant grey and black panels. Not a lot of glitter on the bridge like a lot of the newer space yachts. Simple design. Simpler was better, in my opinion.

Did I have a backup plan if the monitor decided to call Detran? No. Bit of a risktaker there, Rusco. My crooked grin grew crookeder. Seems I didn't even need Myscol to work up the nerve for these scams anymore. The evolution of small time operator, Jet Rusco.

I made my way to the nav com, bent under the console that housed the main nav controls, with spider in hand. A couple of wires plugged into the right places and I'd be done. I shone a light under the cowling and saw the serial number lit in red underneath. Perfect. I punched the codes into the spider and let the magnetic strip latch itself to the cowling out of sight. I'd already entered 661XA, the secret passcode Detran had whispered back in the loo. The thing was smart enough to assume wireless control once it had the codes. A couple appeared, browsing the bridge, voicing their admiration for its roominess, its sleek lines and teal and enamel decor. I had to agree.

The guard had followed me in and was scrutinizing me with more than lively suspicion. "Find what you're looking for?"

I put on a frown. I pulled out a tablet from my breast pocket and punched in some codes into a fictitious fact checker, then nodded and raised my hand. "Checks out, mister. This here's an older model, manufactured at Orizon Enterprises on Falcion. Has had eleven maintenance checks, three owners over its lifetime. All legitimate sales of transactions. Looks like we're good to go." I gave him a clever smile and took a deep breath. Good thing I had Wren back on board radio me background info once I gave her the drive codes. I saluted and left.

With a grunt of relief, I made directly for the loo to chuck out this ridiculous disguise and wash the grease off my face. I unfurled my lovely hair, whisked it back with my fingers, sprayed it with more purple dye. There, back to Jorry Rambo again. Much better.

I came out a new man, but not too quickly. I headed back to Bantam for the final prep.

"All smooth," I said to Wren. Noss and Blest lounged nearby. "Now we work fast. In the next half hour the auction starts. When the buyers go in to bid, our Vega-6 star queen *Alastar* will suddenly come to life, start to lift of its own accord."

"Shouldn't we get the hell out of here first?" asked Blest. "Why stick around?"

"That's the safest thing to do, Blest, but it looks suspicious. Some too-obvious cons taking off before a heist. We'll wait a while here then we'll take our silent leave. I mean, what dope would be stupid enough to stick around as a suspect when he could have flown off in advance? Security'll go after all the ships that left before the heist."

"You're a sly bastard, Rusco," Wren murmured.

"Yeah, well we'll see how sly I am if they catch us. If they find the spider beforehand, we're in trouble. Let's hope that doesn't come to pass. That attendant'll squawk bloody murder and they'll backtrace it to me, or at least, Jorry Rambo."

I set to programming the wireless controller for the spider, setting *The Alastar's* course for Deneb, light years away. Next thing I did was reset the passcode to a new one, Mr_Rambunctious, in case

Detran decided to get cute and alter the course, if he had remote access.

Blest didn't like his part in playing bidding stooge, but then again, he was always tending to be a little bitch. Noss was good to go and convinced skeptic Blest to go down to the floor with him and hodge the bids. "Let's get some more duty free liquor. Nothing's going to go wrong."

"Like the last time?" Blest quipped.

Chapter 8

The bidding had begun. A crowd of three hundred or more must have been herded into that hot, sweaty rotunda, milling about, most standing holding drinks, clutching bid cards, a few sitting at tables at the bar, murmuring the talk of big gamblers and bidders. Noss and Blest joined me near the back as the bidding started. Wren had stayed back on Bantam. She'd played her part and I didn't want her face anywhere near the action. I added Noss to the bid roster and paid the 600 squeeze fee—a worthwhile sacrifice, considering the possible payback—nudging him when I wanted him to raise his card. Blest was just there for dressing. Truthfully, I wanted to keep my eye on him. No better way to do that than to have him right at arm's length.

We pushed our way forward to about mid-central, looking through the glass at the line of merchandise. Detran had his arm around Lew's shoulder at the front on the dais, beaming like a new groom. Bids had started on some of the lower end junkers, and low indeed they were. 80k, 82k…A few people had raised their hands with tentative bids.

The auctioneer stood on the podium next to the CEOs, yammering auction talk through a black mic at a mile a minute,

"Anybody for a *Mars Mink*! Mars Mink going for 83, 83, yes, 83! Reserved to the gentleman in the pink tie, yes, 85 anyone? 85 anyone? Going for 85, who will bid 85? Yes, yes, you there with the busk hat and the bright smile. New, fun, relaxing, hip, gotta love a Mars Mink, she's ready to fly to your doorstep!…"

I grinned and studied the crowd. Flushed faces, speculative murmurs, backslapping, claps, mingled laughter with drunken murmurs. A bunch of kids excited at the prospect of gaining some new toys.

When the bidding skipped to the last of the eight junkers, a surprised murmur rang through the throng. "What of the other ships?" someone cried. I gave a sly grin. Probably Detran canned them because now that his drug scheme had fouled, he gained nothing by selling his ships. But the show must go on. I was curious to see how big wheeler Detran played it.

He approached the mic all apologetic and held up his hands. "Ladies and gentlemen, I regret to say the majority of ships are not for sale. Only two of the former line will be up for grabs today. Sorry, a technicality."

"What's this nonsense?" There came another fierce hum of disappointment and loud grumbles from the crowd.

Detran waved a conciliatory hand. "As a consolation, the vintage cruiser *Lady Lou* will be featured today, as our primary giveaway. Not a bad catch."

"Cheater, Detran. Shamster!" cried a red-faced bidder. "What kind of a cheap stunt you pulling here?"

"Now hold on," cried Detran. "I've never been called a shamster in all my twenty years of doing business."

"Well, there's always a first time."

I chuckled. Good little gambit, Detran. Too bad it's failing.

Detran roared, "Some security people have found a need to check certain of my papers—If you want to blame anyone, blame them. It's out of my control." He pulled at his cherry red nose and snuffled. Flourishing a fake document in a gesture of frustration and wearing that Jim-Bob-dandy flushed face and Aw shucks look, he boomed, "Be assured sales will resume on all other craft at 0400 sharp tomorrow!"

"Now the fun begins." I turned to Noss and silently engaged the spider's remote.

The Alastar broke free of her mooring. Her docking arms ripped away and with it the covered walkway leading up to her.

People's heads turned in surprise. The station's air locks closed in automatic response to avoid vacuum engulfing the main wing. For a second everybody froze. Then pandemonium broke out.

The Alastar floated on low impulse power like a big obedient butterfly ninety degrees to the radial axis of the station. I stifled a murmur as her wings and many dips and angles glinted in the station's artificial light. Noss and Blest blinked in unison.

Gistron's security cameras would show nothing. I'd remain out of sight. It'd remain a mystery to everyone how the starship had made her sudden exit.

I feigned my own gasp of innocence while a klaxon rang somewhere down the docking hall.

I turned to watch Detran's expression.

His face boiled in pure fury. "What the bloody hell—" He patted his side, felt for the missing passkey.

He clawed at grey-bearded Lew's arm. "The woman—" he rasped. "Where is the she bitch?"

"There were a few dames on that last ride out," growled Lew. "Could have been on any of them."

"Go after them, for shit sakes!"

Detran scrambled to pull on the arm of one of his lackeys. Soon all were talking at once into coms.

I couldn't resist wading through the crowd to watch more of Detran's panicked antics. Fun being a fly on the wall.

"Stolen in broad daylight?" Detran blinked. "It makes no sense. Why aren't they going after my ship?" He turned and his big brown hound eyes bugged out of their sockets. "Damn RSA. They instigated this." He reached to his side and his face curled in a mean, prune-like grimace. "I'm sure that bitch must have been working in cahoots with those rotten RSA meddlers."

He turned to gaze in wild contempt at the dispersing crowd. Lew gripped his arm. "Wait, Hal. There's our so-called RSA agent there. He looks as surprised as the rest."

"Then who the fuck...?" Halley's perplexed moon face pinched and mouth pursed in a little 'o'. "Find the woman," he croaked.

"She'll be long gone now," Lew objected.

"Find her!" The big man waved a fist.

Lew stumbled off on a run.

Noss, Blest and I waited some minutes before the bedlam reached its peak then followed with a more leisurely gait after a few who made for the landing dock, perhaps gripped with the thought that their ships would do the same magic disappearing act. None of them looked as if they liked the way things were progressing. We headed up the padded carpetway down the boarding hall to the moored ships.

"Slow," I muttered at Noss. "Don't look so freaked out. You look like your granny drowned your hamster."

Noss murmured an apology while Blest looked at me in dogged wonder, itching to get to Bantam.

We approached the checkpoint and its wire mesh and I nodded at the officer at the turnkey on duty, decked out in his blue uniform. He packed a compact R3 at his hip. He gave me a stony inspection, then scanned us all with suspicion.

Something in the way we looked perhaps, the pasty face on Noss, gave us away. Or maybe it was Blest's challenging scowl.

The officer held up his firearm and blurted out a deep-throated order. "Hold it! Identification."

I blinked. "Is there a problem, officer?"

"Not yet, but you might have one. Pass me your ID, and don't try anything stupid."

"Why us?" blurted Blest. "Those people up there are going through." He pointed to the couple ahead of us.

"We're not running an equal opportunity checkout here, wiseass," the guard grumbled.

Turning to flash a reassuring smile at the officer, I felt the first beads of sweat running down my neck while warning bells went off in my brain. I glared at Blest. My hiss of warning did not reach him or Noss in time.

Noss made a move for something at his hip. The officer whipped out his weapon and tagged Noss in the wrist, shattering it. Noss squealed in anguish as a bright red smear appeared from knuckles to wrist joint.

"Down!" the officer roared. "On the ground, all of you!"

I knelt slowly, my hand reaching for the tiny disc I had smuggled in. I pressed the *arm* button and I made as if to put my hands to my head. I released the disc at the same time and it hit the hand railing and flared up. The guard, momentarily blinded by the bright orange ball, gave a howling cry. Blest charged him. They wrestled, each with their hands on the gun with Blest gnashing and cursing. The weapon boomed yet again, clipping the officer low under the chin. He slumped, gave a gurgle of anguish and fell to the floor as a bright blotch blossomed on his throat. A glazed look appeared in his eyes.

Blest grimaced in a daze. He threw the weapon down on the guard's chest.

I raised my hands to my hair and clutched at it. A moment of despair passed. I shook my head in resignation. "That'll do it, Blest. Drag the corpse behind the kiosk!" I hissed at him. "We've got exactly one minute to get the fuck out of here. This heist is going sour. It was all sewn up."

"Sewn up, Rusco? Not really."

We booted it to Bantam, wasting no time to scramble to the bridge and get the engines fired up. All the time klaxon bells shrilled at our ears. Nobody was supposed to get wasted.

Wren came running out of the corridor, blinking in perplexity. "What the fuck's going on?"

"All's not well, Wren." I fiddled with the nav thrusters. "Get us the hell out of here, Noss. Move! Program the Varwol! And for fuck's sake, Blest, don't do anything more to fuck up the day."

Noss moaned, holding his shattered wrist. Wren hopped to it

while Blest glared at me.

I shook my head in sad acknowledgement. We pulled away from the berthing arms. Impulse power took us up from Gistron on to the stars.

I took Bantam on an opposite course to *Alastar*, our runaway yacht speeding to Deneb, my finger ready on the Varwol.

"Ignore the pain," I rasped at Noss. "Keep an eye on *Alastar's* progress. For Mary's sake, pitch *Alastar* into warp if shots come at her, or some SOB comes too close to tractoring her in. She'll lead Gistron's security bozos a merry chase." I hated to be hard on Noss, but the poor fuck need direction and these desperate times demanded desperate measures.

The first ship came roaring up on our tail. But it wasn't who I thought it would be. Wren pulled up the holo feed and zoomed in. A cigar-shaped fast-runner appeared, tapered on the ends, wider in the middle where the bridge lay. No security logo on her side. Odd.

The message came crackling over the com, on a general hailing frequency. "Jorry Rambo, Jorry Rambo, cut your engines! We've weapons locked on your hull. RSA and Gistron security are aboard with orders to kill, regarding the murder of a security agent."

I scowled. On a whim, I paused, my fingers fluttering over the Varwol slider. To find out what they knew could be expedient.

"Seems as if we have some uneasy people on our back," I murmured at Wren." I spoke into the com. "Don't know what you're talking about, captain. Must have the wrong guy."

A fat face appeared on the visual—Halley's—and his angry face spewing invective rattled the line. "Rambo! We've got your number and we know you're keeping a bimbo accomplice aboard. Turn her in. We might go easy on you."

"What bimbo? Are you mad?" Odd that Detran'd go after me instead of *Alastar*. The word 'bimbo' clued me into the fact that Detran and his cronies had no RSA or security team aboard. "Who am I talking to?" I croaked.

"Name's Halley Detran, you fucknut—organizer of the auction, a name you know well enough, unless you're the most clued out SOB in the universe! Turn that hunk of shit around—"

I killed the channel. "Rude bastard." I never took well to insults. I nodded at Wren. "Okay, let's make hay." I kicked in Bantam's hyperdrive while she engaged Alastar's Varwol. But Halley took a shot at us from behind. A deafening boom hit our hull. The shields held but I watched as the red light flickered on the structural overload gauge. The warp sequence failed.

"What kind of bombs is that fucker carrying?" I murmured. "You want to play, Hal? Okay." I swung Bantam about and grunted at Wren. "Fire at that bastard's ass."

Wren loosed a fareon beam. A jagged streak of ionized light flared from our port and shook Halley's craft till it was an ugly shade of dusky yellow.

"Rusco, get the hell out of here," Blest yelled.

As much as I hated to back down from a fight, he was right. I hit the Varwol control but nothing happened. I gaped again. The red light was stuck at the 'on' position at an eight out of ten intensity. "Now, we're fucked."

"Fix it, Noss!" I growled at him in utter helplessness. He grunted and rocked back and forth, holding his mangled wrist; sweat poured down his flushed cheeks.

I swore again, gunning the impulse thrusters. I took us in a tight loop starboard and aft to avoid Halley's continued fire. We played a game of dodge and dash for minutes until I saw our measly impulse thrust would lose us this game. From the direction of Gistron station came two security bogies, bearing down on us with wrath. Red flares issued from their port cannons. Directly at us. The jig was up.

Noss, bless his hide, started messing with the controls and gave a sharp cry as he diverted the auxiliary power to the Varwol drive. The overload warning light flickered off for a brief instant. I slammed the hyperdrive to engage. The high-pitched whir of light drive was music to my ears. Space and time suddenly flipped; we were gone from this sector.

Staring at one another in stunned silence.

"Any chance of them tracking us?" Blest panted.

"Not unless they have angels or psychics on their side," I mumbled.

They couldn't track us. Not at least with the gizmo cloakers I'd installed in the forward drive vents some weeks ago. More yols down the drain, but necessary ones to keep degenerates like Halley off our tail.

Blest drew a hissing breath through his teeth, "At least you avoided what was turning into be a lethal firefight, Rusco."

"For now. There's always tomorrow. That yacht *Alastar* and the booty aboard'll pay for our losses in Resus. We'll head to Deneb, cook up some schemes to get us back in the green."

"I'll believe it when I see it," Blest said.

I sighed. Noss gripped his hand and clenched his teeth to bite back the pain. "Good work, Noss," I congratulated him. "You saved our asses. Wren, get our friend some regen before his hand turns into a bird's claw beyond fixing." She reached for the extra stash in the hidden bulkhead—stuff I always kept in an emergency. There was enough there to deal with Noss's problem. At least I hoped.

Making enemies everywhere I went. Not a good modus operandi.

Chapter 9

Alastar was off to Deneb and we were out of radio contact until the starship came out of warp. Nothing we could do but sit tight and follow her light trails. My eyes kept scanning the overload gauge. The bright red light kept flickering on, then off, only to fade out for a few minutes then flicker back on again. Noss's efforts to keep a steady trickle of auxiliary power trained at the light drive seemed to be failing.

"Damn it, Noss, what's wrong with the blasted thing?"

Noss shrugged, wincing as the regen did its work on his wrist. "Could be anything. The last hit jarred something loose. Bad connection maybe, a corrupted stabilizer? Take your pick."

I grimaced. "Don't like the overload light coming on. We'll stop along the way, get it checked. Where's the nearest civilized world?" I looked to Wren.

The holo image showed a green gridded layout with nearby suns of various intensities as she consulted the star chart. "Baladar in Kepler's Reach."

"Baladar it is. Damn Hal and his bloody super ship. We'll keep regular shifts at the helm. Noss, you turn in, get that wrist healed. Blest, you and Wren fight over who gets the first watch." I turned to make my exit, moving down the hall to my cabin like a straw man, feeling the strain of the last few days building, a pressure under my temples.

I entered my berth, paused in front of the mirror before the sink, scrutinizing myself. The rugged ruffian look. Hollow pits under eyes too dark and purple to signify anything good. Nor did I like the crows-leg cracks forming around the edges plus the whiskers turning a visible shade of grey. The cynical awareness was still there, of a lone glimpse into the facts of life: after all the blood has been shed and the guns have gone off, only the lies we tell ourselves remain, about what heroes we'd been, and how lucky we were to have survived the day.

One Jet Rusco: a washed-up space hustler roving the stars, well past his prime, trying to strike some balance between having a stable life and making ends meet while risking others' skins in the process. Not the best way to play it. On the bright side, a man with some conscience, maybe scant little, but some backbone, and a shred of basic decency floating around there somewhere, but slim pickings lately. Not the best recipe for making friends, or keeping friends.

Perhaps it was this disquieting reminder of my own mediocrity that brought the greatest sadness, a life bereft of fulfillment, the hollow pit-in-the-stomach feeling while going through the motions of playing bandleader to other grifters on the path hunting for a paradise they'd never find.

A knock came at the door. Wren seemed to have won that fight for bridge leave. "Come in."

I looked her over, liking what I saw in her fresh black and grey leather and all her lioness cheekiness. "Well, this's a surprise."

"Is it, Rusco? You think I don't care for you?" She smirked. "What's the matter, not happy to see me?" She came up behind me and put long arms around my chest. In the mirror's reflection, I saw her eyes agleam, a wry twist to her sun-bronzed brow.

I turned and gave her a lingering kiss. I unlatched myself and led her to the cot then flopped down with a groan.

She came to lie beside me. "Rusco, you look haggard."

"You think? Wake me in two hours if I'm not up." I yawned, rolled over on my stomach and she pushed over to my side.

"What's wrong, Russy, out of sorts today?"

"Too many foul-ups, Wren."

"I can unwind some of those nerves," she coaxed. Running a warm hand over my shoulders, she pinched at some key places, which had me arching in response.

"Maybe you could." I turned and leveled her a meaningful glance. The briefest tigress's purr escaped her lips.

"How many problems can I help you forget?"

"A number maybe, but I'm just a dead weight right now, Wren, not much good for what you have in mind."

"You could be worse off, Rusco—think of Noss, poor bastard. Speaking of which, what do you think of our new recruits?"

"If I had my choice, I'd opt for more experienced people any day. Though I can't fault Noss or Blest for their bravery and coming through with the goods. Though Blest is a pain in the ass most of the time."

She nodded. "I think Blest is going to cause you some more serious problems one of these days."

"No doubt. I'll re-evaluate him and the situation once we get to Deneb. Maybe give Blest his share of the spoils and send him on his way."

She snuffled out a laugh. "Good luck. Blest'll squawk like a rooster—he's such a hard-head and chronic whiner. It's for the better you send him packing."

She tickled an area below my belly that seemed overly sensitive and had me jumping up a few inches. "Hey, I'm supposed to be sleeping here, aren't I?" I turned to hold her.

"Sleep is for wimps, Rusco. You can sleep all you want when you're dead."

I laughed.

She rolled over. "How come you never tell me anything about your life?"

"You want me to turn into one of those jolly boy blowhards like down at the station bar?"

"Well, not that bad, I mean."

"I know what you mean." I sighed, rubbing my temples, trying to think of something. "Okay, picture it, me back in midtown Nepasi, on a nowhere world, the place where I started my security guard gig with a man called Trex. Trex—all fun and games. Boozing, whoring, gambling, you know, shows me the town, the hot spots, the low spots, the dives. Once while he was guarding a hock shop, he wanted me to cover for him while he picked up some stuff, and this wise guy comes up and wants to put the drop on me, thinking me a pigeon he can pump for information, maybe score an angle, seeing as I am new kid on the block. He doesn't know I was born on Jaunus 8, war shithole of every kid's bad dream, and that I grew up on the streets. So he asks me where's the best 'gauge'. Testing me out by dropping the word 'gauge'. Numbnut. Every greenhorn knows the new hip term for illegal tech and cop-channel decrypters and neuron stimulators and all that is gauge. 'Dunno, man,' I say, 'I've got like two hour's experience with the stuff.' So, he starts thinking twice about getting by me and taking me by surprise which is his real play, robbing the joint. He asks me if I'm interested in working for a guy named Makey, as in his boss. Me, twenty-three, a dumb fuck, knowing nothing about anything. I say, maybe, how much? 'Oh, a lot more than you're making at this dump.' And before I knew it, I was getting mixed up in a smuggling ring out of that backward planet. Mean fuckers. They'd drop your grandma for no more than the roll of a cigarette."

"Nice. How'd you get out?"

I paused, my lip working a little knot. "Not proud of it, Wren, but I wasted a couple of those assholes, deputies or zarks as they called them. I snuck out of there fast as a weasel, as in fresh off the planet."

She winced. "Rusco, always running from something."

"Yeah, well, sometimes it's just part of who you are and it's all you can do."

"Maybe."

I frowned. "Now your turn."

She gave her shoulder a small twitch.

"Aw, come on, Wren. When were you ever one to turn down a story swap?"

"Maybe because I don't have a story to tell right now." Her lips pursed, in a masked chuckle or a mock curl.

"I know that false smirk. What are you thinking of? Come on, I know you're recalling something."

"Just an old childhood memory." She let out a cooing sigh. "Never forget the time my little brother left the chicken coop open. A bunch of hens got out, so did two roosters. Then they scooted out of the yard and little Freedy, my youngest brother, went chasing them, thinking they'd get eaten by coyotes or something, and I got scared that he was going to get eaten by coyotes himself. We didn't get back for hours, wandering around the hills, all dusty and scratched by desert weeds and fire thistle. I was only eleven, Rusco. Oh, was my dad ever mad and he gave us a tanning for losing those egg-laying hens.

I grunted. "Very quaint, Wren. Glad you shared that story."

"Okay, Rusco, maybe not as invigorating as your shoot-em-up-and leave em in a body bag yarn, but I'm not up to blood and guts tales right now. Sure, got me some more to tell though."

"I'm sure you do, Wren, baby. Like those zombie creepsters you blew all to hell on Talyon."

She settled down, shook her head and laughed. "Sorry, I get a little defensive sometimes. Don't know why I thought of that dumb chicken story."

"The mind is a strange thing."

"Like shit it is, Rusco. You make this stuff up as you go along?" She pounced on me and nearly knocked the breath out of my tired lungs.

"Okay, I give up. Enough story telling for now."

"How about some quiet girl kisses then? I'm in the mood for looove..." She gazed at me with long, hungry eyes.

"Again? Didn't we—"

"Hours ago. Why, you not up for it?" Her kittenish arch of smile hit me with that level of challenge that stirs a man to bawdy deeds. Rusco, no matter how tired he is, can always rise to a challenge.

I rolled over to pull her to my bare chest. "After this deal is over, you and me have to go on some long vacation. Maybe Palm Monteray. Spas, beaches and warm rays. What do you think?"

"Sounds like fun. What are we going to do with Blest and his buddy?"

"Forget those two. Pack them off to Timbuktu with Winnie the Pooh. They've got each other."

She laughed. So the tired JR surrendered to the magical pump and grind of big, talented, desert girl with all the bells and trimmings to go, and the endless mysteries and unfettered openness that was Wren.

I must have dozed off to warm, bawdy memories of Wren, but then dreaming of shooting off down some wind tunnel like I was going to get blown to Arcturus. High winds were buffeting me every which way. Damn those archetypal dreams...

I was running through the bushes, breath huffing out a rasp. Gilm and his contingent of hoods were somewhere behind me, switchblades, billy clubs and bare fists on the ready. Reg, my buddy, had been robbed, beaten down. I was next. We were the only ones aware of the gang's doings on the east side of the river. They'd kill me. I'd only my wits about me. Precious little. I sucked in a wheezing breath, then another breath, willing myself not to make more noise. Up came a flash of pipe, for my throat. I blocked it, plunged a knife into the wanker's yielding belly.

Someone's hand jarred me awake. "Rusco, get up."

"Wha—"

"Signal came in from *Alastar*." Noss stood over me, blinking like an owl. Wren was nowhere to be seen.

I shook my head as if registering for the first time what he was talking about and where I was.

Noss frowned at the slowness of my brain. "You left your door open. You weren't answering your com."

I let out a moan. "Alastar couldn't have gotten that far that fast."

Noss looked at me as if I were still jacked on Myscol. "You'd better come look."

"Aw, shit." I threw on my clothes and stumbled down the dim-lit hall.

CHRIS TURNER

Chapter 10

Wren and Blest were gathered at the bridge, Blest looking like some ragged, bleary-eyed raccoon.

"What's this about Alastar?" I growled.

"Beached somewhere in quadrant 3.21 AZ." Blest stabbed a thumb at the holo star chart.

I blinked. "That's a fuckhole of a place to crap out in—"

"Right, she must have conked out somewhere at the edge of *The Dim Zone*. Her standard paging signal relayed through the world, Daerzoo. Must be regular transports flying in and out that carried the message through the warp tunnel."

"How far in is she?"

"A few light minutes from Daerzoo."

I sighed.

"You're talking dangerous territory," grumbled Blest. "Pirates, scum killers, freaks. Why don't we leave it, Rusco, try some easier fish?"

I scowled. "Wren and I went through a lot of pains to get that ship, my friend. We need to protect our investment."

"That ship may be worth nothing with the Varwol toast," Blest warned.

"But there's a half mil of Myscol out there," I argued. "If Detran was even half telling the truth, we've got to get it. We're already several thousand in the hole. We'd be stupid not to take a crack at salvaging her."

Blest puckered up his lips and shrugged. "Whatever. Do what you want. What do you think, Wren? Is it too risky?"

"I'm with Rusco."

Noss nodded his agreement.

"You guys!" Blest licked his lips, his red-face burning with annoyance. "I get pissed getting outvoted every time we're on this bridge."

The clock said 04:35 which meant that *Alastar* had been in warp for some three hours. My foggy brain tried to piece together the events. Facts: Encrypted messages are uploaded to servers and travel to other ships leapfrogging across the gulfs, until the messages finally make it to the receiver, the same way. Fact 2, the free store interstellar net shares information across the star systems. Fact 3—

Rusco. Focus. So that meant *Alastar* had dropped out of light drive at 02:00, and a few light minutes from Daerzoo put her something of an hour plus change away from us…Couldn't risk our own Varwol crapping out on us. Which meant—

"Where are we now?"

"Ten minutes from Baladar."

I nodded. "We get Bantam fixed up and immediately warp to *The Dim Zone.*"

On the space dock orbiting Baladar, I rode Bantam in as fast as I dared. We made prompt dock and inquiries for maintenance. We were lucky to land a spot at Reyce's Gut Shop as today they were not inundated with service calls. The head mechanic, a slack-jawed man in blue coveralls, with grease on his chin and rag in his hands, listened to our story with grunts and nods, trying not to grin too hard at my fabrications. I saw it wasn't gaining us anything, so gave an expansive flourish.

"Okay, I'll cut the bullshit. Truth to tell, we were in a firefight in a world I shall not name. Bantam took a couple of hits that knocked something important loose. Can you fix it?"

He nodded and signaled his henchmen. I watched the man as he went to work.

We waited in the reception, pacing like tigers.

He came back wheezing and wiping his hands on a dirty white rag. "Good thing you got it looked at. Left stabilizer shot. Replacement 900 yols, labor 200. It'll get you through the next month. But there's more serious damage to the time-drive mechanism. My scanners picked up a hairline crack in the drive crystal. You're looking at minimum 5k repair job, and three days' work in the sweat shop."

"Aw, shit. Three days?" I groaned. "We don't have three days. More yols down the hole." I waved a weary hand. "Well, do the minimum."

The mechanic nodded and left to talk to his hired hands.

I had to dip into my reserve to pay for even that minimal fixup. Now I was riding on empty. More than ever did we need *Alastar* with its Myscol payout. If I had been a bolder man, I'd risk flying in without the repairs, but experience and wisdom of age told me to temper that impulsive plan. I didn't trust Bantam's warp drive not to leave us stranded out in no-man's land as it had *Alastar*.

We bundled up and set a course for Daerzoo. ETA 1 hour. I hoped the gamble was worth it. We'd be in time—for what?—to get the spoils, hoping no other parties had got there ahead of us?

I had Noss soon adjust our course to rendezvous with *Alastar*. If it weren't for her encrypted homing beacon, we'd have a tough time finding her, like the proverbial needle in a haystack. It was a risk. I just hoped others hadn't been listening in too long.

Alastar loomed up on the viewport against the faraway stars. A defiant old bird of a previous generation—her prow shaped like a hammerhead, her body that of a sleek mermaid with twin tail fins. Her robust Vega-6 drive was not so robust any more. I wonder what she thought of her new owners. I killed the homing signal that had alerted us to her position via the spider.

"Let's check her out and find that Myscol and transfer it to Bantam. How I'd like to get her to a safe port…then auction her off as quickly as possible for real this time."

"Won't they be looking for her?" Noss fumbled with the autopilot. "Crosschecking drive codes, insurance records, the like."

"They can't patrol every port in the galaxy, Noss. Places out this way could give two shits about some heist back on Gistron station."

Noss smiled. His wrist looked less puffy and bruised than earlier, though he wouldn't be doing any handstands too soon.

He murmured, "The ship looks okay. We can keep her on impulse drive to wherever she needs to go in the meantime."

"How long would it take us to get her to Daerzoo?" Blest asked.

"Two weeks," Wren answered. "Give or take a day or so."

"Two weeks we don't have," I mused. "This is *The Dim Zone*, remember?"

"Can't we go over and fix it?" Blest piped up.

"Yeah," I barked, "like the hyperdrive just needs a screwdriver and a bit of elbow grease."

"I dunno, just asking." Blest withdrew, flushed-faced.

"All the same, a few of us'll go over and see what's gotten into her."

Noss and Wren stayed aboard and I took Blest with me on the shuttle: a small oblong, eight-legged craft built for short distant hops from ship to ship. I flicked the spider's remote to engage and opened *Alastar's* starboard hatch. We maneuvered Lander to dock in the starboard port. The steel-grey door closed shut and we hung inside the landing bay while the pressure equalized. The little green light blinked and Blest and I hopped out, guns at the ready. I motioned him to cover me in case there were some unpleasant surprises we hadn't counted on.

We moved to the forward hall, weapons drawn, choosing not to err on the side of caution. The place was quiet as a tomb. Pilot emergency lights showed through a dim ambience. Eerie. A sixth sense alerted me to something indefinable.

We crept up the companionway then stalked the corridor leading to the bridge. I held up a hand to Blest to cool his heels. Something felt not quite right.

I saw that a small white plastic dish lay out on the conference table. A fresh vacuum pack of oat flakes sat beside it. Could have been maintenance crew. But why would they have been so careless when potential buyers were roaming about the ship? It seemed odd.

Blest was about to blurt out something, but I put a finger to my lips.

I heard a muffled sneeze. Also caught a glimpse of the console panel to the left of the nav displaced, as if someone had tried to put the cover hastily back on. So my suspicions were not unfounded. I cautioned Blest and crept over to the wall and kicked open the hatch.

A pale figure, some thirty-years old, sat hunched in the dimness, quivering like a jellyfish.

"Who are you?" I hauled him up. The pale-faced man held up his hands. I recognized him from Halley's crew. "Bloody hell." Blest's gun was in his face, the barrel practically shoved up his nose.

"My n-name's Krel Follee. Don't shoot! Lew told me to make sure Alastar was ready to fly on short notice. To unlock the nav system."

"So did you?" I demanded.

The stowaway shook his head, a pronounced quiver on his bottom lip. A momma's boy, some geek clever with tech, with a high pitched whine to his voice and a nervous tic on the left cheek.

He didn't answer right away and I wondered if his explanation were a cover. His logic made sense but now we had a problem on our hands. "Lucky we found you, otherwise you'd be a skeleton by the time anyone came looking for you."

"Lucky, how? I got your friend jamming a gun down my throat."

I croaked out a mirthless laugh, impressed despite myself at Follee's spunk. "Lower your weapon, Blest." Blest withdrew his R4. I gave an update to Noss and Wren over the com. "Found Halley's geek code cruncher hunched in the forward bulkhead. A Krel Frowlee. Seems our charmer, Detran, didn't check all his inventory before blast off." I chuckled. "One unlucky dabchick stowed away."

"That's *Follee* and I'm not a geek. I'd have fixed the drive eventually. Even if I had to rip every component out of the stupid panel and piece it back together."

Blest licked his lips and grinned. "So what do we do with this jitterbug?" He redirected his weapon at the stowaway.

"Maybe I have a use for him, Blest. Can you diagnose ships?" I barked at Follee. "Can you pull code, break into systems?"

"Sure, I suppose, all of the above."

"It's no 'suppose', Fowlee, you either can or you can't."

"I can," he growled.

"Then I give you a choice. You either work for us, or stay locked up in the brig on my ship."

"But you're thieves and pirates."

"Anything less than what your employer was?" I sneered. "You don't know the half of Detran's evil."

He struggled with the concept, working his lips in a frown and muttering. Then his eyes went wide and he gave a grave nod. "I suspected him. Never liked that puff weasel anyways. Where the blazes are we? Alastar dropped out of light drive in the middle of nowhere. I couldn't do anything with the controls. Hal's passwords were useless. I was lucky to even force open the food hatch as it was."

"That's because they're locked by my spider," I said proudly, holding up the black, square-faced remote.

"How did *you* get the code then?"

I fluttered my fingers and mimed a mysterious expression. "Little pirate magic."

"Yeah, right."

"Don't get so hot and bothered, Fowlee. I'm short on recruits. As I said, you may come in handy and your options are kinda limited. Where's the Myscol?"

"Myscol? What Myscol?"

"Like the stuff your blowhard employer uses to pad his ships with."

Follee blinked. "You mean the medicines? They're in the engine room, right behind the artificial grav generators."

Blest and I exchanged glances and raced for the hold, hustling our friend along with none too gentle hands.

"Medicines," I scoffed. "Where the fuck did you get such a bird-brained idea?"

"Hal said it was for research: a philanthropic move to fight cancer and other deadly diseases."

"Did he now?" I crooned. "Boy, you've got real dibs on the Gullible Gus award of the year. Your pals've been running drugs. That makes you an accessory."

"No way, I—" He gulped.

We reached the engine room. I heard the low hum of the Vega 6 impulse engines, electro-stroke, quasi-sol drives. Neat stacks and coils on her, running vertically up the wall to the silver-foiled ceiling. Follee pointed. "Over there, behind those black, square units."

I nodded and we crowded in close. Blest and I took the butt end of our guns to the fibrofane and we ripped off the paneling. I saw twin rows of clear plastic packs containing pink powder with elastic bands tied around them.

I shoved Follee's head down to take a look. "Does that look like cancer medicines to you?"

He gulped, licked his lips. "Hey, be careful. I'm not your punching bag here."

I ripped open a hand-sized pack and dipped a finger and ran my tongue over it. "Here, try some," I said to Follee with a grin. He recoiled, like a frightened baby. "Mmm good. Pure stuff. Blest, you should try some too."

"Here, you eat it." I had Blest hold Follee while I forced open his mouth and plugged my pink-snuffed fingers past his tongue. He spat and hissed like an angry cat.

"Consider it your inauguration to Myscol." I laughed. Follee struggled and I shrugged. "Won't do any good. Enters the bloodstream fast." Ah, Rusco, you're a real hoot.

Blest, wearing a lizard's grin, thrust the stowaway aside. I even got a rise out of Blest as he dipped his finger in the bag and took a generous dose.

Both our eyes glazed over a bit. I shook my head, enjoying the buzz. "Now, Fowlee, here's how it's going to fly. Your name, Fol, that's your name from now on. Mr. Fol."

"Naw, just Fol for short," said Blest.

I conceded to the name change.

Follee held up his hands. "So you got your stuff! What's in it for me?" His nervous gaze rested on Blest's itchy finger caressing his weapon.

"This is how it works. We look for opportunities. We split the profits down the middle. I take an extra cut, since it's my ship and I assume the risk. We share in the overhead. You try any fast ones, we blow your head off. Or at the very least, finger you as an accomplice for stealing this pleasure craft."

"Sure," he stammered, "but as long as I don't have to do anything illegal."

I took a deep breath and rolled my eyes.

Blest cast me an impatient glance. "Don't think I want to play nursemaid to baby brat here, Rusco. Though, may give me some amusement on a slow day on my shift." He reached over and rubbed his knuckles on Follee's scalp of thin sandy hair and Fol cried out, telling us to lay off him, not appreciating the threats and sarcasm.

We both laughed, feeling good on the Myscol.

We carted out half the product over to the Lander. Less than what I had thought. I guessed about 200 g's by the time we paid expenses and dropped the price down for a quick sale. Split four ways, that wasn't bad.

I hesitated with the other half of the shipment. Changed my mind. Left it aboard *Alastar*. Blest looked at me as if I had a few screws loose.

"Never put all your eggs in one basket, Blest—ever hear of that maxim?"

He shrugged and gave a muffled snort.

With Fol that made five in our merry band.

* * *

Wren met us in the landing bay, passed her eyes over the stash as Blest and I unloaded it into the utility bins. She gave Follee only a cursory inspection. He stared at her with nothing less than awe.

"Hi, Miss, my name is—"

She ignored his outstretched hand and shouldered her way over to me, all business-like. "We've had about 28 hours, Jet, and counting since the homing beacon was up. We should get the hell out of here."

Blest and I kept unpacking the rest of the bags of product as if we hadn't heard. I took Follee up to the bridge. Noss gave him a guarded greeting. Wren trailed, wearing a peeved look. "I'm talking to you, Rusco."

"Heard you, Wren. All in a day's work. You see how much stuff there is? You should be dancing for joy."

"I am, but this place gives me the creeps. Heard horror stories about *The Dim Zone*."

"Worse than your own shithole on Talyon?"

"Well, yes, worse."

I shrugged. "Could be all true, or maybe just wives' tales."

"Right, like mutants carving out brains and using victims' skulls as wine gourds."

I laughed. "That's a good one. Right up Mong's alley."

Follee looked and stared bug-eyed. *"Dim Zone?"* His eyes flicked back and forth. Thick glasses, clamped at the bridge of his nose, fat, meaty fingers, short, stocky frame coming up to about Noss's shoulders. At least he was keeping his mouth shut, unlike Blest.

"So?" Noss inquired.

"Noss, it's looking good, my man. You may be able to retire yet," I said with enthusiasm. Enthusiasm lit by Myscol.

"That's good." Noss grinned and beamed. His smile faded. "What about Alastar? Can't just leave the ship there to get picked clean by scavengers. You know the law of the jungle, Rusco, finders keepers."

"It's a problem, I know." I looked over at Wren, who seemed torn between ditching the craft and flying the hell out of here. Any moment our own warp could cut out even with the recent band aid.

Blest grunted. "Still say we lose her. Too much risk."

My lips curled in a grimace. "Still could get some appreciable salvage for her. I hate leaving a starship behind."

"Who doesn't, Rusco, but—"

"Look, we have to act fast," interrupted Wren. "Raiders could be out there sniffing down our trail right now."

"She's right," said Blest.

"Any other place we can hide her at?" asked Noss out loud.

Blest snorted. "What, at the edge of *The Dim Zone*?"

"Wren, check it out," I urged.

She pulled up the holo register and began zooming in on nearby worlds. "What am I looking for?"

"Asteroids, space stations, moons, planets, mining operations, any space junk that could create a smoke screen for us until I figure out a better plan."

She shook her head. "Nada, Rusco. Wait! There's an abandoned station."

"What? Where?" I leaned over her shoulder.

"Dunno. Some decommissioned space station. No… Too big for that. Look. Holy, Christ, it's a fortress."

"How far?"

"A couple hours away on impulse thrust."

I chewed my lip. "We could warp in, check it out. If it looks promising…" I saw the overload warning gauge flicker. "What the—" I whuffled out a breath. "Those bastards. Mechanics promised me it—"

"He warned you it could go at any time," grumbled Noss.

"Said we'd get a month," I groused. "Hairline crack must be getting wider."

Blest waved a restless hand. "That station could be a magnet for trouble."

"Few other options are knocking on our door. The long and short of it, our light drive's buggered again."

Blest threw up his hands. "That's just fucking great."

I shrugged. "Well, not much we can do about it. We'll have to risk it."

We headed out on max impulse to the station. I tossed the spider remote over to Noss, who used it as a guide to get *Alastar* trailing on our heels.

CHRIS TURNER

Chapter 11

The last leg was the longest and glummest ride I could remember. We were trucking along on impulse with both Noss and I trying unsuccessfully to get the warp drive up again when we came across a blip on the sensors.

"Visual," I hissed.

"There." Noss pointed.

The station loomed out of the darkness. An obtrusive cube with circular pods at either end. But much more than that, a complex wonder of science and technological engineering. Lights glowed on the superstructure. It wasn't completely dark there and that worried me. Automatic lights? Still operating under some weak solar power from Daerzoo's sun? It seemed a stretch.

"Wren, give me more info on this place." The monstrous station had a look of promise—and menace. It looked too new for the age that Wren had quoted earlier.

"It's four hundred years old. "

"No way!"

"Yes way. Name changed from Cyber Corp to Cygon, somewhere in the last few years of its life."

"What else does the omniscient computer have to say?"

"Supposed to be haunted. A ghost station, actually."

"Yeah, haunted my ass," I scoffed.

"Why out here?"

"Some space laboratory. Experiments, controversial research, close to their base of operations, somewhere in *The Dim Zone*. It is said the firm's senior scientist, Dezmin Yadley, assumed control of the company after the CEO, someone named Mathias, went mysteriously missing. The company dissolved, after repeated disasters rained on its labs."

"Give me the visual on the schematics."

Wren pulled up a complicated diagram on the holo display showing several bays, a series of side wings and work areas across four levels, fanning out radially from a massive warehouse several stories high and breasting out on the hangar.

"Last known to have been searching for alien life out on the remote planets, mostly *The Dim Zone*."

"Makes no sense. Why *The Dim Zone*? Why would a cybernetics company be messing around with alien life?"

"Who the fuck knows, Rusco, or cares," said Blest, "we've got ourselves a serious problem here—"

"Yeah, I know, and we're trying to solve it without you naysaying my every word."

Wren squinted and read on. "The firm is shrouded in mystery and scandal. Known for employing unconventional means—escaping government jurisdictions and facing multiple infractions in both ethics and tax evasion."

"Sounds just like our kind of guys." I laughed. "Dead guys I bet now, unless they built some longevity serum."

"No, afraid not. Afraid the company hasn't been active for centuries."

At one time, it had been formidable, now its defensive cannons had been blown to bits or ripped off by scavengers. A gaping hole loomed in its side, allowing a shadowy glimpse into the docking hangar. I motioned Noss to steer us in closer, my eyes peeled for anything untoward.

I guessed Cyber Corp maintained an extensive empire at one time, perched at the edge of *The Dim Zone*. Maybe their fingers had dug too deep in the pie? Found something they wished they hadn't? What had they been fucking with?

Once inside the hangar hole, I trained Bantam's floodlamps down to see what we were dealing with. Noss guided the ship through the darkness. *Alastar* followed behind. We saw a brood of lurking spaceships. Ancient models—Phasons, KV-Levlars with odd, sleek, tapered outerbodies like the V-Ugons of old. Odd that nobody's taken them, I thought. Vintage. Fly on, Rusco. Maybe the station's unsavory reputation would detract any avid raiders from taking a crack at us. But why go after small fry when you could have a whole squad of ships? There were lots here. Though some had drifted from their landing berths, chipped and battered, looking not so lucky in their fight against the ravages of time.

"Those ships aren't chained down," said Noss. "Artificial grav generators still functioning. A miracle after all this time."

"Yeah, fancy that."

The hangar loomed in all its glory. I was impressed by the sheer size of it. Could fit a mountain in here. We traveled through the warehouse of the station and landed at the end of a line of ancient craft that looked like antediluvian freighters. Carrying what?

Wren punched some keys and a green, wireframe grid appeared. It rotated on the holo display to show more bays and hidden alcoves.

"Turns out this station has been a hazard for salvagers and scavengers for centuries."

"Great, a motherload of bad karma." I chewed on my lip. "But maybe it's just the type of place we need—"

Two Skurgian vessels came streaking in from the entrance. The first ship's fire hit us broadside.

"Motherfuckers," rasped Blest. His fist clenched his rifle.

They'd been hiding on the outside of the station's superstructure, stuck there like leeches, blending in like grey-green lichen on a tree's trunk. If we'd been able to warp in here earlier, we could at least have saved *Alastar* and maybe our own skins.

"We can't warp out," said Noss. "Trapped in this goddamn

creepy hangar."

"How to evade these asslicking fuckwads?" I mused.

"Fight our way out. What else?" Blest howled.

"No, too many of them. They'll blow us to shit." I saw two more come in to join their pals as more fire splatter licked out at us. "We've got two ships running on impulse power. Useless. We take them out there, they'll pepper us with bombs. We have to do the unexpected."

"Like what?"

"Dump Bantam and take our guns and go in on foot. We can hole up and ambush them in some cubbyhole in the station."

Blest stared at me as if I were loony. "What? Take on a small army of Skugs?"

"They'll never find us in this maze. At least easily. Even if they do, we'll gun them down—and it'll be better odds for us."

"Great," said Noss. "We go in there, get blown up and charcoaled by laser trip beams."

Blest gave his head a laughing shake. "It's just crazy enough to work."

I got them rushing down to the cargo bay while I stayed behind to reach in the utility bulkhead and grab the silver phaso I stashed there. That slim little silver disc had saved my ass before, the same device 'friend' Mong and his goats had been after since the beginning. Why the freak wanted it, I wasn't so sure. A powerful artifact of ancient alien technology: it could transport an unwary being to hell and back, or if one was lucky, to some other alien dimension. No easy way of getting back from there unless the disc was clutched with fierce force in one's hand, not so easy. I'd been there once and did not care to return. I was damned if I'd leave it for the Skugs to find.

I caught up with them in the hall leading to the hold. Follee tugged at my arm. "But won't they take the ship?" he stammered.

"They might, Fol, but there's a chance they won't. I'll rig some explosives on the hatch, that or give them a mother of an electric shock if they touch it plus something extra for Sunday brunch."

"What if they blow the hatch—?"

"For Christ sakes, Blest, get your ass moving and shut the fuck up for once. These scavengers don't seem to be after ships. Didn't you see the row of them all sitting here?"

"That's because they're dead."

"Could've scavenged them for parts though. Why didn't they?"

"It's a bad idea, Rusco." Blest shook his head.

"You got a better idea?"

Wren waved a hand. "Let's just hurry up for fuck's sake! We're wasting time."

Blest grunted in resignation.

"Suit up!" I growled.

We grabbed the reserve pressure suits off the wall, snugged in and checked each other's helms and air supplies. Follee's face was green with apprehension in the dim lights, reluctant to move toward the cargo hatch. "I don't want to go, Rusco," he pleaded through his mask.

"You want to stay back here, Fol, and get mauled by mutants? Or blown to shit?"

Fire hit our port stern but our shields held. Follee cringed at the idea, shrinking like a bug. "Since you put it that way—"

"Get going." Blest pushed him along. I stuck an R3 in Follee's gloved hands. "Use this. Here, safety on. Safety off. Get it? You point it at bad guys and shoot if some come trying to blow your head off."

Follee gave a vigorous nod.

Wren looked at me, a flushed look of uncertainty there—Are you sure you want this guy along?

No, I wasn't sure, Wren, I answered her voiceless expression but I didn't see too many options here other than signing the poor guy's death warrant leaving him behind.

Noss powered down the ship, save for shields. We rushed to the cargo exit pad, so it left no easily traceable signature. I booby trapped the hatch with my regular batch of tricks—explosives and high voltage. If Skugs managed to penetrate it, we'd be stranded here—an unwholesome thought. *Alastar,* I could do nothing for now. I'd spidered her to a safe landing place a few hundred yards away, couched in thick, gummy shadows.

My breath hissed out a ragged whisper through my mask. We hurried out onto the docking pavilion, keeping to the wall. Blest and Noss gave covering fire while Wren sprinted ahead in a crouching trot to get the air lock to the station open, even as the Skug vessels, beetle-like shapes, swarmed closer. I could tell they were Skug by the lady-bug shape of their hulls, and the crude symbology writ on their sides: a long spiked anvil with a red slash through it. What significance it had, I'd never known. Something to do with some industrial accident that had maimed them.

The air lock, about a hundred yards away, was intact, another thing that puzzled me.

Blest cursed as I hustled Follee along, a slow bastard by anyone's standards. Barked into the com to get his ass down and lie flat on his stomach while fire ripped around us. Wren had the air lock mechanism figured out; *tada,* the doors suddenly jerked open to the square chamber beyond. We would have blasted it to shit if it were too stubborn to open. We dragged our hides in before the Skug blasters could rifle us with holes. They'd be landing and assembling their own teams. Whether they went after us on foot, or went for our ships, remained to be seen.

The chamber pressurized, then the inner lock opened automatically. We spilled out into a hall.

Surprisingly, the air lock wasn't seized. Blasting it as a last resort would flood the whole station in vacuum, but I was guessing the station had backup systems for that.

"The air is breathable," said Wren, "according to our suit sensors."

I motioned them down the dusky corridor to the right, Follee making googly eyes at the state-of-the-art tech. The lumo shields draping the walls, the fibrofane shock and sound bafflers, the intricate myriads of sensors and scanners for contagion, contraband and weaponry, luckily manned by no one in these brave new times. There were even a dozen emergency suits hanging behind glass showcases.

Not far down the hall we peered through more massive glass windows into broken laboratories, shattered tables and lab equipment, benches askew. Bins of chemicals lay strewn on the metal-plated floor; sealants, robot parts, component boards scattered everywhere. It looked as if the place hadn't been walked through in an eon though. A weird, ambient violet, self-perpetuating glow permeated the surroundings, as if some ancient power still lived here and was still in operation. How, I couldn't guess. Maybe solar power still up and running, as I'd speculated earlier? I eyed the grey crystal fibrofane panels on the wall. Dead camera eyes watched us like insects. Noss opened his mouth to speak, but I signaled him to silence.

We hustled down a wide stairwell, another corridor to a lower level that opened into what looked like a giant depot. The space was enormous. The domed ceiling rose unfathomably high. Monstrous shapes, mechanical things, loomed out of the artificial gloom, like ill-conceived ghosts. Wren's jaw dropped, as did Blest's who had curbed his wise-guy tongue for once. We all walked smitten to silence.

I listened for the expected flurry of enemy fire and feet. Nothing. Only a faint, faraway echo of boots on metal—wary and hesitant. Then another, louder, duller thud of metal—like a ship's landing pads touching down. "If we're lucky, we can lose those gooks," I whispered. "They'll go looking somewhere else." Somehow my own words sounded comical and naive in this ancient murk. I didn't believe my own vain hope for a second.

I recalled typical Skug physiology. A cross between a mutant warrior and a walking mummy. Once human, these mutants were victims of some plague or chemical spill disaster. Freaks, albino genetic rejects forced to wear headgear in the form of blue-grey fabric scarfs wrapped around their misshapen skulls. Reputed to have dull white horns peeking up on their oversized heads and tusks protruding from cheeks with black nozzles affixed to noses with wire mesh where mouths should be. If such mutations were accurate, I assumed the nozzles facilitated breathing. Maybe they siphoned drugged up gas there? I didn't want to meet one of the mutants face to face, or for that matter, ever.

Even through the filtered ages of decades, I tasted the faint waft of death here. Ancient death. Old corpses lay strewn about the feet of the mechanical monsters on the steel paneled floor, victims struck down from the look of their eyeless sockets, by some mysterious, brutal force.

My mind traveled back to a distant memory, a time when my father took me to some natural caves outside our home town on Jaunus. Strange how memory is jogged by the weirdest of triggers. I was scared shitless of bats and snakes and anything fluttery and crawly, but my father took me down there anyway, where the drip-drip of water from stalactites and the cloying darkness had my knees knocking. Despite the dank air chilling my bones, he wanted me to get an appreciation for 'nature', its majesty and terror. "All is not as it seems, Jet. Nature comes in all shapes and sizes. Never all just sun and bright sky and fresh air. Mother Nature has secrets that no one will ever know. Observe and find out, if she wishes to show you. You may learn something." And I lurched back as a snake slithered out of the shadows and lashed its wedge-shaped head at me.

My feeling now was not much different.

We took stealthy steps through deep gloom, keeping our eyes off the ancient corpses. Blest kicked at some moldered bones. "Are these for real?" A clattering echo rebounded through the dimness. I waved him to silence. We threaded our way among the hulking shapes of the weird mechnobots, robots of some savage origin, some as high as a second story apartment with pincers for arms and strange metallic outerbodies and turret-like heads. Others materialized in the gloom, as short as midgets only knee high, human, animal, a mixture of the two. The cavernous ceiling rose more stories above than I cared to guess and seemed to exude a maroon-purplish glow from somewhere high above, almost phosphorescent. Whatever these hulking shapes were, they constituted an intimidating rack of armory, scaring the crap out of us all in the eerie light that filtered through the opaque dome.

Chapter 12

I felt a shudder pass along my spine as I threaded by those inert goliaths looming in the eerie darkness. They'd been spawned in a day when technology far outmatched our current science. Now only shadowy hints lingered of the dark age humankind had lapsed into since the last alien war centuries ago. I swallowed the lump in my throat, wondering about that violent, bio-mechanical heritage we'd evolved out of, and of which we remembered little.

Cyber Corp had been messing with robotic experiments, prototypes of weird and wonderful kinds. Aggressive ones, judging from the weapons and guns, the flamethrowers and ray sprayers mounted on the turrets, also the size of those dinosaur shapes and the quality of their armor.

So many mysteries and relics of the forgotten past...The only common thread, invariably, was war and its cruel aftermath—the glue holding it all together.

Here a garden sprawled, as if a horticulture or greenhouse experiment of loose soil and potted plants, there a shattered glass bin of shriveled ferns, long browned with striped leaves and stigmas of curled proboscises. I couldn't help but shiver, almost forgetting our Skug menace.

I tapped on the glass of a certain rectangular glass lab cage, eighteen feet long. Inside was what looked like withered ferns clinging to chunks of dry soil. It appeared as if the vessel had been hurled from a distance; from one of the labs spread along the side walls. Uncannily, the tempered-glass had not shattered.

I tapped on the glass again. Nothing…And yet, I detected a small flutter of movement within.

I gave a hollow laugh. Impossible, Rusco, you're a lunatic. I breathed through my mask. I chuckled, attributing my imagination to the Myscol I'd tongued.

Yet that primitive awareness that lurks at the back the mind and knows something is watching it, tingled my spine. I knew it was something not quite arguably human. So did the others. We all watched in a kind of glazed horror as a monstrous hulk, some twenty-foot-high half-armored ape and scorpion, came to sudden life, a bluish-grey pilot light beaming from its turret-like head. Ridiculous, of course. Not even possible to hallucinate such a thing, but we were the fools striding through a forsaken, molder-ridden mausoleum of the haunted past, and evidently a living vessel for things that should have been left alone.

No time to ponder the chilling horrors of the past. The first gunfire came at us in green energy beams from the wings where we had come. I hissed out a curse and beckoned Follee forward who hunched behind a shoulder-high, four-legged mechnobot with a hideous oversized head and downturned sloping back.

We slunk like panthers to a place where three giant mechnos stood poised on human-like legs, poised in the violet gloom like grim guardians of a tortured past. We hunkered down behind them, taking up ambush positions.

Figures moved in the murk. They came upon us like wildfire, flanking us in a wide semicircle. A small army of horned heads, mummy-wrapped figures with tusked noses came lumbering like stalkers out of screaming nightmare. So, the tales of Skugs were true.

Their sawed off R6s spat blue fire at us.

Fire flare was all around, shredding glass cases, sending bright streaks off the tough armor of the standing mechnobots.

The Skugs grunted through their nosepieces like wild hogs. I saw bits of plant and earth flying up as their fire flares shredded the aquarium next to me. Were those plants moving, or hissing? No, a stupid trick of the mind, amid the sudden carnage and chaos.

I dove for deeper cover, missing a spray that would have ended me.

I gained my feet and stood back to back with Wren emptying fire into moving shapes. Noss and Blest worked in a similar manner. I didn't know where the fuck Follee had gone. Had he fled? Was he dead?

These mutants were going to flank us and take us down in minutes. My head struggled to make sense of it. A flurry of thoughts coursed through my mind. Primitive cannibals these headhunting Skugs, relatives of the Skurgs, drinking blood from carved goblets of skulls. Up to this point, I'd assumed these freaks were just raiders seeking plunder, not the bloodthirsty savages of local legends passed down through the ages.

That illusion was shattered with the rush of a seven-foot giant from my right. He bowled me over, snorting like a bison, and reached out a deformed paw to hurl me against the mechnobot to my left. I let out a wild grunt. My gun slipped from my grasp as I slid down on my haunches. I shook the daze from my skull, rolling and reaching for my weapon. Fingers gripped the stock. Brain hoped he didn't grab and toss me again. I brought the butt end up, whistling steel for a Skug crown. He reached out to catch it in his tatter-wrapped fingers, but the barrel snapped past and clipped him in the skull. For a second he teetered. I caught the whiff of meaty breath and almost gagged. Bloody teeth showed through an oxygen mask. The creature staggered back and shook out the daze, grunting obscenities. I plugged his rat-bastard ass full of holes and he fell face first in a pool of blood.

I looked to the others. Wren and Blest fought tooth and nail to repel a swarm of the mutants. In the flash bursts, I caught glimpses of blood and guts flying. Amidst animal roars and the *rat-a-tat* action of multiple fire, I plugged death into the backs of two freaks trying to take down Wren. They fell, hands reaching high over their shoulders.

Blest turned, looking like a wounded, feral animal in the dimness. Noss was hunched behind him, making use of the cover of an arching mechnobot. His hands were too shaky to aim and his gunfire sprayed uselessly in the fray. They'd die soon. As would we all, if we didn't—

A sudden thought intruded on my mind. The thing had tried to catch me, not kill me—so, capture was their game—They were preparing to gather us for their stew pots or some deeper evil which chilled me even more.

The mechanical monster that had come to life flashed fire from its twin guns sticking from its mouth. The thing scorched a mob of running figures. They disintegrated in a burst of legs, twirling arms and shredded masses of flesh. Into the carnage the mechno moved on its armored legs. It killed, trampled and sprayed fire. For whatever reasons I could not fathom. Powered by some mysterious force? My jaw hung on its hinges. Was the thing killing our enemies because it liked us? No. Perhaps it was an automated angel of mercy?

One of the Skugs went racing back to the hangar. Others followed. A surcease?

A group came loping back, how long later I don't know, carrying long, tube-like weapons: RPGs? Barrel-blasters?

A blast from one of the weapons rocked the mechnobot from the side. The metal thing toppled backward and smashed into another of the glass aquariums housing more of those eerie plants. My hope died.

I gaped in wonder. Some bug-like creature emerged from the shattered ruin of the turret, spreading iridescent wings. A majestic creature, with at least a foot-long wingspan. It was some wondrous dragonfly, or moth, boasting wings of all colors of the spectrum. Had it been hiding in the armored shell all along? Perhaps it had been commanding the armored shell? That was impossible. It sprang aloft, made tentative motions of flight, as if disturbed from its ancient slumber.

Without warning, another new, weird creature emerged from the ruin of the glass aquarium. Part dragon, or flying snake. An eelish lizard was as close as I could peg it. It took to the air with wings of its own—alien, freakish, of a design a stroke of majesty. The creature was much larger than the dragonfly.

The dragonfly and eel seemed to be allies, if such a word could be applied. Within hairs' breadths they flew past each other, crisscrossing without causing each other injury.

I marveled at the aerodynamics, but gazed in horror as the eel-thing swooped over our company. It settled nearby, wrapped its swordfish-like body around a skulking Skug and twisted its head off. The flower-shaped, petal-ringed mouth snatched at the mutant's spinning head and gulped it down in midair, as if such were a juicy snack. The serpentish body convulsed. The lump moved like a blob under the iridescent skin as did a python digest fresh meat. Yet the greedy, fanged-toothed mouth ignored the rest of the carcass.

Something, in the meantime, had affixed itself to Blest's left leg. He shrieked. One of those narrow, striped, petal-like leaves from the nearby glass case. It had ripped through his suit. Cursing and moaning, Blest tried to pull it off with his fingers, but the effort only made it worse.

"Agh!" he howled in anguish. "Get it off!"

Follee and I tried, but we shied back at Blest's next gruesome howl. Wren watched in horror as it curled tighter around Blest's shin. The harder he tugged, the more it clutched, to the point that he grimaced in agony.

"Don't try to rip it off," I cried.

"Easier for you to say, Rusco," Blest moaned. "It's not suctioned to your leg!"

"What the fuck is it?" Wren hissed.

"Don't know." I scuttled away. Something similar tried to latch onto my own leg. I squinted in the gloom, as quivering plants stood on root ends and leaped to attack as do aggressive leeches spring from trees in monsoon season. Something warned me not to vaporize the plants as the Skugs had done. The poor bastards were now getting slaughtered in numbers! "Quick, get away from them!"

Wren shuttled Blest hobbling along to safety, toward the smoking mechnobots.

The dragonfly swooped and slashed at the Skugs with its razor-edged wings. Skug gunfire blasted up at it, but the rays seemed to glance off its wings or be absorbed by its body as a lightning rod channels electricity.

I could not in any way figure out this scene. Perhaps nothing more terrifying than watching a primitive force unfold before your eyes. Magic and terror of the unknown rolled up in one—an alien species flying with prehistoric fervor feet above your head, doing the imaginable.

Wren was uttering a warrior's cry. She aimed a spray of death at a gang of Skugs creeping up on us from behind. I climbed the back of one of the intact mechnobots and dove into the broken window of the cabin, using it as a shelter to peg off raiders.

The bullet-proof armor saved me from becoming a charred crust. Hero Rusco to the rescue. All the while the crazy dragonfly veered around us like some colorful kite out of a nightmare. The creature slashed down on the Skugs again with its razor wings, spraying blood and guts everywhere. A trail of carnage painted the ground in a way that would make a war vet weep. Nothing could kill the insect. It wheeled around, regrouped, slaughtering Skugs right, left, and center. What did the Skugs want with us? A sick feeling came over my gut, as a grisly thought surfaced again. Suddenly it all began to make sense. I gritted my teeth.

"Die, you fucking mutants!" I peppered the approaching raiders with R4 fire, watching a bunch of them drop, their heads exploding in clouds of crimson. I kept them away from Wren and the others—for now.

Whatever it was, the dragonfly didn't like its habitat disturbed. But how had it survived? The place had floated derelict for centuries. No one had disturbed it. Why?

I watched spellbound, aghast as the dragonfly creature tucked in its wings, plunged through the throat of a Skug and emerged out his back, somewhere at the same level as the kidney. The mutant split into two pieces in a glistening spray of guts. That Skug had been skulking up the feet of my perch to get at me.

That butterfly, moth, bat, dragonfly—what the hell was it? I could only guess that whatever CEO Dezmin had done, he had delved too deep and the creatures had nuked this operation, turning it into a ghost station which nobody would touch for eons. Except maybe some desperate travelers like stupid old us. Question was, how could an obscure alien life live that long? I mean, this was some centuries ago, right? Like what were the chances? Had the plants spawned that dragonfly thing an age ago and it had gestated to life just now? Unlikely. A better question was, how had it powered that mechno?

Or even better: what had it eaten during all those years? The hapless flesh of raiders? I shuddered. Maybe it didn't need to eat? Maybe it could get its nourishment from anything? Even darkness.

I shook my head. Conjectures like this meant jack shit now. Jet Rusco had stumbled onto one of the mysteries of the universe, an archaeological goldmine, and here he was blasting everything to shit.

One of the Skugs had the sense to launch a flash bomb at the titanium base of my mechno tower. The metal hulk shook and shimmered with heat then began to topple. Red fire rose around me in the turret. "Shit!" I loosed a long wail of agony as the tower came crashing to the ground. Whump! The impact reverberated through every bone in my body, cracking my helmet, whooshing the wind out of my lungs. I crawled out of my hole, gasping, choking on the dry, tomb-like air. But it was at least breathable. Young Noss or somebody ran out, dragged me to safety behind the other mechnos. I wheezed out another gasp, looked up into a masked face with black hair behind the faceplate. "Not time to die yet," the figure croaked.

"Getting too old for this shit, Wren." The com was staticky, but still legible.

I felt myself slipping, my mind tumbling as I danced with a tribe of Skugs around an ancient fire… The Skugs who were once human. Skugs come to kill us now, saw off our heads and drink blood from our skulls.

I snapped out of my daze. I punched through my faceplate and pulled away the glass fragments. The two alien creatures buzzed about the chamber, twin horrors from another dimension. The Skugs peppered them with fire: blaster burls, ion-fire, heat sinks. This time a flare caught the eel-lizard's wing and ignited it. The creature gave a mournful hiss then tumbled out of the air like a crippled bomber, skidding to the metal grates. It flapped around like some demented squid out of water.

I winced as a bunch of white-grey effluvia gushed from its side, along with a half dozen, strange, fist-sized bulbs, as if the thing were giving birth to a premature spawn, like a phoenix reverse birthing from a worm. I almost heaved. The dragonfly seemed to go berserk at the fall of its comrade. The winged horror dove over to the mangled, sizzling husk and careened into the killer Skugs with fury. A whistling shriek issued from its nostrils and it chopped and slayed with its razor-sharp wings.

A hunched figure stepped out to study the unusual ruin. The figure ran curious eyes over the twitching carcass and the otherworldly bulbs. Follee? Was this for real? The man wasn't dead. He'd been hiding somewhere; hadn't even fired his weapon. In a trance Follee stooped to poke at the eel-like body.

What was with the sod? The fool must be in shock. "Get the hell out of there!" I called.

I saw Follee's hand flick to his suit's belt. Why? I had more important things to do than babysit the fuck. I hustled Blest along who was in a bad way with that thing wrapped around his leg. Follee lumbered after us with a crazy grin carved on his face, as if to touch a dead alien was some novelty. Loony, dumb, loser idiot.

"This place is a robotic glass menagerie of death," Wren rasped at me. "We're better off taking our chances in the ships."

I gave a grimace of defeat, seeing the chaos around us.

Follee croaked, "What about you and Blest? You can't go out there in vacuum with screwed-up suits."

"We'll use the extra ones back at the airlock."

"Think they'll be any good after all this time?"

"They'd better be." I turned to Blest and wheezed out an apology. "You were right, Blest. Bad idea coming in here."

"Thanks a fuck of a lot. Now I've got Mr. Friendly clinging to my leg."

"Could be worse. You could have Mr. Follee pawing at it. We'll get it off," I grunted at him.

"Yeah, with what, Rusco? Your handy-dandy crowbar back on Bantam that has no warp drive?"

"Shut up! Move." I shouldered him ahead with a rough hand and he gave a howl of pain as the thing gripped his leg tighter. I shoved Follee along also who'd caught up with us.

We hustled our way back through the corridors to that airlock adjoining the hangar. I smashed the glass housing the spare suits. We pulled down two black, durable sets of space gear at random and tested the breathing apparatus. The flow of cool air on my skin indicated they were operational. I gave a sigh of relief. Blest and I struggled into the sleek coveralls while Wren and Follee helped Blest into his, taking care not to get near the plant thing which seemed to ever tighten around his leg. We entered the airlock, crouched by the exit door with our guns on the ready, not knowing what to expect.

We came charging out, blasting full out. Two Skug guards went down in bloody heaps, caught by surprise. Wren and Noss ran ahead to Bantam.

I gaped at the hopelessness of it all. Another Skug vessel moved on us, its weapons trained.

"Wren, Noss! Get back."

I turned my head away as Bantam went up in a ball of flames. Wren and Noss were knocked backward, sliding down the metal runway. They picked themselves up.

Shock hit me in a blind fury. Half a shipment of Myscol and a half mil credits of ship up in smoke.

I saw Noss grab up Wren and they hurried to Alastar.

I turned to fire at the ship in the air. Blest tugged at my arm. My mouth dropped when I saw steam coming from the rear thrusters of a Warhawk parked nearby. The ship was stationed beside a Skug craft. My suspicions confirmed.

"How in the name of Jesus—"

"I'd recognize those Warhawks anywhere," said Blest. "See the eagle insignia on the left side?"

"Must have been our friends, the Skugs. Can always count on them. Mong must have put the word out to even the raiders to keep an eye out for us."

Blest groaned. "Either way, we're fucked."

A rustle came to my left. Not Skug but human. A swarthy, slant-eyed, bushy-browed face of a muscled ball-breaker peering at me. "Weapon down. We've got you tagged, Rusco. We don't want to kill you but…"

I gaped. The three black kevlar-vested figures had 'bounty hunter' written all over them. I went kamikaze, spraying fire in their midst, roaring as they ducked back under the struts of the Warhawk. I grabbed Blest, pushed Follee behind the nearest vessel, the beetle-shaped Skug craft.

Blest gave back fire at the enemy, cursing aloud, hobbling on his fucked-up leg.

Looked as if I'd underestimated Mong's obsession with getting his hands on my phaso.

"The phaso, Rusco!" one of Mong's men called out in a raspy voice from the curling smoke. "It's all we want."

I looked left and right. No options.

"You want the phaso, you fuckbitch?" I called. "Catch." I snatched at a kerchief and pulled the disc out of my pocket, careful not to let my fingers touch it while chucking it at the foremost attacker. He went to slap it away from his face. But in that split second his body mushroomed into a shimmering halo of heat and flame. The man fizzled out to nothing, as if sucked into a black hole. The phaso had done its dirty work and fell ringing to the ground. All this after shuttling its victim to a far off, dark and deadly universe or some unimaginable dimension. The nearest thug gaped, licking his lips. A section of the hangar roof caved in and fell on his head, crushing him along with the phaso.

The bounty ranger-captain crouched behind the tail of his ship and stared bug-eyed. "You're dead, Rusco! Mong will skin you alive for destroying that most precious artifact of his!"

"Tough luck," I yelled at him. "Give Mong a personal message from me that he can go fuck—"

Fire bit back at us, nicking off the metal struts of the Skug's landing gear. I cursed, ducked back under deeper cover.

We would have gotten away. All of us would have, if not for ill-fated luck.

To my left came a clink and a roar. I dropped to my knees, tagged a grotesque shape with a full head of horns. The thing sagged, snuffled like a bison then fell in a sloppy heap. I ran and kicked the energy gun from the twitching hand.

Skugs, I hated them all, hated the look of them. This mutant was no exception and still alive.

I peered ahead, seeing gunfire lancing from all angles. A regular midnight fireworks show. Follee breathed like an animated doll, still clutching his unfired R3. Blest stared in shock at our unlikely prospects. Wren and Noss scrambled to reach *Alastar* before she was blown up.

They were fast on their feet, disappearing into *Alastar's* airlock, but we were pinned down. Skugs held down the hangar. No way of reaching *Alastar* without getting shredded by crossfire. Despair crept over me.

I flicked on my com, rasping, "Wren, listen to me."

"Rusco, there're too many of them. Alastar's warp is screwed—"

"Shut up and listen. Take Alastar and get the fuck out of here.

Use whatever drive you have. Forget the shipment. Forget I ever got you into this mess. Sorry Wren. Get Noss to fix the problem, if he can."

"But you'll—"

"I'll make my own getaway on another ship. We'll rendezvous—somewhere—the usual place. I'll draw them away." I cut communication and dragged the fast-dying Skug before the cargo bay. Blest helped me. Maybe we'd need him to fly this thing. I didn't know what condition the mutant'd be in, in the next five minutes. "Into the ship!" I croaked. I dug through his suit pouches and snatched up a grey-red keyring, looking like a wireless hatch control.

"A Skug vessel?" Follee whined.

"Move!" I swatted him with my gun. I'd wasted one Skug. I hoped there weren't others aboard.

"Get in," I commanded the two of them. Pushing buttons on the keyring remote, I got the airlock opening. Follee scurried in to the small pressure chamber beyond. Dumb fucker. If he hadn't stopped to play peekaboo with that stupid eel, maybe we'd have had that extra minute to get to Bantam. Yeah, and maybe be blown up in the meantime. All real useful conjecture, Rusco.

I darted into the mutant craft's airlock after Blest, dragging the Skug last. He didn't look good, his tusked face a pasty white and drenched in sweat. We sealed the door and re-pressurized the chamber. Then we scrambled out the back into the cargo bay. Blest combed the periphery, hobbling on his one good leg. Nobody seemed to be around. The other Skugs who'd manned this vessel must have gotten baked back in the station.

According to the suit sensors, the air seemed breathable so we took off our helms. We shuffled to the bridge, Follee helping me drag the Skug down the hall. A bloody slime pool trailed from his bleeding wound. His breath came as a tortured rasp.

"You can fly this shitbox?" I barked at Follee.

"Y-yeah, I think so. Not so different than an A2X."

"Do it! What are you standing around waiting for?"

He scrambled to attention, flicking controls on the console while mumbling under his breath.

"We can force this mutant to show us how to run this thing," I said, "if I have to wake him from the dead and shove his teeth into the nav panel myself." I looked down at the control panel in growing disgust. Lots of green and red lights flashing amid myriad dials, more intricate than Bantam's console, packed with symbols and script incomprehensible to my eyes.

Follee got the craft moving out of the hangar. Some of the Skugs had tuned into our escape. Their ships lifted off after us.

I grimaced, uttering nasty words. Wren and Noss had *Alastar* up and running, limping along at impulse speed. Christ, their warp was still inactive. What could they do? Skugs took pursuit, three of them, and now one of Mong's Warhawks lifted into the fray. My heart dropped. I looked out onto a dead hope as the station slipped behind us, a massive grey cube with broken antennae and cannons fading in the rear viewport.

The logical course was to engage the Skug light drive and warp out of here, drive away the memories with a lot of drink and Myscol. But the memories of Wren played in my mind, and how they would haunt me to the end of time. The times she'd saved my ass and aroused my passion and caressed my body. As much as *Alastar* was doomed without light drive, I couldn't leave Wren or Noss to die.

With a roaring oath, I smashed my fist on the console aside Follee and ordered him to speed after *Alastar*. He blinked in confusion. To avoid my wrath, he set the craft chasing after her. I manned the warp if things got dicey. I shot beams of fire at whatever came out of the hangar.

An echoing boom struck our hull, high and aft. Echoing hits raked our hull. My eyes squinted at the grey panels above. Blest licked his lips, clutched the table with a white-fisted hand.

"Dodge them!" I bawled. "Follee, keep them away from Wren and Noss!"

Follee was no fighter pilot. Our shields were getting hammered.

But he maneuvered with confident hands clicking the toggles and pushing sliders, guiding the Skug beetle on a tortuous course after the beleaguered Vega 6. Blest watched in white-faced horror.

Although we were *Alastar's* rearguard shield, I saw she was getting hit hard by fiery blasts. Follee hailed her on general frequency. "Noss!" He blurted out in a hoarse voice. "Do you read me? Noss!"

Noss's voice came fluting over the com, a faint-edged staticky rasp.

"About the warp…reboot the time relapse circuit. I know that ship! It must have flaked out while on course to *The Dim Zone*. The reboot will recalibrate the light drive…"

Despite Noss's maneuvering and Wren's fire, *Alastar* was taking too much damage. We looped inside each other's paths. Suddenly there was a wild swarm of enemy ships all around us. Skugs, Warhawks, green, red, yellow, blue beams flaring in all directions.

Fareon fire flashed in wild torrents. A complete soup bowl of chaos. I saw a Skug ship explode in front of our starboard viewport. Then it took out another of its kind, rolling, burning, flipping end over end to splatter shrapnel against our hull. The junk clattered like hail stones. Our heat sensors beeped out warnings as temperatures rose. A thin, robotic voice called out in some guttural tongue, which I guessed was something like, "Danger, Will Robinson, danger. Hull integrity at 30%!"

I targeted anything that moved. Another Skug vessel caught fire and exploded in a blazing ball.

Sudden triumph dawned as the light-drive trails on *Alastar* gleamed from her stern. A rainbow color blazed from her like a light highway turned to infinity. She stretched to a pancake, then was gone.

I howled in glee. "Follee, get us away—"

But my voice faltered as the cabin lights dimmed and the bridge went dark. The ship lurched. A hell of a whump hit our starboard side, knocking us tumbling end over end.

I picked up my feet, scratching my head where it had struck the console weapons' board.

Mong's warship loomed in our viewport. We yawed and rolled. I caught flares coming from the fuselage just aft of his wings. The reserve power came on—an eerie maroon light. Follee gave a hoarse shriek. Blest looked up from the place where he was sprawled.

My eyes flicked to the display. All too well did I know the spider-gripping force of the tractor beam that now drew us toward Mong's much larger vessel.

Chapter 13

I watched Follee in the pilot's chair clutching at something at his side—it's as if he had a monster itch or some nervous tic on his gonads. "You okay over there, chief?" I groaned. "You picked a hell of a time to choke your chicken."

Follee's face paled as our power drained from the main thrusters. They petered out. I felt the sudden g's of deceleration and I teetered in dismay as our ship was pulled toward the larger craft. Its big quad fareon cannon loomed, enough to blow a hole in a small planet. It'd make mincemeat of our shields. Stars slipped sideways past the glass viewport, then a massive cargo door slapped shut behind us.

We were trapped like mice in the enemy's ship.

I heard the clinking and cutting of tools at the hull's hatch. My blood turned to ice as I stared at Blest. "Christ, can't you do anything, Follee? Anything at all?"

"I don't know how to work these shitty Skug weapon controls!" he brayed.

I looked around. Panic swept over me like a bad rash. The electro shock. The explosives. Where were my usual bags of tricks?

I stumbled over to the weapons console, slamming my fist down on the panel before Follee. "Can't we blast our way out of this situation? Take over their ship?"

He stared at me as if I were a lunatic.

"Direct the shield power to the outer hull. Quick!"

Follee nodded. Nearly wagging his head off, he fumbled with the touchpads while Blest stared, green-faced, fists clenched in agony as another wave of pain rippled through his leg gripped by the alien plant. The door to the bridge door burst open in a blaze of blue fire.

I dropped to my knees, bringing my R4 up in one continuous motion. Shots emptied from the barrel. Blest choked out a gasp. He leveled death into the area behind us.

A hulking figure loomed at the doorway, weirdly immune to our fire. He held himself erect, fearlessly confident. Long leather wine-colored trenchcoat trailing with golden eagles on the sides. Wolf furs draped around his shoulders. Hair thick and black as buffalo fur trailing past the middle of his back. The man was enormous. He filled the doorway, must have been seven feet tall. I recognized him at once.

Silent despair crawled over me. A tidal wave of fear and loathing all at the same time, like no other.

The Star Lord.

I fired back at him but he ducked, seemed to flick out his hand and deflect impossibly that burst of fire and absorb it back into his body. What the hell did he have under that leather of his, hyper-kevlar? Plate armor? He wore a sick grin on his wide, sideburned face, eyes windows into nowhere. He jerked his other hand. The weapon sailed out of my grip to slap against the wall. "What the fuck?" I cried.

Staring at my empty palm, I felt a stupor enveloping me as I rolled for cover.

Blest lifted his weapon to loose hell and blast the shit out of the intruders, for there was another figure coming up behind. Blest's fire went wide and ate into the wall, shredding it to pieces. But it was too late. Mong's techno-psi power was in motion; with a twist of a wrist, Blest's weapon seemed to wither in his hand. He gave a mournful cry. The R4 clattered to his feet. Blest blinked, shaking his head, staggering and reaching to grab it. But Mong was a step ahead, kicking it out of his grasp.

Follee was too stunned for action. He just sat there, staring like a zombie. Mong turned to him, a fatherly expression on his face, ignoring me while Blest writhed for cover on the debris-ridden floor.

Two gunman came in behind to waste Follee and the rest of us if we dared to breath too loudly.

Mong grabbed the nearest gunman's barrel and shoved it down. "Wait! I want these people alive."

Follee jerked in a weird way. Maybe it was just panic or madness taking him over. Lurching off his chair, he clutched a dark lump in his palm, the same pod he'd been fumbling with earlier. One of those damned bulbs from the space station. The thing in his hand had been birthed from the dying eel-lizard, pulsing now and shimmering with an eerie expectancy.

Follee gave a harsh laugh. "Stop, or I'll chuck this at you. I've seen what these things can do."

Mong hesitated. His lips parted and his large brown eyes stayed trained on the bulb.

The other two gunman circled us. Raising the bulb in a trembling hand, Follee gripped his firearm in the other, as if he'd never shot a gun before.

Mong motioned. "Who is this momma's boy?"

His nearest henchman shrugged.

I lay on the floor by the debris of the destroyed door, praying for a miracle.

"Come on, boy," the dark figure said to Follee, "you don't have the nerve to shoot me, a Star Lord, do you?" His deep-throated voice echoed through the seashell-shaped bridge.

Follee faltered. The tech man was cracking. Why didn't he shoot? It was unthinkable to just stand there and threaten Mong with that bulb...and yet, Mong did not advance.

Follee hoped to bluff his way through this. Like as if something was going to hatch and attack on his command—even if it did, so what? I remembered the Myscol I'd force-fed him and I did a face palm—a fool gag to play. One that could get us all killed now.

Mong continued to stare down Follee with that avuncular look. It was a look of grave concern, one I remember all too well back on Trellian when he blew my hand off and plugged acid in the stump for kicks. The memory, burned indelibly in my brain, was one I wished to erase. Follee seemed to freeze, as if hypnotized by Mong's mesmeric stare—caught like a deer in the headlights.

"Shoot him, you idiot!" I croaked.

Follee gave his head a vigorous shake then his hand twitched as if to make a move with the bulb.

"Don't—" Mong's warning came too late.

The nearest gunman pegged Follee's nasty little bedroom surprise, blowing off some of Follee's flesh, maybe a finger or two. He sagged with a thin-mouthed squeal. The shifty-eyed gunman whipped up his gun, firing more warning shorts. He leveled blasts at me and Blest when we started to inch forward.

The shattered bulb clattered to the floor like a Humpty Dumpty egg.

I watched spellbound. It hissed, imploded, suddenly sagged inward and rippled, as if bubbling with hot lava. For Christ sakes. It then burst in a splatter of red and green pap, spraying the nearest gunmen with acid, sizzling his leathers and flesh. "What the fuck—?" cried one.

A winged cricket, or some other unnameable horror, burst out of the mash and flew around the room, buzzing and hissing above the gunmen's heads. They ducked, cursing in bewilderment. They swatted and fired at it, but it evaded their shots, hissing like an angry serpent. Without warning, it dive-bombed, burying itself in the face of the first gunman who'd fired at it. He gave a wild shriek and clawed at his face, beating at his nose until it was a pulp of blood and gore in what was left of his disintegrating face. The thing burrowed deeper into his mouth and nose like a termite.

The other gunman gave a cursing yell and rained fire into his comrade, frying both man and winged thing.

"Bloody hell," moaned Follee, staring at the crimson ruin of his palm. He stared around him from one horror to the next, then back to his maimed hand. Fumbling for his R3 which he'd dropped and lifted it to pepper Mong and crew, he gasped, but Mong uttered a hypnotic word and Follee seemed to suddenly freeze, as if beguiled by the Star Lord's impending powers.

"Shoot! What are you waiting for, you dumb fuck?" I cried.

"Try." Mong mouthed the word as if blowing a bubble to a baby. I could see the snicker of triumph curl the lip on his swarthy face. The sightless eyes penetrated into a person's soul. The man's presence was what awed one most. Terrible, unwielding, irresistible. He flicked out a hand in an almost negligent gesture. Follee suddenly flew across the room as if propelled by an invisible force. I heard a snap, then a neck bone break as Follee's back thudded hard against the panels. He slid to the floor, a straw puppet, gazing up in dumb fascination, his spinal cord snapped in two.

I closed my eyes. Now I shook my head in despair and mumbled a prayer, something I hadn't done since my youth.

The other bulb at Follee's side hadn't hatched. Though maybe such a horror could have saved our asses—if only Follee's desperate plan had worked.

Maybe we all should have died back in that Skug tomb of the space station…

Mong turned his feral gaze to me huddled under the nav console; his gunmen's wide-barreled R6s trained at me and Blest.

"I knew," Mong spoke in a sudden raspy voice, "you'd poke your meddling nose forth sooner or later, Rusco. So here we are, each with our unique purposes, though they be vastly different."

"So what's your plan, Mong? Your grand vision?"

"To conquer the habitable worlds, what else?"

"And then?"

"I'll conquer more. To achieve what no other visionary has done in the history of time. Outdo all the warlord chiefs. Even Julius Caesar, Alexander the Great, and Genghis Khan."

"I've heard of those dumb bozos. Good luck. Seems as if you

didn't study your history. Look at where it got them, holes in the ground."

"You're a funny man, Rusco. But a keen sense of humor won't save your skin, especially in so disparaging a position. I should keep you around—sharpen my wits, trading jokes with you. But I feel the gods have punished you in a far crueler way." He stared off into space, as if in some trance or other. "Yes, I believe the gods have chosen a much more grievous fate."

He licked his lips and made a loud smacking sound with his mouth. Blest tried to get up and charge the nearest gunman while Mong was occupied with me. It was a brave but foolish mistake. The gunman twisted and smacked his gun barrel into Blest's head and sent him flying into the rubble.

Mong trudged over and clicked his tongue at him. "Poor fool." He shook his head in sad reflection.

Blest moaned in a sprawled heap. Clenching a fist, he shuddered as delirium took him. His eyes rolled back in their sockets.

Mong studied the flap of plant material curled up high on Blest's leg with new interest. "This creature appears to be an epiphyte of some sort, perhaps a symbiotic lifeform forming a strange and rare bond with its host." A frown graced his leonine face. "I doubt if Mr. Rusco's colleague is getting much benefit."

"It's a fucking parasite," sputtered Blest. "Get it off." He had for a moment drifted out of his delirium.

"Oh, no," chided Mong, "we mustn't interfere with Mother Nature. Such singular phenomenon are examples of a reaction to a super-charged environment."

"You fucks are a real scream," croaked Blest.

I cautioned Blest, shaking my head. "Watch it, Blest."

The gunman who'd fired on his comrade made as if to cut off the tapered leaf wrapped around Blest's shin with his knife, but Mong held him back. "Don't touch it, you fool. The thing'll likely attack you. Watch." He stepped forward, reaching in his leather pouch to bring out a silver vial. He flung a pinch of acid on the curled leaf.

The alien plasma immediately sizzled and a round blotch, like something of a dark eye, widened and glared at the two curious gunmen. Mong nodded. "We will take Mr. Blest back with us to Othwan. He'll keep Mr. Rusco company." He sighed. "An interesting creature," he mused, "but of little utility at this moment."

He sucked in an expansive breath through his nostrils and studied the charred remains of his colleague now slumped in ignominious death with some charred cricket creature half burrowed in his nostrils. "Take its comrade, Balt—the one intact in the form of a bulb beside that other corpse." He gazed at Follee and the now lifeless Skug we'd dragged in sprawled at his side. "Be vigilant in its handling. It may decide to eat you for breakfast."

Balt recoiled. "Sir?"

"The thing exhibits a rare, predatory trait. A hunter that is well worth studying. The thing demonstrates remarkable propensity to protect its habitat, like a she-wolf defending her pups."

"Are you sure?" Balt lifted his weapon.

"I'm a man of research, Balt, you know that. I study the wilderness and all its mysterious creatures, priding myself on my knowledge of predators. Only on the most evolved of creatures do I model myself."

Balt nodded, wincing. With a nervous motion, he signaled another minion who had arrived at the scene. The man fetched a glass case and scooped up the intact bulb.

Mong turned blazing eyes back to me. "A waste, Mr. Rusco." He kicked at the lifeless body of Follee. "I hear you recently disposed of my phaso in most careless a fashion. Alas, a costly error."

I struggled to bring my hoarse voice to life. "Maybe your Skug friends shouldn't have blasted my ship and brought the ceiling raining down on our heads."

"The Skugs, a foolhardy people, will be punished. But there is still the matter of my amalgo—which Captain Baer, sadly, failed to deliver. I fear he is a 'hole in the ground', to use your expression."

"Maybe, how would I know? Should I care? What are these alien gizmos to you, Mong? You're obsessed with the mere sight of them."

The Star Lord's expression grew grave. "To live and breathe air—life is an obsession, Mr. Rusco. Tell me where my amalgo is."

"It's not here," I growled at him. I needed to think, stall for time.

"That is likely true. But it does not answer my question."

I firmed my lip.

Mong gave a weary sigh. "As you wish, Mr. Rusco, we will settle this the long, hard way."

Chapter 14

After a time, Mong turned to Balt. "Give the Skugs back their ship. They can clean up this horrid mess." He gave a negligent flourish. "Tell Lord Raspin of Zuut he will get his 50k yols, minus a 30k damage fee, of course, for his stupid pyrotechnics that destroyed my phaso."

Balt stirred. "Raspin will be pissed. He delivered up Rusco. How many mutants did he lose down there? A hundred? Two?"

Mong shrugged. "Means nothing to me, Balt. Mutant flesh, what's it worth?"

"Unwise, lord—to anger such a primitive warlord—we could face a full blown rebellion against us."

"And what do I care of rebellions? I'll raise a thousand more recruits this year. These fools destroyed my phaso!" The whites of his eyes flashed red. "If Raspin decides to raise his hand against me, I'll bomb the shit out of his little hideaways like I do all dissenters. Every Skug rathole will feed the fires of my wrath. He'll learn to fear the name of *Mong* to his grave."

Balt gave a brief nod. "Very well, sir."

Mong beckoned Balt with a curled finger and strode off the bridge, his furs flapping behind him. He ducked his head under the smoking lintel. Balt grunted and motioned for the other gunmen to haul Blest and me up.

In Mong's wake, the gunmen dragged us down the hall through

the melted hatch whose metal hung in shreds. We marched through the impossibly massive cargo bay then past other men garbed in armor and leather, R6 blasters strapped snug at their side. Steel chains hung from the ceiling from which I saw other ships suspended: captured vessels with similar holes in their sides. Mong stared and strode on; the man seemed to make a habit of trapping ships like flies.

We weaved our way around the impossible maze of ships, out of the cargo bay and down some more halls, with barbaric symbols and panoramas carved on the walls—3D murals of famous ship wars, epic battles, faces of Mong and his lieutenants, warriors of feral disposition in poses of combat. These were a crew of badasses, proud of their achievements. I looked over at Blest. The poor bastard wasn't responding. His head hung slack in the guard's arms. Occasionally he'd mumble an incoherent phrase, probably suffering from a concussion.

We passed a glass viewport and I caught glimpses of faraway stars, and the doomed station, a far point dwindling to nothing. My mind whirled in panic, searching for a way out of this mess. There appeared none. We were weaponless, powerless in a warlord's invincible flagship. I recalled the fareon cannon on its side that could blow holes in planets. The fiercest warlord in the galaxy strode a few feet away in front of us. Impossibly strong. Armed with weird powers. Leader of an invincible fleet of warships hell bent on dominion of all human worlds.

We passed more guards, two now on either side of a U-shaped door. Mong ordered us thrust into an interrogation room, one that looked disturbingly similar to that of stark, grimy quality back on Trellian where I'd lost my hand.

A plain table sat with three chairs to one side. One of those chairs had leather straps on the arm rests. Didn't surprise me.

They tossed Blest like a sack of potatoes on the floor where he lay dazed and groaning. I looked over at Mong with sullen contempt.

He stood facing the wall where a star map glowed with a simple console and buttons fitted below. His back was to me and gnarled, massive hands knotted behind his rippling back. "Now, Rusco, about that amalgo."

I sucked in a breath, ignoring the question.

Mong signaled and Balt struck me in the kidney, causing me to buckle over with a gasp. I lashed out with my machine hand, clipping Balt on the hip, prompting a startled yelp. He smacked me again as his cohorts pinned my arms behind my back.

"The thing was on the *Bantam*," I gasped. "Your bungling Skugs blew it to shit. You saw it yourself."

Mong motioned again to his man, Balt. They had an ingenious way of getting a hostile and unwilling participant to talk. One clamp on the left hand, another on the right foot. One man to apply a squeezing force. Balt clicked a remote which opened a drawer in the wall, withdrawing two black squarish devices as ancillary props with prongs and vises and a base not much bigger than my spider. The fastened those devices to both limbs and kicked Blest in the gut as they walked by. They forced me down into that chair. With the screws tightened, those clamps would have a regular GI Joe confessing to stealing money from his momma's purse or pranks like snitching on a big sis's sexual theatrics with Jocko the Stud while parents were away.

I babbled more, blurting out nonsense, but pretended as if I were jacked on Myscol. They weren't buying it.

"An easier question, Mr. Rusco," said Mong. "Why were you and your crew in *The Dim Zone* at that abandoned station? Seems a long way to venture out on a pleasure jaunt?"

"We were collecting my ship, Alastar. The Varwol cut out."

Mong frowned. "That seems improbable."

"Well, sorry then, for the truth. Maybe I always wanted to tour *The Dim Zone*."

Mong nodded, a sigh of amusement on his lips. "I think conventional means would be better, eh Balt?" He gestured and Balt removed the clamps and hooked his thumb around my baby finger.

Snap. My baby finger hung askew, nearly twisted off.

"Aw, fuck you," I roared. "You fucking ape, baboon, dipshit, fuckbitch bastard—"

"Hush, Mr. Rusco," chided Mong, shaking his head. "Back to my amalgo. Where? You still have to tell me."

I shook my head, uttering profanities, spitting insults.

Balt snapped another finger and I howled in pure agony.

"The amalgo!"

Mong sighed. "We will continue to break every bone in your miserable body, Mr. Rusco, until you tell us where that alien tech is. You're off to a bad start here. Remember, you're of no value to me without giving information." He inclined his head to Balt, who grabbed thumb and forefinger for another twist.

"Wait! Hoath," I yelled. "Go to Hoath."

Better to get it over with quick. I wasn't so good at enduring torture—ever since he'd blown off my hand. It kind of sticks in the memory. Cellular memory and all that.

"What about Hoath?"

"That's where you'll find your stupid toy."

The Star Lord's face twisted in interest. He rubbed his chin. "Hoath...So, it was always there, and you tricked us into believing it was elsewhere." He breathed. "I might have known. Amazing how a few broken fingers will open a mouth."

"Set the course for the Tiga system," he ordered. "And Rusco, you better not be playing games with me, unless you wish to become a paraplegic sipping pablum out of a straw."

We took a ride to Hoath on Brisis 9. Vowed I'd never visit that shithole city again—at least of my own choice. A walk down memory lane, those shabby warehouses out on the north end of town, wrapped in barbed wire, squalor and neglect. The smelly, scummy, sallow-skied excuse of a planet. The local cops, nothing more than crooked mercs, who gave our five Warhawk team a wide berth. Probably savvy of what Mong was capable of. It didn't take much to follow the holo-screen broadcasts and see what such a psycho did to uncooperative worlds that resisted his tyranny.

We transferred to one of his smaller Warhawks by shuttle while the other four escorts stayed not far out of range.

"Where exactly?" Mong demanded.

"Some old warehouse near Baer's." I grimaced, nursing my mutilated hand.

"Which one? There are many."

"Some old moldy place, maybe a mile from Baer's crib." I shrugged. "I dumped the tech in haste. Memory's a bit dim."

"No doubt. Let's sharpen it up. Tell you what, we'll visit every rusty warehouse in this section until we find it, or something jogs your memory."

"I don't know why you have such a hard on for that crap device—Ever try getting your kicks over a woman?"

Mong nodded and Balt, catching the look, biffed me in the face, sending a stream of blood down my nose. Bloody fuck!

"The amalgos are sacred, Rusco, and I'll tolerate no disrespect for them."

There was no point in antagonizing that big lout further. He was going to get his transporter anyway and he knew it. He'd tear apart this universe, killing everyone in it to get it. I was already a dead man. Soon as I gave him the location, bye-bye Rusco.

The ship circled low over a jumble of rusted factories and boarded up warehouses visible through the viewport. A swollen river flowed behind the line of industrial buildings from an era of the past.

It seemed like eons ago when Marty and I had scouted this terrain, planned that fateful heist on Baer's turf. I remembered that scumbucket warehouse, the long, rectangular shithouse with a broken, blackened brick smokestack at the one end. Couldn't miss it. Then there was the other one where I'd hidden the amalgo—a lower structure but with two smokestacks piking up instead of one. There it was. I debated not saying peep to Mong, just stalling him out in this charade, but I could see black death coming my way. When they had to circle back to the same row of warehouses and I squawked out the exact location, torrents of pain would follow.

I lifted an aching hand. "That's it."

Mong nodded. He instructed the pilot to bank.

We docked the ship in an equipment yard behind the warehouse. We stepped out onto the weed-eaten hardtop with Mong's gunmen crouched low, guns trained on the open ground, casing the joint on the odd chance there was anyone about. No one was about. I caught a faint, acrid whiff of Brisis's scummy air. My ears perked up at the purl of the river flowing alongside the service road over the sound of a gentle wind.

Brisis was as I remembered. A brittle coal-sulfur smell lingering in the air, random wreckage and rusty forklifts left to disintegrate, the sullen quiet of a violent past of rage. One of the original slum worlds. Here, only broken factories lurked, steeped in sullen disuse, abandoned dingy warehouses with a creepy vibe. The place seemed eerily deserted.

We passed only broken cement blocks and a corrugated tin watchhouse in the center of the yard, which looked, for all purposes, empty. We trudged up the back and around the side of the warehouse, our boots crunching on the gravelly asphalt.

They herded me along, pushing me in no gentle fashion when I lagged. I was desperate. My mind wandered to Wren. I had a sick feeling I'd never see her again. Glad she got away. Hoped she'd stay the fuck away from Mong.

The yellow sunlight hurt my eyes. Too much time spent in artificial light on ships and space stations.

My blood quickened. I knew once they got their grubby hands on the amalgo they'd waste me. At all costs, I must find a way out of this, throw a monkey wrench in their shit plans.

But how?—I had no weapon. Four against one. Mong and his telekinetic powers were unbeatable. I looked down at my throbbing hand, a comical pretzel of fingers that didn't work, and might never work again.

More flashbacks. Those silly dreams of how I'd wanted to be a rocket engineer as a boy. Before my parents and friends had been wiped out by warmongers storming our planet, before I'd been passed from refugee camp to camp. How I'd resolved to get myself out of that ghetto, ultimately becoming a gangster, the only way to get ahead fast. Look at where it got me. Now I was back on Brisis with a Star Lord up my ass…

"Move, Rusco."

"I have to take a piss," came my sullen growl.

"You can piss later. I want my amalgo."

"I'm going to piss my pants, if that's any concern of yours."

Balt laughed. "Go ahead. We won't much mind."

Mong looked over and cast me an impatient glare. "Go with him."

Balt took me over to the watchhouse, the smug fuck, some twenty paces away, nudging me with his rifle. Weeds and long grass blades poked up through cracks in the tarmac, caressing the tin siding. If I could fake the barbarian out, get one solid hit to the balls or some sensitive place, smash his nose, maybe I could make for that rusty fence and hop it over to the thickets.

With that limp of yours, Rusco, you'd be lucky to make it twenty feet before getting gutshot. And that hand? Good luck getting over a fence.

But they're going to kill you anyways. You want to die like a pig with lead in your brain, or die on your own terms?

Does it matter? Death is death, Mr. Rusco.

Mong seemed to be reading my thoughts, hovering around as I unzipped and heard a heavy boot fall behind me.

"Any problem here, Balt?" his deep-throated voice rasped.

"Nah, just Rusco being an old woman with a finicky bladder, slow as dogshit." He came close and smacked me on the shoulder, breathing down my neck. "That pecker of yours sawed off or something? Hurry up."

I held up a hand. I let warm spray sprinkle the tin siding, sniffed the sulfury air, maybe my last polluted breaths yet. As I zipped up, I darted eyes around the desolate yard. Death inched closer.

"Get going," Balt grumbled. They herded me up to the warehouse, then busted through a boarded up door with the ends of their rifles.

We came into a gloomy equipment bay that I remembered opened up to a loading area. The place had maybe an extra layer of dust and rat dung, cobwebs and reek of spilled oil. Several grubby rooms spread out along the wall. I could see activity here. Bootprints etched in the dust. Somebody had been storing cargo here, and then moving it from time to time. Large wooden crates, dozens of them. They lay stacked against the wall.

"Anything familiar?" grunted Mong.

"There," I lifted a mangled hand to the first room on the left. Toward a battered door, leaning on its broken hinges. They prodded me along, cursing and wrinkling their noses at the musty stench that hit them when they entered the room and thrust me forward.

"Search through that pile," I said.

They kicked through the bags and broken pieces of wood and metal strewn in a corner. From the likes of the broken machinery and tubs, at one time, I guessed, this had been some sort of meat grinding facility or canning factory.

Balt's face lit in a sick grin. The tech was still there—in that pile of junk amid the rat dung and the mice piss. A U-shaped contraption with thin, flat base and parallel plates standing waist-high on either side. Now it was covered in fly shit and rat dung, but still glowing with that dark, sullen greenish hue and emitting that disturbing low hum.

Mong practically fell to his knees in adulation of the precious artifact. "At last!" he rasped.

He held it up in his hands with reverence, lifting it to the grubby ceiling, and I could see the primitive, feral madness in his eyes.

The gunmen looked at him with odd curiosity, but I could see something of the falseness in those grins, as if they too thought their master was more than a bit off.

We came out of the warehouse and set out toward the ship, a man beside Balt carrying the prize.

A voice like a crow's caw echoed off the stone behind me. I staggered in my limp, my good right hand slapping involuntarily to my hip—for a weapon I did not have.

"Hold it, you fucks," came the voice. "Yeah, you!" The voice called louder.

Mong and his men kept walking as if deaf. I turned, saw a thin-faced security guard training his R3 at us at the edge of the watchhouse.

"I'm talking to you!" The man's rifle came up with a click.

One of Mong's men whipped out his weapon and plugged the guard in the brow. He fell in a crumpled heap.

In detached curiosity Balt swaggered over, treading over the body and grunting without a backward glance.

I licked my lips.

Mong beamed. "Mr. Rusco, you've been a good boy. You should be proud of your achievement today. I offer you my congratulations. This is history in the making."

"Yeah, seems so, and I bet that dead guy is cheering you on."

Mong sniffed. "That man will rise again, in another life. Long is the cycle of painful lessons to learn in this life and the next."

"Is it? A little rabbit once whispered in my ear that the call of the screech owl isn't to be considered an invite. I don't buy into your spiritual jabber, or your warmed-over bible shit."

Mong shrugged. "Your loss, Rusco. It means little to me."

"Yeah, well—"

"And now, for the second part of this operation."

"Let Blest go," I urged. "He's innocent in this." I braced myself for annihilation.

"Nobody is innocent in this world, Mr. Rusco. People must learn to accept the consequences for the company they keep."

I tensed, my teeth gritted for bullets to fly.

"Relax. I see you think I am about to snuff you out. No. On the contrary, I have plans for you. I reward those who bring me opportunities. I am not an ungrateful man. I am the angel of death. The ones who get in my way are blood sacrifices who are crushed under the boot of an enlightened future."

"If you say so." I let out a breath of contempt.

"Phase two may cure that defiance of yours, Rusco. If not, there is always phase three."

"Just can't wait."

Mong chuckled, a grunt at the end of an evil threat, a throaty, brooding sound, the closest I've heard to a laugh. In truth...my bluster was pure bullshit and I felt a cloying fear rising as a crest of warm bile in my throat, bursting at the seams, on the heels of a repressed scream.

Chapter 15

Back on the *Vulpin's* bridge, I looked down with wary distaste on Brisis 9, that slum planet of my nightmares as it slowly receded into the background stars. I wished the hell I'd never gone down there with Marty, my old co-partner in crime, and heisted that alien tech some months ago.

Our resident Star Lord seemed a changed man, all ebullience and bright smiles as he directed affairs from the captain's chair. Now that he had a working amalgo, why shouldn't he play captain of the universe? His despicable lieutenant Balt had dropped hints that the other amalgamator never worked, that its green glow had fizzled out long ago and the few attempts at exploration of its powers had denied him access to the alien worlds he so coveted. The box of small, disc-sized transporters given him by his erstwhile captain Baer had likewise yielded zippo, only toxic places of doom.

My hand ached like a bitch, my fingers skewed at unnatural angles. Torturer Balt had seen to a maximum of pain.

"Instruct your men on the amalgo," boomed Mong in his resonant baritone. "Any who so much as touches the device, shall be skinned alive. Is that clear?"

Lieutenant Balt nodded, grumbling an acknowledgement. He beckoned Hadruk forward, the security officer, looking a cross between a bulldog and an ape, given his stoop, glinting baboon-like eyes and the bristly hair on his cheeks and the back of his hands.

The bridge, a dim-lit place with high ceiling, black panels, viewports and holo displays, showed various state-of-the-art equipment. The setup made *Bantam* look like a toy. As Mong directed operations from his raised seat, a crew of nine of his men hunched around various consoles, operating computers and monitoring sensors.

I'd not seen hide nor hair of my shipmate Blest since we'd last journeyed to Hoath. Mong had ignored all my attempts to wrest information on his status. He assured me he was being taken care of.

Mong kept me on the bridge right next to him, like a pet hamster, flashing eyes my way every minute, along with his precious amalgamator, that blood diamond of treasures he'd forced me to uncover for him at Hoath. Mong had stationed it by the weapons console where he could keep an eye on it. The device glowed with a baleful purpose, a sickly green, its parallel plates inviting vistas into nowhere. Exactly what this fuck Mong planned to do with it was beyond me. But I'd visited one of those alien worlds some months ago via the phaso that the Skugs had destroyed—jolted there in a dangerous split of a second—to some freakish landscape with barely breathable air and desiccated bodies. I remembered the sallow dawn lit with strange clouds and aphid-like shapes crawling across the horizon. For all I knew they could have been far-off alien spacecraft—either way, I had no desire to experience such hell again.

Two long-haired men with war helms crested with eagle wings stood at attention by the U-shaped contraption, gripping R3s. Six more manned the bridge, all well-built soldiers wearing deep scowls and leather breastplates with firearms at their hips. My chances of taking any of them by surprise were zero given my crippled hand. As for Mong, well, I'd never gotten used to his intimidating size and strength. His leather and fur-clad bulk, some mythic incarnation of Genghis Khan, cast a cold shadow and exuded a magnetism that never failed to give me the creeps.

"How are our campaigns going in the frontiers?" he barked.

Balt shrugged. "They are going tolerably well, lord. We have puppet figures dancing Azron a tune in the Denista system. Funds and raw materials trickle in slowly from conquests in Bagrish. We grow our Beryllium plants there and on Phenix and other worlds in the Veglos sector. Captain Yisil is producing more warships every week on Susol's moon."

Mong gave a gruff acknowledgement. "Anything else?"

"A continued resistance on Melinar, sir. We have Guptaon under control, her sister planet. We'll blast them to compliance, if needed. But the Melinarians pose a worse threat. I propose we exercise extreme military force, move in on their planet with prejudice."

"Melinar?"

"They have cunning spies, lord. Also advanced tech which seems to have jammed our signals."

"Ingenious bastards, eh? Rebels?"

"More than that, sir. They rile up the neighboring worlds, the Vendecki, who are pooling forces with the Jaiwils on Xistris."

Mong slammed his fist on the console. "This is unacceptable, Balt. We must quell this budding rebellion and crush them all. We'll fly to the Azileus system immediately. Assemble the armada. Full speed. The kid gloves come off. No mercy."

"Very well, my lord. And the jammers?"

"I doubt they can jam an entire fleet." Balt nodded and barked orders into the com to the war captains.

"Prepare the enhanced fareon beams we received from Trellian," Mong instructed. "Have our vanguard outfitted with our most impenetrable armor. The insurgents will learn not to meddle with my plans. They'll be slaughtered. They've ignored our terms for too long and flout our authority like sharp-toothed badgers. I've offered them every reasonable alternative."

Balt grinned. "Too true."

I felt the ship lurch as we warped into Melinar with an armada that would make General Krod's historic fight against the Fineus rebel strike of 2401 look like a baby shower. Mong's ships materialized from the ethers, ships outfitted with augmented tech and now deployed. A thousand strong.

My mouth hung open. I'd never seen such a force of warships. They must have warped in from all over the galaxy.

"Look at their pitiful defenses," gloated Hadruk. "Two hundred Vendecki warships and a smattering of Melinar skyslips—That against our *millardian*? Paf."

Mong spat a wad of phlegm on the deck. "We'll overpower them with our superior firepower. Our armor is better and our new shields juiced with neutron boosters. Strike at will."

The ships sped forward to meet the defending vanguard. The first squadrons branched out in complex, crazy spiraling loops, each army trying to outflank the other. Mong's, of course, having the superior numbers. I cringed at the sight of the Melinarian forces surrounded and crushed.

Mong barked a command, "Order the left wing to bank and wipe out that Vendecki wedge."

"Signals jammed, sir," the weapons engineer cried.

"What?"

"It's bizarre. Like the last time. We were sure it was a temporary glitch—"

A Warhawk went up in flames beside us, now a smoking fireball, prey to Vendecki fire. Another disintegrated in a cindery ruin to our starboard.

Hadruk swore. "We cannot communicate with our fleet, lord! Jamming signal at 90%."

"Where's the source?" Mong bawled.

"We don't know. Conflicting reports."

Mong's face turned beet red. "Find it, you fools!"

The weapons engineer cried in vain, "Sir, they not only jam our signals, but scramble our weapon's systems. Fareons have gone haywire."

Mong blew air out of his nose.

I grinned a sour clown's grimace. Finally a world that could fight back against these mongrel war dogs. I rocked on my heels, relishing to see Mong fall, even if I were to die in the process. I stared down at my mangled hand. If I didn't get regen soon, the nerve damage would be permanent. I doubted dear old Mong was about to outfit me with another robot hand. I clenched my good right fist, the prosthetic, the robot implant, and ached to use it against his ugly face. Maybe drive it into his skull. Kill him in one last stand.

"Report."

"Weapons still jammed, sir. We've traced the sources to two small moons, Twidor and Anxaste, orbiting Melinar."

Mong hissed. "So fast? You knew this before? Why the hell didn't you say something earlier?"

"We ignored it because the signals ping-ponged back and forth, confusing our sensors." The engineer clacked keys on the pad nervously. "We thought they were malfunctioning. I now believe they have dual jammers going."

"Of course they have, you numbskull. How can they jam our signal and keep their channels open?"

"We don't know. They must have penetrated our encrypted messages. Some new phantom tech." The weapons engineer's heavy jaw clamped then quivered under the heavy boom of more strikes on the hull. Multiple enemies were encircling us. I jerked about and snatched a look through the viewport. Melinar and Vendecki craft swirled in dive formations to bomb the hell out of Mong's flagship. "If we destroy any station down there," the engineer quavered, "we destroy any chance of using such tech in our own campaigns."

"If we do not wipe out that jammer, Verlioze, we'll *lose* this fight."

"Shall we retreat, sir?" Balt suggested, his eyes narrowed pinpricks of feral intensity. Bombs erupted around us, though shields for now held.

Mong glared at him as if he were a poisonous toad. "I never retreat, Balt. Never. I win every battle I fight."

"The losses, lord, they could be catastrophic."

Mong's hand came out and grabbed the lieutenant's neck. Balt choked, clutching at Mong's wrist. It was as if the lieutenant'd swallowed a lizard. "Catastrophic, yes, Balt. But risk is inevitable and to be expected. We will win this battle, as I said. Find those damn transmitters." He threw Balt down.

"Take the ship to the nearest source," the lieutenant croaked, massaging his reddening neck.

Another wing fighter caught in flames and disintegrated in atomic ruin.

Hadruk and Verlioze muttered, then Verlioze raised his voice in a hoarse bray, "Our fleet, lord. We cannot communicate with them! Do we just leave them here? Our last command was to attack with prejudice."

Mong's face remained impassive. I looked to see his reaction. He bared his teeth, then said in a dangerously low voice, "For all your sakes, where's the exact source of those transmitters?"

The weapons master shook his head. Confusion clouded his face. "Sometimes they seem to come from Twidor's *Ghost Mare Valley*, other times from Anxaste."

"Triangulate! Send a probe in to investigate and fly back out. We can manually scan its databanks."

"We've done that before, sir—"

"Do it again!" Mong snarled. "Wait! Scrap that idea! Bring *Vulpin* into Twidor's Mare Valley. On the double!"

It was a gutsy move. We left the war front, unable to reach by signal the rest of the fleet. To Twidor we sped at full impulse, leaving the fleet behind to hold the line, or sink against the lockspring tide of resistance. In their glee at targeting Mong's gigantic front line, the defenders failed to notice *Vulpin's* absence.

Within moments, we were passing through the threadbare atmosphere of Melinar's closest moon, skimming across the surface, a grey desolation of changeless hills and valleys. The ship roared across the pitted craters and low rises of crumbled rock and layers of moon dust.

Mong advanced to study the holo readout as if oblivious to the damage his shields had sustained. I wondered what went on in that rattrap mind of his.

"There! In that thin ring of boulders! I see a weak signal pulsing on the scanners."

Hadruk, twisting about his stout, ape figure, said hoarsely, "Our probes must have missed it prior. That, or their signal is now operating at full strength and traceable. Helmsman, turn us about. Make another sweep!"

The 3D projection shifted to higher resolution. A clutch of displaced boulders rose on a low rise. A thin rod nestled inside, its tip poking above the cradle of its rocky protection.

"There's an antenna! Are our weapons up?"

"Fareons are inoperable, sir, but traditional drop bombs are active."

"Blast the transmitter to dust."

"With pleasure," Hadruk grunted.

The landscape incinerated below us and Mong stared in triumph. The ship soared upward into space. The communication static had diminished. Now only the thin garble of screams of dying men carried across the black gulfs.

"Move quickly!" Mong ordered. "To that shithole Anxaste. Since we can't reach our scouts, impulse over to Anxaste."

Vulpin's heavy–duty Vega 8 impulse engines roared under our feet, bringing us to Anxaste, another dead satellite of Melinar—the place of the second illusive triangulated signal.

Sure enough, a high-energy transmitter lay cached within the rocks on some barren moon hill.

"Fire at will," Mong bellowed.

I saw a mushroom cloud erupt on the desolate horizon. A dozen breaths tensed on the bridge. If they undermined the communication jammers, Melinar fate would be sealed…

Seconds passed and communications systems came online.

Mong's lip curled in a vindictive leer and my heart plummeted. It was clear what would happen now—another world lost to Mong's mad vision of galactic supremacy.

Orders were shouted across the com and traded across the air waves as *Vulpin* raced to the battle front.

It was as I feared, his ships, the bulk of which had survived the onslaught of the smaller forces, now united in full assault and communication, drove in a wedge, firing full on into the defending ships, which up till now had held the advantage. Mong's remaining ships, some seven hundred strong, blasted a hole through the thin line of defense. A dozen assault fighters impulsed at max speed down toward the orange globe of defenseless Melinar. The defenders, stunned by the sudden downturn in fortune, brought their ships back to meet the strike. But fareon beams prevented them from making any difference.

I winced as a new contingent of Melinar and Vendecki ships ignited and blinked out of existence. Long range fareon beams made mincemeat of the underpowered craft, firing at double strength.

Our flagship rocked to gunfire, but Mong merely grunted. He knew that his shields, electro-juiced to the max and built for disaster, could dispel any threat. The rebel leader of the resistance, a large Melinarian cylindrical cone with wide brim and tapered stern, flared, its shields at capacity. A sudden red poof lit against the backdrop of stars and the ship disintegrated in a ruin of cinders and twisted metal.

Mong's men on the bridge howled in triumph.

Mong forced me to watch that one-sided battle. The thousand ships he had assembled from lord knows where, all attacked in wide loops, evading fire or absorbing it with their electro-shielded armor, surrounding the relatively few dozen of remaining Melinarian craft. Nothing but wholesale slaughter. In his flagship *Vulpin* he oversaw the destruction, his muscled arms crossed on his barrel chest. As he barked orders to his crew, I saw a whole planet brought to its knees. Bombs fell on the cities of Jezuan and Narsilie—millions dead. Visuals showed green forests and parklands, tenements, roads, bridges, towers exploding in ruin. Suddenly I realized just why no one could defeat those armies, led by that madman. He knew his tactics, was meticulously informed, ruthless as an armored viper. No detail escaped his attention. Almost as if an inner angel whispered in his ear, or some inner sense guided him to victory, complemented with an unerring confidence in his invincibility, even when doom should be his reward, as the present glitch in detecting the jammers had demonstrated. Such sociopaths were beyond domination. Was it even possible to take down a monster as this? I knew without doubt, no one in this galaxy would have any peace or security until Mong was destroyed. Without him, his empire would crumble. His lieutenants did not have the nerve or the spark in them to keep such a bestial war machine alive—Balt, Hadruk, Verlioze, the lot. They were surely all evil, but not of the same stock as dear old Mong and his Machiavellian mind.

The hours passed and were like blows to my senses. A ghastly blur of death toll and destruction. My aching hand was but insignificant compared to the losses suffered that day.

Struggling shapes were at last brought to heel on the bridge and forced to their knees, to grovel before Mong.

Hadruk, the security officer, announced in a triumphant tone that the resistance leaders were dead or being gathered up. "We tractored the remnants of their pitiful army aboard, lord. Caught them trying to escape our net."

"What a surprise," said Mong. "Good work, Hadruk. What's their story?"

"Ambassador Zaud from the world, Melinar, meet Lord Mong, your new master," he announced tonelessly. "And here is Lady Volia who was shuttled off to preserve the civil aristocracy. Some Baroness or Countess or some fool thing—queen or slut to the dead Prince Athrean."

While Zaud bowed his head in cowed defeat, Volia crouched. She was defiant, clad in her silver and red brocade. A limber woman with fiery, hazel eyes, red-gold hair spilling from under a diamond-encrusted tiara. A silver sickle was tattooed to her brow above an elegant face. That face, pinched with anguish and tear-stained, brought a pang of sadness to my heart.

"You've killed our people, slaughtered my Prince and husband. What more do you want?"

"Oh, everything, my lady," said Mong.

"You beast. You've destroyed—"

"I know, destroyed your air defenses, knocked out your communications systems, laid waste to your beautiful planet."

She spat a gob in Mong's face. "I curse you for the end of time!" she wailed.

He wiped his cheek without haste. "You may do that if you wish, Lady Volia. Accomplishes nothing."

"We will not give up! We will never surrender to your crude domination and brutishness. Our people will fight in the streets, though they be broken. They will run guerrilla warfare in the cindered forests till the end of time. You will not last forever, Mong. Sooner or later you will fall!"

"Where are your feckless allies now, Lady Volia?" Mong jeered. "The Vendecki? Who abandoned you at first sign of bloodshed?"

She stiffened and a sullen scowl lit her strong features.

"You can resist," continued Mong, "but you will end up with buckets of blood on your hands. I urge you to speak to your surviving citizens. Advise them to surrender peacefully and these war tolls will stop. Maybe you can even spare some of the war hounds you have hiding in the hills painful deaths. We'll ferret them out eventually."

She turned away, her glistening lips and mouth working. She lashed a contemptuous glance my way, as if I were one of Mong's motley brood. I opened my mouth to protest, knowing the falseness of it and knowing any words would be useless in light of her despair. A wave of nausea and animosity blossomed in my chest, then remorse for her loss and her defenselessness. I realized the full weight of my impotence in this affair. A helplessness that shamed me, being as useless here as a trussed deer before hunters.

"I will lay bare all your secrets, Lady Volia, like your puny jammer circuits. You will learn a new meaning of the word 'invasion'." Mong's lips twisted in a sinister sneer. "Sift through the slave-prisoners, Balt. Bring me all their engineers. I want to know the secrets of this jamming technology. It may be a weapon I can use against other renegades like the Melinarians."

Balt croaked some words into the com.

Mong went on, an explosive exclamation whistling through his teeth. "I have no time to waste on defiant females. You show a spark, Volia, that your husband didn't, dead as he is in his metal coffin, but I think I will hand you over to my lieutenants. They will teach you a lesson in humility. My personal guards have been restless of late. Part of their training is to practice abstinence. Though they balk, it makes them stronger. The odd time I do throw them a bone, they light up like candles. Hadruk! See to it."

The security officer approached, nodding, grinning.

Mong flourished. "Have Lady Volia taken to solitary. She will serve as a useful adjunct in the Temple of Light on Othwan."

Volia struggled but such efforts were useless in the hands of Mong's guards. I surged forward, hurled my hard-muscled body at them, but brawny arms held me back. Fists smacked me down to the metal grates. Mong glanced my way, scoffing in passing amusement. "Rusco, you do have a chivalrous streak in you. Another weakness I must cure you of." He sighed and dismissed me and the woman without a backward glance. Now that the bloody battle had been won, the Star Lord would land his warships at the capital city of Jezuan and secure his toehold, as he had so many other worlds across the galaxy before. Of the Vendecki, I had no clue as to their fate.

"Set a course for Othwan," Mong murmured. He had moved on to other matters, the testing of his amalgamator.

Chapter 16

Vulpin dropped out of hyperdrive and I looked out upon a green planet. A wide river flowed through a peaceful valley. An ordered colony, set straight out of a page from history—Old Earth? with its Oriental peaked roofs, red and white pigments, stucco and wood, set on the lush bank of the winding river? Rice paddies loomed farther back at the base of the hills from what I could see, dotted with workers in the fields, both men and women who clutched hoes and carried baskets.

We banked low and settled on the wide tarmac at whose near end rose a complex control tower prickled with antennae. Several other Warhawks sat docked. A giant hangar loomed about a half mile away, likely harboring a fleet of warships of similar menace to *Vulpin*.

We debarked and several figures met their leader on the landing ground. All wore curious helms of bronze and robes of various ornamental dress, reds, yellows and gold. He waved them off and strode on, beckoning his henchmen to take me and others from the ship, and what looked like several selected prisoners. Balt and Hadruk personally attended to the amalgamator, handling it with utmost care, under Mong's critical, watchful eye.

My step landed lighter here than on other worlds, so I assumed Othwan to be a smaller planet than the more earth-like worlds.

We passed an armed gate and entered the colony, or whatever it might be, and strode past a towering bronze statue: of Mong with forbidding face and arms crossed on chest. We hustled down a main avenue of flawless asphalt flanked by transplanted palms and rare, ancient banyan trees then headed toward an edifice with a red-tiled roof of many dips and valleys mounted with turrets and spires.

I blinked under the warm sunlight, not used to the stark dissonance cooped up in starships and space stations, to this ordered greenery of an unexpected oasis.

What was this idyllic place? It seemed incongruous considering Mong's brutish character. Could it be a haven of his?

Mong seemed to read my mind. He turned his heavy smile of amusement on me. "Not what you expected, eh, Jet Rusco? This is the only settlement on this planet. I discovered it years ago, wild and pristine. Perhaps you'll revise your opinion of me. Every man can have his many faces, and alter ego—mine is one of the aesthete."

I grunted and shrugged. I had no use for scum mass murderers like Mong.

Othwan then, was a private planet he had made his own. An oasis amongst the stars. Lush forest on low-domed hills of green firs mixed with ancient yellow and rust-colored banyans, sheltering a temple community nestled along the banks of a slow-moving river. Odd and surreal. A haven too bucolic for warmaster Mong.

We passed some rock-strewn gardens with fountains, trickling rivulets of water purling through a maze of exotic plants and flowers: cacti, succulents, azaleas, daffodils, bergamots, a myriad of unnameable wildflowers in yellows, reds, oranges, blues and whites. Several pagodas lurked off to the side, decorated in orange and white plaster and wood with eastern motifs patterned after Old Earth architecture. A quiet, hushed atmosphere ran among the trimmed lawns and the manicured bushes. Monkish figures, dressed in violet robes, some trimmed in brown, others in white, moved in respectful gaits. Some from building to building, carrying supplies, foodstuffs, or what looked like prayer books. All tuned to order and perfection, much like Mong's military mind. Though I struggled, given the man's barbaric proclivity, to comprehend how he had the aesthetic impulse to mastermind such a complex.

We came upon another open iron gate, straddled by large sculpted heads, mean-looking, eighteen feet tall, staring down at us from the corners of what appeared to be a grand temple. Not Mong's face, these heads, but some related figure, possibly an avatar, with a look of rapture in his big, bulging eyes.

The temple, raised on low pillars, proved an awesome sight indeed. The mere gravity of it was enough to instill awe in the casual spectator. Perhaps a hundred and twenty feet high, speckled with stained-glass windows. The massive double doors were open. Mong marched up the steps and ushered me inside, as if I were an honored guest. I blinked, stared at him in cold contempt. I inquired about Blest but he ignored me.

The peaked ceiling was eighty feet high, carved and paneled in what looked like rosewood. Pale light shone from both clear and stained-glass windows high above. White marble floors led across a great open space—an auditorium, I guessed, to a raised altar. Cushions for some audience to kneel or sit on and listen to discourse, ranged in piles to the sides. The massive stone altar near the back wall of the temple stood flanked by square columns rising high to support the peaked roof.

Mong strode in with authority. I took reluctant steps after him, that or suffer the painful jabs of his guards.

A fresh balmy air blew from artificial air circulators. Palm trees grew inside, along with other potted plants sporting green and yellow leaves. All in all, a pleasant environment, but the reek of depravity hung heavy. I could taste it, smell it, feel it in my bones, as I paused to absorb it all.

"How do you like my victory shrine?" Mong inquired with a leer.

I could only shrug. I saw men and women coming in through the door to bow before the altar, monks or nuns or some mindless worshipers.

"Don't look so surprised, Rusco. These residents are just showing their respect and allegiance to the new order—the Power of the Light of Ages. As custom dictates, they obey without question. In fact, it is customary for all visitors to bow before the great altar. I don't recall you having genuflected yet." He lanced a meaningful glance my way.

I stood there, stone-faced.

"Bow," he said in a cold voice.

I licked my lips. Coinciding with my better judgment, I gave a slight gesture of head, hating every moment of it.

"Very good, Rusco. A grudging bow is better than none at all. Acceptable at this juncture, but in need of improvement. Ritualistic prayers and acts of devotion go on here daily in assurance of a better future."

"What is that exactly?" I growled.

"A unified universe governed with strength, peace and order."

I snorted. "Under your rule."

"Of course—under who else's rule? Strength must be wielded by the most capable man."

I had to admire Mong for his supreme arrogance. Not a shred of doubt in that feverish brain of his with its vision of manifest destiny. Lunacy at its most depraved. Insatiably cruel, but a mathematical beauty lay in its simplicity. I shook my head. Shut your mind off, Rusco, you don't want to get brainwashed like these others.

I looked above and saw alabaster statues raised on high amongst the columns flanking the altar—half man, half demigod with wings spread wide. Angels of doom? Avatars of destiny? They all had R6s clutched in enlarged hands and maniacal grins carved on angel faces. I shuddered. The rifles had barrels large as bassoons.

Mong nudged me forward. I had to wipe my eyes to ensure I wasn't hallucinating.

Two glass tanks flanked the altar, each with a human male floating suspended in pale greenish liquid. Their eyes stared out from behind the glass, as if they were alive. The tanks reminded me of those I'd seen on a derelict Ring Station out in the Muridon Belt.

"What the fuck are those?" I croaked.

"Watch your language, Rusco. This is a hallowed place. Those tanks are the wave of the future. I've been collecting them, like curios and scientific curiosities. They are like nothing else in this universe! Strokes of genius from a dead race like no other. Once I discover how to harness their power, I'll become supreme ruler of these jaded worlds while you and other dissidents will go to feed a nation."

"I have no doubt about your vision, Mong, and yet, I'm glad to know I will serve the empire in some small way."

He huffed at my sarcasm and breathed in a heady sigh. "Those two tanks I discovered in a remote, abandoned mine station, a Mentera factory, if you will, on Perseus. A rare find."

"No doubt."

"The grim, vacant-eyed fellow to the left is the Lord of Evenness. He defied me at Jaro. The one on the right is Vanxus, a skulking rogue if there ever was one. The blackguard betrayed me at the battle of Brog. Now the two are sacrifices to the Temple of Light."

I moved closer to study the victims and saw Vanxus's lips move in a small curl as a fish might blow bubbles. I recoiled. The blond hair hung suspended and moved with the imperceptible currents in the pale green liquid.

"Are they alive?" I asked in morbid wonder.

"In a way, but perhaps it is better to be dead than grace the waters of the Mentera tanks."

It became clearer to me now Mong's infatuation with the alien tech. These fucks worshiped the technology of the tanks. Maybe they worshiped the whole dead race of the Mentera. I'd heard of them, even seen evidence of them aboard that Ring Station. Mong and his crew must be one of these old Mentera cults still floating around the universe in fly-infested corners...which explained his obsessive fascination with relics, memorabilia and acquisitions of amalgamators.

I stepped back to stop from reeling. He had made some ghastly shrine out of these pickled occupants in the tanks. The dazed cultists wandering about this temple worshiped them on their fancy daises near the altar like statues of Zeus, while their high priest, the mighty

Mong, fed on the living within and became the all-powerful sorcerer. It made twisted sense. In a skewed, monkey-brained world. My head ached.

"Sorry to bust in on your parade, Mong, but what about my hand? Am I supposed to walk around with a bird's claw for the rest of my life? It's throbbing like a banshee. Some regen would be helpful. That or a basic medic."

He waved a palm. "Don't sweat it, Jet. A minor wound, some small inconvenience in the overall order of the things. Distractions as these are fodder for disciplining an aspiring mind. Makes a man worthier to rise above a modicum of pain. You seem a bit squeamish about pain. I had my man Balt go through a heavy rigor on his journey to lieutenant-dom. Now he could care less if his balls were on fire."

"Very good to know. I'll remember that next time I'm applying for position of lieutenant."

"Good rejoinder, Rusco. I like your quick mind. But your creeping cynicism, I don't like. Speaking of which, seems you got your other hand back. Pity I didn't blow the other one off back on Trellian. It would have had me devising more creative tortures than bent fingers to convince you to reveal the location of my amalgamator. But I have better plans for you. As much as you've sabotaged my plans, I've taken a shine to you. That last scheme you pulled off on Belisar One was a bit of genius. Oh, don't think I didn't know about your part in orchestrating poor Captain Baer's demise. I was just fucking with you earlier, drawing you out, seeing what you knew, hoping you'd let something slip about my amalgamator. And you did. I see potential in your hustling and roguish mind that may serve my ends quite well—as much as I'd like to see your hide roasted and blown into a thousand fragments. I'd take as much pleasure in personally torturing you myself."

Mong's true colors shining again. I knew his aesthetic side was too good to be true.

"I spare you this painful indignity," he went on, "because you delivered me my amalgamator." He reached over, gave Vanxus's tank a loving caress, then flashed its victim an affectionate leer. "The Mentera used these tanks to siphon out the life energy of their victims. They had some fancy apparatus for it, hoses and pipes and circuitry and other gadgets beyond our current science. I haven't figured them out yet, but I hope to soon, and use it to augment my own, above-normal strength."

I stared at Mong as if he were an instrument of lunacy. "What sick fuck would even think of doing that?"

"You judge me, Rusco," said Mong. "Remember, judgment is a dangerous thing."

"Where's Blest?" I growled at him. "You plug him in one of these tanks?"

"Blest is currently occupied, redeeming his sins. He raised firepower against me. For that he must suffer."

I winced at the implications. So, Mong's hints suggested that Blest was beyond saving.

"Move out," he commanded.

Hadruk and two others motioned me away from the altar and we trudged down a windowless corridor located behind the altar. Guards prodded me from behind. The light dimmed. I could feel Hadruk's rank breath on my neck.

I heard then a woman's scream. A man's hearty laugh followed and a heavy slap. I turned to see a flash of reddish-gold hair, a figure like Lady Volia's suddenly pushed through a half-opened, double-door in carved teak.

Mong grinned. "Perhaps if you are well-behaved, Rusco, you may experience some of my Orpheum's pleasures one day. 'Tis a novelty."

Almost at the same time I saw a figure who looked like Blest hauled into another room. I could only guess that each victim would be taken to task in the most practical way. The Temple of Light… What a fucking joke! Temple of Pain. Fane of the Loony Tune.

"Perhaps you'll want to rename your hallowed shrine to 'Temple of the Deranged'," I said.

"Deranged. Very good, Jet Rusco, perhaps that is one way of seeing it, but I hope you will be convinced otherwise." He brandished a fist. "Come! The hour is late." He beckoned with a sweep of arm, his voice resuming that cordial earnest mockery that I'd come to detest about Mong.

He drew me aside, his jaw working as if dissatisfied with my attitude toward one so great.

"You have potential, Rusco, but your sly sneaking and vindictive brooding erodes your sense of reality. You are like an old woman trying to get one up on everyone she thinks has slighted her. It's unhealthy. It has made you gaunt and unlikeable, like an old crow cawing for the cheese it cannot have. Withdraw from the past and embrace the future." He raised his hand in a righteous flourish. "'Tis a healthy, healing attitude. My program can help you on the path of your journey toward enlightenment."

"Gee, Mong, would you do that for me? And I only wanted a nice ride away from a nuthouse, on a starship, at first available convenience."

He tsked, shook his head with a screwball gleam in his eye. "Impossible, dear Rusco, I'm afraid you're quite disillusioned into hoping for such a fantasy. Once a guest's landed at Othwan, there is no going back."

I swallowed, the thought chilling me, even more than a prolonged death at the hands of this psycho, a lunatic of lunatics.

"Let us test out the amalgamator. I'm sure it will be of interest to you."

Chapter 17

Mong's men transported the amalgo to the farthest room at the end of the hall and set it in a prominent position against the back wall. It looked like a new-fangled electric radiator. Didn't seem to require any mechanical tweaking either; the flat facing plates continued to radiate their infernal green glow. The plates were wide enough to fit three men striding abreast, no more. None of the others spoke as Mong remained deathly silent for a time. He stared off into space like a Sphinx. "Ever am I searching for their lost worlds," he intoned. "I can use this device to find them. Maybe acquire more samples and apparatuses that will help me resurrect their hallowed race."

A sick feeling grew in the pit of my stomach. For what purpose and at what cost?

Mong nodded to Hadruk who withdrew a light oxygen mask from his side pack. Then he tossed it to me. "Put it on."

Mong inclined his head to Hadruk. "Give me gauze."

Hadruk handed him a roll. Friend Mong tore off a strip, spat on it and tossed it at me. "Look after that hand, Rusco."

Grumbling foul words, I wrapped the stuff around my left claw. Hadruk accelerated the process by forcing the mask's straps around the back of my head with no gentle hands.

"Hey, watch it," I warned.

"Shut up," he grunted.

"As for what lies on the other end of this warphole—" Mong shrugged, held up a palm. "It is a gift, I give you, Jet Rusco, to be first to venture to an unknown realm. The first to explore a new world, a place of vast potential, or perhaps terror and eerie surprise. A crap shoot. Perfect for a hustler like yourself."

I gave a mocking salute while managing a sick grin. "I know, Mongo, why risk your own balls when some expendable stooge can risk theirs?"

"On the contrary, Mr. Rusco, Balt will accompany you on this important mission."

"Good ole Balt? Really? Is he up to it?"

Balt stammered, licked his lips. "Sir, I'm hardly the best choice for the mission. Hadruk is much more qualified—"

"No arguments, Balt. I have thought the matter through. Are you ready?"

"I must prepare my war gear, lord—"

I put on a sour face and pushed forth. "I must freshen up and take a few things with me, like some Black Dog ale and a pint of regen—"

Mong shoved me through with a vicious snarl. I staggered between the space enclosed by the parallel plates and was gone in a second.

Harsh, strident sounds buzzed in my ears as if bees swarmed me from all directions. The eerie plates lit in full amber and an electrical surge passed through my body, hitting me square in the temple. I gave a soundless cry. A white light practically blinded me as I was sucked across gulfs, whole universes, unfathomable distances, through black holes and out the other ends.

I fell an incalculable distance then landed with a thud on a hard surface. I felt disassociated from my body as if I had been atomized. But somehow I was whole and very bewildered, staring out from googly eyes, not knowing where I was. Everything was dark here, with only the sound of the raspy air whistling through my mask. The air felt warmer than before, though edged with an acrid, dry tinge of decay. The mask only assimilated the alien air, processing the surrounding atmosphere as best as it could. My lungs pumped air, but my brain struggled to catch up with the impossible reality.

A tickle of electrical energy played at my back. Balt materialized behind me, like some amber ghost. His electrical signature jolted me forward, spiking me with a stronger current. I lurched to the laws of physics, sprawling on my hands and knees on some type of concrete floor. Balt's form shimmered back to visibility, his atoms reassembled, and I saw that he wore a mask like mine. He kicked me aside, his weapon raised, trained to kill.

We crouched there like white-eyed zombies, breathing in the sepulchral darkness, waiting for some horror to come out at us. But it did not.

We'd left Mong's temple far behind. We were in some new dimension. Behind us, the sister amalgo, companion to the one on Othwan, buzzed with a bee's hum and shone a grim amber. We were in some medium-sized room with a low ceiling, carved out of pure rock—no, it was metal of some sort. I reached out to touch it and it gave back a hollow, tinny, reverberating sound when I knocked. Only the ethereal glow of parallel plates of the transporter gave us any illumination.

We edged our way to the room's end, which was empty save for the amalgamator, perhaps fifty feet away. We passed through some U-shaped doorway with no visible door. I sensed we had moved into a vast space, like a cavern of giants, or some immeasurably large hangar. I looked down upon a frightening scene:

A vast pantheon of rectangular tanks standing upright, like old telephone booths out of Old Earth all assembled in a V-shape, or some deformed star shape. How many? The numbers were uncountable. Hundreds. Thousands? Some tanks were larger than others, and sported a dim green glow, perhaps large enough to hold some large lion or elephant or alien creature.

Balt prodded me along down the walkway that spanned the rim of the depot or hangar, whatever it was in the gloom. I discerned several aphid-shaped ships scattered amongst the masses of those tanks, much different from the Skug vessels, larger, bulkier, like praying mantises, with cruel prows and grotesque, chitinous flukes in their sides.

Christ, what was this place? Another Cyber Corp, some enormous crypt of the past?

Balt nudged me on. We wandered down a low ramp that gave access to the hangar below. I use that word loosely, for I approached the first row of tanks as a man would shamble in a sleepwalk. Ages of dust and grime coated the panes of thick glass. I wiped off a section and peered within. I saw only death. A human skeleton, stoppered, entombed, honeycombed like some primordial honeybee. The saliva in my mouth suddenly tasted dry and sour. Another victim was in no better state. A grinning skull, slumped at the bottom of a glass cage, some relic caught in time. The glass had cracked in several places, as with all of them, as if a foul liquid had drained from the glass sarcophagi ages ago.

A glow of green water radiated up ahead. Balt pushed me along with surly impatience, a hoarse rasp deep in his throat. Two neck-high tanks, stood side by side. Intact. We wiped the glass. I sprang back in horror, recoiling with a snarl on my lips. That tank contained the most repulsive creature I'd ever seen. Some jet black insect, as high as my shoulder, floating on its hind legs, suspended in some god-awful brine, light green like that back at Mong's temple. The red eyes blinked back at me with feral intensity and a claw pincer lifted to touch the glass a few inches from where I stood. As in a trance, I raised a hand and my right finger mechanically touched the same spot that the insect had touched, suspended in that horrible brine beyond the glass. The insect's lips parted and a bubble rose, as if to say something. *Peekaboo. I see you.*

No, this couldn't be happening. Like some lunatic on a funny farm, I laughed at the mad absurdity of it. Balt licked his lips. "Pipe down. So, they do exist. They didn't all die out."

"Does what exist? What didn't all die out? What the fuck are you talking about? What are these things?"

"They are the Mentera. The mutant locusts. Overlords of the galaxy."

I stared again. The hint of wings, the faintest silver on the chitinous back, glinted back at me, as if long ago over the course of its evolution those dwarfed appendages had dwindled to stubs, depriving the thing of its power of flight. "Doesn't look like that to me."

"You wouldn't understand, Rusco. Mong can tell you all about it."

"Fuck Mong," I sneered. "I'm sick of that crazy bastard and his airy hints. Let's get the fuck out of here."

"Shut up."

"We've done his scouting, god damn it. Dead humans, a bunch of tanks, and a couple of weird bugs—"

"I said, shut the fuck up!" He gripped his R6 with a white-clenched fist. I could see the sweat dripping down his bull neck. He was spooked too.

That dome far overhead, it allowed those mantis ships access to the universe. Sealed now. Perhaps that power grid, or control board, whatever the fuck controlled it at one time. I glanced at it again, to the side, with all its knobs and dials. Could it still work? If I could make a break for it, steal a ship—

Balt prodded me with his R6.

This was a graveyard, a mausoleum of death.

This depot once, was a vast factory of something, some repository of human specimens. I knew it, from what Mong had maundered on earlier about. But where in the hell was it? With no windows or portal to something for reference, it was impossible to gauge where in the cosmos we were. We could as easily be inside a small moon as on a space station, or in some madman's dream. The green glow of the weird water of the few intact tanks was the only source of light.

I noticed a cable dangling from the stopper at the top of the insect's tank. It hung to the floor, as if hinting of some feeding apparatus that Mong had described. To feed what—the Mentera? Or the trapped insect to feed something else? Why was one of their own kind imprisoned in the tank?

It was enough to make me retch.

I turned to back away and kept backing up, my entire being sickened by it all. I kept backpedaling, only to smell a more pungent odor of decay. I lifted a hand to shield my nose, nearly stumbled over a body, caught myself at the last instant.

I balked, did a double take, for in that withered face of the human figure, I thought to recognize a person of the past. I gasped. "That's Mitch! I knew him. From way back on Brisis 9 when Marty and I had heisted the amalgo. Poor fuck must have starved here."

"Yeah? Well, he's maggot food now," muttered Balt.

There, at his side, lay the crumpled black and white cap Mitch'd last worn. I remembered how he'd gripped one of those phasos and then poof, was gone, blasted into some forsaken dimension with no way to get back. The phaso ride he had taken back in Baer's warehouse must have plopped him into this complex. Never occurred to him he could get back via the amalgamator in the other room. Then again, how could anyone have known that, or even how to use it?

This amalgo was tuned to the same destination as the phaso that Mitch'd touched. However long he'd clawed his fingers bloody trying to escape this place of lunacy, only the goblins of the past knew. Mitch had no inkling the magic U-shaped amalgamator in the other room could have transported him back.

I scanned the ships that lurked in the dim peripheries among the hundreds of tanks and skeletons. Mantis-like prows with big smooth, curving hulls like monsters of the deeps waiting to pounce. Perhaps one might offer a chance of escape? Yet the beetle-like turrets with their bug eyes sent shivers down my spine.

The place was dead. Not a flutter of movement. It had lain dormant for centuries. A part of me swayed, as if suddenly ready to fall head first from a high mountain. I bolted, trying to chase that image from my brain. Tanks swept by me like phantoms.

Balt gave a sharp yelp and caught up to me and ground me to a halt, pushing the R6 in my ribs. He prodded me back toward the two intact tanks. "Where the fuck do you think you're going? Dimwit. Playing hide and seek on me in the dark? Another stupid move like that and I'll plug you full of shells. Mong will be interested in these tanks."

"He'll likely want to play grabass with old Grover back there."

"Shut up and move. Don't waste my time. Mong should've blasted you from the start. Help me haul these two tanks back over to the transporter."

I blinked as if he were speaking another language. "Your crazy master already has a couple of these."

"So? Not with bugs in them. Move!" He struck my shoulder with his rifle, causing me to wince and gasp.

He kneed me toward the nearest tank, forcing me to start pushing it from behind. I leaned my shoulder into it, groaning in agony as the glass brushed against my mangled hand. The water inside the tank sloshed. I could hear the thud of hard chitin of the insect's shell knocking against the side. It creeped the hell out of me. "Pure insanity what we're doing here."

"Quit your bellyaching." Balt snapped me again with the end of his gun. "You're such a baby. Mong can be a real hardass. Be thankful you have me. He had me lifting concrete blocks with a broken ulna."

"Bully for you. Maybe you two can suck each other's dicks as return favors."

He sprang at me with a snarl of rage, pinning my arms down on the floor with his knees, shoving the barrel of the gun in my mouthpiece. "Only reason I don't blow your fucking head off, Rusco, is Mong'd have my balls for breakfast. Consider this: 'So, Balt, why'd you waste, Rusco?'

'Because he was a dumb fuck.'

'Well, I wanted him kept alive.'

'Yeah, easier said than done—'

Bang—"

"So, consider yourself lucky. Now help me move this piece of shit out, and keep your mouth shut!"

He took an end and wiping my stretched lips, I helped him lug the bulky tank back the way we came.

We got it up the ramp and I pleaded for rest, hissing breath through my teeth through my awkward mask. I shook the pain out of my hand. Balt ignored me. We pulled it the rest of the way to the transporter room. I stepped back. I could see the trapped insect's gimlet red eyes following us in something of rabid interest, as if after so many centuries it had something finally to entertain it. The thing was definitely alive. I could feel the vibrant force of its alien existence pulsing through the glass. Whether it breathed or shat like humans I could barely guess.

Balt prodded me back to fetch the other tank. Hard work. We crouched before the amalgo, gazing at our cargoes, Balt with satisfaction, me sweating and grunting with agony. We pushed the first of those eerie tanks between the parallel plates. The thing fit between the plates with only inches to spare. A flash of light almost blinded me, a sizzle, a flare, then the tank and alien vanished. The plates resumed their familiar dull, greenish glow.

Balt grunted and jostled my shoulder, a signal to help ease the other tank through. We did. It vanished with equal alacrity. Gone. Obviously such cargoes were meant to travel through these transporter highways. Balt pushed me through next. Vertigo hit me like a hurricane. Again that tickling sensation clutched my nerve ends and the dizzying freefall marked a dark journey through some wormhole. Not a bon voyage.

I came too, blinking in exhaustion back in the room on Othwan. Balt shoved me aside as before. It was as if I'd been gone only a second. Balt, the glib fuck, appeared to suffer no side effects. A half dozen eyes raked over us as if we were lab specimens. Hands snatched at the tanks, sliding them to the safety of the nearby wall. Mong, muttering in boyish excitement, gave a sharp exclamation. He pushed by me and embraced Balt in a bear hug. "You're a hero! You'll be awarded medals for this historic salvage, Balt. Those are live specimens—real Mentera!"

"I knew you'd be pleased, lord. Hundreds more tanks are back there. Maybe no more of these live bugs that I could see. The other tanks are cracked and drained of their life-giving fluids. There was a fleet of mantis-like ships." He filled Mong in on all the gory details.

Mong stood rapt and hungrily drank in the information like a kid learning about the birds and bees. "It's a food factory!" he rasped. "A human-processing plant. We'll assemble teams to investigate. The technology is staggering. Look at the accessories on their tops. Full-fledged feeding cables with intact circuitry."

The Star Lord's fleshy lips pursed in satisfaction. Mong was in high spirits. "A gold mine out there. Enough to study for years. Enough to defeat my enemies and ensure my rule of the galaxy."

He let his gaze pass over the nearest Mentera, the black, hulking locust with red eyes, quivering antennae and sharp pincers. His jaw hung in awe. "Incredible. They are such beautiful specimens."

I gazed in horrified incomprehension. Walking, mutant grasshoppers which enslaved humans for centuries and this fuck worships them like some totem god of the past? It was beyond lunacy.

"Excuse me, but am I missing something?" I croaked. "How can a vampire that fed on countless humans be 'beautiful'?"

"They were an advanced race," he declared in a defensive voice.

Was it adoration I heard in that tone?

"They were scavengers. Soul-sucking parasites."

"So you think," Mong sneered. "But they knew how to establish their supremacy and become all powerful."

"As you intend? You're insane!" I peeled off my mask and threw it on the floor.

Mong flashed me a sadistic grin. "Perhaps, Rusco, but I prefer to think of myself as a visionary. Your opinions of me mean less than dogshit. Congratulations on your first salvage. There'll be more to come."

Chapter 18

Hadruk had two lackeys escort one broken-fingered Rusco out across the common grounds. Pagodas and prayer halls nestled amidst banyans, garden fountains and trim lawns. We waited at the stone terrace of a minor shrine for some time. I couldn't make heads or tails of the archaic deity to which it was dedicated. We traded no words and they kept me under close watch. Mong met up with us and dismissed his men. He beckoned me with a gracious hand toward the main lecture hall with its red-and-white peaked roof. I studied the man's swarthy face, wondering what went on behind that complex skull of his.

"What now?" I asked. "No new journey to locust land?"

"Since you have shown sense," Mong said, "you'll get a bonus. I invite you to attend the lectures of the 'brotherhood', the brotherhood of the future."

"Where's Blest?"

"Your comrade's being taken care of. Quit asking about him. I plan to make a better man of you. That's what you're here for...for that you should be grateful."

I snorted air through my nose. None of the residents ambling about, monks or nuns or whatever they were, seemed to have any official status here or occupation. They wore no weapons at their belts. All were plainly dressed, in smocks and robes without frills and for the most part quite ordinary. But I could tell something was wrong with them. They walked funny, like stilted starlings, and they looked out of their eye sockets sideways, as if something had been done to their brains.

"No guns?" I muttered.

"Firearms are prohibited at Othwan," Mong explained, "with the sole exception of me and my lieutenants."

"Hmph." I absorbed the information. "Not so good when a disciple goes ballistic and clips the headmaster in the forehead."

"You've a morbid imagination."

"Well, you can thank my mother for that. Her genes."

Mong ignored the remark. "Step up the pace, Rusco. We've a big day ahead of us."

I noticed loudspeakers strung up on every building. From time to time a singsong voice would come over announcing the time of day:

"One o'clock and all is well! Residents of the Brotherhood, please proceed to Prayer Hall #1. Seva duty, as a reminder, will commence an hour earlier, since the Celebration of Silence is slated for 2100. Brothers and Sisters must observe absolute silence until 0900 tomorrow morning."

I chortled.

Mong turned me a scowling look. "I run a tight ship here, Rusco. Schedules, rules, strenuous physical activities, group sessions. Discipline invites obedience and cultivates an ordered mind."

I gauged the territory, its lush opulence, careful attention to detail. Not a grass blade out of place. Ever an escape plan brewed in my mind. We stood roughly in the middle of the grounds. The odious 'Temple of Light' sprawled behind us, about five hundred yards to the east, laced in fine mist from the river. About the same distance to the west, the elegant prayer hall of acolytes loomed. Various pagodas with peaked roofs and ornate wooden scrollwork carved on their lintels, spread across the grounds; residents or followers milled about in numbers, steadfast in their business which seemed solitary and internal, judging from the glazed-eyed faces and the bird-like mannerisms.

The background whine of cicadas dulled my senses, as did the odd hoot of a grey tree monkey, or something like it, swinging in a nearby banyan. My mind absorbed the various-colored birds and the large butterflies flitting from bush to bush. All a so-called utopia.

The common ground or lawn, with its various bushes, terraced walkways, white-walled shrines wrapped in ivy, small gardens with fountains and ornamental boulders, created no less the illusion of a peaceful community. The final, definitive touch, the small, burbling creek that bisected the oval grounds and ran down to the river. Behind us terraced paddies rose before the domed hills of Othwan.

Mong beckoned me. "Here we are, Rusco. You'll like it here." We approached the prayer hall where a group of individuals stood, conversing in hushed tones and holding books.

"Listen, Mongo, I don't want to swap bible stories with your hermits and balding pilgrims."

He touched finger to lip. "Is that what you think of them, my *meslars*?"

"What in the hell else are they?"

He nodded and snapped his fingers at one of the members of the group—a brown-skinned woman with hand drum and small, wizened, chipmunk eyes. "Kazu, come here please."

The shaven-headed lady approached, all gleaming pate with stubble bristling from her chin. The drum vanished and hands pushed together in a loose scarlet and green robe.

"Yes, lord?"

"Take Mr. Rusco to the 'inauguration' pagoda. See that he's cleaned up and outfitted properly. I'm thinking it's time he learns the Seven Serums like the other recruits. Truth, Pain, Vice, Love, Hate, Renunciation, Emptiness. How they slip off the tongue. I have a feeling, *Pain*, with a capital P, will be Rusco's bugbear."

"As you wish, lord." The *meslar* bowed. She had a glazed look of emptiness, as if juiced on something. Myscol? Some happy drug? I hated that pervasive hush about these men and women. Looked like a bunch of busy little badgers. The men probably hadn't gotten laid in a decade, if they'd ever been laid before. Judging from the look of 'Kazu', I didn't blame them.

"I think you're proud of that hair, Rusco," remarked Mong. "We'll take it off today sometime. You will wear simple clothes—an acolyte's smock, gown and garb and say goodbye to your 'streaked purple' look. Acolytes undergo strict ordinance, ritual, fasting once every ten days and every day only one meal and no food after sunset. Toughens a body up. Needless to say, no extracurricular activities among males and females, as it dilutes the power and purity of worship."

I gawped. What a bunch of baloney. "How do you expect to win over any recruits to your pagoda club under these strict rules? What if I have the hots for Kazoo?"

"It is traditional, Rusco, the way it has always been. Study the religions and sects of the past. My advice for you is to follow the ordered regimen. The penalties for disobedience are severe, as you can guess. I hope this gives you enough of an incentive to take the program seriously. I expect nothing but enthusiasm and acceptance of the teachings."

Mong turned to leave, but paused with a thoughtful look. "I'll let you in on a secret—because you gave me the amalgo, I tender you this 'gift' my master told me about years ago. It was about emptying one's mind, going deep inside and probing the deepest layers of being. I laughed at my master, disrespected his mystical message. The last laugh was on me. I tried out this 'spiritual purification' and my mind became empty, one-pointed, a powerful instrument of execution."

"Sure, Mong. I believe you. I really do."

He clapped his hands. "So, shall we? You're first up in the Medicine Wheel. Really this is a favor I'm doing you. If you do well, you'll rise high in the realm of the brotherhood."

I wagged my head in bright enthusiasm. "It's everything and more I've ever wanted to do in my life."

Mong slapped me on the back. "Excellent! Sister Kazu will brief you on the technique. Please keep your eye off her behind." His expression grew dark, and the Mong I knew returned in full force. "Do anything you want here, Rusco. But do not ridicule the teachings. My wards do not appreciate it. They can be downright nasty when due respect is not bestowed."

I gave a nod, seeing no need to goad Kazu or these other fucks into torturing me as Mong already had.

Mong strode off. Was the man confident I wouldn't get into trouble? I laughed. I heard the chanting deep in the prayer hall. Low, guttural sounds rendered in monotones in some language foreign to my ears. A shiver of unease ran through my body. The rumbling unison of the subdued figures portended evil purposes and practices, endorsed by Mong.

"This way," Kazu said, a singsong lilt to her voice. She beckoned me toward that house of chanting prayer.

I held up a hand, trying to keep my eyes off her wonderful ass. "I need to take a dump badly. Where's your crapper?"

She frowned, then nodded, pointed to the communal facilities back behind where Mong and I had come from. I took my long-legged strut there but she stalked along with me, her busy chipmunk face working hard.

I turned and leveled her a cold glare. "In private please, Kazoo."

She pinched her lips in a frown. "I'll be waiting back of the facility hall. No funny moves, Rusco, for your sake."

"As you wish, Kazoo. I'll be the embodiment of purity and chastity."

She scowled and stared at me with hard eyes.

I shuffled off down to the patio-stoned terrace bordering the communal facilities. When I was around a bend, I gave a grunt of satisfaction and tossed off my polite bearing.

I peered at my broken hand, grabbed my index finger, counted to ten, pulled hard, yanked it straight. "Motherfucker!"

I waited until the ripples of pain had subsided.

Sweating in profusion, I left the background agony behind and hissed air through my teeth. I waited a full two minutes, then yanked on the finger next to it, straightened it as best I could. Then the pinky. More waves of pain. I dug through the dense shrubbery, gritting teeth and cursing, then found some tough twigs, enough to make a crude splint so my fingers would at least not move. Some of the stems of these green leafier plants I could use as string to tie my fingers together. I smelled like grasshopper spit afterward, but it was better than suffering from chronic, crooked finger syndrome for the rest of my life.

I scanned the layout of the grounds once again. The compound's gates and six-foot-high barbed-wire fence were well-monitored. There was some ringed tower over to my left behind the prayer hall, a lookout post that likely housed sentries on the eye alert for wandering, recalcitrant acolytes. I caught a glint of movement there, rifles, binoculars? Mong had said no weapons were allowed here, but then again, what did that mean? He said his lieutenants bore arms. Maybe he wasted precious lieutenants guarding the place, gazing out on the yard, on the watch for troublemakers like me.

I doubted I'd have an easy time reconnoitering the hangar some mile or more off. Though something told me, I'd have to discover what was inside, at least use whatever was there to make my escape, like a ship, for example.

Not much I could do now, with old Kazu pacing and gnashing at the bit a few dozen yards away.

After slashing cold water on my face, I returned to the dutiful *meslar* who led me across the lawn to the chambers adjoining the prayer hall. Four *meslars* took me to a room, some sort of dressing room, and off came my ponytail and purple-dyed hair. They garbed me in orange and brown robes like the other novitiates. I ran my fingers through my crop of bristles, whistling through my teeth. Last time I had a buzz cut, I think was in my rebel years. Or perhaps when I had to jack that space trailer out in Gazeus, posing as an energy monitor or some damn thing. Could have been both. Did it matter?

A blur now. Change, Rusco, change. At this point in your life, you're due for some. What's a little hair gone, compared to a broken hand and some torture?

Kazu shoved a book in my hands then flashed me a stern glance. "You are looking better, Rusco. These are the first Five of Seven Serums on the Path of Attainment. Please memorize them and adhere to the strictures."

"Says who?"

"Says Master Mong."

I scoffed at that. "Be a cold day in hell when 'Master Mong' gets me to—"

"Silence. Your opinions are of no value here. We have a 31 hour day on Othwan so you'll find our program especially strenuous. We will proceed to the inauguration. You may join the current group of acolytes."

The loudspeakers emitted a gong-like resonance, a call to attendance at the prayer hall.

We assembled in the auditorium. I saw figures from all quarters gathering, moving like robots. I could only think of moths fluttering toward a bright light. Perhaps a hundred and fifty initiates, men and women, mostly men. No children. Kazu shuttled me inside and gave me the once over while passing me to the ten monitors dressed in long white and brown robes, then she took a place at the front.

I grabbed a cushion from the side like everyone else. We sat in cross-legged silence. Plunked on our cushions facing the front in an ordered grid, with exactly two feet between each novitiate. The spaces were marked in red tape on the polished teak floor.

The prayer hall was smaller than the main Temple of Light, one third I'd say, with a proportionally high ceiling and white stuccoed walls with varnished pine beams scrolled with ornate eagles, falcons and majestic birds, none of the disturbing, warlike elements of the former temple and its lurid glass tanks. In fact, this hall stood in stark contrast, following the old Zen tradition of minimalism I'd seen on other terraformed worlds. I put on my best smile and mask of cooperation, listening to what old Kazu had to say.

"Close your eyes," she said gently over the lightly amplified speakers. "Focus your attention on the third eye point. Empty your mind. Let your spirit relax and slip into emptiness. Let your breathing come to a placid rest. Relax into a deep state of inner silence."

There were sighs and shifting of legs, noseblowing and coughs. I looked around with a crooked grin.

A stern monitor eyed me and approached with a sharp gesture. I held up a hand, nodded, squinting as if to comply.

"Focus, pilgrims, focus," Kazu said. "Mong's mission is a bright blip on your horizon. Your future is at stake. Let the inner tranquility transport you to a higher dimension."

I yawned. It was nice to get a breather after all the intensity of the past days, hunting aliens and killing Skugs, but after a while I could not help my mind from wandering. I kept wondering how I could garrotte Mong and flee this nuthouse while these fucks sat in their mental masturbation with eyes closed. If I could sneak out and make a break for it... I opened one eye. A simpleton's plan, Rusco. Monitors ranged the hall, scanning the rows of acolytes with cane whips in hand. These whips had metal-edge flails. I could see them glinting in the dim sconce light. One poor schmuck at the front had the bad luck of wavering in his seat and a flail came slashing down on his shoulders. He let out a miserable wail. The female attendant who had administered the blow grunted then raised the weapon again. The guilty aspirant sat up in rapt attention. A painful lesson on the path to enlightenment.

The others stood with backs ramrod straight, keeping silent, maintaining equanimity, if not in more rigid attention now. They pretended as if nothing had happened. A weird scenario, if you asked me. Gave me the chills. Suffice it to say I stayed quiet and played the obedient monk. I did feel a new strength come over me as if there were a concentrated force of mental power in that hundred and fifty or so gathering doing their mediation, but soon a thousand qualms plagued my brain. Where was Wren? I doubted Blest or Volia were sitting as comfy as I was.

Twice I caught myself nodding off, barely saving myself from a cane-lashing.

The session came, thankfully, to an end, though after what seemed endless hours. We filed out, many of us blinking like owls and looking very zoned out. I had to admit I did feel refreshed, more than after a good sleep. My ears buzzed with the sounds of silence. There was a peculiar alertness to my brain as if I sensed every sound around me, even the cicada huddled behind the manicured boulder. Maybe, just maybe, I needed more sleep and this tranquility was my natural state?

Or maybe Mong had some subaural brain stimulators or brainwashing devices running on half power in that Zen cult room of his? What the fuck did I know?

The sun hurt my eyes after coming out of that dim lighting inside. I sure couldn't wait to get back to prayer session for more breath-taking excitement. The romp through cricket world on amalgo transit seemed almost a letdown compared to this nail-biting adventure of sitting with pins-and-needle ankles for hours on end. That said, I would not want to trade places with Lady Volia or Blest any time soon.

CHRIS TURNER

Chapter 19

There was a lot more going on here than just passive monks going about their business, conducting hokey prayer habits. Activities abounded… Climb a ladder and stand straight on the top of a high pole, teetering with vertigo. Then jump from said pole that towers over the cement below. The bungee cord would catch you before you mashed your face in free fall. Anyone with a fear of heights was dead meat. I was about a six on a scale of ten, so was not as unfortunate as some. Men and women blubbered like babies, bawling their eyes out, retching their guts, white as ghosts, fighting tooth and nail not to go up that ladder and stand on that one foot square pole with the wind blustering. But Mong's enforcers shuttled them up and pushed them over if they chickened out. Somehow it shattered their nerves. Did it accomplish anything outside of breaking those individuals' spirits? I doubted it. Just another form of torture.

The activities continued. The browbeating, the physical conditioning, the brutal hand-to-hand combat. The repercussions high in cases of cowardice or failure. Also of interest, the fire walk. Walk slowly and you were doomed. The undersoles of your bare feet scorched by red hot coals. Move fast and keep an eye ahead on the target and one has a chance. Slip and fall in that 8' by 30' pit of ash and cinder, as one poor schmuck did and had to be carted away yelling with agony, the whole left side of his body charred and smoking, and you'd be sorry for not taking better care. Those who thought to dodge off the path were cane-whipped along by *meslars* on either side. Nowhere to go but forward. Mong had an endless supply of new recruits, so he didn't care if a few got damaged beyond repair or lost their minds. "It's the warrior's way," he quoted at a prayer session he had come to attend on one of the following days.

I growled under my breath. "Sick fuck."

"Anything to add, Rusco?" Mong's ears perked up with interest like those of an alert hound. "Please share with your brothers and sisters."

I remained sullen. How I'd like to put a fishhook in the mongrel's brain.

There was *Seva* too, a term he had coined from some ancient term of spiritual service. Out in the rice paddies, watering and weeding in the hot sun. One to two days a week, working for the common good.

A soothing voice rang over the loudspeaker, announcing that a time for rest had come—one hour, and that evening prayers would resume after.

A small grassy rise set back from the fire pit caught my eye. A solitary figure sat with a grass blade stuck in his teeth staring off into space. I approached and plopped myself down beside him, hoping to find out his story. He squinted up and I sighed. "I think of all the he-man exercises, the pole is the scariest of all, on account of my fear of heights. Something about plunging off into thin air. It unsettles the soul. For a spaceman I reckon that's a bad thing."

He replied in a dead voice, "This fire-walking stuff's not too bad once you've got it under your belt, or done it once or twice." He looked at me with minor curiosity, assessing me with his bushy brows lifting and a scar over his left cheek twitching under his skewed eye. Something about him tipped me off—I knew he was not like the others. A glint of deviancy showed in that skewed eye.

I stared in earnest at the bald man they hauled off from the fire. The bottom of his feet were fried, smoking. "Certainly he'd disagree."

"He didn't listen to Sister Kazu's instructions."

I laughed. "Name's Rusco."

"Zan Vulder. What brings you to Othwan?"

"Oh, a little birdie chirped in my ear, told me about this little utopia out here in nowhere-land. Mr. Mong took a big shine to me. Practically made me his bed mate since the get-go."

"You don't say?" Zan sighed. "One of those?"

"Yep, and you?"

"Master Mong's captains initiated me into the pleasure of the brotherhood quite a while back. Recruited me from Bagrish when they 'assimilated' my home planet. Broke my brother's legs, raped my sister. They told me I'd be next if I didn't join his brigade of zealots. Said I had 'all the qualities of excellent battle breeding'. 'Fine-quality soldiery'."

"That's quite a compliment. Guess we all are indebted to Master Mong for some reason or other, bringing us here together." I tipped my head at him. "Long live Master Mong."

"Yeah, long live Mong." His voice was edged with venom.

The exercises continued into the evening after the final prayers and picked up again the next day until we were a battle-weary and sleep-deprived bunch. Then we were shuttled back to the prayer hall to listen to those monotonous liturgies of Sister Kazu and her company of *meslars,* chiming off items of dogma that Mong called Teachings.

We settled upon our usual cushions and I steeled myself for the usual rubric of dogma and drawn out lectures.

"The soul and spirit are one. They must be fed by constant purity and discipline.

"The mind that is weak and the body that is impure are ones that languish and die in a state of sloth.

"We must vanquish evil. Must hear no evil or see no evil! Let us put forth our vows and learn the moral conduct of warriors! All in favor say 'Aye'."

"Aye!" came the crowd's forced, automatic response.

"Open your heart and mind to the path of wisdom as espoused by Master Mong!"

"Aye!"

"Cherish the teachings of the elder age. Let the brotherhood envelop you!"

"Aye!"

"Work hard, be humble. Serve and be faithful! Never let the darkness or the temptation of deceit enter your heart!"

"Aye!"

And so on. Maxims after maxims and mantras and affirmations with it, a vestibule of brainwashing, enough to come slopping out one's arse like diarrhea on demand. I wouldn't give a wrap of dirty baby wipes for half this stuff. Hours upon hours of slogans and half-baked spiritual syrup, until I was bug-eyed and my ears burning and wanting to shut out the world around me and put a blanket over my head and curl up and die.

Mong had a nice little setup, I'd give him that. A brain-washing crib as cute and cuddly as any unofficial, high-end think tank engineered by any autocratic government. He'd select the most promising recruits, make them lieutenants, train them to fly those nice little Warhawks out into the wild blue and blow planets to shit and nuke any suckers who didn't want to play ball with him, cede their native land and governments. People who'd die for the cause, grinning, faithful to the end to dear old Mong. How could a man demand so much loyalty? In the same way all the dictators, did it, through personal magnetism, an iron fist and classic conditioning. Genghis Khan, Nero, Stalin, Wasgon, Farseid, a hundred others, though my tired brain couldn't conjure all the mad, sick fucks throughout history who'd done it, and succeeded, for a time.

Grey skies graced the horizon that day and the following day. Zan caught my eye and approached me at the refectory as I cleaned up my tray of standard beans and rice fare. I gave him a dutiful nod of acknowledgement, tired and exhausted from the day's rigors.

"If a man were to think of getting out of this place," he hissed, "he'd think fire in the hole." He jerked his head in the direction of the prayer hall. "Some wild animals must have made a gap in the fence, been in and out eating from the garbage bins filled with all that delicious food you just chucked out."

"You're suggesting burning the joint down?"

He shrugged. "Just saying." He walked off.

I rubbed my chin.

As I was well on my way away from the refectory, Mong came sauntering by to check up on me. I gave him a salute. "All well on the battle front, general? Enjoying your little batch of insects from a new dimension?"

"You know, Rusco, we found an alien species there never before seen. Trapped in one of those tanks. To describe the creature would do it no justice. Suffice it to say it had six tentacles attached to a greyish-black bulbous body with no visible face that we could see. Even I have the good sense to stay away from it."

"A wise choice. These little nuggets of wisdom come from long experience. They leave one in the best of health."

"Too true, Jet Rusco. Now to your health? Are Kazu and her people seeing to your comfort?"

"Kazu is simply marvelous. Couldn't be better, especially my hand." I held it up, showing my makeshift splint.

Mong gave an ear to ear grin. "I'm glad of that, Rusco. I see you have used your ingenuity to accelerate your healing. Bravo. That's testament to a man of resource."

We both laughed in our own dark way.

"What do you think of our program?" Mong asked.

I drew in a slow breath. "Where to start?—unique? Rigorous? Zany? A wild ride? A jaw-dropping experience? Bullying, invasive, a blatant mind fuck?"

Mong cleared his throat. "Privation, torture, hardship, renunciation, spurning luxuries and passion is a means to an end. If a man can see with a crystal clear mind, without frivolity and excess, he will rise above the rest. Burdened by them he will be distracted. You show promise. That's why I spared your worthless hide. I could use someone of your multi-talents. Purpose can focus a man's will, one-pointedly on a goal. Anything else may fail."

"You're a hypocrite, Mong. You indulge in these power-mongering no-nos on a daily basis. Who is it who controls vast wealth gained from war and plunder? Do you not waste worlds as if they were fly paper?"

"I need not justify anything to you. I've passed my tests. I've dug my destiny. I can do whatever the hell I want. That's why I can wield power from anywhere I stand, and why you are in the monk's robe."

"Good point," I jeered. "Just playing devil's advocate."

Though I wasn't and Mong knew it.

Just keep playing this stupid game, Rusco. Dial it back, or you're going to get yourself killed. You're still alive and if you can keep your brain intact, you may get out of this tin can in one piece. Look for a way to get out of the pickle jar and save your ass.

Mong could see the gears working in my head and gave a moody scowl. "Rusco, I'll not insult your intelligence. Most of this structure is set up as a conditioning farm, like what Pavlov did with his dogs." He held up a hand. "I know what you're thinking. A certain primitive part of the brain responds well to conditioning. The reptilian brain, the primal core of what drives us. We drill our initiates into obedience, so that when I tell them to act, they move without question. If I tell them to jump, they ask how high. I give them basic proficiency of body and mind through rigorous training then a diminishing confidence in themselves by forced association with the group and affiliation to our cause. I make them what I want of them. After training, they respond favorably to stimuli; good deeds prompt rewards, bad deeds prompt punishment. It's a formula quite tried and true; maybe even dull and monotonous, but in truth, quite effective."

"So simple that even an ant can follow it," I added.

Mong exhaled. "Study the ant, Rusco and you'll learn something. A creature that never gives up, never! Even when 90% of the hill dwellers are destroyed in a fight with a rival horde, they go on biting and gouging, protecting their eggs and territory. Such tenacity, such strength!" He lifted a hand. "If only humans could exhibit such concentrated power and competence. We humans would do well to study the insect species, Rusco. If a mere ant were the size of one of us, they would rend us limb from limb, crush us in their mandibles like soft fruit. Like these dormant Mentera, you have seen. They—"

"They lost the war."

"You are mistaken, they didn't. They are merely hibernating, biding their time in their cocoons, safe from the ravages of war before they will be resurrected. I may be the only Star Lord to resurrect them as my minions. You'll see. The Mentera left enough of their technology behind to preserve their species forever."

A cold shiver prickled my skin. I hoped to hell Mong was far off in that assertion.

He gave me an odd, faraway look—the look of the fanatic—as he strode off to confer with his prayer monitors.

Dumb bastard. I'd drive an ice-pick in his brain before this was all over.

Maybe not tomorrow though, Rusco. As illusively innocuous this place looked, it was a regular Fort Knox. Sneaking out at night from the barracks would not be an easy task…in fact, it proved downright foolhardy. One sod tried a sleepwalking gag and I recalled the dull wails and whimpering as he was caned from head to toe. He later revised his story to 'getting out for a breath of fresh air' which earned equal whaps and slaps. Night time was an obvious no-no to make a getaway; the grounds were then at their most heavily guarded.

Rotten pricks. I reflected on the week's activities with a grimace. The Seven Serums—what a bunch of shite. Seven Validations of Reality: Truth, Pain, Vice, Love, Hate, Renunciation, Emptiness. Each day of the week we'd visit one meditation, or 'Serum', centering on the profundity of existence. *"Focus your tiny brains, miniscule ones. Focus on one spirit medicine."* I couldn't take much more of this shit. Soon I'd be spewing Mong's dogma. It was time to act.

Chapter 20

Three days passed with much brooding over escape from this prison. Early in the day, I heard the roar of fifteen Warhawks buzzing overhead. They vanished in the clouds, their engines fading to oblivion. Seems as if Mong had taken a significant number of his warships with him.

Perhaps a good time to initiate an exit plan.

I contrived to scout near the fence Zan had mentioned earlier on pretext of a morning walking meditation. Sure enough, the wire mesh had been pulled back and a gap about a foot off the ground gaped for a lean man to worm his way through. Very convenient, especially for a man who had lost much weight at this fat farm. Good on you, Zan.

An easy enough diversion, Zan's scheme—torching the prayer hall. Any of the other structures in the compound would be too minor a distraction, so would sabotaging the Temple of Light be a call for suicide.

The nagging voice in the back of my head warned me about how hackneyed such a plan was, but for the life of me, I couldn't think of anything better. Hard to come up with a quality plan in a micro-controlled environment with a mangled hand.

The refectory would be teeming with its regiment of robots at midafternoon, precisely 3:30. The prayer hall would be empty, or near empty. If I could sneak out, do my deviltry and be off with none the wiser, I might be able to pull this caper off. Shamble to the hills, any hidey-hole would suffice, better than being stuck in this madhouse, captive to Kazu, the meditation-meister.

A section of the west fence was unguarded from what I could see. There'd be fewer *meslars* now as the lunch bunch tucked into their flavorless fare, seeing as it was the only meal of the day—one of Mong's innovations to make recruits more disciplined, and better fighting, loyal, iron-willed machines. Or half-starved, sleep-deprived zombies eager for scraps and any chance at betterment.

I took an early exit, chucking out my beans and rice, grimacing with distaste at the soggy paste. Didn't doubt Mong spiked the food and water here with a brainwashing compound. I snuck out to the prayer hall. The doors were always open, for keeners who wanted to get in some 'extra meditation' or some shit like that. I crept to the front altar where Kazu usually delivered her guided meditation. Long burgundy tapestries hung from ceiling to floor behind the altar, starched and stiff. A kerosene lamp burned away amidst assorted knickknacks: candles, incense, medallions commemorating Mong and other soul-stifling memorabilia. Very convenient. Minimal electric lights outfitted this place. Old school.

Snatching a glance over my shoulder, I grabbed the kerosene lamp and kindled the fabric behind the prayer altars. The wood paneling and spray-painted stucco would go up like tinder. Because the devotees loved this prayer hall so much, they'd naturally not want to see it go up in flames, so they'd come running to douse it in a bucket brigade. A perfect bit of cover I needed to get away from this funny farm.

I paused at the door long enough to see flames licking up the wall. My lips curled in a grin. In minutes this place would be a raging inferno.

I turned and ran across the green, my stumbling feet taking me to the west fence and the gap I'd scouted earlier.

I wasn't half way there when a figure came sprinting up next to me—must have seen me scurrying away. I turned, baring my metal fist for a strike, halting in midstride.

Zan hissed at me. "You actually did it, Rusco? You're crazy! Mong will skin you alive."

"You only live once. Are you in on this, or do you want to go back to playing disciple at prayer meet?"

He grinned. "Hell no. Let's blow this scene." He charged after me.

We hurried to the fence and squeezed through the hole, Zan first.

Shouts and activity drifted from behind.

I looked back to see a bright funnel of flame eating at the prayer hall's roof. Frantic figures scurried around the doomed building like beetles, waving hands and shouting commands. Fools!

We took off toward the river, abandoning the plan to strike out for the hangar.

We didn't get a hundred steps before Mong's security people were all over us like muggers in a back alley. Intercepted us from a place down the fence. Didn't take them three seconds to figure out who'd pulled the fire stunt either.

I took down the first wanker with my bare right fist, though two more came at me with truncheons. I kicked out with fury and lashed out with my metal fist, smacking down a big brown-robed figure, elbowing another in the teeth with as much Jet Rusco street fighting 101 as I could: keep your head down and keep punching. Never let up on your guard, unless absolutely necessary for a winning hit or you're going to get creamed.

Three of them surged in to smack us down, but not kill us. A significant detail. Three more lay groaning in the grass with broken bones.

Yet my fucked up left hand would not win me this fight and with no weapon I could seriously do little against these shitheads' superior numbers. My strong right hand made contact with another face and I relished the crunch of cartilage and bone. I lost track of Zan in the melee. Floundering arms and legs were all around me.

"Get him down," snuffled a robed figure. Blood dripped from his cheek and flattened nose.

Four of them overwhelmed us at last and twisted my arms behind my back, smacking me hard in the gut. Another whacked me a couple of times in the face.

"Don't damage him, Paneu. Mong'll want to have words with him when he gets back. The last time some new recruit got frisky and made a break for the river, Vorcox roughed him up good and Mong brutalized Vorcox for playing the overzealous policeman."

Five more came huffing and puffing to our side. I saw Zan pressed in the ground a few feet away. The *meslars* hauled us gasping and cursing to the refectory, now a place of operations for dealing with the fire. Armed men stood around trading bitter words and questioning *meslars* and disciples.

A half a day must have passed, maybe more. I wallowed in a blur of memories, hazy voices coming in and out of my fuzzy brain.

Through vision half blurred I saw Master Mong stride in, wearing a Star Lord's crown and nursing a lion's snarl. I guessed he'd preempted his mission just to try to save the cindered prayer hall.

One of the captors who'd taken me down jerked a thumb in my direction. "Fire boy here and his crony tried to get to the rice paddies. Likely wanted to loop back and make a break for the hangar. Figured if they'd made it past the first fence, they could double back and steal a ship."

Mong shook his head. "You never cease to amaze me, Rusco, with your juvenile antics. It almost makes no sense to me."

I looked over at Zan, crouched in a ball, cowed against the wall. Why'd I listen to that shaven-headed idiot?

"Sometimes I think there is some genius to your moves but mixed with these dumb, rat-brain schemes makes me pause. How are you even still alive? Did you actually think you'd be able to make it past a battalion of trained men not a mile away? I thought you a man of some resource, that you'd devise something more innovative?" He frowned, a heavy sigh pulling down his lips.

I shrugged. "Well, desperate times demand desperate measures,

don't you think, Master Mong? You would know something of that."
I grinned, spat out a chipped tooth and a thin spray of blood. I
remember regurgitating some dumb line like that back on *Bantam*
when Noss's hand had been chewed up.

Mong clicked his tongue. "It saddens me to think you've
corrupted innocent minds into committing arson. Brother Zan is a
loyal member of our Brotherhood."

I broke out in a laugh. "Brother Zan would cut your heart out
and eat it if he had the chance."

Mong stared at the rebel who sat crouched, scowling with a sullen
gleam in his black eyes. "Perhaps. The truth will be ironed out in
time. I am confident in Zan's loyalty despite your claim."

I shrugged. "You can keep on believing your fantasies."

"I see my tests have failed," he cut in. "I expected you to try to
escape—I was wondering when and how. Surely not some lackwit
effort from the master of mayhem, Jet Rusco."

"Well, now that we know the truth, it's cause for celebration. Just
a dumb grifter in need of Sister Kazoo's teachings."

"Get them out of my sight," he barked. "Take this wiseass to the
Chamber of Redemption. Zan too."

Chapter 21

They dragged us to the Temple of Light, several doors down the hall from where Blest and Lady Volia were held prisoners. I guessed Mong kept all his subversives here.

Before a lofty iron-bound door, Zan and I slumped with armed guards on either side. Balt and Hadruk were among them.

After a time, Mong arrived in a black mood, murmuring curses through his teeth. He stared at me, as I looked up at him, sullen and red eyed.

"You disappoint me, Jet Rusco. I told you about my rules—no escape. What do you do? Try to escape." He exhaled a caustic breath. "I've been far too lenient with you. It's been an expensive mistake. I fear I've done you a karmic disservice by not counseling you properly."

I grinned in a crazy daze of unreality. What the hell was he talking about? I contemplated his words in my hazed, beaten-up condition as Balt kicked the grin off my face and a new level of pain tingled through my nerve centers.

"A few prayers first." Mong declared, beckoning us curtly into the main chamber of the Temple of Light.

Rough hands hauled Zan and I forth through marble halls, high-ceilinged as a basilica's. In truth, an odd and surreal display of opulence not generally known in these depressed times. As if I saw it for the first time, the Temple of Light's apse loomed before me. Seen from another angle, graced with dreamy, multi-colored light filtering through the stained-glass windows, to illuminate the altar screen gilded of only purest gold inset with pearls. Paintings were strewn lazily on its walls of war scenes, inspired by works of art from long ago Earth.

Before the altar, Mong muttered a few desultory words at the macabre tanks. "I must clear my mind of this fiasco. Balt, Hadruk, be my witnesses. Bow and meditate, Rusco, all of you. Pay obeisance to the old gods!" He bowed his head in silence. Minutes passed. At last, marching footsteps drifted to our ears behind us and a massive, square-shouldered man dressed in leathers and furs like Mong swept forth stiff-legged. He had a troubled frown on his flat-nosed face.

Mong tilted his head up. "What do you want? Why disturb me now?"

"It's the planet Sargon, sir. It is—"

"What of Sargon? Full report."

"Seems they took the Vendecki lead and fired by propaganda—"

"What, Freduk, what? Spit it out." Mong glared at him.

"I'm afraid, the Sargonians triumphed and managed to seize Keryutti, the capital city."

"What of our outer defenses?" Mong barked.

"Lost. Bastions crumbled."

The Star Lord's fist clenched. "I gave you full command. What of the squadron of attack ships I deployed under your leadership?"

"Repelled, sir." Freduk winced, his lip downturned. "By some unknown force field." He quivered. "More Vendecki tech. We believe they were colluding with the Melinarians."

At the mention of the name, Mong sucked in a long, slow breath. He moved toward the altar on tired feet, his boots echoing ominously on the marble. He stared at the memorabilia there for some time, the medallions, incense holders, the hallowed cups and carved, commemorative bowls, lit a candle and looked up into the ancient, dead face of his stone god lost in the mists of time. He murmured a few words then withdrew, turned his weight full around.

"You idiot! May Yrzin punish you for your incompetence." He lifted a hand and in barely concealed wrath, the guilty lieutenant Freduk's eyes bulged. Blood pooled around those lids and his face shriveled, crimson with fluid.

Freduk slumped in an unruly heap. "Clean up this trash," Mong said with disgust. "Throw his body to the eagles and buzzards on the other side of the river."

Balt nodded.

Mong scowled. "If I had have been there, Balt, instead of playing policeman to Rusco's stupid high jinks, none of this would have happened."

"Agreed, lord. Give the irritant to me. I will kill him, slowly and painfully. We will be rid of this pesky canker."

Mong swelled in irritation. "No!" He gave the explosive order with impatience and walked away, waving Balt off. "Rusco will come with me. He will not get off so easily."

The Star Lord seemed to master his anger; once more he resumed the warlord in control with a face of relaxed manner, if such could be said for a psychopath like Mong.

"Come," he said to me in a curt voice, "I will show you what you could have been and what you both could have had."

I traded glances with Zan. Mong took us to the *Orpheum*, that garish chamber decorated with barbaric fountains of gold and animals carved in marble and twined around the legs of its statuary. Pearl-gray waters were stocked with rare tropical fish. Amongst the splendor, lounged a dozen diaphanous silken-clad beauties of all races. I saw Volia there, drugged out of her mind, sprawled on silken cushions with her mouth and legs open amidst tropical plants. Others, men and women, drank from golden goblets or fanned their dainty faces with exotic feathers. Mong's concubines? Or perhaps for the general use of his privileged captains?

He mustered a sly smile. "Yes, Rusco, sloe-eyed nymphs from Alphanor, geisha girls from Nashene, courtesans knowledgeable of a hundred pleasures and tricks of the trade to drive a man out of his skull. Pleasure, ecstasy beyond his dreams." He grinned, an animal grin. "And you thought I was a eunuch. Pah!" He shook his head in wonder. "Yet you have disqualified yourself from all this." He swept an arm in a grand, mocking gesture. "You have repeatedly broken rules and proven yourself unworthy. Phase 3 is now upon us. I must take necessary action."

We returned in swift order to the hall sporting the iron-bound door. Hadruk unlocked it and set it creaking inward, then he and Balt thrust Zan and me inside.

Balt held back my flailing fist while Hadruk secured Zan. This secret chamber I guessed was Mong's inner sanctum, only the privileged few got to witness it. He'd set up a mini altar here, though several degrees creepier and more sinister than that of the Temple of Light. A strange primal drumbeat echoed from deep within the candle-lit gloom.

The man seemed to have a thing for altars, pious sod he was. Here he had not only his two tanks with live Mentera on display but two extra ones, one which contained Blest, staring out of his glass cage like a deflated grouper. My jaw sagged in dismay. Likewise Zan uttered a croak of despair. I almost had to turn my head, seeing Blest like that, but my own morbid curiosity would not let me look away. His dirty blond hair floated like seaweed from his scalp; he hung suspended there like an underwater scarecrow, his legs floating a few inches off the floor, one leg turned a deep shade of yellow where the parasite still clung, his thin lips parted in a O. That blank expression, the eyes staring, his unblinking gaze all unnerved me. Slowly his pale hand lifted and a small bubble rose from his open lips. I gave a crow's squawk of panic, struggled for sanity to return to my brain and stop the dry heaves from coming. A grisly sight, yet, truth be told, the scene didn't surprise me.

Breathe, Rusco, breathe.

My gaze flickered to several ropes suspended from a beam above. Light chains too looped around that high beam and dangled from the ceiling. Some of the rope ends were frayed and bloody.

I licked my lips. Did Mong do public hangings in this dark crypt? I rejected the thought. That Zan and I were worthy of such an easy death seemed unlikely. I sucked in another breath and willed myself to be strong. How much worse could it be than a few broken fingers?

Much worse...stuffed into that spare tank.

I stared at the usual assortment of adjuncts and curios spread on Mong's altar. Candles, incense, sacred texts, mortar and pestle for grinding alchemic substances and aromatic herbs or other odiferous things to toss on a candle flame. Secured in a glass case sat the bulb that Follee had coveted and had once clutched in his trembling hand. A brown, fist-sized pod with rough skin like a coconut's. A reminder to me that Mong kept all his weirdest curios here—relics, grotesques, commemoratives—a place where he inflicted the utmost pain upon his favored residents.

The drumbeat grew louder. Without warning a big brown-faced man, looking totally stoned out of his mind, came ambling forward, tapping what looked to be a deerhide drum with his tanned palms. He sat before us wearing a trance-like grin. Bristly, black-matted hair spread from the scalp—Oriental, like Mong, of some mixed race of old Earth lineage.

Glaze-eyed, I opened my mouth to speak, but Mong spoke first. "Boauk is a faithful servant of mine, don't mind him. Listen to the drum beat, Rusco. Let it draw you toward the inner world of mystery."

"I'll get right on that," I said.

Mong chuckled and flashed me one of his hideous grins. "You jest, Mr. Rusco. But maybe you will not be joking an hour or two from now."

I motioned to the two grisly tanks of Mentera arranged at the front. "Running out of space to put your pets?"

Mong smiled. "The Mentera demand further study. As do these tanks, before I install them as permanent fixtures in the Temple of Light. I hesitate to release the creatures, knowing their diabolic tendencies. How to study them without emptying their tanks? A little conundrum that troubles even my formidable mind, so for now they will remain tucked away in this little cubbyhole."

"How fitting. I suppose we could use the company."

Mong stared at me, a sullen grin twisting his face. "I see my Redemption Chamber has not fazed you much. That shall change. Your meddling and sabotage at Othwan has set back my research a month or two."

"Sorry to hear that."

"Condolences acknowledged. Now to our program."

"Wait!" I grumbled. "I still don't get why these bugs are in their own tanks. Didn't you say they fed on humans?"

"I did." Mong sighed. "These specimens were likely criminals, punished to serve as a type of cannibalistic nourishment for their fellow locusts. Sacrifices—given as sluts to the state, so to speak—not peculiar, if one studies history. The irony is, these prisoners have outlived their overlords, cruel jailors they were."

My skin prickled. Not unlike others I knew.

Mong motioned. "Blest, as you can see, is cooling his heels in one of the feeding vessels."

I nodded. "I imagine the waters are quite chill there. So, Blest is dead. Does it give you a particular thrill?"

"On the contrary, Blest will return to the land of the living soon, as shall you, to continue the rigors of my discipline. Blest's penance is not yet up."

A cold ball of fear knotted my gut. "Death is death, Mong. Why mince words?"

Mong flashed me an enigmatic glance. "You don't believe in the other worlds, do you, Jet? The life after death?"

I snorted. "Do you?"

"It is not for me to preach. I know the truth. Whereas you do not."

I gave a grunt of exasperation. "This ancient religion you market to your stooges and that you model your 'learned' teachings on does little to convince me of anything. Nor is your unreal world of drugged up cultists and yes-men you've recruited to fly your warships and carry out your dirty work, credible."

"Is that what you conclude?" Mong inquired with amusement in his eyes. "How's this then?" He clenched his fist. The walls started to shake. He closed his eyes. A rumbling as fierce as any earthquake grew. The tanks rocked, their glass panels jiggled, waters sloshed and Zan started to whimper and whisper prayers in all the languages he knew. My eyes darted about in instinctive panic. Did the man have control over the elements?

"Does that interlude not convince you of its reality?"

"I do not understand any of these voodoo tricks of yours."

"Not voodoo, Jet Rusco. Science and physics. Intelligence and power mixed as one. I am the first of the true augmented humans." He saw my skeptical, grimacing look and smiled. "These circuits I've implanted amplify my telekinetic powers. I've had many engineers working on the ins and outs of the problem for some time."

"An augmented arm then."

"Yes, Jet Rusco."

He pulled back the brown leather on his right arm and exposed bare skin. He peeled back a flap. I saw dense circuitry there that went up and probably past his elbow.

"As well as being left-handed, I have ESP and psi power. I am considered demonic and a warlock by my own people. My mentors recognized my potential from an early age on my home planet, Vasgon. Some of them worshiped me, others persecuted me. I had to slay most of those who became too ambitious and tried to use me for their own ends. Their mistake. I had the augmentations custom-built to my needs." He raised his augmented hand, flexed it, and I heard a clicking from within. "You marvel?" asked Mong.

I gave a curt shrug.

Mong closed his eyes. Flicking out his finger, he sizzled a small hole in the far wall. Black smoke billowed out from the indentation.

"A nice parlor trick."

"It's more than a trick, Jet Rusco. I see you have a machine hand too. But much cheaper than mine."

"We all don't have access to unlimited funds." I stared at his flexing hand, feeling a wave of nausea as he made to demonstrate more.

"I think it's time to see how you fare in the lower realms, Rusco. Prepare for an awakening."

Quicker than a snake, he smacked the palm of his hand into my solar plexus in sync with the next boom of the drum. I felt a tingling queasiness in that flat fleshy part of my gut below sternum and centered between my rib cages. It sent an avalanche of pain through my nerve ends—taking every breath out of me. Something else with it—my tenuous link with reality. My waking state world disintegrated as I was thrust into an altered consciousness.

Chapter 22

I could only vaguely discern the past privilege of having a body, gasping, sweating, feeling the pain of what it was like once to be human. It made Myscol seem like a kindergarten field trip.

Visions swam before my eyes. Souls of the dead. My dead mother in her shroud. The guy I killed with an ice pick back in that bar out in Brefus on a chop job. The dozens of others who had perished by my hand. All crawling around my bug-infested skull, floating out of mists of nightmare. All the close scrapes in every hole and seedy dive. My hand exploding into bloody bits. The hundred climaxes with nameless flings on the road. The infinite light years travelled through the star highways—the restless spirit that followed the body of Jet Rusco. All peaking in one final climax. Then nothing.

Blackness. No body. Jet Rusco, effectively dead.

But a vestige of the old Jet Rusco still remained, drifting soundlessly in some freakish ether on the gulfs of time.

Somewhere I was still alive, like being in an obscene tank perhaps, but not connected to anything, or any reality. I was everywhere at once, but nowhere at once, and it scared the living bejesus out of me. I couldn't get out. I couldn't flee anywhere. Only the basic truth of existence was laid bare before my mind's eye.

Cold…empty…space.

For how long I floated in that caustic vapor, a dead, spiritless zombie, I do not know. I could have floated there for a million years.

What meaning does time have in such bodiless realms? A human thought, some mere idea, or figment of imagination, as insignificant as a grain of sand or a single atom, floating in space and time which might become a thought bubble of tomorrow.

Maybe only a split of a second was I in that realm. The mind can be a funny thing. The conscious reality that we cling to in this waking life is tenuous, that stuff we take for granted in our pitiful drop-in-the-bucket existences. The merry-go-round soup bowl we live in.

I'd never really understood it so clearly until now. I could still not describe it, since it was so abstract and timelessly alien as time itself—and so frightening. The expanse so enormous that it brought to light in chilling clarity how puny the individual awareness truly is.

In a blur, I came back.

"Wha—"

"Easy, Jet Rusco."

I came back into my body, sucking in a rasping breath. Mong sat before me, grinning at me like a grim reaper. "How did you like your little ride?"

"What the—fuck are you?"

"I am the angel of death."

"You're a psycho-demon."

"I was already well-versed in the forbidden arts before you were sucking on your mamma's teats." Mong's jaw worked in satisfaction. He blew air through his nostrils. "I had hopes for you. But it's time for you to die. Maybe then you'll understand the truth of it all." He nodded to Balt and had him plunk me on my ass and hold me steady.

He stripped off my monk's robe to the waist. With my hands lashed behind my back, he stepped behind me, brandishing a glinting bowie knife. Without preamble, he cut deep into the muscles of my back.

I howled with pure agony. He took no notice of my squeals. He merely threaded leather cord into my slit flesh and looped the strips round my chest, tossing their ends up over the high beams above. As an afterthought, he wound my ripped robe around my back to contain the flesh and blood before he pulled me up like a stuck calf with his massive strength.

Regrettably I came to know the reason for those ropes now hanging in front of his obscene tanks.

Dangling and twirling like a slaughtered buck, I gasped and gurgled. How my flesh could withstand the pressure, I did not know. Perhaps a testament to Mong's setting of knot and cord, looping rawhide around my chest to take off some of the pressure.

He stared at me in a mode of abstract curiosity, as an ever inquisitive scientist would who wonders how his lab experiment is faring. Not with eyes of sympathy, but of detached interest. How long could Jet Rusco handle the pain? How long before Jet Rusco wailed, shit his pants, cracked, gibbered like a lunatic, convulsed, cried? Most curious of all was Mong in seeing where my edges lay, the thresholds of reason before the other world of lunacy and death.

"Surrender to pain, Jet Rusco," he murmured. "'Tis the only way to survive. Fighting will only get you deeper in the mire."

"F-Fuck you, you shit fucking bastard sadist," I spat out between my gritted teeth, the pain rising to indescribable levels. I closed my eyes. Utter agony had my eyes rolling backward in their sockets like a crazed yogi, hoping that a split second's death would release me from this flesh-tearing, mind-numbing pain.

But death would not take me. Mong knew it as he knew his brutish handiwork and he was master of torture.

That figure of doom withdrew from my flickering, darkening vision, but my sense of reason knew a monster was still nearby. Next came Zan's turn, the recruit who had shriveled to a husk, shrunken to a worm in some crab shell of fear. He thrashed and whimpered but there was no getting away from Mong's bestial justice that would envelop Zan in seconds. In less than five minutes, we were like two stuck hogs twirling slowly and gently from our fishhook, rawhide lariats in Mong's special house of horrors.

Through pain-streaked eyes I could make out the clear glass tanks below us. The trapped insects inside looked like black-tarred puppets, much different from this vantage: toy specimens out of a cartoon lab. So did Blest's blond-matted head appear like a comical jack-o-lantern as he floated in his pale brine a dozen or so yards away.

Mong loosed a moody sigh. "Let me tell you the story of my mentor, Rusco. He was Zastras, a cruel man and practical man, with many innovations. We had a particularly grueling time one fine day in late summer. I remember how he strung five initiates up, one by one, dangling from rawhide straps like yours from the stout branches of certain cypress trees.

"I was one of them. A time like no other—brimstone and fire stretched across a limitless fire plain; pain and pleasure mixed as one in a long silent continuum. Suspended over the fire one minute, then dunked in ice-cold water the next. Some of us he dunked in pools of fire weed; others, he incited flesh-nibbling fish to bite at our toes.

"You can see I am much less imaginative than Zastras. I saw men with ankles bared to the bone. Zastras was a dark humorist of his time, assuring that his victim would live, that the skin would grow back. Strung up there like beasts, we would believe anything.

"Oh, Zastras was a funny man! One of the old guard. There will never be another like him, rest his cursed, black-hearted soul. Lucky I have not so macabre an imagination, Jet Rusco. Still, you will beg me to stop, you too, Zan. Both of you will beg, and I will smile and watch you squirm like maggots."

Mong burned loathsome incenses, clouds of sickly sweet vapors, rank as mushrooms from some jungle hell, and his doped up drummer beat those skins with ever fiercer force and wilder intent while the Star Lord stood by, nodding with much toe-tapping and finger-snapping as the fumes of myrrh and absinthe, cinnamon and sage struck my nostrils in a vague fury of madness during my time of torture.

Cold water dripped on my brow now from a tap he had installed high above. He lit a crackling fire underneath my toes. Both sensations were eerily approaching the threshold of pleasure now. One counterpoint to the edges of sensory overload of the other.

Reaching such places, he tapped new regions that the pain-pleasure sensors could not reach. All the while his mellifluous voice swirled in my hazed brain, spewing out dime-store philosophies, cheap, preachy aphorisms, endless lessons, patronizing, hackneyed teachings, moralizations, sermons, which hovered on the edge of my consciousness.

Every sin I'd committed roared back to me in full technicolor during those moments of pain. I screamed them aloud in a hoarse voice, as did Zan, who was half dead while Mong nodded, explaining in quiet tones that this was perfectly normal.

He gave a snorting sigh and rubbed his temples in thought. "I will leave you two for some time. But I will return to record your progress. My interest waxes high in this affair. I want you to reflect on a basic point. What drives you? What is your purpose in this universe? To what end will you go to fulfill your lives? Men and women have pondered these basic questions since the beginning of time, when we rose from the lower species and became masters of the planets. Still, we have no more clue of an answer to these questions than when we rutted in primitive caves as common beasts. Questions perhaps much too abstract, Jet Rusco, considering the direness of your current situation. At a base level, you'd be thinking, when do I get cut down from here? When do I take some regen or narcotic to dull the heart-ripping pain? But life is pain, Jet Rusco and Zan Vulder. When do we ever take time to contemplate these grand questions? Maybe in our darkest dreams and most intimate moments of pain. I leave you with these questions."

Mong's words echoed in my beleaguered brain. The pain had gone far beyond any sane man's threshold and yet we hung there like freshly slaughtered deer, our bodies numb. I saw a giant man-insect in the form of Mong leave us in that godless torture chamber, a place of windless darkness that had no windows showing vistas to skies or stars. My vision blurred and before I lost consciousness, I cursed Mong and all his breed of *meslars* and monkey-guards to eternity, cursed them to suffer the worst hell that this universe could offer.

Chapter 23

Light years later I remember strong hands prodding my body and testing me to see if I were still alive. Those hands stopped my slow twirl around magnetic north. A fatherly figure with compassion in his eyes peered into mine while capable hands lifted me from my swinging perch and unlashed the hated leather from my pierced back. Those same hands cradled me as if I were a baby, popped off the top of the nearby empty tank and let me fall into the chill green water with a plunk. Struck dumb, I floated there for some time, unable to move my arms hardly an inch, and my body a wall of stiff rubber while an unfathomable pain racked the mutilated flesh of my back. Those hands pushed my head gently under the pale green water while I choked, struggling weakly, like some limp shrimp beached on a lonely shore. My lungs filled with water. Muscles spasmed as all muscles do when faced with perilous conditions, or in my case, death. My legs and weakened arms thrashed, struggling to raise my head above water and gulp life-giving air. But the arms of that impossibly tall figure held me firm and with his fatherly strength and ever compassionate sense, drowned his deformed child with no future.

Twice I died on that day. Jet Rusco, twice deceased.

I hung there suspended like a jellyfish, or some unlucky crustacean in the sinister water. It was eerie, but magical. The numbing pain that had once burned my body like a firebrand subsided to a dull ache, then to a warm tingle, some soothing balm of long-lost techno-science. A background elixir of warmth and massage. I was on a blessed Myscol trip!—to the far stars!

My eyes flickered open. I looked out upon a dim panorama of opaque filminess, blurred shapes, distorted distances, much different from when I came in. Through eyes not my own, it appeared a grainy world out there. The Star Lord stood idly by as he watched me with detached interest, as a father does his child caught with his hand in the cookie jar, as if nothing could be more natural than watching a child drowning in alien brine.

The water on my lips tasted terrible, salty and fermented, a peculiar rancidity, impossible to quantify. I saw my arms float up. My hands looked as if they had starfish-like fingers. That's because they were broken. The splint had come off, the wrappings peeled off long ago. My fingers were not as crooked as they'd been on entering the tank. Knob-knuckled, yes, like some old codger with severe arthritis. But remarkably whole. I could move them, barely. The water seemed to act as a paralysis agent, making my nerves sluggish and unresponsive. But I could think, and the mind of old JR was as active as before.

What to think? Well, a million things. Dwell on the past. Be stuck in a cage of the mind forever. Remember those medicine teachers of Mong's somewhere back in the pagoda babbling on about the endless chatter of mind when one first sits down to meditate? I was a drowned man floating, but alive. A punishment worse than death.

All sorts of random items flitted across the landscape of my mind as I stared out from behind the glass.

What were these plant tendrils wrapped so tenaciously about Blest's leg? What was that bulb that hatched the flying cricket? The thing that killed the Skugs and Mong's mercs.

The alien plants must have given birth to the flying things—the dragonfly and the eel-lizard, then the flying cricket. How? A poignant mystery. I shuddered at the implication, thinking again of the gross leaf twined about Blest's leg. The poor sod must be going out of his mind.

I closed my eyes. Shielded whatever remained of JR from the demons that would eventually take him. I let my mind travel inward, like those insistent monks had instructed me back in the prayer meetings. I flashed back on old memories, truths, lies, to past lives. Or were they past lives? Or just tricks of the imagination? The images, compelling enough, entailed fighting enemies with swords and gunpowder and electric wands then R4s, enemies so cruel and detestable that they threatened to bring down the empire. One minute I was a hero, then a broken-legged soldier, next a traitor, then some nameless beggar wandering the ghettos, slumming for scraps in back alleys. Was that this life, or a previous one? All a blur. My lingering dream morphed into the boy wanting to be a rocket scientist and save the world, then it flickered out like a candle flame to something else. The bombs of the warmongers fell ravaging my home planet, leaving thousands dead, and the camps and the flight of madness occurring afterward, a nightmare like any aftermath of war, but it all started to make sense. I saw the dance and drama of my life multiplied a million times over in the lives of countless others. Just little puffballs of existence flashing in and out of time, with little significance to speak of in the overall picture.

The quintessence of me was but a tiny drop of water dribbling down on the vast leaf of time. Dripping down into an immeasurable pool of life, to be drawn out, consumed, reborn, recycled into some new matter and new phenomenon. Humbling to see this, and yet disturbing to catch a glimpse of what could be reality.

And I thought and I dreamed and I brooded in the green liquid as the days and the weeks drifted by.

Out of my suspended animation I sprang up in a groggy rush. The sounds of murmuring voices and the sensation of touch drifted nearby. I flexed my hand. The fingers moved with full power. No more did my knitted flesh or my bent fingers throb. As the water had the power to nourish the occupants in the tanks, so could it heal flesh and broken bones. As long as the individual wasn't dead, the liquid could perform the miraculous.

I felt rough sandpaper hands slapping at my moist cheeks. Words struggled to come to my nerveless lips.

"Steady does it," said the figure who pushed finger to my lip. "Well, Jet Rusco, how do you feel after your first rebirth?"

I stammered.

"It will take some minutes to readjust. It won't do to talk. Look at Zan over there. Comatose. Afraid the poor lad couldn't cope with his suspension. Alas," Mong sighed. "I will have to throw the wretch back in the tank for a while to regain his wits."

"Wha—" I sputtered, my lungs heaving with the effort of taking breaths of life-giving air.

"You have questions, I know. We will repeat this exercise, until you are cured of your insatiable desire to defy me. Blest is up next on the ropes. Each of you will take turns in the Mentera bathtub. The liquid heals all wounds, no matter how grievous. We will start the process all over again, then the pain will run deeper. Much deeper. Treat it as my gift to bring you to a level of awareness higher than what you have already attained. It is written in the Budo scriptures that enlightenment can come through pain."

"F-Fuck you, Mong," I croaked. "You rude fucking sadist. I s-shit down your throat and piss on your scriptures."

The Star Lord sighed. "Blasphemy. Disrespect for the wise ones. Very bad. Behavior as this demands cleansing." He signaled to Balt.

The fucker lieutenant grabbed me up like a sack of potatoes and tossed me back in the tank, making sure my head was sufficiently underwater for enough time. I struggled, screaming bubbles from my lips. No use. They drowned me, again.

Whole days passed in snail-crawling increments. The prolonged immersion had me fading in and out into weird and grotesque, infathomable worlds.

Again I contemplated the truth of the universe in an alien tank, an irony that did not escape me. For all purposes, I should be dead, physically and spiritually. Then it hit me...as that voice from deep within the psyche broke through the filmy layers of encroaching darkness and spoke in an echoing blur:

The Star Lord will destroy this universe. Such is the duty of an angel of death. He is a cancer that must be excised, hit in the most vulnerable place—through his adulation of the crickets. Your life's purpose is not to sit encaged in brine, Jet Rusco. Do you not see it? Do you wish to suffer torture indefinitely like a chained beast? You must kill him. You must kill deftly. By striking at the core, the weakest link...

I'd come to believe Mong was invincible, but the monster had a weak chink in his armor, as did anyone else. It was those damn bugs. Mong worshiped them. They had no love for him. Why should they? I'd seen the evil glint in their eyes when he came sidling into the room and their brooding red glares trained on him. If I could escape, loose those creatures upon the compound, maybe there'd be a chance...But how, Rusco? You're in a tank with half your back ripped open.

All those ruined worlds out there, all the people crying for emancipation from slavery, death—can you help them?

So the devil sat on my shoulder, whispered in my ear. *You have to take a stand.* So drenched in cynicism I'd been for so many years, shooting my mouth off and myself in the foot with all my breezy sarcasm and my clowning around, I hadn't seen it. I thought being a rocket engineer was my role of roles. A hustler not long after? Scammer? Gangster? Big man with the big ship?

Your purpose lies before you, Jet Rusco.

Even if it kills me?

You're already dead. Twice remember?

But I'm in a tank.

So, get out of a tank.

And there was a flash, a glimpse, of some reckoning between me and Mong, a final showdown, just me and him on a distant planet. The details were crystal clear. My mind, lucid as a ten megawatt bulb saw the rocks, boulders, the fields and the peasants hoeing their onions and yams in the fields, eking out a meager existence off the impossibly arid land. These past lives, these future lives, whatever they were, they were a hell of a trip. I'd stick to Myscol if I could.

So, floated to the surface, one of those crazy visions and conversations one has with his alter self, which make a lot of sense in a storybook fantasy but not in real life.

The tanks, the failures, the fuckups, the slits in my back—all these were the universe's way of forcing me to see reason, to do my duty, and fulfill my life's purpose. The voice spoke again. What are you, a crazy bastard? Yes. But the path burned clear as a lighthouse's beacon before me.

I'd have to bring down Mong if it was the last thing I did.

Chapter 24

I must have floated there a lab rat for hours, days. Who knew in this artificial, freaked-out world?

When Balt next removed me from my tank, Blest was out of his watery prison. He sat trussed like a wet hog, his back tied to a square wooden post. Zan twirled in my place hung from the beams, his shaved head lolling on his chest.

"Time to dry for a bit," Mong remarked, rubbing his chin in earnest thought. He motioned to Balt. "See that they're taken care of. I have tasks that require attention offworld. Blest's punishment will be less severe than Rusco's, so he'll need time to dry out some more."

Blest's leg had turned a deep green from shin down, a source of amusement for Mong. He studied the strange creature, the flap of leaf wrapped around Blest's shin and tsked his tongue. "Old Greenie seems to be still latched on for good, Blest. Aren't you a lucky one? He's taken a liking to you. Pretty soon we'll have to start calling you Mr. Greenfoot, or 'Jolly Green Giant'. Or how about Plant Toe?"

Blest moaned.

Balt gave a chortling laugh.

"Let's leave our sleeping beauties for the time being, Balt. They need to catch up on some well-needed rest."

Before Mong left, he turned and raised his hand. As I blinked, thinking to hear a sound behind me, he whacked me in the solar plexus again, hard with the flat of his palm, that magical palm that sent me spinning into a world of oblivion. Some new universe, some new dimension of pain, horror, and illumination.

Maybe it was angels I saw, or consummate devils. Winged beings, half anthropoid, half alien, with voices croaking like frogs, breathing sighs of wind, whispering horror in my ears. They hissed macabre tales of the universes we know not of, both unseen and the seen. I protested in a voiceless murmur, wishing their voices would leave my mind, but they did not. Only laughed and carried me far away to realms unheard of, places beyond the sphere of time and space that defined the witchery of the amalgo. Call me a liar, Jet Rusco, but this was real! Perhaps it was the same place where the filthy locusts built their diseased technology. I wished for no reminder of that terrifying world, that other world that Mong brought me to again and again.

I died another time, and I knew the power of Mong's devils. His depraved gods. And I wished to hell I hadn't.

   * * *

My waterlogged brain woke again, struggling to drive sense back into the flaccid cells. Mong and his minion were gone. Only Blest and Zan remained where I'd last seen them. I guessed this would be one of the last times we would all be together in any conversable ring, so we'd have to take full advantage of the situation.

I hissed at Blest who lolled about eight feet away. "Pst…can you hear me, Blest? Are you still conscious?"

He moaned. "Go away whoever you are…"

"Blest, dammit!" I cried. "Look at me."

He stirred. His eyes blinked and gained focus. "Oh, Rusco. I must have died and gone to heaven. It's you. Are we back in Bantam yet?"

"*Bantam?*—you idiot. The ship's dead. Remember?"

"Oh, right. Where are we then? Oh, I'd better not ask. Why are you tied up like that? Wait, I'm tied up too." He shook his head, struggling to make sense of the physical evidence, as if he were an amnesiac, his eyes goggling every which way.

I gave a wretched sigh.

"Rusco, you wouldn't believe it," Blest said in an excited cackle. "The funniest, damnedest memory. Me and my buddy Rog were out cruising at Pegri's tavern. We'd just come off training shift, wanted to let loose, hit the pubs, and we had this bet, see who could get laid first...old Rog, braggartly bastard sicced himself on this quiet, solemn-type sitting in the dimness o'er by the window. Real killer broad. Turns out she was a robot, can you believe it—"

"Shut the fuck up! You're rambling, Blest! Focus! Can you reach your bonds? Twiddle them with your fingers?"

"Don't rightly think I can, Jet. Why, you want a hand job? Ha ha."

"Would you knock of the hillbilly shit?" I gave a sigh of impatience.

Blest started to slip back into his delirium. Drool dripped from his lips. His head lolled.

"Snap out of it! For Christ sake, Blest. No time to die yet."

"Wh-what?" he grunted. "Go away. Fuck off, Jet, I want to sleep."

"Plenty of time to sleep in your damn tank, dumbo. Listen to me—"

"I told you to bug the fuck off, Rusco."

"Listen!" In a fit of sudden anger I focused the brunt of my frustration at him and there came a sudden zing, like an instrument popping strings. Blest's head jerked back then he snapped alert with a sharp cry. "What the hell was that? Rusco, you don't have to get sore. Stop chucking things my way."

As my eyes darted around, I was as startled as he. I shook my head. This chamber was booby-trapped, beyond a house of horrors.

I turned my focus toward Zan, who seem to have roused from his painful hangman's hell. He hung up in the rafters, dangling from the beam. "Zan, talk to me," I hissed.

As Zan twirled, his one skewed eye bulged my way, blasted me with a look of despair. "D-did I ever tell you how I made it to

Othwan, Jet?"

"Think you did."

"Nah, the real story." He winced and took bite-sized breaths as he hung from those cords knitted in his back. I empathized with such pain, like a pork loin dangling from a butcher's hook.

"We were on an attack ship. Mong ordered me to blast the small ship that my mother and father were escaping on."

I closed my eyes and looked away.

"Yeah, that bad, Rusco…Well, Mong—basically, he killed my family, my brother and sister. The man has means…technology, influence, black magic."

Zan was preaching to the choir. I'd witnessed too many bouts of Mong's black magic. But I needed to keep Zan talking, engaged in the present, if he were to be of any use, which at the moment, didn't look likely. "How'd you get that scar under your eye, Zan? What happened?"

Zan snorted, grimacing. "Mong's guards cut me to make an example of me."

"What'd they do that for?"

"I violated the bell rules."

"Really?"

"When the bell rings…we're all supposed to…assemble for teachings. I was a little slow."

"Got us all jumping like trained seals."

"Seems so." Zan's face curled in anguish. "What about you, Blest?" Zan croaked. "Seems you've dropped out of the—conversation. Nothing more to say about Rog and his sexy robot?"

"Forget Blest," I grunted. "He's out of—"

"Quiet. Someone's coming," Zan hissed.

There came a clinking at the door. Hinges creaked and Balt, the sick fuck, came in, carrying a large bowl, which might have held food.

"Dinner anyone?" Balt called, sauntering forth with a breezy chuckle. "Oh, I see you're occupied. I'll just leave these fine treats here on the bug tank. Fresh owl gizzards, chicken liver, raw snail.

Mmm-mmm. Whole bowl of it. Prepared raw for maximum protein."

"Why don't you try some yourself, Balt?" I suggested. "Mong's prayer circle always emphasizes sharing and goodwill."

"That's true and mighty kind of you, Rusco, but I'll pass on the victuals. My stomach's a little off today. I'll stop by for a little chat though."

"Mighty neighborly of you."

Balt frowned. "Those thongs look infected, Vulder. Think the skin on your back can handle it? Might rip off more of your shoulder."

"We're all getting used to it by now, Zan included," I broke in, hoping to cut Zan off and stop Balt from getting riled up.

Balt huffed out a grunt. "No fun here, Rusco, this is boring. Think I'll be on my way now. Good luck, kiddos."

He left, closing the portal behind him with a loud thud.

"Fucker." I pinched my eyes shut with a sigh. "Where were we?"

"Ready to die, Rusco, what else?" Zan gave a horrible groan. "Let's lay off the chatty Cathy stuff. I'm dying over here."

"Listen, we can defeat this Star Barf. We have to—"

"What? Scream a little louder?"

"Listen, Zan. Blest, you too. Dammit. Let's dig in our heels here. We can beat this fucker if we cooperate. But if we whine and grouse about it we're toast. There's three of us, plus these ugly bugs in the tanks, that makes five."

"Now you're—the one's sounding—like a lunatic," Zan croaked.

I gave a hiss of exasperation. "Blest, are you with me? Blest?"

Blest had slipped off into some lotus land. His head jerked up with a jolt.

"Rusco, I had the most brutal, fucked up dream."

"Another?"

"They come at me a mile a minute."

"Lucky you. Must be the fluid in the tanks."

"You think? This one was of me drowning in a swimming pool. Bugs—fishes—they all were nibbling at my toes, eyes, arms, legs, taking bites out of my ribs…except it was no dream, Rusco, it was real, and my buddy Rog and the rest of them were all bagged up in that tin can of a space capsule on a training mission. They'd crashed-landed. There was nothing whole left of them when the rescue unit came after they'd washed up on the shore, capsule and all, Rusco. In the middle of nowhere. Damn it, that really happened! Rusco, are you listening? Don't look at me like that. They all died in that crash. It's in the report. They found the ship crumpled up on Maelstrom's beach. Rog, Ven, Peri and Noose. Should have been me. Earlier when our ship was cracking up, we drew straws to see who'd live. I got the lucky straw, took the single chute, there was only one left after the explosion.

He shook and shivered like a man suffering from dengue fever.

"Not much left of Peri and Rog after they got eaten up by those fishes. They nibbled at them, man—those fishes ate them like corn meal! Damnedest thing. But here's the weirdest part. This time I was the one who got all chewed up and Peri was the one who escaped…as if the scene played a million times over in my head in every possible combination of survivors and losers." Blest convulsed again, and this time his eyes rolled back in his sockets, his mouth agape, showing white teeth and drool spilling down his chin.

I grimaced, remembering the glimpses of past-lives flashbacks during my own time in the tank, much less with Mong's whacks to my belly, and I didn't doubt that what Blest was saying was real. Each scenario a new alternate reality in some dimension somewhere. Blest's tragic tale was as close as I'd ever get to the real Blest and any clear understanding of his haunted past.

When Blest slipped off into unconsciousness, I heard the recurring moans and cries of a woman in a chamber somewhere down the line, possibly through an upper air vent. Perhaps they were Volia's or perhaps other pleasure victims of the Orpheum.

Chapter 25

Mong had gotten a tad more creative lately and rigged an interesting variation of the hook and hang punishment. This one had me hanging from my toes, with my back to a pole, strapped at the waist. He claimed it would make me smarter, in a crude way, all that blood flowing to my head, plus seeing the world upside down. Did a man a world of good, he said. A party bag of laughs, Mong was. Hadruk had done the tying, not Balk who was the designated rope man. One of the rawhide knots ultimately slipped while Mong was out on errands, the one on my big toe, which allowed me to thrash with one freed-up foot against the knots of the first.

A significant breakthrough. With that foot I scraped a hell of a lot of skin off the other toes in the process, but after a painful amount of cursing and grinding, I managed to get the other foot free.

So, I was swinging ass over end, trying to worm my way free with waist still tied to the post while Zan was cheering me on in his hoarse way, practically dying up there in his hangman's noose. While I was practically choking from being bent over double at the middle, my hips like a pivot with my spine still stuck to the pole. I did manage to squirm out of that hold with the extra leeway I had with my legs free.

I was squatting on the ground now like a pinched toad, panting, with only my arms bound behind my back. Not too bad for an old timer. I staggered up painfully, pushed my back to the post, rubbed the leather cords against the corner of the wood, all drenched in a feverish sweat, knowing that this would be the only chance I'd get to get the fuck out of this mess. Snap, snap. Enough friction to cut one of the cords then the other. Freedom!

Not too shabby. Some torn flesh, scraped toes and wrists, nothing I couldn't handle. My ears perked to a fumbling at the door. I ducked, swearing as the iron frame groaned inwards. I hobbled the best I could behind the nearest Mentera tank, dreading the proximity to that vampirish creature and hoped whoever was coming hadn't seen me.

It was Balt and his eyes flicked to the vacant post. Up came his rifle. "Rusco? Where are you? Come out, wherever you are." The torturer grinned, aimed his rifle at the posts, peering crosswise.

I clenched my prosthetic fist, trying to stay hidden behind the hunched form of the locust suspended in the tank. Whether I got shot up or I didn't, old Balt was in for a bit of rough and tumble.

This Redemption Hall went back quite a ways into darkness. I didn't know what was back there. Didn't want to find out either. That was Balt's business and his first guess as to where I'd fled. He probed the silence, squinting into the dim shadows with a bulldog's scowl on his face. "The more games we play here, Mr. Rusco, the more painful it gets for you. Big Mong's not here to protect your silly ass. He gave me full license to use excessive force should there be civil disobedience."

Good for you, Balt, you smug fucker. You can call 'civil disobedience' on me all you want. *It ain't over until the fat lady sings.* I came scuttling back like a land crab from behind Blest's tank, hoping to get closer to Zan who hung like a bug on flypaper.

Balt must have heard that scuffle of movement because he came beetling back like a scarab, clutching the end of his gun and using it as a club to take a big whack at me. He missed. I ducked the butt end of the rifle that came smashing full into Blest's tank.

The glass splintered and water spilled out in a tidal rush. A whole side of the tank fell outward and Blest came sloshing out on his knees, gasping, choking and spewing putrid green water out of his gullet.

Balt charged me with a deep-throated roar. His full weight caught me head on, and I grunted, bowled over, croaking, smacking my metal fist in his face, jamming fingers in his nose, his eyes. The man was not human to have a grappling force like that. Any other strike would have split a man's skull. I struggled with him. The man's ape strength was enough to make me crumple and I could feel my backbone starting to give. I saw Blest out of the corner of my eye, staggering woozily to his feet while I fought on with less and less hope.

"Kill him!" I wheezed. Blest suddenly came stumbling like a straw puppet with the feeding bowl clutched in a fist. He clocked Balt on the back of the head.

Balt grunted. I felt his grip slacken. It gave me time to get my fingers into his eyes again. He roared, grabbing my wrist. I chopped him in the throat. Blest smacked Balt again with the bowl just above the ear. Balt went raging maniac and charged Blest, rolling on him like a bear. The alien plant leaf which had up till this time been stable, suddenly unfurled, doubling in size, whipping out like a serpent. It latched onto Balt's midsection like a cincture, squeezing the breath out of him. He writhed and howled, clawing at the thing, only to get more wind sucked out of his lungs.

I kicked at his head. Blest stayed well back from the constricting force that had plagued him for so long. The sudden intrusion on its stable habitat had pushed the plant parasite to violence.

While Balt twisted and howled, I hissed out a vindictive laugh. "Never forgave you for busting up my fingers, Balt. Not too smug now are you, you fucking bitch-ape? What's that, can't hear you?" I ground my boot heel into his flailing hand, stepping on it so hard I heard it crunch. He grimaced in agony while struggling in the wet glass.

I motioned to Blest. "Here, help me drag this fuck over to the tanks." Zan watched the battle out of the corner of his eye in a groggy haze.

We dragged Balt by his heels, taking care not to touch the alien plant. Under no circumstance did I want it to leapfrog to either of us. We upended Balt into the tank formerly occupied by me. He sputtered foul brine and splashed like a fish but he slipped under water, having no more will to fight, clutching feebly at the constricting leaf robbing him of further strength. Before the lieutenant sank to the bottom, his lungs filled with water and he stared out of his glassy cage with lips parted in an O like one of those black bugs in the vessel beside him. Oh, how Balt glared out from behind that glass! If I could only snapshot that scene.

We crouched on our haunches, panting. I reached over and patted Blest on the back. "Good work, friend. You came through as I knew you would. We were always a team."

Blest babbled an incoherent word. "This is fucking madness, Rusco. Where are we?"

I slapped him on the back. "Madness or not, seems your vine critter came in handy after all."

I gathered up my boots, then snatched up Balt's weapon, gripping it in a sweaty palm with an air of triumph. There'd be some serious payback for old Mong now.

Blest stared at me with suspicion glinting in his eyes then at Balt's twitching form in the tank. "Why put him in there? Let's kill the fucker and get out of here." He grimaced as Balt convulsed in his watery prison.

"He's already dead, Blest. No way to change that."

"Don't like him swimming in there, Rusco. He ain't dead, and you know it."

"I know what you're thinking. Let's not mess with things that aren't broken."

Blest shivered, as if recalling an odious memory of his own tank experience. "That damn plant thing constricted me like a bitch, Rusco. The green devil water gave it more strength."

"Yeah, well be thankful you're out of there and rid of it now."

"For how long?" He started to shake like a recovering Myscol addict and I had to grab his shoulders and shake him like a wet blanket and slap his cheeks a few times.

"Snap out of it! We have to move, Blest. First, let's gather up Zan. He looks to be in a bad way."

We cut him down from his swinging post, then unwound the leather from his wrists and got the groaning man up onto his feet. His back was mangled up, sure, nothing we could do there. But Mong had spared him the usual agony of extra deep slits this last time. Zan swayed on his feet, moaning, looking around in confused horror.

"Amp up your game, Zan," I said. "We've got a journey to make." I shook him as I had Blest. Seemed it helped. Zan wasn't in great shape. I considered dropping him in one of the spare tanks to heal him up better but I grimaced at the idea. No time, and even if I could hold him by down like a rat in that witch water, by the look in his eyes, I knew he'd not go in easily.

"Steady him, Blest. I've a little last minute business to take care of."

"Like what?"

Over to the remaining tanks I hobbled and took the butt end of my rifle in a firm hand. With all my force, I smashed the nearest Mentera tank.

Blest's eyes bugged out in horror as the glass cracked and green fluid trickled down the side. "Are you fucking insane?"

"Chip and Chong are inseparable," I declared. "We separate these bitches and we create a whole new dynamic, don't we? It'll sharpen up our old friend Mong. He seems to be a big fan of trials and tests." I leaned in and smashed the glass again with triumph and rage.

"What about us?" Blest croaked. "You plan on getting snipped by their claws?"

"I'm not messing around here any more."

"Easy for you to say, Rusco, you're—"

The next strike hit the cracked glass square on and the locust came spilling out in a spray of green water and glass. The thing rolled then coiled up in a dense, black heap. It lay there sprawled, its antennae quivering before the broken tank. Then the dwarf wings fluttered in a burst of movement. The power of flight seemed lost over the passing ages. It scootched up on its hind legs into a beetle-like crouch, making weird clicking noises with its mandibles.

Blest recoiled. Zan's mouth moved in a hoarse scream.

"Let's get the fuck out of here," I cried, "before Chip starts to get antsy."

We hobbled like three broken musketeers to the exit.

On the way, I caught a brief glimpse of the glass case on the altar, the one that housed Fol's alien bulb. A brief hesitation had me wincing before I smashed the glass case and snatched up the bulb, the same that Follee had taken up on a whim from Cyber station.

"What are you planning to do with that?" croaked Blest.

"Stuff it up your ass, what do you think?"

"Rusco, these things are fucking dangerous."

"Exactly. Now move."

We thrust our shoulders to the door. Nothing. Tight as a spinster's crotch. Locked. Why wouldn't it be?

Blest sighed, blowing spittle past his dry lips. "You could have tested the door before you woke up Chip."

"Hindsight, Blest, hindsight. The key must be in Balt's purse. Guess that's what his firearm is for." I lifted the gun barrel.

"But the noise'll—"

I blasted the fuck out of the mechanism before Blest could argue. The door sagged open.

"There, see? Now shut up or I'll put you back in the tank with Balt. Everything'll work out." I grinned in satisfaction as I used the rifle to widen the gap to reveal a dim-lit hallway. Broad marble tiles sheened in the sconce light. Zan huffed out a laugh then hissed a breath between his gap-teeth.

I nudged the others out into the deserted hall. Thank Mong's ugly gods there were no guards. I risked a glance backward and saw our little bug friend, Chip, righting itself, staggering over to his cricket buddy in the nearby tank in a bent-legged crouch.

Time to bug out from this crib.

Chapter 26

Shadows crawled where I motioned the others down the temple hall. Fewer wall sconces lit the broad passageway. Only portraits of Mong and his warriors and ancient warlords adorned the walls. A small air fan chugged away. I started to move toward the exit then recalled a face devoid of hope and a woman's legs splayed over silk cushions. I halted, mumbled a curse, and backtracked.

"Where you going now?" croaked Blest. "The exit to this shithole is back that way, isn't it?" He stared around grimly then rolled his eyes. "Oh, Rusco, you've got to be kidding? Don't you get enough skin from Wren?"

Blest and Mong had me pegged, yes, I was a stupid, chivalrous sucker. My true colors coming out. "More than enough skin, Blest. But for now, move."

He flung off my arm. "Who the fuck are you to give me orders?"

Maybe I should have pistol-whipped Blest for his insolence long ago or left him on Gainor. My brain wasn't totally sharp-edged this moment, nor was I the greatest tactician. Too many rival emotions, desperate plans and hopes, crossed signals. Too many damn things that could go wrong. Good to see that Blest was returning to his normal obnoxious self. But dammit, we had one chance at freedom and seeing blue skies again! I didn't want to blow it or lie awake at night, thinking, well, Jet, if you had only tried to save the noble lady who had the guts to stand up to Mong, instead of scurrying off like some damned coward with tail tucked between his legs intent on saving your own skin…

I heard the staccato rap of gunshots ahead.

"Down!" I cried.

The roar of ship engines surfaced above, then sounds of explosions rocking the temple's massive roof.

"What the fuck?" Blest stared white-eyed at the ceiling. "Mong got a little fireworks celebration for us?"

"No, those are fareons," rasped Zan. "Attack ships."

"Maybe Mong's got a little training exercise then in motion?" I mused.

Something smashed into the roof and the whole temple shook down to its foundation.

"Maybe he's made himself a few enemies?"

"Come on!" I squawked. "No better time than now to get out of here."

Commotion reigned up ahead. Three figures came running toward us, rifles in hand. Two trailing—youngbloods. They cast tense glances over their shoulders, at the *meslars* who pursued them. I halted, Balt's confiscated weapon trained, reluctant to fire on them.

Good thing I didn't. The foremost, a tall, shadowy figure loped up out of the dimness, moving like an agile cat. I recognized her at once. My God…my heart leapt. Could it be?

It is you, you glorious sight for sore eyes.

She turned and aimed her R4. Mong's *meslars* came waving truncheons at the three. They crouched and spat gunfire back at them. Two fell. One of the fanatical survivors kept running with truncheon raised. She blasted him to shit.

Wren tossed me a better rifle. "You look cute in bald, Russy. But you're harder to find than a beetle in a barnyard."

My jaw dropped. Not the grim affirmation one'd expect, but the lean figure was a balm to my beleaguered spirit. "Good one, Wren." I rushed over and gave her a fierce embrace.

"No time for kisses, Rus. These temple laymen are all lambs but

Mong's hard-boys are out, crawling all over this place with guns."

I motioned them forward. "Back down the hall. How'd you find out where we were?"

"I asked the hired help, nicely."

"Yeah, I'll bet."

"They're still picking their teeth up off the ground," said one of the youngbloods, a curly haired gunman garbed in grey khakis and kevlar.

I gave a curt nod. The short-barreled R6 I'd taken from Balt I tossed to Blest.

I made a signal to move on with quicker speed. Wren blinked, indicating the exit was back the other way. Blest just sighed and shook his head. Knowing time was short, I herded the others on, urging them to silence. The corridor curved in a bow around the back of the temple. Stairwells led to lower levels. I bared teeth at those places, wondering how many more torture chambers Mong kept in this ill-begotten place.

We crept down the hushed halls, Wren, Blest and the others at my heels. A vengeful leer was carved on my face as we halted before the iron-bound door worked with ornate inscriptions of naked bodies plunged in orgiastic positions. I gave a quick nod. We blew the mechanism and burst through, our guns hefted. The place appeared deserted, but through the thick billows of reeking incense, I perceived goblets of stale wine and ale lying strewn all over the marble floor amidst the decorative fountains. I caught a shiver of movement in the back. Cushions and embroidered blankets sprawled on plush divans; heads turned at our approach and naked bodies twisted.

Amid the rank haze, I stared and found her spread-eagled under a drunken captain whose croak rose to a bull's roar of defiance.

The naked, struggling figure underneath him kneed him in the groin. The man groaned, one hand groping for his weapon. Wren opened fire and he fell in a rapidly-spreading pool of blood.

Frenzied shrieks echoed about the stone chamber. Several of the dazed women rolled off their couches, uncertain what to do. Volia staggered up, pulling a fleece cover around her half-naked, olive-skinned body. She looked broken in some indefinable way, but I glimpsed a defiance still burning in her hazel eyes and a growing contempt for her captors and a raging desire for vengeance. I shuddered to think what those animals had done to her in here.

I moved forward to gather her up, snatching up a long fur coat draped on the side of a couch.

"Who's she?" grunted Wren, motioning her gun. One of your girlfriends?"

"It's Lady Volia—"

"Leader of the Melinar," Volia croaked. She coughed, staggered up to her full height, fumbling to accept the garment in my hands. She leaned heavily on me and I caught the musky smell of sweat and sex. She wrapped the black-furred garment tighter, hugging the trim contours of her body, the smooth round of hip and curve of breast I'd glimpsed earlier. She was half drugged with something, still zoned on local poppy or some drug no doubt. Probably the least of what Mong had forced on her. Her eyes stared funny, all glassy.

Wren seemed to pause. "Your people are here, Volia, trying to rescue you."

She nodded, gave a weak acknowledgement.

"What of these others?" Wren motioned to the scattered few in this smoke-hazed, degenerate orgy grounds.

A half dozen other women shied away from us. The riddled corpse spooked them and had them cowering back against the wall in even greater fear. "If you want to come with us, hurry your asses!" Wren called in a crisp, no-nonsense voice.

None of them responded, only quivered in doubt and fear, retreating to their shadowy corners.

"Broken as whipped dogs." I shrugged in resignation. They were too far gone, too brainwashed and terrorized by Mong's sadistic abuse. It was sad. I took a few halting steps toward the exit.

Blest's moon-face blinked; he started to shiver again, still prey to convulsions.

"Blest, snap out of it." I slapped him then gave him a reassuring pat on the back. "We have killing to do."

"Yeah." He shook off whatever was buzzing through him and took a firmer grip on his R6. Zan was doing better, though he was looking terrible. Pale-faced, bloodshot eyes, jittery hands.

Wren looked the epitome of health. Ready to take on a small army.

I shuddered to think what I looked like. Probably a ragged scarecrow with a shit-eating grin pasted on his gaunt-ugly face. I rolled my eyes. Quit mucking around, Rusco. You auditioning for a beauty pageant here? A second's daydreaming and it's graveyard time for you.

Another half-baked sot sprang to life from under a blanket on a nearby divan. His hands clawed for me. I kicked him in the gut, whacked him with the butt end of my gun as the snarl died on his lips and he fell in a soundless heap.

I stepped over the body and motioned to Zan. "Forgot to make the introductions. Wren—meet Zan. Zan, Wren."

Wren waved her gun at the two young recruits. "These ugly mutts are Voj and Grild." The whites of their eyes showed against camo-blackened faces, matching toothy grins.

Zan shook his head in confusion. "Rusco, who are these guys? What gives?"

"This is my swat team, can't you see? If you want out of this prison, follow her lead."

Zan gave a low whistle. "You've got friends in very high places. Or some guardian angels protecting you."

"I followed Mong's meditations, remember?"

"What's our plan?" Blest growled, facing Wren.

"Get to the ship," she said. "Noss is out there waiting for us. I told him to hide the ship not far away, on the other side of the river."

"Good," I said. "What is it, *Alastar*?"

"No, a new one."

I shook my head in wonder and could have laughed for joy. "Wren, I applaud your resource. Good play. Can you reach Noss?"

"Of course." She tapped her invisible earset. "All on a safe channel."

"A bold move, considering Mong's ruthlessness."

"It was the only opportunity we had. Paid some mega yols out of your drug money for secret intelligence. I'd been watching Othwan like a hawk for weeks, then I saw the Vendecki move in. They must have used some force field to penetrate Mong's defenses and used it to repel the host."

"Heard them surge in," I mumbled. "Sounded just like Mong's bat fighters making a stealth swoop on a defenseless world."

"The Vendecki can't hold these brutes off forever. We'd better hurry."

In that moment I realized the fortuity of Wren's presence and loved her all the more for it. The gal was saving my ass again. All of our asses. She'd been watching the planet. Liquidated the assets to buy and equip a ship and track down Mong's movements. The Vendecki strike had been a bonus, providing the perfect cover to move in. Probably by trying to spring Volia, they'd gotten neck deep in Mong's murderous warships. I hoped they'd stay alive long enough for us to get to our new ship.

We slunk with speed down the hall.

The sound of sudden bootfall thundered behind us. I swore. Angry voices, shouts of doom followed. Somebody must have gotten wind of the expo of carnage back at the Orpheum. I turned to level fire at the pursuing figures, a half dozen or more.

"Rusco!" I felt a sharp tug at my arm. Wren.

From up ahead, two ghastly shapes scuttled straight for us. Anthracite figures out of a ghoul's nightmare. *Chip and Chong.* I almost shat my pants. Wren raised her gun to blast them to atoms. I elbowed her gun wide.

"What did you do that for?"

I pulled her off to the side and we hugged the wall. Blest, half out his wits, lifted his trembling rifle.

I slapped his gun away. "Don't kill them!" I barked. The two locusts scuttled forth on their hind legs, antennae twitching, but as anticipated, they fled past us as if having a definite mission in mind. I could see in their red glinting eyes the malice and vindictive wrath, armed with centuries of old animosity for whatever the fuck else. The ancient memories that brewed behind those insectoid skulls, could not be known. They were infathomable.

"Let them face Mong's guard," I hissed.

"Why, they're—"

A crunch of bone precluded words. The two black shapes pounced on a defenseless *meslar* armed with a truncheon.

The first locust's strike was lightning fast. Lashing out a slimy appendage, it hooked the man while its partner snapped off the man's arm at the elbow. Another pincer reached for the man's jugular. The victim gave a blood-curdling shriek as his life blood spurted on the marble floor.

The creatures sped away on their hind legs, heading toward the Orpheum and the place where I remember Mong kept the amalgamators…almost as though they were drawn to a homing beacon like moths.

I had to turn my head away as more crunching sounds came drifting back to the tune of men's screams and hoarse wails of agony and terror.

The insects scuttled on, leaving a trail of dead in their wake. Feisty and efficient devils, I thought.

"What are they?" hissed Grild.

"Come on!" I rasped. "Let's get the fuck out of here before those bugs decide to beetle back and bring a horde after us." I waved my R4.

"Where did those things come from?" Wren called.

"You don't want to know, Wren, believe me."

Blest was too dissociated from pain to do anything but mumble doom and gloom. Volia, paralyzed with shock, was having trouble registering any of it. Zan had already inured himself to such unnatural violence, having seen and experienced enough grisliness to last a lifetime back in the Redemption hall.

Events were fast sliding out of control. I knew I had to get a grip on reality and get the fuck out of here.

No such luck. Fierce shouts issued from down the hall—Mong's men, perhaps even Mong himself. The heavy tread of clopping boots and running figures came to our ears. We were blocked in. Enemies in front, enemies behind. Too many to deal with, even with our guns. Some of us would die. Maybe most of us. I looked around in utter desperation. Where's your bag of tricks now, Rusco?

On a sudden inspiration, I shuttled Volia and Zan to a door and into a room, hoping to hell there was nothing lurking there to cut us to ribbons. Blest and the others loped behind; Wren brought up the rear.

Nothing. Nobody. Just a shrine room dedicated to some obscure god, one of Mong's pantheon of creepos.

We crouched in the murk, the whites of our eyes showing and our breaths held. The shadows were thick at the far end of the chamber. A lone, sputtering candle set on a low altar cast long and wavering shadows upon a grim warlord's face carved on the stone wall.

We passed precious minutes hunched in the dark, crouched like mice, trying to stay out of the cat's jaws. Weapons trained at the door, we prepared for violence. Blest tried to hiss out some unsolicited advice, but I waved him to silence. Too many bloody amateurs spilling ideas in the stew pot. Too many foes around us. I could hear harsh, enemy voices echoed from under the crack of the door. We couldn't hide here forever. Decision time. I was about to give the order to head out and let us take our chances in a mad scramble in the hall when I heard more voices and figures doubling back this way. I winced and waved the others back, though they huddled close at my shoulders. I stuck my ear to the door.

"The locusts, sir. They've escaped!"

"What do you mean, escaped?" Mong's voice rumbled in a throaty roar. "How the fuck did that happen?"

I heard the man groan then another groan. "There's more, sir. Balt's in a tank. Drowned."

There was a pause until Mong bawled, "Rusco! I'll kill that fucking bastard. Go, look for them."

Now the proverbial shit was about to hit the fan.

The sound of running feet echoed up then the sound of panting breath. Another harbinger of doom?

"They've killed six men, sir! With pincers and claws. One guard mauled but still alive, told a gruesome tale. They fight like demons. The Mentera. Hooks, claws, squirting venom from pointed teeth. The *meslars* died badly."

I opened the door a crack and saw Mong's eyes widen with fury.

"Find them," he hissed through gritted teeth. He flung out a hand and the wall sizzled as if acid had been thrown at it.

I scowled and pulled my head back. If those fiends could keep chopping up Mong's brigade, we might have a slim window of opportunity.

Staring back through the crack, though, I swallowed hard. This was a precarious situation. Multiple enemies. Nowhere safe to run.

Another voice panted and huffed in fear in the hall. It sounded like Verlioze, Mong's weapons master. "The Mentera have slipped back through the transporter tunnel, sir, the sacred amalgo."

Mong gave a bleat of rage. "Go in after them then. Get them back!"

His henchman swore. "Can't. The device's jammed. It's inoperable."

"Those fucking grasshoppers." Mong clenched a fist. "They must have shut off the amalgamator from the other end. Now we can't go in after them. Can't even visit that wondrous world again."

Another voice, sounding like Hadruk's, jeered. "Still think they are the greatest thing since sliced bread, Master Mong?"

I heard a slap as Mong backhanded him. Probably Hadruk.

Though I couldn't physically see Hadruk. "Shut up, you ignoramus. Until we know the Mentera did it purposely, we'll give them the benefit of the doubt. Maybe the device just jammed and it can be fixed."

The struck man sneered. "You're a bloody fool if you believe that, Mong. Hypnotized by this ancient bug cult of yours and this brotherhood of 'light'. You're losing it and you can't see it."

Mong pulled out his weapon and smacked Hadruk hard across the mouth, drawing blood. Hadruk grinned and jumped him. The security officer got a good grip on Mong's face, clawing at nose and lips, before Mong, with his bare hands, grabbed Hadruk by the throat. Hadruk sagged, struggling like an ape, but was no match for the Star Lord's unnatural strength. With the crushing brawn of ten men, Mong's augmented arm lifted him off his feet. There came a sudden crunch and ripping of flesh. Mong snapped the man's neck like a rotten branch and tossed the security officer's corpse aside. I winced. So much for Hadruk.

If those fiendish crickets could get one of those ships running…I balked at the thought.

Mong bellowed, "Don't stand there like a bunch of stuffed dummies, you fools! I want that amalgo fixed and I want Rusco brought to his knees. Find him and bring him to me. Someone will answer for this and die."

Verlioze licked his lips.

Mong gave a feral roar. "Now, you fucking idiots!" The Star Lord's orders rebounded off the stone and wood like the boom of a cannon.

The temple roof rocked to new blasts.

Mong looked up and he shook his head in frustration. "Leave the corpse," he spat. "Come with me. New plan. Those fools on defense are doing next to nothing to stop this inane attack. Let's make for the ships. We'll deal with the rest of this mess later."

The sound of echoing bootfall faded down the corridor.

We bolted out of the room, sidling in an opposite direction.

Hoping for a back exit, we threaded our way like thieves through the wide, dim-lit corridors. Far too many of us though for stealth.

But stealth wasn't necessary.

CHRIS TURNER

Chapter 27

We burst out of the doors in a shambling crouch, our guns on the ready. Out onto the temple grounds we poured, with Wren in the lead, the roar and whine of jet fighters overhead and the scurry of running feet and anxious shouts all about. The light was fading from Othwan's opalescent sky.

Enemy ships ranged the sky. How they had penetrated warlord Mong's security net was still beyond me. More tricks? More last minute secret tech?

Volia and Zan were having a hard time. They had no weapons. I stayed back to cover them. Wren instructed Voj and Grild to move ahead and act as front men, clearing the way. It was their chance to prove themselves.

They hopped from boulder to garden bush, keeping their bodies low, rifles aimed. They motioned us ahead; the coast was clear.

The Temple of Light smoked behind us, a thin chute of flames rising from its caved-in roof. Now a gaping hole smoked in its nearest side, the once-proud spires teetering on drunken angles.

The grounds in the vicinity of the hangar writhed to a beehive of activity. Men in khakis firing R6s. Ships roaring overhead. Vendecki skyslips, smaller Melinarian fighters buzzing by. I could see Mong and his men scurrying away in an opposite direction while the Warhawks were on the move ready to pick them up. One landed and as bombs dropped, lighting up the green in crimson fire, they dove for cover. Mong's plan to board was thwarted.

I still couldn't believe the Vendecki had slipped through Mong's defenses leaving them this unaware and exposed. Must have been one hell of a force field.

I draped an arm around Volia's shoulder, seeing the white, dazed look of confusion in her eyes. Like another dream, Rusco, no different than the one hanging from Mong's torture rope or floating in his Mentera tank...

We made it to the open green, a few hundred yards just shy of the charred prayer hall. That was as far as we'd get. I could see Mong's men were converging on us, coming out of the woodwork like termites. Doom stared us in the face. So, it had all been for naught. Wren screamed orders into the com. Maybe she couldn't hear over the roar of the destruction. Where the fuck was Noss?

The savage sweep of heavy engines blitzed the compound. Cone-like shapes and elliptical hulls of the rebels drew up and away while others landed air strikes.

A grenade clattered six feet away from us in front of a ruined fountain. Wren tackled Zan out of the way; I pulled Volia down behind a statue. Shrapnel webbed the immediate area; splatter hit the marble base behind which we crouched. The blast nearly took out our ear drums.

Vendecki and Melinarian ships roared across the sky, deafening us further. A fierce dance of death played before our eyes with pursuing Warhawks which numbered in the dozens. Selected rebel craft dropped paratroopers to extract Volia from the temple. What a colossal fuck up! Brave souls, those would-be rescuers. I saw they hopped from cover to cover like us and the terrified cicadas and rained fire into the fray. Volia gestured frantically. None of them could see her. I debated trying to do a kamikaze run across that no-man's land to tell them we had her, but it'd be suicide.

Wren shouted into the com. "Noss, bring Eagle 4 around to temple pickup! Now! The back door!"

"Can you signal the Melinarians?" I rasped at her.

"All their channels are blocked."

I shook my head in frustration.

Groups of rebels sprang from blackened shrines to trade fire with Mong's defenders, with the rebels intent on storming the main temple to rescue Volia. Bombs dropped from above. The tops of pagodas disappeared. We crouched, hoping we could last without getting peppered full of holes until Noss could bring the ship around. So much for Mong's halcyon, idyllic world.

So much for us too, if we didn't get away from here fast.

Clutches of men fought guerrilla style, launching grenades and spraying fire, ducking, scrambling for new toeholds of cover. It was Resus all over again.

Fareon beams lashed out of the sky. A sleek ship with gleaming hull roared down from above.

My heart leaped. An Alpha 9 fast runner? Could it be? My old ship, *Starrunner,* back from the dead?

No, only a copy.

'The next best thing," Wren rasped.

I shook my head in bewilderment. No time to ponder. The ship landed a few hundred yards away, trim and grey with ox horn-shaped prow and rough diamond shape at stern.

It might as well have been a thousand yards away though. A squad of ground troops identified me among the company and moved in with guns booming.

A hoarse yell hovered on my lips. I turned kamikaze and leveled R4 mayhem into the figures that came charging us. I waited for oblivion to snatch me, riddled with fire and the force of energy pulses. But it did not. In a last defensive move, I fell flat on my stomach. Fire clipped the earth all around. I plugged round after round into the noise and confusion. Through the smoke, I saw Mong striding amid those running figures, a gigantic, barbaric, black-clad leather brute with furred cap. I knew the jig was up.

Gunfire grazed my side. Not possible to escape hits. I reached down, felt a wet stickiness at my ribs. The pain was minimal compared to the animal agony of Mong's hangman's torture. Still, I'd need regen soon. I saw a dream image of Blest hobbling behind me somewhere, catching some shrapnel fallout in the burst of fire power.

He and Wren jogged together, or rather tottered, lurching ahead to dig in defensive positions closer to the descending ship. They dove into low shrubbery. They would get eaten to bits in seconds if they didn't find better cover. Volia and Zan, weaponless, hunched like whipped puppies behind them, white-faced, resigned to death while *Starrunner's* engines blew dust and grass all over the place. Voj was down, riddled with bullets. Blest's leg had caught a slug. We were not going to make it. *Starrunner*, resurrected, loomed a hundred feet away by my estimate, near some broken fountains and a sizzling stream. The ship lifted and tilted. Seeing our plight, Noss angled her in to shield us from the savage fire of Mong's militia. I realized we had missed the narrow window of rescue by mere minutes, despite Noss's clever maneuvering. Bigger ships loomed on our rear horizon; they came chugging toward us.

The alien bulb lay at my side, slipped from my waist belt. With my head tucked low, I launched it, mumbling a prayer that Mong and all his deranged brood would taste bitter death. The frightening thing left my fingers, lobbed like a grenade at the first group of running figures only a few dozen feet away. They lay into it with fire, thinking it some freak grenade come to shred them to bits.

A big mistake.

The bulb exploded in ruin and fragments of its coconut shell bubbled like lava. They turned away to shield their eyes from what they expected to be hideous shrapnel. But from within came unimaginable horror. A winged, misshapen creature, some demon spawn with six starfish arms equipped with sucker pods of sandy-brown color, emerged from the chaos. It was different from the other birthlings, nothing like the dragonfly killer or eel-lizard that had attacked and munched through the Skugs, or the black cricket horror that had burrowed into Mong's gunman's face.

What spawned the endless variation of this creature from its plain

Jane bulb, none could ever know. This one was like some cross between a sea urchin and a bat, if such were possible.

Fully grown and buzzing with anger, it now dove like a demon possessed upon the hapless minions of Mong's troop, slicing holes into them with its barbed-suckered appendages. It tore through a gaping man and came out his back, leaving a fist-size hole where his heart should have been.

"Holy fuck," I gasped.

Mong shouted orders, barely ducking and dodging a lunge and slice and dice by the creature. "Stand down! Don't fire at the thing! It's one of those alien freaks. It'll only kill us if we attack. Kill Rusco over there—kill all the fugitives."

Mong lifted his augmented arm. Immediately I felt a sharp tingling surge course through my joints, rattling my nerves. I flopped about like a fish, but such was my hate for Mong and all his sadistic powers that I vaulted up, gun in hand, spraying fire, cursing him for the end of time. I directed every atom of my animosity and feverish hate at the man.

"Eat buzzard shit, you bloody scumbag, fucking tyrant."

I watched his arm jerk in a spasm and then his figure double over. With a roar of rage, he straightened then I blinked in puzzlement because my rapid fire didn't come anywhere near the sod, but I was already stumbling to my feet toward the ship on the heels of Wren and the others, heedless of the gunshots whizzing around us.

I cried out in pain as more stray beams grazed me, but they didn't kill me—at least not yet. Wren was still shrieking into the com. The others were on the move. I staggered toward them, one hand clutching my ribs, the other my R4. We all raced to safety. In that fateful minute, death and life hung on a thread while the creature from another world made hatchet work of Mong's men. If not for its deadly savagery we would have been rat bait from the get-go.

We made it through the cargo hatch before it closed and Noss was fast in getting us airborne and the hell out of there. A squadron of Warhawks were on our tail. No doubt Mong was ordering his gunners to exercise maximum force.

We lurched inside and crawled deeper into the dimness, choking on the smoke and clutching the straps along the wall while Noss weaved us on a rocky tour with fareon fire slamming the hull.

I stumbled on duck feet toward the bridge, my ribs on fire, while Grild stayed behind to tend to Zan and Volia. Blest? I don't know about Blest.

Wren hissed in dismay. "You need regen."

"Screw the regen," I rasped hoarsely. "We need to save this ship—and our hides."

We staggered onto the bridge. Noss beamed at me from behind the pilot's console. "Welcome back, Captain."

"Get this bird out in deep space, Noss. Good to see you."

Reunions were short. We had bogies on our tail, deadly ones. Both Noss and Wren were on it. Wren slapped herself down before the weapons console. I assumed nav. Noss weaved us in impossible circles high over Othwan's forests and lakes as flash bombs spilled around us like confetti at a wedding. Wren blasted blue hell back at the warbirds behind us. I knew Mong had those superior shields installed, making his vessels nearly tank-armored, so our fire-power would do less than nothing. Dodge and dip was all we could do while we ran the dangerous gauntlet on impulse power. Noss was doing a capable job. This new, suped-up starship was ace, but I could see we were not going to make it through this hell unless we did something very damn tricky. I set the course for Veglos. My hand strayed to the Varwol slider. I pulled my fingers back at the last instant. Gripping my side, I was wracked by a sudden spasm and felt the crippling wooziness of shock threatening to tumble me into an abyss. A monumental bad feeling hit my gut hard—one flick of that lever and it could be the end of us. Planetary gravity and warp drive do not mix, cadet Rusco. Any junior flyboy can tell you that. There had to be another way.

The Vendecki line of battleships ranged the inner edge of the planet's atmosphere. There was a right, mean space fight in progress. A hundred Warhawks stood arrayed against much the same Vendecki numbers. No other choice but the hard one. The reckless one. And that meant—

"Noss bring us into the eye of the storm."

"What?"

"There! Straight into the war zone." I stabbed a thumb at the holo nav.

Noss blinked, he hesitated; at the last moment he caught my drift. Steering *Starrunner* straight into the Vendecki front, he fought the controls, negotiating an obstacle course where hundreds of ships weaved in and out, firing fareons and launching bombs at Mong's Warhawks.

Volia came staggering onto the bridge. She'd bypassed Grild's ministrations and stood before us, her breath a hoarse rasp. "Where are we?"

"A million miles from nowhere soon, sister—or we're space debris."

She gazed at me, looking somewhat better than before, though her wide eyes teared at the number of her own Vendecki and Melinarian allies locked in heated battle with Mong's forces getting battered by Warhawks. She let out a hoarse cry. "Tell them you have me, Rusco! Innocents are dying in the air, on the ground—for me."

I grimaced. The rebels hadn't responded to us on secure channels. I swore and patched her through to the general emergency frequency.

A staticky voice rasped over the com, "General Azun here, Lady Volia, Countess of Melinar. Are you alright?"

"Yes! I am, General. I'm aboard *Starrunner* right now with a fellow named Rusco. Get your people out of there!"

"Roger. We've confirmed visual. All rescue teams are on the abort. Set a far course and tell Rusco to fly *Starrunner* to safe haven!"

"Affirmative. You too, find safe haven. Please abort this crazy mission."

"Negative. Operation Tiger is underway. We've committed and we'll never get a better chance to destroy Mong's hideaway, though many of us may die."

"You will all die!" she wailed.

"With all due respect, beloved Lady, we are all dead with Mong ruling the free planets. Over and out."

I grimaced and clutched the nav. Volia wrung her hands in despair.

The two Warhawks on our tail battered us to hell. Our shields dropped to near zero; a few more direct hits and we'd disintegrate. Before us loomed a phalanx of rebel ships holding off the attackers. We passed right through their great wall of defense, through fire and flame and roiling ships and the topsy-turvy madness of full out war. Fareons grazed our shields and had us buffeted around like puppets. Noss and Wren went skidding out of their seats.

Before the shields blew, I hung on to the console and engaged the Varwol. Death was at our doorstep. Our fate lay in the hands of Othwan, but Othwan's witchery was less risky than flying with our shields down. *Starrunner* flew just on the cusp of warp meltdown this close to planet's gravity, but we were in no position to be choosy right now.

For a split second, the ship seemed to come to a dreamlike halt. Then we hung in space like time thieves. A brilliant white blast lit the cabin, like a small supernova, then a fan of multicolored light trailed behind us, shearing by our viewport as the familiar rainbow of an enormous light highway set us moving to the far stars.

Then only silence.

Free, at last from that bastard's clutches! It was almost too surreal to be true.

A part of me, a grim, primal part from way back in incarnations of my war-torn past, vowed that the next meeting with Master Mong, if ever there was a next, would not be under such one-sided conditions.

Chapter 28

We passed the metal tin of flesh-regen around our company. I could feel its magic working as I lifted my torn monk's robe and ladled the smelly orange paste on my ravaged ribs. The stuff was good for cuts, tissue tears, small organs like a missing ear, damaged tongue or even major skin damage, but generally not for regenerating bones. Except the heavy-duty regen like we had. The pulse weapon that'd tagged me left no lead in my guts, fortunately, only burns, so the regen worked at stitching the flesh together, sparing me the agony of pulling metal out my hide. Luckily none of us had heavy-duty bone issues, outside of Blest with his busted shin. We'd have needed Mong's tanks for worse injuries. We said little and were indeed a glum party, though we had everything to be grateful for—being alive. There lingered the secret fear that Mong was still about lurking like a ghoul around the next corner as we raced across the cosmos at hyper warp speeds. Where was the lowlife? Why had he let us escape so easily? What happened back on Othwan?

Grild sat apart from the others lost in a world of his own. I passed by and gave him the tin, wincing with the sting of my own wounds. "Dry up those cuts, Grild. Don't let them get infected."

He took the tin with a heavy grunt of little enthusiasm. "Voj bit it down there."

"I know. I could see you two were friends."

"He was a loyal ally and a brave man." The young man's eyes were bloodshot, his fleshy cheeks grime-smeared. Ordinarily, a youngblood like him'd be apple-cheeked under that camo cover. A definite defiance on that tough face with the flat nose and the flared nostrils—a kind of proud, physical fighting ancestry that went way back, perhaps to the stone ages. I could see why Wren had chosen him.

"How much of our booty is left?" I asked Wren.

She shrugged. "When you didn't show up at Gainor, our usual place, I knew you were either dead or they'd captured you. I really hoped not dead. The information came at a high cost, Rusco. There's virtually nothing left."

I gave a wheezing sigh.

"You've got your life to thank for it, so be grateful."

"I'm getting used to it."

"You're bleeding still," she pointed out.

"Ah, just flesh wounds," I mumbled. The regen was working, but slowly, and waves of hot pain stung my side, arcing from rib to rib as the flesh knitted together. I'd become almost immune to pain after Mong's long cruel sessions. Wren lifted my blood-soaked smock and balked at the scars building there. Good thing she hadn't seen me before the tank dunking.

"Forget it." I pushed her hands away. "We've other things to worry about. Throw me some more regen after Grild's finished, I'll slap it on and be done with it."

"As you wish." She took the tin from Grild's upraised hand and tossed it my way. "Got extra just for you, Rusco. Knew if we did find you guys in one piece, you'd be needing it."

If I came across as an unhappy man, it wasn't because I was not glad to see Wren. I just wasn't in an affectionate mood. No one could blame me. Torture and too much senseless death kind of does that to one. Deadens a person to the finer things in life, like a wholesome, caring woman. I looked over to Blest who had the look of a lost soul. Couldn't blame him either. Degradation and torture had made him a withered husk. Guilt hit me that he'd suffered too much for my sins at the hands of that sadist Mong. Follee dead too, Voj dead. How many more casualties before this was all over?

Wren reacted to my melancholy. "Going to take some getting used to you with no hair, Jet. The one and only Jet Rusco, bald as an eagle. Who'd have thought?"

"Yeah, well there're always changes happening in the universe."

"I take it Mong was not gentle with you?"

I made no comment.

Blest interrupted with a surly snarl. "Very nice chitchat, lovebirds, but how did you get the drop on us, Wren?"

She shrugged. "We gave it exactly twenty minutes to get you out and warp to safety before Mong got wise and crushed us like bugs."

"And you managed it," I said, "minus a few flesh wounds."

"Speak for yourself," Blest said, rubbing his slow-healing injury.

"With your funds from the Myscol payout, I purchased this new ship, an Alpha 9, as you see—" Wren swept out her arms "—also bought reliable intel that pinpointed your place of captivity at Othwan. We also learned some rogue planet was going in for a strike against Mong—at his monk's retreat to steal back the Countess. If it hadn't been for the Vendecki's diversion, I would have given up, thrown any rescue plan aside as suicide."

A dead silence. We were happy to shut up for once and just stare at nothing.

We took our time outs and rested in our cabins. Noss and Wren took shifts watching the helm as we sped through the light highways on our long journey to Veglos. Why Veglos? Well, where else? Volia still hadn't said much, staring in her vacuous way in a cloud of shock. Likely processing her part in the whole affair—the Vendecki assault, the conquest of her planet, the death of her husband and her old way of life. A chunk of the Countess's soul had died on Othwan and I'm reckoning it had for Blest and me too. She kept to herself, said little, nursing her wounds. Zan was Zan, still blank-eyed and a partial zombie after being strung up on Mong's chicken wire so long. He'd not had the luxury of a tank healing to repair his wounds and relied solely on regen. Blest had taken some serious leg damage, which was no secret to any of us. Like me, he'd been stoic about his pain and the regen recovery process. Luckily we had the extra duty regen, costly as it was, otherwise Blest's shin would have been a lot sorrier than it was right now.

Zan and Grild had bonded and played mindless games to pass the time. *Crockseye* and *Bad Leader*—computer board games with AI players to up the ante. Wren and I had a lot to catch up on, but there was a distance between us. Of my time with Mong I spoke little and was evasive at best. Though she managed to catch pieces of it from Blest who spoke in grunts and whispers from time to time but was at best unreliable. Next time she saw me she was all hushed up and our eyes did not meet, as if she were reluctant to trigger my depressed moods or broach any sensitive territory involving physical torture. I let it stand at that. I wasn't even prepared to talk about it to myself. I couldn't imagine how Blest was coping with it. His video games and rough-guy talk worked to some degree. As did hiding behind a Scroogely-curmudgeon persona and mask. As good a protective mechanism as any.

Volia later approached me and others on the bridge as we munched on assorted goodies in nutrition packs: veal alfredo, spacer's ghoulash, tofu teriyaki, all washed down with instant coffee. "I want to thank you for what you did, Rusco. From what Zan and Blest said, you went out of your way to get me, at risk to your own safe getaway. Is there anything I can offer in return?"

I shrugged. "Nothing I can think of."

"There must be something—"

"After being in the Mentera tank, there's nothing much matters any more, Volia. Materially anyway."

She frowned, confused at the tank reference. I gave her a ham-faced grin, opening my mouth to say something then thought better of it.

Volia touched Wren on the arm. "I am indebted to you too,

Wren. If not for your dogged persistence and courage, we'd all still be slaves down there."

Wren nodded. "We'll drop you wherever you want to go, Volia. I'm guessing it won't be on Melinar."

"No," she said, with a rueful shake of her head. "The capital, Baki on Vendecki soil should be fine."

Wren hesitated. "Isn't that a little close to the war front?"

"We're still allies in the uprising against Mong. Like it or not, I'm leader of my people and the titular commander of this war."

Wren swallowed a mouthful of microwaved lamb. "Not envious of your position in life, nor eager to trade places with you, Volia. But if I were in your shoes, I'd keep up the fight for freedom. I'd do everything in my power to take down that murderer Mong."

She flashed Wren a moon-eyed stare. "It's as if I know you from somewhere." She blinked and shook her head. "All of you. As if we've been here before and done this in another time." She shook her head again, wiped her brow of sweat. "I must be losing my mind, or experiencing some major case of deja-vu."

Remembering my flashbacks in the tank, I guessed it was contagious. Maybe good old Mong'd plunged her into a tank and she didn't remember it?

A tear drifted down her cheek. "After all the tragedy, my people slaughtered, my husband…" She couldn't say more and turned a desolate gaze upon me. "I misjudged you, Rusco. When I saw you there on that ship of Mong's, I thought—only a brutish thug, one of his trained animals."

"Yeah, well, you know what they say about first impressions."

"I see a good man in you."

I laughed. "I wish I could frame those words, Lady Volia, and put them on the wall here. Somebody appreciates me after all. Hear that Wren?"

She grinned.

Volia grabbed my wrist. "Rusco, we could use freedom fighters like you. Join us. Come to our haven. There're more than a few rebels down there you'd take a shine to. We need support, your kind of gutsy, off-the-wall leadership."

I smiled. "Sorry, Volia, but think I've about used up my nine lives in this lifetime."

Blest's snort seconded that opinion. No sooner had I acknowledged Blest's dog-eared sneer than a sharp pang hit my heart as I remembered my vow to take down that fucker Mong. Grudgingly, I remarked, "But I'll take you to Baki at least and listen to one of your talks. If you need help flying supplies in, or black market war props, I could help you out—for a price, of course."

She gave a crooked grin. "Always the businessman, eh, Rusco? Consider it a deal. Your services are more than welcome."

Chapter 29

Down on Baki we congregated in a huge war hall at Independence Square. The place held eight hundred or more avid supporters, a mix of Melinarian refugees and Vendecki sympathizers. Volia spoke up in a resonant voice:

"Freedom fighters of Baki, comrades and allies, your enthusiasm and steadfast courage gives me great joy. Though my own planet Melinar fares ill under Mong's occupation, I see you have held out and survived. For that I commend you. Loyalty and unity are the greatest assurances for a brighter future that a leader of the people can ask for."

Her noble presence inspired loyalty. I could see that. First time I'd seen her all cleaned up, her hair shining brilliant hues, bleached pure gold this time under a silver tiara, her cheeks flushed a rosy pink and eyes bright sparkles of fervor, of a nationalism that was, truthfully, one of my least favorite qualities in her. But if it gave these beleaguered people hope…hope against an impossible enemy who I, as much as any, wished to see vanquished and trampled in the dirt, then so be it.

"If not for these brave men and women, I would not be here. Let me introduce my friends—Jet Rusco, Wren Zalan, Noss Brekia, Blest Surok, Zan Vulder and Grild Malsi."

We stepped forward on the low stage in turn and presented ourselves.

Sure enough, we were heroes, even as the deluded Vendecki continued to hold out against Mong's tyranny and the frightfully large number of his attack forces posted at nearby Melinar. Perhaps Mong's crew were thinking twice about advanced Vendecki tech poking up out of nowhere and launching an attack on their doorstep, the same insurgents who had nearly brought them to their knees at Othwan. All the same, I kept glancing out the diamond-shaped panes, waiting for the dive bombers to strike—Warhawks and missiles to come blitzing and dropping on our asses. Maybe even Mong's agents were spying on this little congregation right now. Part of me, did not want to think about that, or even be here. Too close to enemy soil. But I'd promised Volia I'd come and I did not want to live in fear all my waking days...

A standing ovation erupted amongst the gathered rebels for our part in the rescue and daring escape. I had to grin, shaking my head in surprise. Never would have imagined an accolade like this, nor had I ever been hailed a hero before. The opposite, by many. It felt good, to tell the truth. The others, taken by surprise, laughed and looked around, trading gratifying looks at one another. Though Blest sported his perpetual frown and just shrugged it off in his usual way.

More speeches followed and Phel, the master of ceremonies, the top-ranking war officer of the Melinarians, stepped forward. An olive-skinned man of mixed Melinarian-Vendecki descent, he was all white teeth, a stiff ruff of grey-peppered hair. He launched into a spiel of how Vendecki forces were working with the defeated Melinarians to liberate their sister planet from tyranny. A valiant saga of how the forces were rebuilding themselves, new ships being deployed and manpower raised; they would conquer and turf out the imperial dictators of Jezuan before the next moon.

Yeah, right, dream on, Phel. Pure rhetoric, but it seemed to be what the audience wanted to hear.

Later at a more informal gathering at one of the VIP tables in the bustling war hall, Phel topped off my glass with fine wine and asked me point blank what I thought of the whole Vendecki program.

I shrugged, not knowing how to answer in front of the others.

"Come on, Jet. Aren't you sold yet? Won't you and your crew fly for us? Volia here has spoken highly of you and of your interest in helping us, offering cargo transport of arms for fair market value."

I looked over to the Countess who wore a devil's grin on her flushed face. "They seem to love you," I said.

"Unlike many aristocracies, I believe that leaders are accountable to the people."

Phel added, eager to promote his cause, "We're mounting an assault on occupied Melinar, Jet," he said in a conspiratorial tone. "Our hope is that Mong's forces will take the bait. We'll be more than ready for them this time."

I blinked as would an owl. These people surely had a death wish, or they loved to flirt with disaster.

"We'll retake our home world. This time with a better plan in mind and more allies."

"Are the Vendecki in line with this?" I asked.

"Yes, they're fierce allies."

"To take on Mong will require a lot more than a few allies and some tough talk about general deployment and rah-rah."

"True, Rusco, but we have friends throughout the Larga system. We underestimated Mong's power. We're asking for help from all quarters. Like yourself. Are you on board?"

I hesitated.

"How do you single out his ships with your jammer?" Noss asked, breaking the silence.

"It's complicated," said Phel. "Do you want the long answer or the short? Harg here, our com expert, can explain—" he snapped his fingers, called over a grey-haired man with a tall drink in his hand.

"Never mind," said Noss, "I'll assume you've worked out the deployment issues."

"Our engineers, like Harg here, and other Melinarian experts, are working on a foolproof version of the jammer. A retractable antenna cached to a depth of 500M. Even if Mong or enemy patriots nuke the area, our automated defense system can raise and lower the antenna to changing war conditions."

"Sounds good, but—"

"Where, on Twidor?" I barked, "and that other wasteland moon? How do you manage that? Mong and his rats'll be watching those moons like cheese at a rathole after that last bout on Melinar."

"That's the beauty of it. They'd never guess that we'd employ the same defense tactic twice. We've run cloaked ships in and out and dropped men and equipment down on Twidor to work in the Dusk Caves, digging, burrowing, shielded under the rock from his onboard ship probes and scanners. The antenna'll be the last thing to go up—and only when we need full jamming capacity. When it's operational, enemies can't indefinitely keep firing on it or patrolling the area. We've redundancy transmitters and backup antennae installed in bunkers across both moons."

"It's a better start," said Noss. "Why didn't you think of it right from the get-go?"

Harg, the signals engineer, answered, "We didn't think Mong or any ally of his could track and destroy a transmitter so quickly. If the transmitters had been up longer, we'd likely have destroyed his armada."

"An honest mistake."

"That cost far too many lives. Let's hope it immobilizes them for good this time."

"I'm still not clear on the overall plan." I rubbed the heel of my palm on my temple.

Phel gave an impatient flourish. "We stir up the pot on Melinar, Mong goes in to retaliate and we jam their signals. The plan's success relies upon the fact that Mong hasn't cracked our jammer infiltration codes. I'm worried his enforcers might have fleshed it out of our captive engineers. But the good news is, we never gave any of them a full schematic of the tech. Mong's crew could theoretically piece it together on the fly—but that'd take—"

"A lot of ifs and probables here, Phel," I interrupted.

"I know. That's why time is of an essence." He turned to Volia and flashed meaningful glances at both of us. "So, will you fight?"

"Hold on. I never agreed to—" My mind flashed on the post and tank in the Redemption Chamber then I clenched my teeth. "I'll help you out."

Volia stirred in her seat and set down her glass.

Wren gaped. "Are you sure, Rusco?"

"Not really, but—"

Wren's eyes fluttered. Blest just gave his head a little shake and took a fish's gulp of wine. Grild and Zan seemed indifferent, resigned to whatever fate was in for them, going whichever way the wind blew. By the look of their hollow stares, I could tell that their lives were at an impasse, governed by the toss of the die.

Conflicting thoughts poured through my mind. Not the least, Mong's words drifting back to me, that dim time on *Vulpin's* bridge, *"I never retreat, Balt. Never. I win every battle I fight."* Perhaps the Vendecki ruse was the deadly hammer that would drive steel into Mong's flesh through that chink in his armor.

And then, maybe it wasn't.

* * *

Down in the underground hangar on Vendecki's moon, Hedra, we oversaw the clandestine loading of boxes and assorted cases of rifles, R4s, gauge 3 power packs, land mines, shell absorbers, flamethrowers, anything we could get in the hold of *Starrunner* and other starships to help the rebel cause on Melinar. We wore standard grey Vendecki khakis with Vendecki logos pasted on our breast over high-grade Kevlar. Black boots, crash helms, refitted R4s at our waist, the whole shebang.

Phel approached me, wearing a moody frown. "New plans, Rusco. Forget the scheduled arms drop. We need fighters in the air at 0200."

"Say what?" I stared at Volia who'd come by and overhead.

"Conditions on Melinar have turned for the worse," she said in a strained voice. "Mong's amped up his persecutions, accusing

Melinarian spies of being the ones who dug up the location of Othwan and brought about the invasion of his sanctuary. I just watched the video feed." She uttered sorrowful croak. "Slave camps, interrogations, brutal torture. Mong's captains have examined all our technically skilled engineers and scientists. They ply them with truth-serums, discarding them like garbage once they've served their purpose. Their minds are fried from drugs and repeated drills. The Vendecki endure no less savage scrutiny. When will it stop? It'll never stop! Not until that madman is put down."

"I agree with you there, Countess. But easier said than done." I rubbed my jaw and looked around at the smattering of ships, pilots, crew and engineers. "You expect to take down a sociopath and a well-greased war machine skilled from day one. You have largely untrained rabble here and some low-tech ships. You don't even have fareons installed. Mong hasn't gotten to where he is without substantial resources."

"You underestimate yourself, Rusco—and us. You had him! *We* had him—we had him worried, and we escaped from his lair right under his nose."

"A lot of luck and diversion there. With more luck to go. How many died?"

Volia sighed. "Our ratio was 4 to 5. That puts us at a 20% total fatality figure. Most of the forces escaped unscathed in that shootout. We decimated Othwan. And we're ready to counterattack."

My eyes could not help but gleam with temptation, unusual for even me. It was an impressive statistic. I looked to Noss and the others who'd been silent this whole time. "So what do you have? What's your plan?"

Phel pushed closer with his teeth clacking. "Mong's fallen for the bait. We've confirmed knowledge of his next attack. Nineteen brave men and women died to bring us that information. We mustn't squander their sacrifice. We'll use the intel for max gain to strike Mong where he least expects it!"

"All fine and nice. A motley crew of disorganized skullbashers.

Angry dissidents whose friends and families have been tortured and killed by that mongrel, all fired up to fight an impossible fight."

"Yes, that's what we are, Rusco, you've summed us up all too nicely."

I grinned. "You're at least an honest, pushy bastard, Phel. This rabble is my kind of piss and vinegar folk."

"Great to hear." He brightened. "Because you're going to lead Reaver Party 3."

I let out an explosive breath. "What the fuck? Where did you dream up this hare-brained idea?"

"I know your type, Rusco." Phel narrowed beady eyes on me. "I did some digging on you. You've got nothing else left. Your life's worth shit now, a shambles, debt up to your ears, bounty hunters in every sector looking to cash in, with that alpha dog hounding your heels, nose up your ass."

"Wait a minute! I agreed to run transport, no more—arms in, soldiers out—for pay. An even 5k was our deal."

"It was, but it's gotten bigger than that."

Eyes were on me. I heard the pound of my heart in my ribcage.

"You have the chance to take him down, help millions of people! Why pass that up for some lesser role, playing baggage jockey over here? You and Wren and the others are among the few rare ones in the galaxy who've ever defeated and escaped the Star Lord."

"And we'd like to keep it that way."

"We need you!" he cried, grabbing my shoulder.

I looked at his hand and he licked his lips and withdrew it, realizing he'd overstepped.

There passed a moment when a tense silence passed, when my life flashed before me—all the times I was a little shit disturber, seven, eight? breaking everything in the house, lighting things on fire, playing tricks on the neighbor's cat. Suddenly time jumped and there were shell shots, explosions, my parents and friends fried by flash bombs—then, like the tenebrous haze in the tanks, a zap of light, illumination, I knew after all this searching that I had a real purpose…as if my life leading up to this point had been only prep, paving the way for this one desperate act. It was crazy. But then again, everything in this mad universe was crazy. A big, mixed-up, shit-for-brains soup of craziness.

"It's 10k yols, if you pull it off," Phel said, intruding on my thoughts, "and Mong is taken down and destroyed."

"Well?" I looked at the others.

Wren shrugged, gave me her 'could take it or leave it' look. I sighed, knew they wouldn't go for it.

"10k bonus each," Phel said, realizing he'd have to sweeten the pot.

Wren's and Blest's eyes flickered. I saw a hint of interest there, and a touch of greed in Blest's.

So they were on board. I grinned and nodded. "Okay, Phel, it'll surely fail, badly—but what the fuck."

Phel beamed and slapped me on the back. "Good call, Rusco. You're a good man."

"I keep hearing that," I said with a frown.

Phel spoke into a com. "Team leader, move out. We have 24 hours to pull this caper off."

Chapter 30

The camoed grey moon rock flap slid aside and *Starrunner* burst out of the cave on Hedra. Five convoys at our heels impulse-thrust away from the desolate lunar plains into the deepening blackness of space—older Alpha X's, but capable of speed and looking beat-up and retro enough to pose as beleaguered rebel craft fighting for a doomed cause.

"Team leader to Sparrows," I rasped into the com. "On my signal."

"Roger, team leader. This is Sparrow 1. Give us the word."

I kept an open channel. Once we escaped Hedra's gravity and were in the safe zone, we'd make the jump to Melinar.

Phel's voice came over the encrypted link, his grey-peppered hair tied back in a bun. "Remember, you're bait only. When Mong's defense guard are alerted and paralyzed by our jammers, you turn and attack them. Until then, maintain defensive positions. When jammers are at full capacity, no mercy! Blast those maggots to shit! The bulk of our fighters will warp in and join the slaughter."

"Roger. Over." I signed off with a grim sigh. Grim plans for grim times.

"T-7 minutes. Remember," I told Wren and the others, "we warp in, make it look like a drop off of arms to the Melinar rebels. No land action. The risk is minimal. At the first sign of trouble, we zigzag then warp the fuck out of here. We hope their little jammers do the work. Then in comes their fleet to finish the job. We're just extra change in the overall equation. Remember the payout—big payout."

"Gift wrapped with pretty little red ribbons," quipped Blest. "Wonder what can go wrong?"

"Nothing'll go wrong," I said to him. "Do your job, have your gun on the ready in case we need backup."

"No one can pay me enough for this shit, Rusco."

I ignored him, spoke quiet words into the com then to Wren, briefing her and the others on procedure. It seemed as if this op was all sewn up, almost too clear and clean. That queasy feeling in my gut sensed something havey-cavey and that things would not be so easy.

My hoarse whisper echoed into the com. "Now."

In a blast of brilliant light, *Starrunner* arched through the Varwol tunnel into Melinarian space. We materialized outside the grav danger zone. Melinar hung below us, a distant turquoise disc, its twin moons bright on the far side of their orbits. The five other convoys materialized beside us, dim grey craft, looking very ragged and wary. I loosed a breath of pent up exhaustion. Word had been dropped to Mong's spies that Vendecki sympathizers were planning a run to grant aid to the demoralized rebels in the Jezuan hills. I didn't doubt Mong's watchdogs would be arriving soon. Very soon. Noss readied *Starrunner* and we set a course for Targan, the square continent in the middle of the vast ocean Praxeus on Melinar's far side where the conquered city Jezuan lay on a jagged coastline.

Hulking shapes were suddenly all around us. Fifty Warhawks— dark gunmetal grey predators, cannons locked on us.

Black-hearted Mong had fallen for the bait, faster than I thought, incensed at the piercing thorn in his side at another Melinarian uprising.

The Star Lord himself was there. His ginormous flagship *Vulpin* loomed into view. I'd recognize that bloated hunk of scrap metal anywhere. Its twisted control towers and bullfrog midsection, rear radial boosters and energy thrusters gave me the shakes. Some hundred or more cannons sprawled fore and aft from every angle of its prickly hide. Didn't surprise me. The bigger they are the harder they fall…Well, wonder if they leaked the news that Jet Rusco was on board leading the expedition. Likely, the fuckers.

Fareons arched out at us almost instantaneously in green and violet menace. Our shields dipped to an appalling low. One of our convoys rippled in red, then exploded in ruin, her shields weak or malfunctioning.

I grimaced in astonishment. "Jesus, Noss. What's going on? Now, Phel! Fucker, get those jammers working!"

It seemed Phel wanted to draw out the Warhawks more, lengthen the charade. Perhaps the jammers were fucked? What was one sacrifice? For a second, I thought we'd been had.

But *Vulpin's* fareons did go haywire and stray fire lashed out from her cannons and ignited one of Mong's own lead craft that was firing on us. I smacked my fist in my palm. Wren locked fareons on the nearest ship in the enemy line. Noss kept *Starrunner* on a sweeping tangent over the warcraft's hulls—a risk, even if we avoided their haywire beams, yet maximizing the damage we could inflict on them at such close range. We rained destruction on their hulls, penetrating their mega shields with repeated bursts. I waited for the rest of the Melinarian fleet to show up with their Vendecki scrabblers.

But they did not come. Or at least not too soon. I saw a hundred Warhawks blitz into existence from various parts of the galaxy and they sent flash bombs after us—salvos that had not been affected by the jammers. Our shields would not hold out for long. The rebel fleet materialized at last. The fireworks began. But this was a different type of fireworks. Little glowbugs on the underdog side burning and biting the big blackbirds. From grey, tiny fuselages pricks of red light lashed out and slammed into the larger Warhawks.

Enemy craft lit in orange and yellow and foundered as their shields gave way.

"There!" I cried in triumph. "Target Mong's shitty flagship! Spare nothing! We have no better chance than now. Do it, Wren!"

She opened full fareons on *Vulpin.* The superstructure rippled, a complex metalworks of folds and dark, twisted cannons and com towers. Rebel craft from all angles opened fire on Mong's mother ship along with others of the fleet. We pelted them with all our megavolts could give, and the enormous craft started to list and fall in orbit toward Melinar.

"Hot damn!" I cried. *Vulpin* flared, pitched and rolled and continued her descent toward Melinar and we raced after her.

Phel's voice came rasping over the com, "Do not go in, Rusco!"

"Bring your ships over!" I cried. "Mong is falling. We've got him. We've already got our weapons locked on his rude bastard hide!"

"Can't. We're too busy fighting Warhawks and having a hell of a time of it."

I could see on the ship's holo tactical that the Vendecki craft were taking heavy losses from flash bombs and were prey to Mong's superior numbers. Sparrow 1 ignited to starboard; the last two of our team lay heavily taxed by enemy fire.

"The warbirds have no com," Phel shrilled, "but their limited reserve weapons are still wreaking havoc on us."

Flash bombs and convention torps. I gave a miserable sigh.

Wren hit the override switch for reserve fareon power. "That bastard Mong's going to get away. Too many slimy tricks up his sleeve."

"Not if we can help it," I growled. I peered over at Noss. "Can you bring us in close enough?"

Noss grinned.

Sure enough, *Vulpin* jettisoned an escape craft from the starboard port as she hurtled planetside. I boomed at Noss, "There!"

Wren targeted the shuttle.

Phel grunted in amazement. "A blip has appeared on our scanners. Wait…No, we do not see him anymore. Mong must have curled around the shadow side of the planet."

"No, we're tracking the bogie jettisoned from *Vulpin*."

"Rusco, I forbid you to go down there—"

I cut the channel. Enough of meister Phel for one day. "Fire every volt of fareon juice we have into that bastard's ass, Wren!"

She unleashed full fareons. We streaked after the fleeing shuttle, a dark bottle-green shape with bulbed prow and twin fins. Straight to the dimming planetside the shuttle spiraled. We entered Melinar's atmosphere. Glowering scarlet hue of early evening fell on the rich landscape. We skimmed over the featureless plains in pursuit of the shuttle.

Vulpin nosedived several miles in front of us then smashed into a large paddy field. A bright blue explosion marked the crater of her entry. The shuttle cut through the smoldering cloud and roared skyward, barely saving its hide. Wren's continued blasts hit it square on, shearing off the rear fins and sending the fuselage spinning out of control. Corkscrewing, it crashed at the side of a hill at the edge of an arid field, smoke trailing from its crumpled fuselage.

As the haze cleared, we saw three figures emerge dazedly from the blackened husk. Magnified resolution revealed one hulking shape, garbed in half-scorched leather and furs, staggering out with two of his henchmen. All were disoriented, blood streaming from their faces and arms. Wren's holo screen showed higher resolution and her fingers twitched over the fareon blaster.

I reached over and grabbed her hand. "Wait!" I rasped. "As much as I want to nuke that bastard's ass right now, we can take him alive! To suffer a thousand deaths for the ones he has given to so many others."

She exhaled an exasperated breath, but the others nodded in agreement.

"Give us air coverage, Noss. An eagle-eye's view. We're going in on foot. Keep us apprised of any unpleasant surprises. We don't want any predators biting us in the ass."

"Roger that."

Starrunner settled beside Mong's broken escape craft, at the rising hill to our right. Noss checked shields and disengaged the rear cargo door. We glimpsed the crash survivors struggling up the hillside on the holo display.

"Zan, you stay behind and help Noss with weapons and nav. Your back wounds are still not healed enough to do a land op. Wren, Blest, Grild—come with me. We go in on foot."

We had no need for masks. Intrepid pioneers had terraformed Melinar centuries ago, with big air generators, water synthesizers, and feeding crops and flora liquid nutrients once transplanted from earth-like worlds.

The four of us stepped out, fully equipped, with R4s, Kevlar vests, coms, helms. The air had a dry distinct tang of slightly tart fecundity, but not unpleasant. Bird song was nonexistent here. The smoke from the escape shuttle had frightened off any animal life. A sudden rank, burning waft of melted metal and gas fumes hit us head on. I motioned Wren and the others up the slope.

Mong and his surviving crew had stumbled up the hill into a grove of weird, strangle-branched trees. Though the word 'grove' was a misnomer. Alien flora at best—a petrified forest. Large tracts of thick-boled trees rose up the crumbling slopes, creating a perfect haven for ambush. I weaved among the tan-colored trunks of the broken landscape, urging the others along through the unyielding limbs.

Almost immediately I hunched under the heavier weight of the planet's gravity. I didn't have the same spring and jump in my legs at all.

My boots crunched on the gravel-like soil. I heard the distant shuffle and crunch of boot heels and heavy breathing up ahead. Fugitives, not far away.

I gave the signal. We split up to flank them. Wren and Blest took the east, Grild and I took the west, up a steeper, rougher tract with strange flakes of shattered, mars-red rocks. At one time these trees had been living things, but now they were dead, only dry spiky, spidery remnants of a forgotten past.

The runaways had split up too, judging from the scuffling echo coming back through the alien flora. A shrewd tactic, to limit the chance of getting tagged.

I wanted Mong badly. I rasped into the com. "Noss! Do you have a read on them?"

"Negative. We lost air coverage... Wait. Two pulses. Lifeforms at A23.61. Sending location…"

"That's them." I firmed my lip. "We see them in our helm scopes. Unless they're indigenous deer, it has to be them."

Mong and his company had no chance. When the rebels blew his fucking, wretched Warhawks out of the sky, neutralized every last one of his killing machines, he'd have nothing. This cat and mouse guerrilla war we were playing then would be pointless. But a nagging uncertainty still tugged at the back of my head. What if those jammers failed? What if Mong's ships came streaking down out of the clouds and incinerated us instead?

I swallowed hard. What mess did you get yourself into, Rusco? Did you think it would be that easy? Your impetuousness may have landed you in a bigger jam than last time.

Voices of doubt. Ghosts of fear. I shook them from my mind and moved ahead, nudging Grild in the ribs.

A deeper feeling hit me, struck now with the growing suspicion that if I didn't catch Mong here, we'd never get him. He was a monster larger than life, an ulcerous cancer armed with an unnatural tendency to escape justice. I could envisage his hulking frame disappearing in the soil forever, like an everlasting termite, hiding, escaping the justice he was due.

I was not going to let that happen.

Like weasels we moved in undulating, semi-crouched positions while the dim light of fading day filtered through the spiny twigs, lending an eerie unreality to the lands around us.

I heard Noss's voice hiss over the helm's com. "They're moving away from you, Jet. But we don't have great resolution up here. Grainy. You've got to cut them off at the next ravine—A25.44. I can't blast the area without taking you out too."

"Affirmative, Noss. Keep scanning. Let us know of any anomalies." I kept my voice to a bare whisper.

The petrified twigs, like crazy fractal patterns, obscured our view. Surreal this landscape. As from a dream I studied the impossible foliage—a massive primordial canopy that blocked out the little light remaining in the sky and left only a dull golden-amber staining the shattered earth floor.

Distant gunfire echoed hollowly through the trees. Impossible to gauge distance with all these stony echoes in this strange geography. The sound bounced off trunks and ricocheted to other places, prompting even a professional soldier to draw false conclusions.

With less confidence than before, we stumbled forward.

We'd gotten no further than a bend in the knoll when fire bit at us from out of nowhere. Grild fell, uttering a moaning cry. He lay face down in a riddled heap.

I grimaced, dove out of the way just as more deadly fire ate into the trunk behind me. I crouched in the dusky light, a wary wolf, my heart pounding. No hits, but I could hear my blood pound in my throat.

Grild wheezed, shifted his gaze toward me. He snuffed out a trickle of blood from his nostrils. He was in a bad way. I motioned him to silence, and to stay still. No way of getting to the man. He was six feet away. Damn it! Mong or one of his gunmen was closer than I thought. He was covering the area with a marksman's expertise. How could I have been so fucking stupid? That fiend moved more stealthily than any predator. Now the hunted stalked the hunters.

Chapter 31

I inched forward, creeping on my stomach at a snail's pace, moving toward shelter amongst the petrified roots. I felt like a foreign grub here, with my R4 trained—hoping it didn't clink on the flaked shingle, alert for any sound or signal.

Grild gasped behind me. Poor bugger. What could I do for him? I'd get my head shot off if I tried to double back and minister to him. What good would that do either of us?

Where the fuck was Mong?

How far I crawled through that rooty hellhole like a miserable worm, I don't know, but it was far, and I could feel Mong's or his marksman's hawk eyes trained on me all the time. Why'd he keep me alive? I knew he could have plugged me anytime. I had no idea where they were. He could be hiding behind the next trunk or crouched behind some shattered boulder, anywhere in the heavy, dusky, growing shadows, waiting like a ghoul for me to slip up. Where the fuck was he?

"Wren," I hissed in the com.

No answer. Maybe she was playing possum too on purpose, staying dark.

A stone turned several feet away to my right.

"Looking for me, Jet Rusco?"

I whirled in the red shale, my gun raised. I sprayed out a stream of fire and Mong leaped back in all his charred, blooded glory, sheltering behind a massive rocky trunk. His rifle pointed out. My fire ricocheted off the rippled bark and took out large chunks of the petrified wood he crouched behind, spewing flakes every which way.

"That's a waste of bullets, Jet."

Closer he limped. I sprayed more fire but missed. He ducked back behind another tree, less wide than the others, but enough to conceal his ape-like frame. He'd timed it so he'd make it. I gave a silent curse. I panted, my eyes darting wildly from trunk to trunk. Maybe the fuck'd already hopped to a new hiding place while I rubbed the grit out of my eyes. I wouldn't doubt that his injured leg was crippled enough, but he could still walk on it. Bloody hell! Didn't surprise me.

A metal barrel spat a few rounds at my heels—just to tease me. I wormed my way more desperately along, the blood hammering in my skull.

My rifle caught on a rock and I heard a grunt of triumph somewhere to my right. That last glimpse of him I saw: his face so placid, untroubled, it unnerved me. As confident as the wild animals that once roamed this forest habitat.

Thirty feet separated me from his last location as I scrambled behind a tree of my own, barely avoiding his return fire. I kept my head and body under cover and my gun low. I dared come no closer. I knew the man's illimitable power. Even maimed, he was a threat. A surge of raw panic tickled up my spine. My mouth felt like a dried prune, a sandpaper desert. Mong was a force to be respected. Any fool could see that. My breath rasped in my throat. The worst stranglehold of fear was on me, having a monstrous tour de force so close. The ultimate psychopathic sadist...

A vision sprang in my mind. The lurid memory from back in the tanks when I experienced that horrible case of deja-vu. I saw myself again on an alien, freaky hillside on a faraway world, facing down Mong. The same as now.

I heard a familiar voice wheeze out a tired breath. "Yes, Jet, one must be careful when he hunts the tiger. Star Lord and con man—

here we are—Hustler wanting to be Star Avenger. No need for quiet. My colleagues will keep your friends busy for some time, so we may converse freely."

I peeked an eye out from behind my trunk. I could not see him. I pulled my head back.

"I must commend you for taking down my flagship and shuttle. I don't know how you did it, but I guess you managed to reinstate the Melinar jammer. Very good. Funny how I dismissed that tech. I don't know how you defeated Balt either and liberated the Mentera. But I can guess. You capitalized on my mistake. Kudos to you, Jet Rusco! Ingenious and spontaneous. Perhaps my teachings were not in vain after all. Balt will stay in his glass prison; in fact, he has moved to primary exhibit in my new 'restored' Temple of Light on a different world, far away in the Butala sector that nobody will find. You'll have to visit it sometime. I've renamed it 'The Temple of Wrath'—in dedication to all the worlds of this filthy system who will pay for rising against me."

The man was talking far too much. Why? I snatched a quick look over my shoulder. The gunmen I expected to come leaping out, fry me from behind, were not there.

Mong must have caught the movement for his lips curled in a blood-smeared grin. Double bluff. My head spun. The man was mind-fucking with me. "You don't seem to be in any position to uphold that claim," I croaked.

Mong clicked his tongue. "Armies can be replaced, Rusco. Ships can be rebuilt and amassed. Like the rich man who loses all his money. Within a week, or two, such a man has rebuilt his empire stronger and bigger than ever."

I raised my weapon.

Mong gave a cynical flourish. "Let's dispense with our toys. I propose a duel. A test of strength and will. We compete with only physical and inner components. The best man wins. Are you game?" He tossed aside his rifle in a clatter of metal on stone, his R9, a rare and deadly weapon, smaller and more efficient than my R4.

Why would the sod do that? Was it jammed up or kaput? Or just another mind fuck?

"I'm not that stupid, Mong." I clutched my weapon tighter.

He narrowed his eyes. "Just stupider in other areas. I see you had the fool plan of trying to take me alive." He shook his head, smirked again and clicked his tongue. "That narrow ambition is revealed in your eyes. Hero Rusco captures Star Warlord! Pah! You still have a dreamy sentimentalism to you. Nor have you lost your old crone's desire to get 'one up' on your enemy. Shame on you." He exhaled a long breath. "Let it go, Jet Rusco. It'll only kill you, like a pig with a skewer in its belly." He motioned his right arm, his augmented arm, to unleash some foul telekinesis on me.

But a sharp burst of fire caught him sideways, slamming the other weapon he was trying to draw from his half-burned furs. The R3 vaporized in his hand and I whirled out of hiding and sprayed fire as I looked to see where the flare had come from. Who was it? Wren?

Mong rolled, grunted, and was up on his knees in three seconds, lifting his augmented arm, as if he'd caught in his grip some of that vicious fire flare.

He gave a wheezing sigh. "Do you need a woman to fight your battles? Die, you miserable coward! You're not deserving of my instruction." He flicked up his augmented arm.

I felt a terrible stinging pain course through my bones. Unbearable agony. As if I burned from inside. My fingers could not clutch the gun's trigger. I fell, gasping, clutching at my abdomen, gasping for air as the rifle fell from my nerveless fingers.

The stinging pain reached an apex. I fought nausea and unconsciousness. Blackout and death. All of a sudden, I snatched myself erect, struggling to save myself from falling into that deep abyss, staggering like a straw figure, with the cellular memory of all the times I'd withstood the depths of his torture, hanging in the Chamber of Redemption. I twisted to face him and used my inner force to redirect that hateful burst of energy from his synthetic limb back at him. How, I don't know. It was as if the Jet Rusco of old went away, and another Jet Rusco of the future took his place, some ancient incarnation of a dead, blooded warrior who raged and gave me the power to wield such formidable magic against a primordial enemy. I focused the energy with my mind, knocked Mong backward, sent him spinning on his heels.

His lips parted in soundless cry. "Wha—" It was like a sound a child might make who sees too late the vicious dog come bursting out of the neighbor's yard.

I snatched up my rifle, sprayed him with death-wielding fire. His right limb disintegrated in a ruin of machine parts and synthetic flesh. The limb hung severed from the shoulder.

His mouth dropped into a silent rictus. And yet, a flicker of amazement touched those swarthy lips, triumph even, that his magical teachings on me had worked—but also fear, for the first time in that man's brain, that defeat quite possibly loomed at the hands of his unwilling pupil.

Powers, it is said, come into the body through penance, or out-of-body experiences. Maybe they had?

Mong wheezed out a hoarse gasp and dropped to his knees. "I— sensed it back on Othwan. I gave you that power, Jet Rusco, would you bite—the hand that feeds you?"

"I would cut out your heart and feed it to the crows," I barked at him.

He nodded and sagged, his head lolling on his chest. Broken wires and white plasma oozed from that smoking shoulder socket, the mechanics of his augmentation. "I have trained you well," he croaked. "You've made me proud. But still you are only on the first rung of the ladder."

Bootfall echoed from behind the nearby trees. Wren approached breathless, training her gun on the weaponless, mutilated man.

I reached for her to steady myself. "Glad to see you! The others?" I croaked.

"His point man is dead. Blest is back there scouting the perimeter for the other one. Where's Grild?"

I shook my head. "Grild's not good. Back there too. Shot up."

Wren winced.

The whine of engines buzzed down through the treetops, echoing over our grim, bloody pasture. Not the deep-throated roar of Warhawks, but the higher-pitched thrum of Vendecki fighters. I could have jumped for joy. Mong's world was crashing down on him, his luck turning sour. I was fucking glad. Mong's eyes bulged, with a white flare of disbelief. He could be conquered and lose.

Blest came limping out of the swatch of trees. He stared at Mong and gave a crooked grin. "So, the mighty Master Mong isn't so mighty any more."

"Any trouble with our friends?"

Blest shrugged. "Sorry to say, the last loose runner has offered his body as fertilizer to dandelions."

I breathed a sigh of relief. I croaked into the com, "Noss! get over here, we need backup. Grild is down. I repeat, Grild is down." I turned to Blest. "Blest, run back and see if you can find him. I didn't leave him in a good state." I motioned in a vague direction and tossed him my extra pack of regen. Blest gave a crisp nod and hobbled away.

Wren wheezed out a hoarse breath, her weapon still trained on Mong. "I saw this bastard through the trees and fired from long range. I must have clipped him. I thought you were dead when you crumpled. What happened?"

"Mong fucked up and you and I blasted him." I debated telling her the whole story of how my inexplicable powers had deflected his killing blow but quickly decided against it.

She stepped over and lashed out a boot to smash in Mong's teeth but I quickly pulled her away from him. "Careful, that viper's—"

Even as I spoke, Mong's left hand flashed out and snatched up a long bowie knife from under his furs. The edge caught Wren's shin and drew a thin line of blood. She leaped back with a shriek, whirled and spat fire at him, catching him in his legs. He howled, yelping like a wolf. I surged forward and kicked the weapon out of Mong's last good hand as he tried to use the knife to cut his own throat.

"No unheroic behavior at this late hour, Mong! Die like a warrior, for Christ's sake. None of this hara-kiri shit," I sneered.

In a snarl of rage, he clawed for the knife, blinking back the agony from his ruined legs. "You have not won yet, Jet Rusco. You forget—the Mentera. The ones you let escape from the tanks. They'll bring back others to this world. You revived them from their slumbers—" he choked out a gob of bloody phlegm "—I would bet my life on it."

He half pulled himself upright among the sprawling roots with his twitching arm.

I wanted to plunge that knife into his throat, rid the universe of him once and for all. But my heart sank in my chest, my eyes glazing in horror. Ships blitzed over the sky. I was lost in a daze. A dangerous one. Mong scrabbled before me, seeking escape, looking for some way to end this life, but I would not let him. I hopped back to tower over him with my weapon cocked. He croaked, wearing a grin of lunatic rage on his grime-smeared, blood-dripping face. "Do it, kill me!"

I shook my head and watched him crawl his way toward the cover of trees, like a sick animal that slinks away to die.

I heard the cries of animated figures through the screen of trees, snatches of dim conversations, shapes of villagers emerging with hoes and rakes and shovels, seeking vengeance on the one who had caused them so much misery. Doubtless they'd seen the smoking wreck of Mong's flagship and put two and two together.

Wren lifted her R4 to go after him and finish him off, but I held her back. "Let the villagers have him. It's a worse punishment than the quick death he desires."

Wren lowered her gun and clasped me. "It's about time for that holiday vacation. Didn't you mention a spa on Palm Monterey?"

I held her close. I caressed her lovely, dust-filled, smoke-reeking hair. My eyes glazed over. "No beaches, Wren. Anytime. Nothing near water."

She stared at me. "Okay."

We both looked back with chill horror upon Mong's retreating shape. The man's psi power was flickering out fast with such grave injuries. A blank look of resignation had come over his face as he peered back. Not physical but spiritual. His confidence had withered, knowing his forces were being wiped out and his invincible fleet was teetering on its last legs. My pulse hammered. Revenge was here and now. And yet, such a bitter dessert. Why did it feel so cheap and savage? Being in those tanks and enduring Mong's torture had opened me to a starker perspective of reality—it had given me powers as yet unexplored. True, my life as it was, would change. For better or worse? Who knew? Time would tell.

Villagers came plodding out of the dimness, yelling, gesticulating, a small army of them. Hundreds. Dust-streaked vindictive faces with eyes glaring in hate, following Mong's slimy trail of blood. I shuddered to think what they'd do to him.

Wren and I looked to the sky, hearing the roar of Vendecki ships blitzing across the darkening dusk-blue followed by more skyslips of the Melinar guard. The Melinarians would not get their revenge today before these villagers took theirs first.

A vague unease stirred at the base of my throat. As Wren and I hustled off to find Grild, I could not dismiss Mong's last grim warning of chittering Mentera skittering through the amalgamator and back to their dead power plant. Who after all, had let the flesh-eating crickets out of their cages? Maybe you need to clean up your mess, Rusco. If those crickety little bastard grasshopper fucks were to get one of their ships running...The disturbing thought faded and became but a grey smear on the fringe of my mind.

I shoved the worry aside, touched Wren's shoulder as we loped through the darkening trees. Live today, Rusco. Live in the moment. Today the living is free and easy…

ABOUT THE AUTHOR

Chris is a prolific author of fantasy, adventure, and science fiction. His writing spans many genres: heroic fantasy, sword and sorcery and speculative fiction.

Browse Chris's books:

http://www.innersky.ca/books/home

www.ingramcontent.com/pod-product-compliance
Lightning Source LLC
Chambersburg PA
CBHW020623020726
47494CB00001B/18